God, because you have seduced me...
...I will seduce mankind on earth!

THE LAST TRUMPET

Book One of the Tablets of Destiny Trilogy

ANTHONY RODRIGUEZ

Cover photo by David Morgan

ISBN: 1451508417
ISBN-13: 9781451508413

ACKNOWLEDGEMENT

I would like to thank my family and friends, in particular my father, whose love of writing perhaps surpasses my own; and my friends Matt Geise, Evan Hines, and Joe Casarona for their patience and support. I'd like to thank Brandon Colson, whose poetic vision of Christ dancing with the Devil in Eden helped give rise to Nick Bliss; David Morgan for being with me on this insane adventure from the very first chapters; and special thanks to both Javier Muñoz and Wayne Gibbons for inspiring me with their muse... encouraging me to find my own.

I'd like to recognize the professional assistance of my editor, Michael Denneny, for his patience taking on a novice; Tommy Ranizewski for his help proofing; Gary Gissler for keeping me sane; and of course David Morgan for the incredible cover art of Andres Concilio.

Finally, I need to thank David Guilbert for enduring my obsessive devotion to this art...je t'aime!

For Javier

CONTENTS

PROLOGUE

Northern Iraq – August, 1999

The land between two rivers, mother Mesopotamia, a white cargo van bounced on four worn tires down a secluded pass infamously known as the heroin road, the smuggler behind its wheel was hopelessly lost. The man dropped his head to the steering column, looking for the vanishing path in the sand, but found nothing. Growling to himself, he hit the wheel hard. It vibrated. His wild eyes began to scan the horizon for some landmark, anything to help him find a way through those wastes. Without warning light exploded in his face, as the sun broke over a peak and stabbed his sight. He raised one hand to shield his face from the glare. In that instant there was a thunderous crash, as a burst of black feathers exploded across the windshield in a flurry.

Chaos ensued.

The rusted suspension of the van began to hurl about, out of control. The smuggler jumped in his seat with panic, swerving erratically across the roadway, and back again. Pushed to its limits, the old axel twisted in on itself. The front right tire made the sound of a gunshot, as the van's breaks quickly seized, and the three remaining good tires slid to a stop. Metal groaned, as gravel and sand rose into the air around the chassis like a whirling shroud.

Before the blinding cloud of dust that enveloped him could settle, the smuggler jumped out of his seat, shouting Kurdi expletives into the air. He scurried around quickly to the blowout, and stared horrified at it for a moment. The heat was insufferable. It baked the surface of the van, producing a ghostly shimmer that rose from it like a spirit passing to another world.

As if from nowhere, a second wild-wind appeared. It picked up even more dust, spinning it about the wreck. The man took a long, unsettled breath – it shuddered in his throat. Nervously, his eyes rose to scrutinize the rocky peaks in both directions. Then he stopped, startled to see a human form standing motionless on the hills above him, watching and waiting it seemed. The smuggler hesitated a moment, unsure of what to do. One mistake in that place and the Angel of Death would be the only thing coming for him. He raised one hand and waved. There was no reply; the figure simply turned away. The lost Kurd moaned, watching the mysterious silhouette hobble over the crest of the hill, its curious form descending away from the light.

The dust devils abruptly beat on the side of the van one last time, viciously, before everything around him became dead calm again. He stood for a time, worried and wondering what to do with his cargo. If he left it there on the road, it would likely be found and stolen. If the authorities caught him with it, he undoubtedly would be hanged for the offense. Even if he escaped capture, all of that was nothing compared to what would happen to him should his employers find him empty handed. He could only guess what torture they would visit upon him.

The anxious man huffed, cursing God for his plight. Not knowing what else to do, he kicked at the dirt and headed up the hill to where he had seen the stranger standing. It took him some time to climb up the rubble, but finally breaking over the summit, he was relieved to look down the other side into a wide, green ravine. There he saw a stream that broke from rocks and pooled at the floor of the basin. The brook fed a patch of inviting palm and long grass. Dark birds darted about the feet of the trees. Thinking perhaps he had seen a herder shuffle over the hill, watering goats in the safety of that oasis, the smuggler decided to risk an approach. He carefully made his way down to the water and the swaying trees that seemed to curtsey in the wind. Not a soul was to be found.

As he drew nearer to the pool, he saw a group of ravens pecking around the water's edge. They paid little attention to him at first. It seemed an ill omen given the turn of events. As he stumbled to the waterline, the birds scattered. Their banter rose above the reeds to scorn him for the intrusion. He ignored their cries, prostrating at the sandy brook to splash water in his face and take a long, indulgent drink to chase away his worry. A few feet away, a single remaining bird scratched at the dirt, as if digging. The man stared. Something odd caught his eye. Just beyond the curious creature he saw a quick glimpse of structure. It was a pair of tall stones rising upright and a long third slab resting atop of them.

The smuggler rose and slowly made his way toward the stones. Reaching them, he examined the smooth, worn surfaces. The entire structure looked like it had been there for eons, perhaps only in recent months exposed by the cleansing stream and dry wind. He brushed grime from the top slab. The rising dust made him cough. On the stone he saw rough cuts and a notch that he guessed was to channel blood. A chill went down his spine, while the ravens let out another choirs of contemptuous calls seeming to protest his sacrilege at their altar.

An unnatural stillness gripped the moment. The shadows around him grew long and assumed an eerie feel, time seemed to stop, and the wind fell breathless. He stood in dread as the face of the sun began to blacken in the sky above him, swallowed by eclipse. With it, the light of the day rolled up like a scroll. Only the ravens were bold enough to heckle and jeer at him where he stood. The world felt as if it might end at any moment.

Without warning, the earth grumbled. His feet became unsteady and he swayed there a moment, before his footing gave way beneath him. He fell. Clinging at the earth frantically, his body dropped, twisting down into an opening pit. Only God knows how long the passage in which he fell had been lost to that wilderness; it crumbled around him, drinking him into its mouth of dark rock and gloom as he tumbled to the bottom.

After landing on the hard ground, he lay still for a moment in the dust. Gingerly, he turned to right his stiff and battered limbs. His eyes began to adjust to the shadows. Slowly, he came to his feet, brushing away the dirt and looking around, trying to re-orient himself in the dimness. His head was spinning. As his sight cleared, he saw a passage ahead, and light. He frantically drug his feet toward the glow behind the doorway, pressing his body against the stone slab, trying to push it inward. It resisted. Straining with all his might, he shoved and shoved. Finally, as if by command of fate, the stone gave way and he stumbled inside.

There the smuggler found a single room carved out from the rock. In the center of the space was a slab of black granite, ornately carved. It was etched on the side with symbols that he couldn't identify. His eyes widened, horrified by what it held. Laid out on the slab was a hideous body, mummified by the dry heat. The remains were wrapped in rotted wool and soaked in a tar-like pitch. The face of the corpse was covered with a thin cloth that ran around the head and up over the chin. He noticed part of the skull was still exposed; it was plain then that both sides of it had been crushed.

Out of the gloom, he heard a scuffling sound come from behind the body. "Please, help me," a raspy hiss followed the noise.

The smuggler jumped backward. He turned to run, terrified by that place.

"No, wait!" the voice pled.

He paused, stunned by the words, as a stranger gradually emerged from the darkness toward him. The man was ghastly. Upon his head was a crown of thorns that dug into his skin, creating bloody lesions on his brow. His body seemed like a walking corpse, not unlike the one on the slab. As the figure drew nearer to the smuggler, his arms were outstretched, holding two oblong stones – as if making an offering of them. He crept closer and closer, finally fixing his eyes to the body on the stone. Reached the remains, the stranger hovered there, sobbing with awful grief. Then he looked up suddenly and pushed the strange relics out, gesturing they be taken by the smuggler.

The man hesitated, looking at them with uncertainty; then he quickly snatched the stones and turned to run, unsure from where the courage came to do so. *This is surely a cursed place*, the smuggler thought to himself, dashing away. With the stones in hand, he raced through the doorway and scrambled up a rubble filled stairwell he could now make out, past the settling dust. From back down in the shaft he heard the tormented figure yelling after him.

"The hour of the Devil's return grows near," the voice called. "Take those accursed stones…you will know what's to be done with them when the dark exile comes."

More sobs filled the tunnel. Then a name came from the dark underworld.

"Habil, my poor brother" cried the tortured soul. "Please forgive me!"

When the smuggler reached the surface again, the eclipse had passed. He was not sure how long he had actually been down in the sunken shaft, but the sky was bright and the ravens were gone. The world looked new again. He glanced down at the black stones in his hands and noticed that they were covered in a red fluid; it looked like blood. Panicking, he stooped into the brook and frantically washed his hands in the cooling water. But no matter how hard he tried to wipe them clean, the mark left would not come off.

Part One: The Devil's Prophet

'Iblis,' God said, 'why do you not prostrate yourself?'
"I will not bow to a mortal whom You have molded from dry clay
and of black loam.'
'Get you hence (then),' said God. 'You are accursed, the curse
shall be on you until Judgment Day.'
'Lord,' said Iblis. 'Reprieve me until the Day of Resurrection.'
'You are reprieved until the Appointed Day,' answered God.
'Lord,' said Iblis, 'since you have seduced me, I will tempt
mankind on earth, I will seduce them all...'

The Koran, Al-Hijr 15:23-32

1

TWENTY-THIRD AND EIGHTH

New York City – October 1999

Manhattan had become an island of perpetual light in the waning years of the twentieth century. After dusk the long shadows were chased away from their rightful dominion by lit towers and neon signs. But that contrived reign of brilliance was frail, like a garish crown that's luster could never reach all the way down to the city's stoops and alleys. The spectacle of the glowing skyline taunted the gods of the night, who took recompense upon the evening's mean streets for the slight. That is why Nikolai Bliss felt at home amid the city's lost souls, for Manhattan's excesses enticed exiles of all kinds – immortal or otherwise – when the purple dusk faded to gloom. During those dim, menacing hours, New York City's deep reaches became the Devil's own.

A cold and wet veil nestled over the city, as Nick lurked about the shadows of the Westside. He stepped to the street and stared downtown to marvel at the line of buildings with their high halos. Just as he did, the traffic signals strung along Eighth Avenue flickered to green, drawing a line of cabs toward him in single bound. Their reflecting headlights bounced and pivoted on the slick roadway.

For weeks Nick had been drawn out by some sinister presence. Its power was everywhere that evening. He drifted to a nearby subway entrance and leaned back against the green paint of the stairwell, sating himself with the lingering inequity of the air. Slowly then, he raised his head and glanced uptown, eyeing the canopy of radiance that hung over the buildings there as well. Strobes and flashing signs from Times Square flared in the distance, like the rage of lightning in a storm. The blaze across the night skyline reminded him so much of what was – for him – unreachable. Manhattan lacked the spectacle and elegance of Heaven, but it was still the closest thing to it Nick had ever seen in the mortal world. *Men are resourceful... if nothing*, he thought.

The dark exile shook, took a deep breath, and pivoted upon his glumness, turning uptown toward Hell's Kitchen. When he stepped from the curb, a playful pack of men nearly ran him down. A youth in their midst stared at him. Nick felt a chill as he bore his eyes back into the boy, calling to him with ethereal longing. He would never admit it, but in spite of his animosity toward humanity, he did truly covet mortal consideration. Young, lovely men fascinated his vanity. It pleased him that such inconsequential creatures desired him so, and he took perverse pleasure in spurning their want. His rebuke of their longing was retribution against the nameless-god for the slight Heaven had visited upon him. Nick would make humanity hurt for its yearning, for its craving to be loved, in the same way he had been tortured by the loss of everything that had been important to him.

Pulling his coat tightly about his body, he moved toward the curb and leered a little more in the young man's direction. Their eyes locked. The handsome youth just stared back, inviting Nick. Then there came an abrupt surge of power. He shivered as the yearning in the atmosphere between he and the boy parted away. An ominous dark-energy ebbed and flowed between them; taunting the dark exile with its enticing lure – drawn to such gloom as he was. A shadowy presence fell over the street; its essence spilled about. This very power was the source of transgression and iniquity that had lured Nick out all week to feed. He reached with his ethereal wits to scry the bizarre wake it created there; he hungered for it.

As Nick's instincts sharpened, he managed to lock on to the source of the dark entity. He was surprised by what he found. A mortal thrall of the Pythia was carelessly intruding upon the streets *he* claimed. These were faithless creatures that turned away from all ethereal light; their humanity subsumed in monstrousness as they consorted with the minions of the dragoness known as Tiamat, Queen of the Abyss. Eons had passed since any of these true enemies to God was brazen enough to come so close to Nick, risking its end in his angry retribution.

Contrary to the legends that many men believed about Nick, he was not in fact a serpent – even though he could not be counted among the faithful either. He occupied his own, solitary existence; apart from the sorted intrigues of either Heaven or Hell. More often than not both sides left Nick alone, but strangely

particular kind of restraint could not come from a simple thrall; it was beyond their power. That kind of spell had to originate in a greater source, one that was reaching for him from the brim of Heaven itself. The dark exile thrashed furiously against the gripping force, as the thrall slipped away into the night, freely loosed upon the mortals there. Nick was incensed. He could do nothing now to stop it from feeding.

A cloud of radiance enveloped his body and time stopped its flow around him. He was drawn up and away from the streets of Manhattan. It was as if he were being towed aloft by three powerful chains – one alone not enough to bind him, but the three together seeming inexorable. He wrenched irritably at the ethereal shackles again, so as to let whatever force lay at the other end know that it played with the fury of a dark fire.

"Accuser," a voice abruptly called to him.

Nick blinked and shook his head, astounded by that name. No one had called him so for thousands of years. He turned slowly to face the sound. Three unassuming figures were sitting on the steps of a dwelling, carved out in the ethereal landscape. There the bright, clean air of Heaven's outer boundary became a shock to his system – *he* could go no further. Nick looked around bewildered. The street where he stood was fitted with polished cobblestone that appeared to have been worn down by the ages. Stretching down the path were mud-brick hovels, one piled atop the next like stacked boxes. The scene evoked a warm memory of home, before his fall from the grace of his beloved.

Nick quickly walked toward the figures and gazed down into the awkward smiles of the three – angels of Heaven. They sat at first coyly drawing in the sand before them with sun-bleached twigs. All three rose to their feet as he drew near them, but only the center seraph extended a hand in greeting.

"Iblis," he said, "it's been some time since we last spoke." His youthful face was soft and gentile. Its comely glow settled Nick, whose body still rushed with the excitement of hunting the thrall.

"Gabriel?" replied Nick.

Gabriel smiled and nodded back at him. "You remember the Guardians don't you?" He motioned toward the other two standing with him.

"Lord Jinn," they said together, using the ancient title of court for a ranking angel of Heaven. Then they bowed their heads ever so slightly in respect. Their smiles nervously lit up, and they blushed as the handsome exile met their gaze.

Nick was a little taken aback. These two guardians of mortal men – one of the innocents and the other of the righteous – had not been members of the court when he was as yet in the nameless-god's good favor. Their formal deference at that moment surprised him, and yet they seemed tense in their greeting. His frightful reputation clearly haunted their steps as they stood in his presence, face to face with the infamous rebel of Heaven. Nick possessed a dreadful mystique among the angels, which both thrilled and unnerved them all. He was the first Jinn to ever refuse that requisite instinct they had to please God; that made him appear inscrutably desirable – a wanton taboo for them beyond even what his own pride and vanity understood.

"Javi and Devi," he replied, nodding back. Then the Accuser turned his gaze back to Gabriel. "What is this? Can't you see I am exacting penance from the unclean? I have no time for pleasantries with you... release me from your binding. I have God's warrant until the last days of men to do as I please."

"Come now," replied Gabriel, still holding Nick's hand and drawing him closer. "What could be of more consequence to you than a visitation from satans of the Lord, unruly Accuser?"

Nick looked at them with disquiet. "Yes, I see...a triumvirate of messengers, no less. I must be getting old. It only took three of you to bind me."

Gabriel smiled at Nick and glanced over at the other two timid Jinn. His gesture seemed to say to them, 'I told you so of his airs.'

"And don't call me Accuser, Gabe," said Nick harshly. "I hate the sound of that title and of what it reminds me." He pushed the gentle angel's hand away, as hard as it was for him to do; he actually relished Gabriel's touch.

"As you wish, Iblis," Gabriel replied.

"My name is *Nick*...you know that. What do you want?"

"A word is all, my old, much loved friend."

Nick looked at Gabriel suspiciously. "Does your Lord know what you three are up to today, cavorting with the likes of Heaven's unholy exile? Is this not forbidden?"

"Times have changed. We were...well...really I was asked to bring you a message from the draftsman of divine design, Micah. I brought the Guardians along because assistance is clearly needed for what we must do today."

"You need aide of what?"

"You said it yourself," Gabriel retorted with a playful grin. "You can be a little much for one Jinn to handle." His reference was weighted with innuendo.

Nick narrowed his eyes, thinking his brother was teasing him now, but the Accuser would have none of it; his mood turned dark.

"Now Gabe," he hissed, "the last time you brought me 'tidings of good-joy,' I seem to remember you rather enjoyed our sorted liaison." Nick pushed the veiled reference even harder, trying to embarrass Gabriel back. "You like it rough I seem to remember... don't you?"

Gabriel's face turned bright red. "Don't be so vulgar, Nick. It was simply a playful joke between us. Why must you always be so cruel?"

"Because you like to taunt me with what I have lost...you know what I would have of you. You are a tease, Gabriel...a little cock-tease."

Gabriel glanced back at the other Jinn before he spoke, anxious for the Accuser's honesty. But they both knew the truth of what Gabriel felt about the Accuser.

"Nick," Gabriel said with a sudden air of authority, "you must recognize you still have friends among the Jinn. We don't approve of your path, but we certainly sympathize with your plight. Please don't be this way…I am here as a friend, not just a satan."

"Your sorted compassion comforts me," snorted Nick, in a cruel tone.

Gabriel stiffened his stance and tried to appear unmoved by the attempt to wound him. The other two angels reached across to support him, placing their hands on his back and extending into him power to confront Nick's menacing stature.

"You know, it has never been your anger that unsettles me…not like it does the others. I know you all too well. It's really your displeasure toward me that injures." Gabriel paused, his eyes filled with hurt." I have always lov…"

"Perhaps I've never given you enough pause to fear my fury, Gabe," Nick cut him off suddenly.

Gabriel grew cross.

"Don't take out your indignation on me. I've always been in your corner…you know that. Stop being this way. You can be such an ass when you feel you aren't in control. We don't have the time for this, Nick…pull it together!"

The dark exile begrudgingly froze in his place, realizing the lovely angel was right. This unease was unnecessary between them. He reached across and kissed the annoyed Gabriel on the forehead – to beg forgiveness. Nick could not in truth stay irritated with

Gabriel for long, but only *he* could talk to the Accuser that way and get away with it.

The gesture calmed the air.

"Forgive me, brother," Nick said sheepishly. "As always I am too quick to anger."

The three youthful Jinn looked suddenly relieved. Javi and Devi marveled at Gabriel's influence over the exile's disposition.

"Walk with us now, please?" begged Gabriel

"I really need to get back there. I am kind of in the middle of something."

"Yes, yes, I know…I will put you back more or less where you were, so you can go about that dreadful business later."

"Fine," Nick said with a short, hot breath. "It seems I have little choice. Where shall we walk?"

"This way is good, I think."

Gabriel turned and took Nick's arm, reclining his head against the dark angel's broad shoulder as they went. A calm-quiet settled around them. Nick did actually relax, leaning into the embrace. In the Accuser's heart, the warm feel of Gabriel so close delighted him. *Something must really be amiss in Heaven,* Nick thought to himself, *for this small comfort to be permitted to me.*

Gabriel extended his wings around Nick. They walked slowly up the path, deeper into the ethereal apparition of the old city.

"So, what does that smug, know-it-all Micah want of me?" grumbled Nick finally.

"Mostly what he always wanted of you," replied Gabriel. "Your attention I suspect...he covets something of you. Still, today there is another matter he would have us discuss, besides what he envies...one of great importance to you."

"He desires something of me? What the hell is that suppose to mean? "

Gabriel stopped and looked up at Nick coolly, composed as all of Heaven could be. He was surprised that Nick did not realize what each and every angel desired of him– that one, true purpose for which he had been crafted. Nick was the consort to Heaven's throne with his splendor, his beauty intended to please the longing of God himself. Nearly every Jinn wanted Nick for his own because of it, and his bad-boy repute only made matters worse over time.

"We all know what he really wants," replied the lovely Jinn. "Envy is as close as he can get to it."

Nick actually blushed.

"But enough of all this nonsense about jealousies and lusts," said Gabriel. "It is unbecoming of our kind...even for you, exile."

"Really?" snapped Nick, turning up his nose.

"*Really!*" returned Gabriel forcefully. "Let us speak of it no more."

Nick realized there was no purpose in sparing with these Jinn. He should relish the moment. They walked in silence for a time.

At long last Javi nudged Gabriel, pushing him to get on with their mission. "The message from the scroll," he whispered demurely.

Gabriel flinched at him with a tiny bit of annoyance for the intrusion. The dark exile was just so enthralling to be near, he didn't want the moment to end. But Javi was right of course, they should get to the point of their mission.

"Another time of tribulation is at hand," said Gabriel. "It is the appointed hour of God's judgment, the seals upon His plan for destiny are being broken as we speak...each affords a prophetic message to someone. Micah says the fifth scroll is for you."

"Me?" barked Nick, looking back at him a little confused. "What are you talking about?"

"Do you recognize this place?"

Nick stopped and looked around, realizing where the messengers had brought him and why it all had seemed familiar. "Oh hell Gabe, what are you trying to do to me?"

"Hell precisely, Accuser," replied Gabriel. The Jinn waved his hand and in an instant all four of them stood atop a towering structure, looking down over an ancient city.

Nick turned pale as comprehension fell over him. "The Second Temple," he said under his voice softly.

"It was here the Lord made His choice...here where He denied you that second time. It is here it begins again for you...the final time."

"Why are you doing this?"

"I am telling you it's time, Nick. Micah says you *must* be told. All the seals will soon be broken, the edicts of Heaven read. He says you will understand what this means and sends you vision. "

As Gabriel spoke, he pointed to two ghostly figures about twenty feet away. They stood at the very edge of the rooftop. One of them was Nick himself. It was a projected image from the past, from when Joshu – the personified God – walked the mortal earth.

"Please, Gabe, I can't do this," implored Nick.

"You must remember, Micah says. You must choose."

"Haven't I endured enough?"

Gabriel simply pointed to the vision and could say no more. He was only the messenger.

Nick turned and walked toward the images, his steps hesitating as he did. He felt the bolstering hands of Devi and Javi upon his back, not physically, but in the way they had offered aide to Gabriel a few seconds before. He turned to glance at them both. They reassured him with their smiles. Nick realized Gabriel had not needed them half as much as Nick was about to, that was what the angels had really intended.

The sound of raised voices reached Nick, and he called on everything within his being to keep from breaking down. His heart sank.

♦

"What you suggest is blasphemy, Niko," said the small-framed Joshu. "If you were not Jinn you would be stoned for such words. Stop, lest someone hears you."

"Call it what you will," barked the image Nick saw of himself, "but truth is truth! Go ahead...

throw yourself from this mound of rubble that these worthless creatures call your temple."

"*My* temple? Do you hear yourself ? You are insane!"

"I am one of the satans of God, Josh, of course I am insane…but it's the kind of insanity that you cannot expel…the way you do the demons from your pitiful Ebonite followers in the streets down there. It's the insanity of deep desire that plagues me…love is truly a form of madness. Look at me!"

Standing back, near the three messenger Jinn, Nick suddenly felt very sick as he watched the memory playing out before him, that image of himself atop the temple in Jerusalem so many years ago, pleading desperately with the only mortal he had ever loved. The recollection had always haunted him, but to see it in the way the Realm of Essences gave his memory animated life was simply too much. Nick felt as if he might retch then and there.

"Why do you torment me with the sacrilege of such talk? I have loved you…like Jonathan's love of David in the scriptures…a pure love, greater even than that of woman. I have set aside the false law of the warriors and priests in doing so and risked much. What more would you have of me, Niko?"

The Christ began to weep, his face sinking into his hands. He still struggled and worried with what his relationship to the Devil signified of his fate.

"Me have you do?" shouted Nick, his rage building. "What are you talking about, Josh? This is your doing…you brought us all here to this time and place…for what purpose I still don't grasp. But you *are* God. There is no other way for me to love a man. I am made for you and you alone…that is how I know!"

"I don't understand your cruelty. You say you love me and you will turn away from your rebelliousness, your slanders… but now you speak unimaginable blasphemy."

"All I know is I am tired of being set side. I have missed you so much over the last three thousand years. I cannot stand it anymore. Please, Josh…see the truth…for me…for us!"

Nick's voice boomed over the temple like a dark storm.

"*STOP!*" screamed Joshu. "I shall really jump from this place. I warn you!"

"Do it," snapped Nick angrily, "and we will be done with this pretense that you are simply just another prophet. You will see what you are, and take me to love again…to be yours as I was intended."

The image of Nick fell to its knees with that last plea. He also began to sob inconsolably.

All of creation hung on the words of Joshu, who was deeply shaken by the dark angel's impossible proposition.

"Be gone from this place, seditious Jinn…you defile it with these profanities," he said in tears. "God only sent me to sweep away the lies of the unrighteous kings and priests, who corrupt the truth for their own gain. From this, you would suggest that I am myself a god? Do you realize what that would mean for me if it were known to others that you think this? You would deliver me into their very hands with such treachery, Niko."

"Please, not again," cried Nick. "I cannot bear to be sent from your sight this way, Lord...I don't understand why this is happening."

"I cannot be Him that is God, Niko. There is but one Lord... to suggest otherwise is beyond sanity. God is not to be tested in this way. Since you will not relent in this foolish irreverence...you must go from my sight. I will not have it."

"No," begged Nick's image again. "Do not turn me out of your presence now...I love you. I need you. I will do whatever you command, but deny the truth. Don't you see? Let me help you look inside yourself... conjoin with me, so you can see He has taken the semblance of man within your flesh. Yes, it seems improbably, but it makes complete senses to *me* now... for I am redeemed in this way. I will submit as I was commanded to do thousands of years ago....but to you, here and now!"

Nick fell flat to the ground, prostrating himself before Joshu, bowing low to that god made man. But it was simply too much for Joshu to grasp. Nick must go.

"I banish you, unclean spirit," moaned Joshu into the air, his heart breaking, but resolved to do what he felt right. His fear of what others might think of the Devil's temptation was simply too great. "Leave this holy place, exile of Heaven, and never return to me with your sedition!"

The image of the rebellious Jinn trembled atop the temple at the Lord's command. All was lost to him again; exile was once more his recompense for love. Nick turned back to Gabriel and the Guardians, unable to look at the vision of his second expulsion any longer. They too appeared broken by the sight. Tears of grief filled the eyes of the angels, as they watched with sympathy Nick's anguish play itself out.

Without a word Gabriel nodded, urging Nick to look back again. When the Accuser finally worked up the courage to do so, he found they were no longer atop the temple. They were standing at the edge of a rubble-strewn hill called Golgotha. Three men were stretched out upon wooden crosses – the center of the three was Joshu himself. His head was slumped forward in torment.

Slowly, the broken figure of the crucified god, dripping in blood and misery, raised his head and spoke into eternity as if baffled by his plight. *"Eli, Eli, lama sabachtthani?"* he begged understanding for why he'd been forsaken.

Joshu gasped, as if with the last impressions of life, but in truth death could not claim him that way. In pain, he finally realized Nick had been right all along. Joshu reached deep inside to draw upon his power, to break the cross and set his foot upon the earth. But in that instant, the dragons sprung their trap. A soldier at the foot of the cross – disguised by enchanted dark glamour called a snakeskin – reached up and viciously ran a cursed spear into Joshu's side. The weapon had been forged from the bite of the Queen of Chaos Herself...it would be forever called the Spear of Destiny for its purpose: to kill an avatar of God.

Joshu screamed in anguish across all space and time, as the deathblow had been delivered. In the apparition, the image of Nick stood in shock as the young demigod's eyes widened and he exhaled his last agonizing breath. The Accuser could do nothing to save him now.

The real Nick shuddered and came to his feet as he watched his beloved Joshu dying before him again. The image suddenly rushed forward in time. Next he observed the Pythian thralls in Roman uniforms take the body of his Lord from the cross, sneering with glee at their victory. Nick recalled being stunned as to how it could be possible that Joshu was dead in that way. It made no sense...he was the Son of God. It would take Nick many long years to understand how they had pulled off his murder, with the enchantment of both the glamour and the spear. Guilt would consume the Accuser, as it was in part his neglect that allowed them to succeed. He had let Joshu down by not defending him when he could, thinking it was the only way to get the Christ to realize the truth about his power.

The images before Nick faded. He was standing only paces in front of Gabriel and the other Jinn, his back still turned away from them. The dark exile was filled with a wild rage more terrible than could be imagined. Gradually, he felt someone take his shoulder from behind. Nick started, but his attention could not be fully distracted from his wrath. Each of the three Jinn heralded a final message to the Accuser.

"He needs your help, Nick," said Gabriel from behind him.

"Micah says the time of the second Deliver is coming near," followed Devi's voice. "A prophet will be sent to you."

Javi then added, "the opportunity for which you have waited since that day on the temple draws near. Choose Accuser."

Nick spun around to find the three angels were gone. He stood in the streets of New York, the darkness all around him again. He was cold and wet, flush with the rage of seeing Joshu taken from the cross by the Romans. As his wits came back to him, he remembered the mysterious beast stalking the streets of the city for a victim...a victim like lovely Joshu. He pulled himself together and fed by rage, the Accuser dissolved into the night to pursue his vengeance upon the bloodthirsty thrall.

Nick's stomach rolled as the putrid reek in the street settled over him. He stretched out his mind and reacquired the ethereal presence of his quarry. The Accuser had another very special ability among angels: the power to glimpse forward and see malevolence's unfolding. It was only the hint of a dreadful fate that he could foresee, but usually enough to make out how it would strike. The simple divination was actually a vestige from his former role as Heaven's inquisitor. If Nick could foretell the details of transgressions moments before they occurred, he could be there to witness them as well. What better way to exact divine justice, than to see the offense himself? He could also choose to intervene if the spirit moved him, but he rarely ever did with men. He felt they rather deserved their lack of fortune, deserting them to fate's frequent cruelty.

Like a great bird of prey, Nick's wrathful instinct focused in upon the beast. He knew he had to move quickly. The dying image of Joshu feverishly fueled his resentment toward all of the Pythia. And this time it triggered a need to do more than simply exact penance after the fact. Now he did feel compelled to prevent the beast from actually carrying out its intention, no matter what the cost. The Accuser's mind was made up; he would not let it feed…he would evoke Christ's mercy in memory of his beloved.

Nick pushed his mind to center it two steps ahead of the killer, where he might glimpse in his forethought the attack. His vision was limited and also oddly wavering for some reason, as if interrupted by some other force. He had only seconds to spare – the threads of mortal fate were thin and fragile.

The thrall had moved up Ninth Avenue and ducked down a dark block, toward the entrance of a well-known nightclub called Twilo. The establishment was actually a favorite haunt of Nick's, making this incursion even more personal than it already was. Cabs churned up the block from in front of the club, as a din roared out into the street each time the doors opened.

Nick was still two blocks away from the thrall. He picked up his pace.

Lurking in the distant dark, the thrall reached a section of street opposite the club's entrance. There he stood for a moment, watching the crowd at the door, reaching out with his mind and probing at the people as they filed out one by one. He was looking for something there. The side door opened. He smiled to himself all of a sudden. *That one*, the beast thought. *He feels just like that immortal son from Golgotha so long ago. He should do the job well for now.*

Turning in Nick's direction, the beast looked around nervously. It knew it was being stalked, and bolted from the spot leading Nick away from the club. The Accuser rounded the street just in time to see its beastly form steal from its perch, to follow a blonde youth out a side exit. Destiny had somehow marked the boy, whom Nick could now fully envision in his foresight being brutalized.

The Jinn had to move fast. He ducked into an alley just ahead of the club entrance and stole into the gloom, as rats scurried from a pile of trash nearby. The vermin rushed from the spot behind him and abruptly turned on their hunches to look at the dark exile. A fine mist began to blanket the evening, giving the night air an eerie appearance. Nick bowed his head and threw his arms to his sides. The sound of rushing air suddenly filled the alley. Two great wings spread themselves at Nick's back. They were the source of the unexpected churning gale, kicking paper and dust about the alley. The wings were long and elegant, colored purple-black, but for the very ends – each stained with unmistakable white tips.

Nick bent at his knee and with a great surge of strength, thrusting himself straight into the air. He vanished from sight, with the rats still scurrying about the alley where he stood; a single streetlight gleaming in front of them as they ran.

Down the other side of the block, the thrall finally caught up with the boy, who only at the very last minute realized someone had stolen up behind him in the darkness. The beast grabbed him by the arm, and then across the mouth. He pulled back hard to fix the young man against his own massive frame. The boy flailed at first, but the struggle was hopeless; the dark mortal was simply too strong. Then the thrall nudged his face against the back of the boy's neck, just behind his ear. "Stop squirming, faggot," he said with a strange, unrecognizable accent, "or I will stick you right now."

The young man froze, as the thrall pulled him into an opening between two buildings, out of sight from the street. The beast quickly pushed him face first into an alley wall, pinning the boy against the brick. As they stood alone in the dark, the thrall released one arm and ran his free hand down the small of the boy's back. The young man shook. The beast held it there for a second, touching the fine hair of the youth's skin just under the shirt. The sinister creature was stirred somehow, cruelly. It forcefully pulled the young man up by the crotch, splitting his legs open. The boy whimpered. Hearing the sound, the thrall chuckled out loud. It reached around to break open his linen pants, wrenching the thin cloth free. The slacks fell away, exposing the boy's naked buttocks.

"Good little bitch," sneered the thrall. "All the easier."

"Please don't," whispered the boy in dread.

The thrall dropped his own pants in a single motion, and proceeded to prod the boy's legs open. He pushed hard on the boys back and thrust viciously inside. The young man squirmed and cried out again, his head suddenly rushing with a flurry of strange image.

While the pain of penetration distracted the boy, the beast reached into his coat and retrieved a long, jagged knife. The thrall hesitated for just a bit to savor that cruel moment. As he did, a large wolf-like hound appeared from behind him, looking more feral than tame.

The thrall gestured at the dog with wild-eyed awe, as if to insist matters were under control. "Is it clear?" he asked.

The dog paced on its forward legs, hesitated, and turned to vanish into the shadows again. Smiling with that, taking the hellhound at its word, the thrall slowly raised the blade to finish the job.

The boy only became aware that his attacker had maneuvered a knife under his chin when he saw it flash in the pale glow of a streetlight. He writhed to break free, conscious now that this would end in his death if he could not finally escape. The thrall's body tensed, as the knife began cutting into the boy's flesh. Panic seized the young man. He shook and his eyes blurred, as he urinated on himself from the absolute terror.

The thrall jerked his thin hair back, with a hard wrench, to face into the dark sky. The trapped boy tried to scream one last time, but nothing came out of his mouth. Then from nowhere his eyes caught a frantic sweep of motion in the gloom above him, as if the night air had become composed of black fabric wrestling in the breeze. There was a pulsing rush, a driving beat that seemed to descend upon his senses. He saw two white flashes amid the darkness. They darted back and forth in front of his eyes, pulling apart, then wrapping back toward each other with flowing elegance.

The pain at the boy's neck abruptly ceased, and his body came free from the weight of his attacker. He let out a sigh and at the same moment heard a tremendous crash from behind – something large had been cast into the rubble of the alley. He pivoted round on his heels, pants still at his ankles, to see two massive wings splayed before him. The black, white-tipped feathers extended to their full length, shook a moment, and then folded neatly away into a man's flapping leather coat as if by magic. All that the boy could see from there was the back of a stranger's head and shoulders, walking away toward the sound of the crash.

Nick had broken the thrall's arm as he twisted the knife free of the boy's neck. He was furious with himself for not getting there sooner. The thrall had come so close to killing the boy. The Accuser reached and grabbed at the beast, elevating it headlong into the air, and tossed it again to the opposite end of the alley with brutal force. He was like a cat playing with a half-dead mouse on the pavement. The thrall flew into a pile of loose lumber. There a sharp wedge of wood penetrated his upper leg as he fell. The exposed splinter was only inches away from his still erect penis. It was now covered in blood. The shock of Nick's unexpected retribution clung to the beast; its master had not warned him as planned. The Pythian lords had offered the beast up to the Devil. The thrall's attention was split between the pain of the wood protruding though his thigh and the menacing presence of the dark exile. His eyes glanced franticly back and forth as if trying to assess a course of action. He stopped finally and fixed his dreadful stare on the Accuser's shadowy brow: the face of damnation.

Nick turned his head as he reached for the twisted man's coat. He grabbed fast and pulled him up to stare wide-eyed into the doomed thrall's dismay. As he did, the splinter of wood pulled free and the beast screamed. Nick looked hard into him, penetrating his mind – for not until right then did the Accuser recognize him. The Jinn's stomach seized.

"*You!*" growled Nick. "You filthy son of a bitch, how is this possible? You are the thrall from Golgotha... Longinus. *You* are the on who killed Joshu!"

The thrall's face filled with dread. This was exactly why he'd been chosen. A brutal rage built in Nick. He looked the man up and down, then reached over and thrust his fingers in the wound on his leg. Longinus screamed again. Nick quickly filled his mouth with scrap of loose lumber, shoving it half way down his throat – then weaving with his fingers through the flesh in the leg laceration, the Accuser grabbed at the bone of his thigh and snapped it like a twig.

Longinus' muffled agony filled the night air. The sound could curdle blood. *There is not enough pain in this existence for you,* Nick thought into the thrall's mind. *But I can be very imaginative.*

The Accuser ripped open the Realm of Essences and dragged the beast inside, kicking and screaming, away from the boy. There in that place, Nick took his time to torture the thrall, methodically breaking each and every bone of his mortal form until he could feel the brittle splints between his fingers over and over. His rage was insatiable.

The Devil' retribution took what seemed forever, for in that place such pain could be timeless. That's why Nick took him there; the Accuser wanted the beast's suffering to last on and on. Each time life seemed to slip away from him, Nick restored his breath, prolonging the pain. Seconds drug on as hours, but the dark exile knew he must eventually go back to the boy. When he was done savoring the torment as much as he could, he raised the thrall to his face and smiled.

"No grace for you this day," he snarled.

With that the Accuser pulled the beast back into the alleyway on the material plane, through a dark portal, appearing once more before the attacked youth, the boy's soul could not be fully healed unless it saw this justice. To the horrified young man no time had passed there. It was just a quick flash within his otherwise hazy perception; only the bloody, quivering pulp left of the thrall hinted that something gruesome had transpired somehow in those passing seconds.

Then Nick spoke out in a ghoulish tone to the thrall. "Your own deeds have drawn a veil over your heart. Your name is marked upon the pages of Sijjin... the book of sins," he said banefully. "This is the end you have earned...I am given right to take vengeance upon the unjust and to separate you from the light."

Nick pressed his lips against Longinus' twisted mouth and inhaled. The ever-lasting breath of life escaped the dark mortal, as Nick consumed his hateful soul in a single breath. When he released the broken fragments of body, the flesh about its bones turned to dark earth and the remains fell to the ground in a heap of powdery clay. The rain fell and dampened the dark earth that was once a man. It trickled away into the gutter as a fine steaming stream, disappearing down a nearby storm drain.

The young man stood there, nude at the waist, wet and shivering in his own urine. As the Accuser approached, the boy's knees buckled a little. His eyes followed Nick, and his lower jaw began to quiver as he tried to speak.

"Please, don't hurt me," the young man managed to mutter.

Nick was filled with pity. *Such pathetic mongrels they are...but so fragile...so lovely at times,* he thought to himself admiring the boy's beauty.

Then cautiously, so as not to spook the boy more, the Accuser walked over and stooped in front of him. He reached to the ground and tugged at the boy's pants until they were up and around his waist again. The young man looked shocked at first, then relieved.

Nick flung off his coat and wrapped it around the boy's shaken frame. He reached to smear away a trickle of blood along his neck; then gently kissed it. The wound closed, as if by some miracle.

"It's not deep...we can clean it up in a bit," Nick said, grinning warmly at the boy.

He brushed a gold strand of hair from the youth's eyes and gazed deeply into his soul with his ethereal mind. The youth sensed something slip away from inside of him. For an instant, he felt safe in the strange man's arms.

"Who are you?" asked the boy, looking up into Nick's dark stare.

"Would you believe me if I told you I was the Devil?" Nick replied with a sarcastic frown.

The youth just shook his head.

"Then don't worry who I am right now. You are safe...that's what matters."

"Thank you," said the quivering boy, averting his gaze.

"Come on, let's get you out of those damp pants," said Nick, his voice almost implying something lewd.

Fear returned to the boy at the sound of Nick's tone. He seemed suddenly unsure if he would be a victim yet again at the hands of another dark stranger.

Nick deflected the boy's frightful look, somewhat annoyed. The Accuser shook his head and took the boy by the hand, thrusting it down the front of his own pants. For a second the young man resisted. Then a look of shock came over the boy's face.

"There now," said Nick, "nothing for you to worry about? Your ass is quite safe."

He pulled the boy close to him and turned him toward the street. There, Nick hailed a cab. They ducked inside it, settling into the backseat as it sped away, nudging out the other cars along the roadway.

From the gloom left behind, the wild looking dog that had concealed itself jetted into the street and trotted after them. It cast no shadow in the streetlights, dissolving into the night.

2

THE DEVIL IN THE DETAILS

Nick rushed the boy uptown to Columbus Circle. There they exited from the cab and made their way into the side entrance of a plush building. The tall marble walls seemed to stretch up and away endlessly, resembling some forgotten temple sanctuary. A doorman sat flipping through the pages of a newspaper. He glanced up to Nick's face as the Accuser sped by, holding the youth tightly to him all the way to the elevator.

The doors opened. It almost appeared as if the car had been waiting. Then the ragged pair stepped inside and flew into the steel-girder clouds of Manhattan.

When the elevator doors opened again, Nick ushered the youth to an apartment, and placed his hand on the door to magically release the lock. The young man seemed to hesitate. It was at that moment Nick felt something powerful stir, as if he had bumped a basket of vipers. He brushed off the sensation in the urgency, tugging at the boy's arm as he led through the open doorway.

The foyer into the apartment was dark. A shaft of light from another room sliced across them as they entered a long, open hall. Nick wanted to use his psychic mind to push into the young man's soul, curious about what he might find there. Questions burned for the Accuser about what the boy now knew and understood. *Why did Longinus single him out with such intention?* Nick wondered.

There was a familiarity about the young man, a feeling that aroused Nick and yet he could sense only raw emotion through his storm of thoughts. Awkwardly, the young man reached up at Nick with his own mind. The Accuser backed away slightly. The boy seemed unaware of the strange new power the attack had afforded him. His eyes glazed over as if in a trance and he brushed Nick's lips with the tips of his fingers.

"Niké...God's victory," he whispered ominously.

Nick went cold, his fears were confirmed, the beast *had* conjoined with the boy – used ethereal power to force its way inside his fragile essence. Mortals could not normally conjoin ethereally, not without help anyway, and there was the boy nudging with that very power. Then without warning, the young man collapsed lifeless into Nick's arms. The Accuser reached for a towel and wet it from the faucet. He wiped away the grime and dried blood about the boy's face, after that he pulled gauze from the cabinet to dress the tiny cut on his Adams apple. Delicately, Nick stripped the unconscious boy's clothing away, his fingers ached to touch the youthful turns of his body, but the Accuser resisted that impulse. He slowly raised the young man up into his arms and took him to a nearby bedroom. There he tucked a downy bed cover around the youth's shaken frame and stroked his brow softly, casting a deep spell of ethereal repose over him to chase away the dark dreams.

❦

The nameless boy lay asleep for several hours on the four poster bed. White linen and pillows rose around him like clouds.

The Accuser sat in a chair next to the huge window of the bedroom, just staring at the young man. To Nick, the boy looked so placid and pure. The light of day streamed in, giving the room a calm ambiance. The young man suddenly edged his face deeper into the pillows for a moment, relishing the softness, before he opened his eyes and looked straight at Nick.

The Accuser glared back into his deep blue stare, unflinching like a great cat suddenly freezing when sensing quarry. Nick's hands were drawn together so that his powerful forearms looked like the arch of a massive structure. He tilted his head low and peered over the tips of his folded knuckles; it made him appear so very menacing right then.

The boy looked confused for a second about where he might be. Then he stopped and took some time to study Nick, noticing how handsome the dark stranger actually was in the light. A surge of yearning chased away his uncertainty – despite some part of him that warned he should know better. The two held each other's stare a long time without giving away their mutual want, neither trusting that feeling right then.

The silence grew awkward. Nick took a deep breath and spoke softly to break its unease.

"Are you hungry?" he asked.

The boy looked away, thinking about it. The details were slowly coming back to him. When he did respond it was simply to nod his head up and down. Nick waited, glaring; the boy shivered from the scrutiny. He could sense the Jinn's raw power.

"Well," said Nick, "let's get some food into you, shall we? What I want of you can wait until later."

The boy froze. Dread returned.

Nicked stopped and frowned as he sensed the boys reaction, not so much out of irritation, more from exasperation. The Accuser knew exactly what he was thinking.

"I thought we established *that* is not what I am after from you, mortal. However, it would be useful to know a few things…if you don't mind…so relax. I don't want your ass."

Nick paused.

Yet, he quickly said in own his mind.

The events of the early morning came rushing back to the nameless youth. He sat straight up in the bed with an anxious bounce. The images of his attacker flashed in his mind, along with the feel of the blade at his throat, then the humiliation of the rape. His eyes turned glassy with tears, remembering the pounding concussion of wings overwhelming his senses and the image of Nick consuming the thrall. He stared into the Jinn's deep, black eyes with dismay.

"Who are you?" he asked, with a quiver in his voice.

Nick waited to reply, narrowing his eyes. He let the silence shake the nameless youth's resolve a little before he answered the question. "My name is

Nikolai...Nikolai Bliss, but my friends simply call me Nick."

Again drawn out silence followed the dark angel's words.

"What happened last ni...?"

"You were attacked by an agent of darkness and nearly killed," Nick cut him off quickly. "Had I not come along when I did, you would be sporting a second smile...instead of the shaving-nick under that bandage."

Nick pointed the dressing on the boy's neck.

The young man raised his hands to touch the bright gauze. He appeared startled by physical evidence that the events he recalled were of no dream, or party-drug induced hallucination. His eyes dampened at the corners.

"How can any of this be? That man that attacked me...you killed him." Then the boy's eyes grew round like blue globes. "You had wings.... you...."

"What's your name, may I ask?" Nick cut him off quickly again, before he could say any more.

The boy stopped and looked away, casting his eyes to the window to catch a glimpse of the cityscape. Nick turned to follow his line of sight, perplexed at first by what he might be seeing. He realized quickly the boy was deflecting the question, his mind in a daze, disassociating from the trauma. *How awful it must all seem for him to suddenly see into the mind of darkness?* Nick thought to himself, looking at the city along with the boy. *Nothing in life will ever appear the same.*

there, nothing at all. It rattled him. *Man, was that ecstasy I had bad or what?* he thought to himself, looking for any excuse to avoid the improbability.

There was a sound from just outside the door, he glanced at it a moment. Trying not to think about the impossible confusion he felt, James shook off the last bit of dampness from his hair. He rose, took a deep breath, and pulled open the door briskly – determined this time to be a little more engaging for his dark, handsome host. To his surprise he didn't find Nick, but the youthful Nafees instead.

Both young men jumped with a start, and took a step back.

"I am sorry," said Nafees anxiously, "*Assalamu alaikum*...peace to you, friend. I was just checking to see if you needed anything." His mysterious accent was thick and alluring.

James blushed, unsure of what to do. "No thank you," he said, smiling politely.

The houseboy looked back and retuned the grin, seemingly thankful not to find James annoyed.

"I've had dinner prepared for you, when you are ready," said Nafees. "Simply come down the hall to your left...you will find the door to the deck there."

James nodded.

Nafees spun about swiftly and vanished down the hall. As he walked away, the servant's mysterious, fluid motion intrigued James. It was almost as if he were a contrived creature. James waited a few seconds to make sure he had gone before heading down the hall, venturing into the apartment. Moving out into the open, he began to realize how enormous the place actually was. *It must take up the entire floor of the building,* he thought to himself. *It's a sin to have this much space in the city.*

Each room was perfectly clean, almost sterile. The furniture was mostly modern, with sleek wooden frames and tight square cushions. Bookcases and tables all appeared simple, clearly understated. The art was extraordinary – a little opulent, but tasteful. As James moved from room-to-room, he saw lavish tapestries stretched over the walls, large marble sculptures adorned many corners; there were even cases filled with antique clay-figurines.

From the main living room there was an amazing panoramic view of the city. One could scarcely imagine its grandeur. It took in the George Washington Bridge to the north and ran all the way southeast to the Empire State Building. Set out between the two iconic landmarks was the sprawling green sea of Central Park, rolling out at his feet like a carpet. He had never been in an apartment like it before. Then gradually, his gaze was pulled from the view out the windows to another sight: a massive marble sculpture that adorned the center of the living room.

The carving was at least six feet high and twice that in width. The entire edifice gave the impression that the room had been built around it, but he knew that would have been impossible. The image was of an inverted angel, his great wings stretched out across the floor, spread as if he were falling head first to the ground. The shoulders and upper arch of wing were cut-off at the floor, to give the sense that they were actually embedded, or at least recessing into it. One arm was cast back away from the body, the other covered the face. Its chin thrust forward into the chest. The torso and legs were flung upward into the air and in between its legs was a handsome sample of manhood that stood at attention. The image was erotic, but at the same time there was something tragic about it. James could not decide why that conflicted feeling seemed so intense.

The young man stared at the statute for a long time, before Nick spoke from behind him. "It symbolizes the betrayal of love," he said. The Accuser's voice caused James to bound forward, toward the stone sculpture. He spun instantly to face Nick. The boy's fair complexion turned red from embarrassment.

"I am sorry, I just got lost…this place is so huge," James stuttered awkwardly.

"No you didn't," replied Nick, "but it's fine. You are right to be curious, as I am of you. Now come with me." The Accuser turned away, moving into the apartment, toward the terrace. James followed closely behind him, passing Nafees as they stepped into the walkway.

The houseboy looked up from the corner of his eye with a wary expression.

It was a clear evening. Both men sat on the terrace of the building and stared as the pink-purple sky faded into gray. The patio was so high not even the sounds of the street seemed to reach them there – only the reverberation of the brisk breeze jetted about their heads. The two men sat and picked at their food for about twenty minutes before either seemed ready to say anything. Finally, Nick cleared his throat and tried.

"So do you have any idea why that thrall was after you, James?"

"Thrall? What's that?" His voice registered annoyance, as he looked at Nick, mystified.

Nick stopped picking at his food with pokes and stabs.

"The man who attacked you, did you know him? Was he after you for any particular reason that you know of?"

"How would I know?" snapped James defensively. "He just came up on me as I left the club. Clearly he was some kind of sicko. What more is there to know?" He paused for a second, realizing something.

Nick stared back, as if to beg the boy share what he was thinking.

"Damn, I gotta get tested…don't I?"

Nick reached across the table and touched his hand. James felt a warm sensation. Then Nick looked down at the table nervously. "You're fine," he said.

James was unsure how to respond. He didn't know why, but he believed Nick.

"It would surprise me if this was simply a random attack," Nick went on, "he was of the Pythia…they don't do this sort of thing for kicks, James. His attack

seemed desperate, but intentioned somehow. I am
very curious why he was after you in particular."

"I'm sorry, I don't quite follow you. Are you
implying you're surprised he would pick me out of all
the other boys there he could have gone after?" asked
James, looking wounded.

Nick shook his head. *Mortal vanity,* he thought,
how strange? He studied James a moment. "No, I did
not mean to imply that at all," he replied, trying to
ease the boy's insecurity.

"Well, what did you mean?"

"Look, James, what the beast did was intended to
frighten and humiliate you while it fed...it's a very old
tactic for them. There is history here, a practice that
goes back thousands of years."

James looked at him, not sure what to think. His
mind raced and butterflies rose in his stomach. It all
seemed insane.

"They establish an ethereal connection through
intercourse," explained Nick, "and fan the flames of
fear through it to feed off the dread. Once sated, they
cut the victims throat to consume the life force. It's
actually a perversion of a different kind of ritual, one
that affords connection to the divine, not death."

"What is this? It all sounds crazy," James groaned
as he shivered.

"Not really, it's quite practical and efficient.
Intercourse is the strongest form of connection two
beings can achieve, either to share great intimacy or
horrifically consume. It's reminiscent of the dark
sacrificial rites they once performed in worshiping

their queen. It is actually the true sexual transgression spoken about in the early laws that the old priests twisted to mean something else. Blood ritual and forced sex between men is the real sin...not that of true intimacy."

"Really?" James asked, becoming aroused somehow.

His power flared with desire. The Accuser ignored the ethereal advance, pretending not to sense it.

"This particular thrall," added Nick, "was going to a lot more effort than would be expected to simply feed, as if it were looking for something specific there in killing you perhaps. I knew him, something is not right...he should not have been here."

Nick slowly looked back at his plate, shrugging with a strange look. He resumed eating, not realizing how cold and apathetic he seemed to the boy. His description of the attack unfeelingly appeared little more than quaint dinner conversation, not the improbable horror that it was. The boy had suddenly heard enough.

James stopped eating, and looked fiercely at Nick. The breath of wind seemed to pause for him.

"O.K...do you mind telling me what the hell is going on here," he spouted. "If you know all of this stuff...why are you interrogating me? I was the victim here."

Then James put his fork down and stared wide eyed at Nick; making sure the sound it made when it hit the table was good and loud to show he was being emphatic. The pitch was like a chime. "I have no idea what you are talking about here," the boy added, "and I think I'm owed an explanation...one that is not so frigging crazy."

Nick stopped eating, mid-bite, fork in mouth, and looked back at the troubled boy with bewildered eyes. The sarcastic, taunting poise of Nick's body language – to say nothing of the fact that he half laughed at James – enraged the young man further.

"Excuse me," snapped James, "do you mind not looking at me like I'm a child...like this is an everyday thing? I just had a thrall, or whatever the hell you call it...stick his dick in me and try to cut my throat. You come along and toss his ass across the alley like he's a rag doll...kiss the dude, doing I don't even know what to him, and *then* he falls into a pile of shit at your feet. So, if you don't mind...stop looking at me like *I'm* the freak."

James's head seemed to pivot and sway as he leaned back in his chair. He folded his arms.

"Dirt," interjected Nick coolly.

"Dirt...shit...whatever," barked James back at him. "This is to say nothing of the fact that you come sweeping in there like some big fairy on two black wings...at least that is what I think I saw... black wings. Where are those wings anyway?"

James pauses mid-tirade and took a deep breath. He moved to look behind Nick, as if to see something. Nick's smile turned to more of a stern glare. Then James raised his eyes, his expression turned accusing. "And why don't you have a dick?"

At that Nick grinned so hard that his grit teeth peaked out from behind his lips. If the young man had not so positively enticed him with his little diatribe, the dark exile might have been insulted by such mortal insolence, but Nick found it oddly endearing. "Now, that was a mouthful," he mordantly chided the boy. "Let me see if I can help you understand all of this a little better...*puppy*."

James straightened up in his chair.

"First, and most importantly," Nick exclaimed, "I do have what you call a dick... one more profound in purpose than anything you can begin to comprehend in your simple mortal mind. When I fuck with it James, it's intended for much more than what yours is...and I might add that I know your type very well. You don't have much inclination to use yours for what its intended anyway...so wipe that smug grin off your face."

James's nostrils flared and his eyes got even wider as the Accuser spoke. He was not afraid of Nick from where he sat, despite sensing he should be. That bravery was short lived however, once he heard what Nick had to say.

"My wings are in the same place as my dick... ethereal beings do not need to sport our appendages everywhere we go, like you little mongrels. We have a degree of tact. And lastly, I am *not* a fairy...I am a divine-elemental. I prefer to be called Lord Jinn by the likes of you...but Archangel of Exile will suffice, if it helps you understand all of this better...whelp." Nick leaned back in has chair pleased with himself.

James simply stared straight into the abyss of the dark exile's eyes. Shock slowly began to register there again. The boy began to feel sick to his stomach.

"Now, as for as the thrall…I reduced him to ash and soil when I consumed his soul. What all you cretins are made up of…dirt. Sadly, I can only feed from the life force of the damned. I don't corrupt souls, my little friend, as some would suggest, but once they are sullied by the Pythians…they are fruit for the picking!"

James looked horrified at that last remark, as it became all too clear who his host actually was. It all added up. "Are you actually trying to tell me you're *the* Devil?" James asked nervously.

Nick picked up his fork and started to eat again, as if not moved at all by the accusation offered as a question.

"*The* Devil is a little formal for my taste and not all together what you think," he said, with his mouth full. "I am not the author of evil…God's immediate family gets that distinction…but yes, I am the first of his pets to ever say 'no' to him outright. So, a devil in your estimate, for what your kind understands of it. Still, all of this is beside the point, James."

The boy sat stunned, frozen to his chair. He wanted to run away right that instant, but could not. At least he dared not. "This is crazy," he said with resignation. "You're out of your mind. I can't believe I'm hearing any of this."

"Yes," replied Nick, "I have been out of my mind for thousands years now….again, that is beside the point."

James was white as a ghost, the effects of the trauma returning. Nick was suddenly ashamed of himself for being so callus and cruel about the matter, knowing it all had to be a very disturbing notion to the boy's sense of his world. He sighed and tired to undo the harm. "Look, James," he said softly, "I am sorry… really. I know this is hard."

The boy looked down into this food, as if to notice something there. He shivered.

"You have to excuse me," explained Nick. "I am just not used to being spoken to by mortals with such," he paused a moment, "frankness I guess is the word I am looking for. I suppose that I should be more sensitive to what you have been through in the last day and how this all shocks you, I am sure. Please, forgive me."

"That's putting it mildly," replied the boy. "Why me?"

"Yes, well I don't know why you specifically, James. That is the reason I was hoping you could tell me anything you might know about the attack. Thralls are not just any thugs and they don't attack randomly, even to feed…especially around me. And they *know* I am here. For this one to hunt the way it did, it had to have a very clear intention. We had a personal score to settle, this little shit and I. So the best I can figure is that you clearly must have something they want, my friend."

"Who are they?" asks James.

"The Pythia….thralls, grigori-demons, and dragons…all creatures that serve the great, dark dragoness," said Nick. "Her name is Tiamat, the primordial beast which is the true source of all wickedness in this existence. *She* is the author of evil… the true serpent of the garden."

James shifted, restless in his chair. If he were not so completely sure that he was now sober and *had* seen what he knew he had the night before, the boy would have stood up and walked right away from Nick that very instant. But there was something so deeply compelling about this dark stranger. James believed every word that came out of his mouth, despite not wanting to. That unsettled him.

Nick could see the misgiving in his eyes. "James," he said seductively, as he looked at the boy and tired to allay his dread with enchantment. "I know you are asking yourself what the hell you are doing here with me at this moment…when everything you have ever been taught is to fear and loathe what I am, but you are in very serious trouble. Right now I may be the only ally you have."

"What do you mean my *only* ally?"

"It's complicated, but when this sort of thing happens the Pythia generally kill their victims outright. Their collective safety would forever be at stake if they did not consummate their wicked habits for feeding with death. At the same time, you are now tainted with their mark. You may not be safe from Heaven or Hell." Nick leaned back and rubbed the back of his head. "Let me ask you something strange, James… do you sense anything different about yourself today? Are you able to see or understand things that yesterday you were not? "

James averted Nick's gaze and stared at his food again. The boy was searching deep inside his soul. He took a deep breath and answered with deliberate words. Nick could feel a shift in the young man's nature as he reached inside to touch that strange new part of himself. The dark exile's attention was drawn to every move of the boy's lips.

"It's as if I have been in a dim forest," said James, "never able to see past the encircling trees. All my life I sensed things out there…really I did…but could never quite make anything out from it. Now, I feel him inside me – the thrall that you speak about – and he is strong, very strong. The trees appear to clear, slowly thinning away as each hour passes. As they do, I am catching a glimpse of a new world."

He looked up sadly at Nick. "And yet, none of this makes much sense to me right now. It's all a fog of mixed images and feelings."

"The mortal veil is lifting for you…it's a dangerous thing to be touched by the power of the serpents."

"Are you saying I'm becoming something bad from this, Nick? Should I worry you will take my soul now?"

"I only ever do what I must," said Nick. He looked a little cagey, but his eyes were uncompromising. "There is more to becoming Pythian than simply looking into the dark-heart of iniquity, you must also *choose* to be one of them. But their way is alluring and often appears the right path because you want it to be, beware them, James. There *is* a correct way to do things as well as a wrong."

James pressed some advantage he sensed in the wavering of Nick's voice. "Funny, if I take you at your word and you only do what you are supposed to do," the boy replied, "why are you sitting here a rebel against Heaven in the first place?" James leaned forward into the face of the Devil as he spoke, not sure from where the sudden courage came.

The Accuser tensed. *This one is no fool,* he thought, lost in the boy's potent blue stare. *I like him... a lot.*

※

After dinner, Nick and James went back into the living room where the great winged statue stood. Nick followed behind the young man closely. The sky outside was velvet-black at that hour, and the lights of city were like sharp and shiny diamonds in a case. Nick sensed little out amid the night streets. He wondered if it was the calm before a storm, or if in fact something in his own sense of things was stilled. In either case, it was too quiet.

James stood transfixed by the statue. "Is this really supposed to be you?"

"Yes." Nick replied with a quiver in his voice.

James heard the shift in the dark exile's tone and turned to face him. For the first time he became aware that he could intuit what Nick was feeling. "At dinner you led me to believe," said the boy, pointing at the effigy, "all of this was some kind of cruel misunderstanding. What is that all about?"

Nick walked to the edge of the room. It was now his turn to stare off into the vastness of the city. New

York was a kind of wasteland, a human desert. It was so large and impersonal that a man could be alone despite standing at a street corner with thousands of others around him. Nick was just another soul lost there. He drew a deep breath and spoke. "The truth is I was betrayed by God." Nick paused a moment, not sure how the boy would take that suggestion.

"I see," said James, looking down at the ground.

Nick tilted his head as if to implore something of the boy, before he pushed on with his story. "I was told to do something I could not do...something I was specifically made *not* to do. When I refused it, I was cast aside. The statue is a little dramatic for my taste... your kind has a flare for that."

"What did God tell you to do that was so impossible?" James asked, genuinely bewildered.

Nick walked to James and loomed over him. His dark eyes drove into the boy. James felt weak in the knees. "Have you ever needed to love someone and could not?" Nick asked. James' face grew pale as he fumbled in his head for an answer. "I mean met someone who was everything you thought you should want to love, but for some reason no matter how hard you tried, the feelings would not come?"

"Yeah, I guess I have," the boy hesitantly replied. The Jinn could tell James was confused.

"Well," added Nick, "God commanded me to give my total trust and loyalty to a man, a mortal made of clay, but I simply could not bring myself to submit my heart to him. I had served faithfully at God's side for over twenty-thousand years...from almost the very beginning of this present age, which we Jinn call the seventh cosmic-day of God's reign. I was the first of my race. The essence of our kindred is total obedience to Him. So much so that to disappoint His favor is a fate worse than death for us...life forever without love."

Nick's eyes turned very sad.

"I don't understand," replied James. "Why would God instruct you to love someone if you could not?" He wondered how any of this could be believed.

"Good question, I'm still trying to figure that out... living in this nightmare of loneliness for thousands of years...never able to feel joy like I did then."

Nick looked deeply into James' clear-blue eyes, as if he were searching for something. Had the haughty mortal Adam touched him the way this boy seemed to – perhaps things would have been different. In the still desire of that moment, wrapped in Nick's sad longing, the boy interpreted his penetrating look as an invitation. James clumsily reached up and kissed Nick.

The Jinn jumped backward, shocked and timid, pushing James away as he did. At first James was hurt by the rebuke, but the instant that feeling fell over him it vanished when he saw Nick's face. The hurt there was so deep in the dark-browed angel's eyes, that James could almost touch his despair.

"I'm sorry, James," said Nick. "I did not mean to lead you on, if that was your impression...I...I.."

"It's O.K," James cut him off. The boy felt a little ashamed. "I just got carried away...I'm the one that should apologize. I don't normally do that. It's just you seemed so... I don't know...vulnerable I guess?"

Nick made an uncomfortably face. It was one of those moments for the dark exile when all his resentment over where mankind had left him sank away and he appreciated one of them for what they could be. "Are you saying I look desperate?" he asked with a nervous laugh.

"No, that is not what I meant."

"Yes it is, and you would be right...I am."

James looked down at the floor. "You don't like boys, do you?"

"I actually don't have a preference in that way, James," Nick somewhat lied. "At some point I will tell you about how attraction really works for ethereal beings, but right now it's more important we figure out why that thrall was after you."

James' expression took on a look of consternation. "O.K, well it's like I told you, Nick. I never saw the guy before."

"Did he say anything to you?"

"Besides calling me a faggot...no, not really."

Nick shook his head, it made no sense. "Well, we must be careful now in any event. You clearly carry a mark from that beast...they may try for you again."

"What do you mean, try again?" James nearly came out of his skin.

"Take is easy. I will be shadowing your every move from now on." Nick's look was sinister but cute in a way, more mischievous than cruel. "Trust me...I am a thrall's worst nightmare. The trick is to figure out what they want, and show them you are not worth the effort of getting past me."

James turned his head slightly and looked at Nick from the corner of his eyes. "So you never told me, Nick. Why do you care so much about me?"

"I care that they are after something here, that the dragoness sent this specific thrall to hunt in *my* domain. That gives me great pause. She is afraid of only one thing in this universe and you are clearly connected to that somehow…if not by purpose, then by chance now. Otherwise, such a powerful thrall would not have been so bold to openly stalk where it knew the vengeance of God waited. The truth is this seems almost contrived for my benefit, and that concerns me as well. I have reason to think there is more at work here than just chance…something is beginning…something dreadful." Nick remembered Gabriel's warning.

"What would that one thing She fears be, Nick?" asked the boy.

"The Son of God…the nameless-one made flesh," he replied.

"What would I have to do with the Son of God?"

"One never knows with your kind, James, but whenever either of He or She takes an interest in one of you…it is generally for a reason."

With that James tuned back and looked at the marble figure again. He suddenly wondered why this image was anatomically correct. Nick had made it clear he did not normally expose that aspect of himself to mortals. Did the artist know Nick in a way the Jinn would not admit to? James' silence seemed to unnerve the dark exile a little, who somehow knew exactly what the boy was thinking.

※

As the night deepened, Nick and James went out to the deck again to look at the lights of the city. The moon hung so full over the Hudson that it appeared unreal to James. The breeze was brisk, but remarkably warm. Slowly, Nick turned to the young man and examined the calm features of his face. The boy's blonde hair danced in the wind. *God, he is so beautiful,* the Accuser thought to himself. Nick could not help but wonder what it was about this boy that so captivated him. Mortals rarely affected him with such longing.

Trying to allay his feelings, Nick turned his attention down to the city, twisting his mind to make sense of it all. New York was immersed in sadness and fear behind its glitz. All any thrall needed to do in order to sustain itself was simply loiter there, feeding off the pulse of despair that flowed up and away from every corner and street. No need to hunt and expose ones power. Proximity alone was enough to nourish the dark bottom-feeders of the city. It was in fact why Nick made the city his home – it was easy for him to feed in the very same way. *So why would Longinus, of all the twisted thralls, dare come here to feed in a way that would stand out so obviously?* he wondered.

Slowly, Nick began to string together what Gabriel had told him about the coming tribulation with this strange, erratic behavior of the Pythians. It was all too convenient for his taste. *Still, even if this is all in fact somehow connected to what Gabe told me,* he pondered. *Why this mortal, with his nagging familiarity? There is something more at work here that I am not seeing.*

The Accuser turned ever so slightly, and looked at the boy from the corner of his eyes again, probing at the edges of James' mind with his own. He wanted inside the boy, but sensed he dare not try now. It was an eerie feeling of foreboding that haunted James' aura.

"Tell me about yourself, James. Where are you from?" Nick asked finally.

James was taken aback by the turn in conversation as well as Nick's abrupt shift in mood. There was such seductiveness to the Jinn's voice. *Is this some kind of spell as well?* James thought to himself. *He is clearly capable of so many things. Is he using me for something?*

"Long Island, a little town there called Sayville," the boy answered.

"Ah yes, where the ferry goes to Fire Island," Nick replied. They both paused, and then laughed together at the unintentional play on words.

"My mother lives there still. My dad died when I was a kid." James added.

"What brought you to the city?"

"To dance…I was with the Metropolitan Ballet for a while, but I injured myself. I've struggled ever since, doing odds-and-ends…working at restaurants or bars."

"That is quite a transition, from the Metropolitan Ballet to a bartender."

"Yeah, it's been a real humbling experience."

"I can imagine…trust me, I know what it is like to have your wings clipped."

James looked at Nick pensively. Somehow he didn't think the comparison was accurate, knowing what the Jinn had meant.

"Nick?" James asked softly after a moment.

The Accuser turned his head a little – his eyes looked menacing, despite that not being his intent. The wind stilled.

"Do you hate God for doing what He did?"

The Devil's frightful look faded to a pale frown; the expression was a sullen. Bit by bit he turned his body toward James full on, and let out a sigh. His entire form seemed to shudder as he began to speak.

"No, James, I don't hate God. I miss Him more than you can begin to imagine. Everything I am belongs to Him; exile is anguish for me."

James looked confused for a second. He could tell Nick's heart was breaking, but how he knew that he wasn't sure.

"Love is a funny thing for the Jinn," Nick said sadly. "We are eternal creatures, living almost without time…outside of what you understand of existence's attachments. The bond between a divine entity and what it brings fourth into existence is more powerful than any attraction mortals can understand, it transcends simple material terminology."

Nick looked toward Heaven. James hung on his words.

"God had a wife very long ago," the Accuser went on, "his one true love. He lost her to chaos, the designs of the dragons. His loss has affected the entire universe ever sense."

James' eyes grew wide. That idea seemed strange.

"When he lost her," added Nick with a tiny smile, "He made the Jinn to fill that gap left in His heart. He made us all to serve and honor Him...most of my kind still does to this day."

"This is so overwhelming," replied James. "You are telling me that first, not only there is a God – which I never really was sure I believed in the first place – but then that there are other god-like immortals. Stranger still that the angels were created because God's heart was broken over His *wife?* "

Nick snorted a little, amused with James' wonder. "Kind of all that, yes...but He made you for the same reason, James...to love and fill the void of loneliness. Is that really so bad?"

"So you are seriously trying to tell me God is like bisexual or something?"

Nick laughed even harder at that questioning observation...for the boy's need to equate sacred affinities with the mortal conventions of gender and sex.

"True love is not as simple as your kind makes it out to be, James. Love is too vast a thing to try and capture with just words. I know it is hard for you to fathom. The best thing to say is that I was fashioned as a specific kind of 'spiritual concubine'... made to love in *His* means of intimacy. What you mortals think of as sex is really the reflection of a much more complex ethereal exchange. Since mortals don't

normally experience conjoining at the level we do…
you misunderstand and misuse it."

James understood that much at least. He nodded
at Nick, agreeing men did not seem to comprehend
true love. He didn't anyway.

"After the loss of the goddess…even we Jinn were
simply not enough for Him and the depth of loneliness
that He suffered. So, he made you and your kind next,
with your ability to choose to love. For him, choice
likens you in spirit to the immortals themselves and
thus He values your love above all else."

"Above your love?" asked James.

Nick looked down at the street below him, his acute
vision taking in every detail of the dark avenue. He
grew very still. "Yes," he said sadly, "especially above
my love…that seems clear."

They both just stared into the dark a while.

After a time, James spoke again. He really wanted
to know more, despite being able to see all these
confessions were weighing heavy on the dark angel's
spirit. "So, how is it that if there are really other gods –
we don't worship them too?"

"You are not theirs, you belong to Him alone.
Your kind has tried in the past to worship others,
but because He is author of your being, He is most
concerned with your lives. To the others you are
simply things with which to toy, especially in trying to
manipulate Him."

"I don't understand something, Nick," interjected
James. "You don't seem like a bad guy at all. How is it
you are considered the source of all evil?"

Nick coughed at that, catching his breath and looking up at the moon to avoid the boy's gaze... thinking hard about the question before he said another word.

"Some of the Jinn were created for other purposes... beyond simply to love God. We each consume dark energy, which finds its source in the malice of the dragons. There were several of us created specifically for the various malevolent emotions, each corresponding to an element...like me with fire, and each corresponding in turn to a negative energy upon which we primarily feed. I consume hate... it is my lot in life to devour the deepest spitefulness in men and immortals. When I fell from God's court, I did not give up my role...I have continued though the ages, a dark vigilante, consuming the enemies of God. But over time, men have come to associate me with the very evil I feed upon, much in the way they confuse my brother, Michael, with death itself. He does not bring death...he consumes fear of it. He is the messenger of peace at the end of all things. And yet, your kind thinks of him as the actual harbinger of mortality. You've all come to see me in a similar way, as the source of hate and malice, which is the root of all sin...despite my not being that at all."

James looked at Nick skeptically. He wanted to believe him, but it all seemed so convenient and convincing. This was the deceiver of men after all.

Nick saw his expression. The boy was unsure he sensed.

"I don't blame you for what you are thinking, James. There is in fact more to it. I have not always been without malevolence myself in many ways, especially where mankind is concerned. Still, was I not there in *your* moment of fear, before Michael, to excise the poisonous hate from the thrall? I could have left you to that death, which must count for something. I drew from you his hatefulness; that is why you do not now find rage in your heart...I took it."

"Well, you are right in that much, Nick. I am thankful you came along when you did. I guess for now we'll have to just leave it at that." The boy looked at the floor. "I have to be honest...I can't say I trust you yet. I'm sorry for that. I think it's important I be honest now. Still, I don't think you are a monster either."

Nick looked relieved. Whether he wanted to admit it or not, it did get to him that men thought of him as one of the beasts that caused malice merely because he did not act under the sanction of God.

James paced back and forth nervously in his own steps, searching for what to say next. "So who was this goddess? What happened to her?"

"Astarte? She was imprisoned, so to speak"

"What did she do?"

"Nothing," replied Nick. "She was actually kidnapped and forever changed. The change that overtook her is a kind of captivity. Our Lord is not without his enemies among the immortals...chief among remains the dragon Aboddon Naga, the hateful one called Leviathan, who rules the sea of the underworld. He abducted the goddess and took her to a deep place under the dome of the earth...to hurt God."

"Freaky shit!"

Nick looked over at James with a strange glare. "What?" he asked.

"Freaky shit…this entire thing. If I had not seen those wings of yours with my own eyes…I'd say you were into some serious drugs, Nick."

The Accuser laughed once more and edged closer to James. A bizarre, sad expression overcame the Devil.

"What's wrong?" the boy asked nervously.

"Nothing," replied Nick, shaking his head as if had been struck about the ears. "You just reminded me of someone for a second." Nick's heart ached.

"Oh God, I'm afraid to ask who that might be," James responded sarcastically, not intending to be cruel, just playful about all the ensuing drama.

"Don't then!" Nick irritably snapped back at him. The Accuser turned and walked a few steps away to stew in hurt.

❧

Not far away from where Nick and James stood, a grigori named Azael sat at the edge of a bed in a tiny apartment. His imposing, nude body filled the space. He took a long drag on a cigarette and exhaled, the smoke filling the room. Next to him a young man lay in the bed face down, sobbing. The sinister turned-Jinn leaned back and ran his hand down the boys back, admiring a series of welts that he had himself just inflicted.

The boy cringed at his touch. "Please, don't hurt me again," he pled through his tears, "just leave me alone."

Azael smiled and leaned forward to whisper in his ear. "I am afraid I do have to hurt you again, beautiful," the monster smugly growled.

He grabbed the young man's hair and pushed his head into the corner to where the bed was set against the wall. He shifted himself up and splayed open the boy's legs. The boy whimpered. The great weight of the beast pressed down on the tender frame of the youth, smothering him. Then he extinguished the burning cigarette on the boys exposed neck. The young man shrieked, calling out for deliverance from Christ.

"That's it," Azael sneered, "keep calling. God won't hear your pitiful cries, but the Devil is bound to soon enough."

Standing back at the building ledge, Nick was fretting over what he thought was James' thoughtless remark. Out of nowhere, he felt a sudden wave of human pain reach him – a jab of dark power clearly intended to taunt his jealous rage. His body tensed and his face turned pale, the Pythia were loosed upon the city, seemingly unafraid of the Accuser's hand now.

James wanted to take back what he had said. It had simply been a joke, one he realized was a little inopportune, but before he could open his mouth to beg forgiveness, Nick had sprung up over the rail. James was shocked to see the Jinn throwing himself

connotation, abused by mankind as it has been, but that is another story. Still, *we* take pride in what we are and how we love each other as a ritual form of devotion to Allah, despite what others think."

"I am beginning to see nothing is as I thought."

"True I am sure, but Allah has many secretes that none of us fully know or comprehend. Mystery is the way of things…life would not be worth living if all the paths of fate were fully known."

James twisted his head a little as he looked at his real host. "Are you another angel, Nafees?"

"Me…a Jinn? No, not at all."

"Then who or what are you…if you are not an angel?"

Nafees grinned at James and reclined his head against the silk covered pillow upon which the boy sat. He said nothing for a few moments, as the room grew even colder. The moonlight streamed into the apartment and seemed to cause Nafees' dark completion to glow.

The strange immortal spirit was not a large framed creature, but his body still seemed strong. He had a lithe, sensual look about him. James noticed how his long hair shone in the pale light, pulled back behind his head into a tail and held there by a string of ornate beads. A strong desire took hold of James to touch the bindings, but he controlled the sudden impulse.

"I am born of the earth and sky. A lesser immortal if you will…the ancient word used for my kind is elohim."

James shuttered nervously, realizing that Nafees was literally bowing at his feet. "You mean like some sort of god?"

"I would not say that, James," replied Nafees. "There is only one god as God, He begetteth not, nor is begotten, and there is none like unto Him...even as human, Deliver, His humanity is absorbed by His deity. The term 'god' carries too much misunderstanding for you mortals to really be the word I would choose for my kind...but yes I am made of eternal essence...a lesser divinity in a great and dignified family of spirit. Still, let's not allow names like 'immortal' to come between us. Allah is all our king and master, directly or indirectly, if you count yourself among the Sons of Light."

James was getting used to being blown off his feet by mystical revelation. Somehow he sensed this was not the last astonishment that would come to him in the days ahead. He noticed the binding on Nafees' hair again, for some reason it kept drawing his attention up to the man's face like a charm.

"The beads of Astarte call to you...she beckons you to partake of her offerings."

"Nick spoke of her...God's wife?" James' voice rose with excitement.

"Alas, speak with more reverent sorrow, James... she will never be that again."

James cast his eyes down, embarrassed.

Nafees rose from where he stood, and walked to the bookshelf, where he took a small wooden box from the ledge. He carried it back to James. Slowly, he unbound his hair and it fell into his eyes. A sensual grace ran off of it as if poured there by some divine power. "Here, let me make for you a gift, as it was for me once," said the immortal cleric.

"Oh, I couldn't," said James, shaking his head anxiously. "You have done enough for me here already."

"I insist. The beads call to you for a reason. You need the peace of Allah's beloved now I think, like few men ever have. She is a path to His grace."

James nodded, trying to grasp the strange things he was learning. It was still all beyond him, he thought.

After Nafees unstrung the beads from the binding in his hair, dropping them into a blue porcelain dish, he removed a small spool of string from the wooden box. The thread seemed to glisten, as if it were made of some mysterious metal. The youthful immortal laced out several feet from the spool, which he wrapped gingerly around James' ankle. It felt warm, and soft to the touch. With meticulous care, Nafees began to weave the string and beads into an ankle bracelet. The gesture filled James with wonder. As Nafees crafted the gift, he spun a melodic tale with his soft and tranquil voice...enchanting the boy.

"In the beginning, there was Allah. He became the source of light, separating himself from all gloom. With Him and yet of Him was Tiamat, the darkness of the void. They were both without form, like two endless, raging rivers twisting about each other. Their essence ebbed and flowed in timelessness. Then Allah chose to reach for Her and She for Him. In the

instant they touched one another, all being burst forth in a great conflagration of light."

"But Allah and Tiamat were not of like-mind, light and darkness became quarrelsome companions from that moment on in time. Tiamat argued with Allah, regarding Herself as His equal and sought to be on top of Him in their conjoining. When He refused Her that place, She escaped like a dark tempest and became the depth of nothingness we call the Abyss, the primal ocean of Ti'amatum."

"Before She fled however, Allah spoke into Her the greater immortals... the mother of earth, Kishar, and the sky lord, Anshar. The earth mother in turn bore other lesser immortals, the elohim, who serve Allah as extensions of his one, true being. It was from our ranks His first beloved came... Elat Astarte, the goddess consort. She embodied love and wisdom... around her all beautiful things were fruitful and took shape. It was Astarte who gave rise the two trees of Eden, as a dowry for Him... one of everlasting life and the other of infinite wisdom. Around them Allah raised high walls to protect Heaven... it was good, and He blessed all he saw."

"But Tiamat was envious and so out of spite... mocking Him... mocking His spoken creation and its fruits... She begot serpents from her own flesh and among them She too took a consort, Aspu. He was an angry, violent spirit because the noise of the other immortals, what Allah spoke, agitated and enraged him. The dragon was such a depraved beast that for his wrath he conspired to kill all the elohim."

"So Allah sought out the serpent's wickedness and struck him dead with a powerful sword. Tiamat mourned Aspu's destruction, hating Allah for visiting wrath on them. She in turn sought vengeance, a blood dept. The dragoness sent

Her son, the impotent leviathan named Aboddon, to trap Astarte forever in Sheol, the deepest vaults of Ti'amatum. The leviathan stole her away by tricking her into consuming dark manna, the fruits of death. In doing so, Astarte became bound to the Abyss for all time, a spirit of the underworld in the prison of Sheol."

"Allah went down the paths of the dead and using His power over destiny defeated many dragons, but he could not bring Astarte out of the Abyss. She had become one with loss, the mother of graves...her soul lifeless like an empty womb. Allah grieved so fiercely that he vowed to never again take an elohim as consort. He commanded that none of us among immortals were to ever assume the form woman again, so even Kishar keeps the appearance of stone and sand below our feet."

"Then Allah made the Jinn, and after made man, filling them with all His love and joy like vessels molded of clay and loam. But the spirit of Astarte did not pass away as He thought...to this day it lingers in the two trees as a seasonal gift...the smell of honeysuckle on the breeze and the sound of birds on wing. She is love and wisdom itself, through her we reach joy...we reach the grace of Allah. Whenever your heart is filled with desire for your beloved, young James, you are touching her, and she reaches for Him with that ecstasy...His beatific-vision."

As Nafees finished the tale, he also completed his work about James' ankle. The beads were snuggly fastened and seemed to radiate a strange enchantment. The boy admired the craft and its delicate weaving.

"These are very special beads," said Nafees. "They are blessed. I cannot tell you of their importance, truly

I don't know. They are charms that yield a different power to each person who holds them. Only when the time is right, will Allah show you their purpose. For now, simply take them as a mark of friendship between us."

James smiled at Nafees with such appreciation, he thought for a moment he might cry for the power he felt within the gift's embrace. "Nafees, that story was so beautiful and sad. I am not sure I understand it all," he said.

"There is so much for you to learn...that is for sure," replied Nafees. "Your eyes are only newly open to the truth of Allah as all our Beloved."

"I suppose," James conceded, realizing how much his world had been turned on its head. Here was a celestial priest revealing to him more than he could fully grasp at once.

"I will tell you," added Nafees, "the veneration of Allah through the Queen of Heaven is a lost faith, but for the few devotees that still follow me. We have a special role to play in the things to come and have had to adapt to changing time, waiting for the sign to take up our swords for our faith again. I am a humble cleric now...my power as an immortal diminished, but my devotion to Allah remains steadfast. This anklet will be our token charm to you...many of the Rafiq ware or use the beads. We also mark the flesh to distinguish our suffering for Allah. You too have suffered at the hand of the dragons, young James. Now we will always be here for you, but I warn you...you must be very careful if you leave here tonight. The minions of the dragon are at hand and are dangerous, from what Nick told me…you should be wary."

Nafees watched James intently, wondering what strand of fate had brought him to them. The signs had said to look for a prophet by way of faithful Jinn, Gabriel he still believed. Yet this young man seemed touched by an ethereal silhouette that was as powerful as any seer he had known. All of a sudden a faint buzz emanated from the boy, like a bee trapped in jar. James fumbled at his tattered pants and pulled out a small pager – forgotten there in all the rush of drama and intrigue.

"I was wondering when someone would be looking for you," said Nafees.

"It's my roommate I think. She must really be upset at me for not coming home." James looked up at Nafees. The boy seemed so lost and confused at the moment that the immortal cleric wanted to reach out and embrace him to soothe all his fears.

"Can I use your phone?" asked James, with a worried face.

"Certainly, it's over here."

After Nafees pointed the way, he left James alone in the room. He paced, sensing the boy would want to leave, despite all he had seen. Letting him go into the chaos of the night would be the cleric's greatest leap of faith in centuries, one he must make. Nafees was restless; his hands shook as he stooped to sift about the contents of an old trunk.

A few moments later James stepped back into the room. "That was my roommate alright," he said. "She was furious. My friends have been calling. No one knew where I went after I left the club."

The immortal cleric said nothing, only nodded stiffly and handed James a pair of jeans, along with a warm sweater. If the boy was going, the torn linen pants he had come in with were simply not suitable for the street now. "Here," he said, "I assumed you would need to rush out. I really don't recommend it right now...but I can understand that you have things that you must do...fate clearly calls you. Nick cannot shelter you from that fact forever. You must embrace it and the intention that Allah desires of you."

James looked a little uncomfortable, not sure how to respond. "I really do have to go, at least to meet one person. I lost my wallet. I never even noticed it was gone in all the fuss. I really need it...it's the only ID I have."

"Understandable," said the immortal.

"Some guy called the apartment and left a message saying he found it in the street," James explained. "I just called his number...I arranged to meet him. I'll just run home, grab some stuff, and meet the guy close to my place."

"Would you like me to call someone...to have them go with you?"

"No, thank you. It will be fine."

Nafees looked at him with concerned eyes. His gaze was somewhat frightful.

"Nafees, I believe this is all really serious stuff... honest. How can I not after what I've seen? But I just can't stay cooped up here. I'm a big boy…I can take care of myself."

Nafees just tiled his head up and down once. *The boy has no idea yet what he is up against,* he thought to himself.

"Here is my address," added James, as he reached for a pad of paper. "When Nick comes back, tell him I'm going home and this is where he can find me." James held out the paper. "All I have to do is meet this guy and get my wallet. After that I will go back home and wait. Really, it'll be fine…I'm a big boy."

James quickly tugged the jeans up around his waist and pulled the sweater over his head. He was adorable, despite the baggy, miss-fit clothes. He stuffed his keys and pager into the front pockets of the jeans and made for the door. As he was leaving, Nafees pushed a wad of twenties into his hand and scowled.

"What's this for?" James asked shyly.

"The cab home…if you don't have your wallet, you don't have money."

James did not like to take cash from friends, even to borrow, but it was an emergency. "Thank you, Nafees," he said sweetly, "I will see you soon…I promise. I will bring back your clothing and pay you back."

"I know you will…you and I are bound now… remember the charm? It's called a Rafiq as well. It means 'beloved friend' …companion, if you will. Here is my number and the address to the apartment, should you need it."

James looked at the card. It was made of some kind of plastic, not cardboard, very professional looking. It had a single phone number in one corner and the address to the building in the other. Directly in the center of the card it spelled out the name of the order. He grinned at the strange immortal.

"Remember the Rafiq when you are most in need and Allah will be there with you, as will we all, James."

James made a grateful face as Nafees opened the door. Within seconds the boy was down the hall and in the elevator. The cleric's own face became very severe, he was deeply concerned about the boy going out on his own, but he knew he had to let him go. *He must find his own way to us now,* thought the cleric. He knew Nick would not be pleased at all, that was for certain.

A warm breeze enshrouded Nick as his body pulled into a tight, aerodynamic dart. The great surge of his wings pushed the air back and away as he descended toward the street level. He closed his eyes, letting the cool gusts flow over him, as if he were indulging a ritual cleansing. He winced for what ached deep at the core of his being, that part of him that could never be purified in any way. It burned at his very center.

Back on the apartment terrace with James, an indescribable dark-surge had crashed into his psychic essence. It was a cry piercing the ethereal realm; the screams of yet another young mortal Nick sensed caught in the grip of the Pythia. *What the hell is going on now?* he thought. *What are they after here all of a sudden?*

Particularly worrisome to Nick was the fact he'd had no prior sense of this attack in his ethereal forethought. His sense of impending malevolence seemed disrupted somehow; it flickered and faltered as he looked to it. He scanned the cityscape with intense celestial perception, looking for the source of turmoil. It was at this point he realized the incursion was from more than a simple thrall. It was a dreaded grigori...a turned angel.

The Accuser was not himself a turned angel, as popularly believed. He occupied a different, rather distinct space. He was more of a refugee from Heaven than an actual rebel against it. Nick's proud disobedience was a far cry from what characterized the plight of a true grigori, for when an angel turned, it did more than flout divine will. It twisted its power against God himself, commingling it with darkness and chaos. Nick was more than a match for any single angel or even a host of thralls, but a grigori was another matter altogether. He shuddered at the thought of facing one alone, struggling to understand what need of him they might have in all this. These incursions seemed almost to provoke him, first by going after James the way they did and now by whatever this new demon wanted. Gabriel had said the end was near. Now the evidence was plain to see, even without the Herald of Heaven's warning. He could feel the grigori torturing its hapless victim, creating deliberate torment that echoed out into the night like a beacon – a ploy to draw him out, no doubt. *Why are both sides suddenly so interested in me?* he wondered.

Nick fell into a dive, increasing his speed as he concentrated on the scent in the night air. He honed in on it slowly, like a shark tasting blood in the water. The air was saturated with terror and hate, making it easy to trace the evil even without his forethought. Using his wings to brace his decent, he stopped in mid-flight where he could almost touch the dread with his hands. He hovered for a second, staring through a half-open window. All was still. The attack was over he could tell; the disturbance the demon created abruptly fading. His wings beat silently in the cool air, as the curtains inside the room fluttered. There was no motion or sensation, just the horrid smell of burnt flesh, and sex. Nick extended his power carefully about the edges of the space. *Nothing*, he thought, *the grigori is gone.* He figured going through the window at this juncture was unnecessary and overly dramatic. Still, he needed to get inside somehow without either startling the boy or disrupting the ethereal signature left by the demon. "The door will have to do," he said aloud to himself, working out a plan.

He thrust up with a single stroke of his wings and shot out over the buildings crowned with their tangled web of TV aerials. Then he eased his way to the ground, landing in an alley that was nestled between the apartment building and a bar next door. The light of the street reflected in the pooling water of the alleyway, it shimmered at his feet. With very intentional steps, he emerged onto the street and glanced down the pavement to see the speeding traffic of Eighth Avenue, with its streaking yellow cabs and dissonance of sound. He turned slowly, concentrating on the pain to find his way toward the boy.

The Accuser moved onto the sidewalk and to the front of the building. His nimble feet jumped the few steps easily enough. With precision, he used his power to pierce the lock. Ever so gently, he turned over the tumblers in his mind and one-by-one they came free. He pushed the door open and slipped inside like a shadow. The smell of urine filled the foyer; he ignored the odor and started up the stairwell. As he did, Nick was relieved to find that he could not detect the presence of the demon anywhere close. Still, he moved with caution, making his way up the stone steps, each worn thin at the center, carved into a dip.

Two feral looking dogs emerged from the basement entrance below where Nick entered the building. They glanced at one another, opening their horrible maws and letting their tongues slither over foul teeth with glee. Their mouths made a kind of twisted smile. Waiting a few seconds, they glared up the stairs toward Nick, then turned, and bolted away into the shadows of the street. The passers-by were seemingly unaware of them as they pounced along the avenue into the night. One beast scaled an oncoming cab effortlessly in a single stride and vanished in the midst of the traffic above it. The other scurried after, tail bent and tucked between its legs.

Nick reached for the door of the apartment, not wanting to probe too far ahead and give away his approach, in case the demon might attempt to strike from hiding. He extended his vision just enough to sense the air that hung there. He found only the boy. Nick turned the knob and the door-latch gave way. There the young man lay sobbing, in shock, and completely unaware of Nick's arrival.

The Accuser cloaked himself in obscurity to insure he did not startle the young victim as he approached. It was increasingly obvious to Nick that the boy had been tortured for the sole intent of luring him there, just as he had suspected. The angel drew upon all his strength and inhaled the fury polluting the room. With vigilance, he looked to the boy's injuries. First, Nick sat on the bed and put his arms around the young man, who was shaking like a leaf. He saw the brutal burns on the boy's neck and the savage bruises across his back. The Accuser mashed his teeth. The boy pulled away from him the instant they touched, but Nick reached out with his power and eased his anguish. "What happened?" he asked softly.

The young man turned up his face to Nick slowly, tears filled his eyes. His lower lip quivered as he spoke. "I met him online, in a chat room," said the injured boy. "He told me he lived around the corner. I was just so lonely."

Nick frowned, he at least understood what the boy was feeling. "Go on..."

"When he got here, he just attacked me...he held me down and made me. I told him I did not want to do that, but it only made things worse."

Strange, thought Nick, *none of this behavior of late adds up for the Pythia.* He looked deeply into the young man, to perhaps catch a glimpse of something the demon may have left behind, like with James. There was nothing. The grigori had simply tortured him. It had not conjoined with his mind, nor even tried to feed from the boy. "Did he say anything to you about what he wanted?"

"No," the boy whimpered, "he just kept hurting me and saying the Devil would come for me soon."

Nick clinched his fists. There it was...what he feared...it *was* on his account. *But why?* he wondered.

The boy put his face in his hands and began to sob uncontrollably. Nick decided not to press any harder, it was doubtful the youth knew more. If the Accuser acted quickly, he might be able to pick up a hint of the beast's presence within the ephemeral world and trail it to its next move; that was if his senses would hold out a little longer. Nick was unsure why his power was fading the way it was, so he would rather face the Pythians sooner than later...before he could not do it at all.

"Is there anyone here who can help you?" asked the Accuser.

The boy looked up and nodded. "A friend lives downstairs".

"Call him," said Nick, bending the boy's thoughts. "Tell him to come now."

The young man picked up the phone and dialed. Nick could hear the faint ring, then the voice.

"Hello?"

"Jim?" asked the frighten boy.

"Yes."

"It's Nathan upstairs, can you come up? It's an emergency...I need help."

"Sure, I will be right up...you O.K?"

"No," sobbed the boy, collapsing into a fetal ball.

"I'm coming right now," replied the panicked voice over the phone.

Nick took the phone and hung it up. He placed one hand over the boys face. "Be calm, help is on the way," he said. The Accuser drew as much fear from the boy as he could, like poison from a wound. The young man stilled, seeming to slip in and out of a dark sleep. "When you wake up, you won't remember me."

The boy moaned and with that turned away. Nick slowly nudged the door a crack, he opened a portal into the ethereal plane and slipped through it.

"Don't let the Devil take me," the boy mumbled anxiously as Nick vanished.

Once Nick's physical form dissipated into the gap of the Realm of Essences, he stretched out his mind and tasted the energy that flowed around him. The demon clearly wanted Nick to sense him. *The power signature is certainly Jinn*, he thought, *but I can't make it out...the traitor is moving away...downtown.*

He froze.

Not one demon....two grigori! Nick's mind raced.

He quickly reappeared in the alley, and stood outside the apartment building. The assaulted boy's window was above him. Looking up, he saw shadows of motion on a shade. Help had come. Nick was relieved. He turned and walked along a path through the trash of the street. Glancing both ways, he sniffed the air like an animal. *Nothing*, he thought.

Nick debated in his mind whether to move downtown where the beasts seemed to be headed, or go back and get James. *Mysterious thralls... visits from Gabriel... more grigori on the loose*, thought Nick anxiously. *The signs are clear, it is time perhaps.* It was obvious both his sins as well as those of the world were catching up to them somehow.

Nick sensed that he would be caught between the judgments of Heaven and the ambition of Hell – war as coming. He began to second guess the hasty decision to leave James at the Rafiq apartment.

As Nick realized these were in fact the last days coming to fruition, he was not sure about to leave the only other lead he had about what was unfolding solely in the hands of Nafees' fanatic knights.

The dark exile paced, trying to set his mind at ease, working through his anxiousness. In spite of his worry, the old cleric was in fact the closest thing to a friend Nick had in his existence. The Accuser had known the priest for eons, but his loose alliance with the elohim had actually only begun in more recent times – as immortal existence goes. Over thousands years, the cleric had ruled a vast collective of sacred precincts that were dedicated to the goddess, Astarte. The temples stretched from Babylon to Egypt at one time, and in them the mortal priests performed primal rites of conjoining. Nick had actually shared in a ritual-bed on more than one occasion – seeking its power – but found no peace in their spell of ziña.

In those days, it was common practice for mortals to make offerings at a temple, and after conjoin with a priest of the goddess in ritual, reaching through them as vessels for the ecstasy of God. It was after Nick's failed attempts, Nafees told him that he would never find solace in the rite until he opened his heart fully to men.

The Accuser of course refused such a thing, spurning all but God directly. But Nafees had been true to his word – from that time forward, Nick did come to trust the cleric's sincerity and they had a deep bond. In fact it would be the Accuser who later helped Nafees' followers escape the night the Levitican temple warriors burned their holy places in Jerusalem, and cast them out. On that night the Rafiq knights and the Accuser came to appreciate each other's plight in exile.

But these were different times. Nick was not so sure who to trust.

The Jinn dodged a line of traffic on the street, as thoughts rattling about his head. There was so much that did not make sense of what was going on, but the truth was that nothing leading to God ever really did for him. While the Accuser paced, he caught the sudden glimpse of a familiar face out of the corner of his eye, sitting just inside a café and staring at him pensively. The instant he saw the figure, his ethereal senses sprang to life. Nick strode into the little side-street shop to stand near his chair.

The Jinn grinned up at him as he approached.

"I'm surprised to see you here," the Accuser said smugly. "Did Gabe get the message wrong or did you need to rub it in a little more yourself, Micah, now that my reprieve approaches its end?"

"Same old Iblis, oh I forget...you still insist on His pet name for you...Nick, right?"

"What do you want? I'm a little busy right now and don't appreciate this sudden obsession you all have with me. I got your message...no need to come yourself to remind me I am condemned."

"Things are even more out of sorts than I realized when I sent the Guardians," he replied. "We need some help and I thought perhaps I could ask a favor of you...since you have nothing to lose." The angel's expression was grim, but didn't reveal more than his nervousness for the need to disobey God in coming to the Devil.

"Out of whack for whom?" sneered Nick.

"Whom else?" Micah snapped back, "the one who makes all of destiny's plans. It seems your little – shall we say – 'rebellion' has caught on even more these days. The deck is being shuffled again, and we cannot count on all our soldiers this time around. The dark-matter of the universe is growing...ethereal power seems to be diminishing in its wake. The Jinn are turning away from God."

"How is that my problem?" Nick snorted. It was then it dawned on him; this was perhaps why his foresight was failing. It was not just *his* power that was weakened. He pulled back a chair and sat. What the Draftsman had to say was worth hearing.

Micah was created from the mind of God, a manifestation of extreme power that existed outside time and space. He was the custodian of the eternal plan and he was the only one other than God himself privy to much of destiny. Still, Nick knew God kept things even from him. The angel of design was out of his element now, lost as God's plan apparently spun out of his control.

Nick found all of this terribly amusing. He was used to being cut off from God, but the remaining Jinn must be utterly unnerved by such a fate, as darkness grew around them. Still, he did not buy that any of this was really his fault, even for a second. Nick knew he simply was not that important to God.

"So if destiny is off track, why do you need my help?" he asked.

"Like I said, because you messed it up in the first place," answered the Jinn with a flip voice.

"Don't fuck with me."

"The Pythia have swayed more of the Jinn. This does not factor into the plan I was shown. Our kind was made to obey, and somehow you have managed to instill in the others a sense of entitlement toward their own selfish end. It's gotten out of hand with the others; while you at least went your own way, and kept to yourself…they have gone so far as to consort with chaos…with Her… other Jinn have turned and become grigori."

"Ah, that's bad," replied Nick coolly. He did not want Micah to know he had already figured out more of the grigori were loosed on the world. "So what makes you think I haven't done the same thing myself? What would I have to lose from finally going over to their side?"

"Because I alone know that while you are a self absorbed rogue...too long favored by the nameless-god before He put you in your place...you still love Him more than you do your own hated existence. But don't worry...I can keep your masochistic obsession a secret, brother."

Nick glared at him so intently that the two of them locked embraces within the ethereal realm itself. Micah pushed back hard at the Accuser of God to fend him off, but the hand of justice was stronger than any one power that had ever been fashioned in creation. Nick pinned Micah's wings, straining there in anger against him for what seemed an eternity. The weaker Jinn finally signaled he would yield. They released each other and both withdrew their power from the ethereal realm.

"I have things to do," said the dark exile as he rose to his feet, grasping Micah's arm to reinforce his supremacy. When Nick went to pull away, having made his point, Micah opened the mind of God and power flushed through Nick's being. Visions of such intensity filled his head that he was wracked with pain and yet he relished the feel of God inside of him again.

Nick let go, stumbled back two steps, and shook his head. Micah's expression became wild-eyed. "You are not as tough as you think you are on your own, don't ever forget that, Accuser," said Micah.

Nick realized suddenly that locking wings inside the Realm of Essences had given Micah an opening. He was an exile, none of the court could freely help him with ethereal sight without drawing the wrath of

God...but Nick could *take* it from them if he wanted, because he was stronger. Micah had deliberately provoked the Accuser in order to have an excuse to submit, so as to allow Nick into the portent of God's mind for just an instant. There he saw more of the obscure design that was playing out, which Micah had intended for him to see all along. "My God," said Nick. "James...he is immersed in dragon fire."

Micah rose to his feet, his face almost pleading. "Stop Azael and Shemhazai," he barked, "before they screw up everything. You need that boy!"

James took a cab home to his apartment on St. Marks Place in the East Village. For the entire ride downtown he could not shake the sense that he was being followed. As the cab pulled up to his apartment, James pushed a ten dollar bill into the cabby's hands through the tiny window that separated the front from the back. He stopped to look at both sides of the seat to make sure he had everything, chuckling to himself as he realized he had nothing to lose. "Keep the change," he said with a groan.

As he climbed out of the cab, the air was still and stuffy. He entered the building and went into the loft, calling for his roommate. She was nowhere to be found. He stood in the living room, shaking himself. He couldn't believe what was happening. Out of habit, he switched on the television; the white-noise comforted him when he was alone. Rolling through the channels, he stopped on the image of a strange, petrified body. He stared at it for a second, before shuffling back to his room with another sigh.

There the boy rummaged through a pile of unwashed laundry, looking for the duffel bag he knew had to be buried someplace in it. When he found the bag, he took off the borrowed clothing and stuffed it inside; then fumbled through a drawer, taking out and putting on a pair of his own snug jeans. After that, he reached for a faded NYU t-shirt, which he pulled over his head and adjusted for the fit. The threads of the shirt were fraying loose around the collar. James admired the ragged look in a mirror on his wall, smirked, and turned away anxiously.

With bag in tow, he walked out into the living room. The television blared in the background; the same image was on the set.

"The bitumen-tar pottery shards," said the narrator, "found at a site scientists call now 'the Burnt Village,' match those discovered at other sites all around northern Iraq from as far back as 3,000 BC. According to archeologists at Leiden University, who are studying the distinctive use of the tar-like substance, the organic pitch was used because it was believed to have magical properties."

James stared at the image of the mummy, wrapped in the mysterious pitch, not able to shake the strange sense of *de ja vu* it produced. He managed to glance away and see the red light of the answering machine blinking furiously. *Could that be Nick already?* he thought.

When he moved toward the machine, the narrators' voice on the television seemed to grow louder, as if trying to regain his straying attention. "The use of bitumen as a binding substance was also found on the mummified remains of a body near the city of Arbil in Northern Iraq…at a location being called by locals, the Tomb of Habil. In this case, the bitumen does appear to have contributed to the startling preservation of the mummified remains…."

James hit the play button on the machine and the tape rewound frantically. It beeped, the familiar voice of one his friends from the club boomed off the tape. He turned down the television with the remote to hear the message better.

"James…. it's Randy…where are you? You took off and no one has heard from you since. You little tramp. Call us!"

Such a drama queen, James thought to himself switching off the machine. *What could happen?*

He paused and let the thought sink in for a second. Then the boy laughed to himself anxiously as he flipped off the television, and turned to leave the apartment.

"If they only knew the truth," he said out loud to himself seconds later, skipping down the stoop.

⚘

The Caribbean Round was slammed with people, just as it was every Monday evening at that time. The café was one of the more popular places in the village, not far from NYU and in an area of town where many up and coming celebrities took up residence. The bar made for a perfect mix of young intellectuals and trendsetters – always alive with beautiful people and a famous face now and then. It was there James knew people, and there he felt safe to duck out of the stale air of the city, trying to forget the entire mess into which he felt he'd blundered. *What could be safer than the Round?* he reassured himself.

The boy walked right to the bar as he entered. He saw the usual crowd huddled about it. Even the regular Monday-bartender was there, a beautiful Australian girl named Meg. James loved her friendly smile and flirtatious banter; she always had a crack for him. As she sauntered over to where he stood, her blonde hair bounced and flowed around her lovely face.

"Hey, handsome," she said to him as he plopped on a barstool.

"Hey, Meg!"

"What's wrong with you?" she asked. "You look like you've been to hell and back."

James gave her an uncomfortable grin. "I think I actually have been," he replied, chuckling. She shot him an inquisitive look and added to his nervous laugh with her own.

As comfortable as the place felt to James, he could not seem to shake the unease, and it was for good reason. Despite his intention, darkness *had* followed him in to his familiar watering hole – closer on his heels than he could ever have guessed.

Azael and Shemhazai cloaked their forms and passed into the crowd like shadows, lurking menacingly, but wary of trouble. They knew Nick was close after them. Their brutal diversion uptown with one of his pets would not keep the Accuser preoccupied long.

"You pull another all-nighter at Twilo, James?" asked Meg.

"What do you think," he said, rolling his eyes. "I would die without that place every Sunday."

"You are such a crack-whore. You know the cops want to close that place down for drugs. You be careful in there, party-boy."

"Yeah, yeah, Meg, I know…that damn Mayor has been after all the clubs ever since he chased the mob away from the docks. They don't have anything better to do with the cops now accept hassle gay boys."

"Just be careful, they'll eat you up in jail. Don't be dealing that shit again."

"I won't, Meg, don't worry…I learned my lesson. That is all behind me now." He paused and looked around. "Where is Jon tonight…seen him?"

She pushed a frozen cosmopolitan in front of him, his usual drink. "I don't know… I haven't actually seen him in a few days."

"Well, I guess he's going to stand me up again. He is usually here Mondays…he has Tuesday's off."

"James, you need to get over that messed up boy. Trust me…he doesn't know what he wants. He even hits on me…and for real too…I can tell, not like your silly ass teasing."

"Yeah, maybe," James said as he spun to face the crowd. "But God, he is hot...I could forgive his messiness for one night." James sipped slowly on the drink and gave her an evil grin out of one eye. "I have to meet someone tonight anyway...can't flirt around." He turned to face her again, wide-eyed. "Oh my God, you will never believe what happened to me, what a fucking mess...I lost my wallet...this guy is bringing it to me here." James paused and got a funny look on his face.

"Maybe he'll be hot!" he said, distracted by the idea for a moment.

"You are impossible, James," she snorted, as she turned to serve the next customer.

He frowned at her with a devious look. She was right about that much. He looked around, glancing at the clock over the door. *Where is this guy with my wallet?* he wondered impatiently.

At the door, a lean and rather shifty looking man walked through to the entrance. He surveyed the crowd, noticed James, then moved to the bar, tapping the boy on the back. James turned to face him – startled at first – but then abruptly put off by the man's unassuming exterior. *This guy looks harmless enough,* the boy thought himself to allay his anxiety.

"James Kyle?" asked the stranger.

"Yes...are you Marco?"

The man glanced into the crowd tensely and nodded. James followed his gaze, but before the boy could see where the eccentric little man's eyes had gone off to, Marco returned them to James' face.

"I found your wallet in the street," he said. "No money in it...but your ID was there. I thought I'd get it back to you."

"Thanks," replied James, "don't worry about the money...there was none in it."

The man handed it to James, and in a dark corner of the room the two grigori watched. They were waiting for the sign that things were clear, that the boy was truly alone.

"Hey," said James, "I want to give you twenty bucks...and let me buy you a drink for your trouble." He handed the guy the folded bill. The man quickly snatched it away with his stubby fingers.

"Thanks, but no time for a drink," he said in a shrill voice, looking uncomfortably out at the crowd again. "I got to be someplace."

James followed his line of sight yet again, but still nothing looked out of the place. The man was starting to creep out the boy's senses.

"O.K...well, thanks for bringing me the wallet then," replied James.

"No problem," said Marco with a strange, sickly grin. He spun and hurried away.

James watched him vanish. *Strange dude,* the boy thought to himself, *this city is so full of freaks.*

Azael saw that James' attention was fully drawn away by the thrall they had sent with the wallet. "Wait for me outside, Shem. This won't take long," the turned angel hissed. "I will fix what Longinus screwed up...it was a mistake to use him that way."

They nodded at one another, then pushed into the crowd in opposite directions – Azael making his way for the bar and Shemhazai for the glass door. They both wove a dark spell about them as they did.

Moving amid the crowd, Shemhazai slipped outside. He agreed they had made a mistake by letting Longinus pick the victim, but no one else would have distracted the Accuser as thoroughly as the thrall that killed Christ. While he was not at all convinced James was the seer that they were looking for – if he was wrong, and the boy was in fact – the error undoubtedly had played right into the Devil's hands.

James saw a sleek, broad shouldered figure approaching him. Azael's outer form became very attractive, taking on the glamour of a snakeskin. His alluring eyes were pinned to James as he drew closer. The boy's libido instantly overrode any and all good sense, as the disguised Jinn stole up and stood next to him, waiting for something it seemed.

James put on his shy routine. Meg saw it from the corner of her eye. She just shook her head.

"Hello beautiful," Azael said to James, his eyes pushing deeply into the boy's.

James dropped his chin, to be coy. Azael sensed that he did not even have to extend his coils of seduction; the boy would welcome his dark embrace.

Meg walked over and gave James an eye, while slipping a napkin in front of his new friend. The man was striking. James certainly got his share of attention from the hottest men in the bar, but she knew it always led to trouble for him.

"I will have that," said Azael, pointing at James.

She tipped her head with a sarcastic smirk and turned toward the dispenser. "I bet you will," she said under the roar of the crowd, as she went to get him the order.

Meg's attention was off them only a few seconds, to stream the frozen drink into a wine glass. She banged it gently on the rubber rail to settle out the air; then slowly pivoted back in their direction. They were both gone by the time she reached the spot.

James' glass sat empty.

"I am going to kill that little pig!" she said out loud, looking to see where he had gone off to. It was just like him to stiff her for a drink over a quick trick.

Azael followed James into the tiny bathroom, and locked the door behind them. As the boy walked over and stood in front of the mirror, turning his head to invite the tall, dark stranger closer, the turned Jinn stepped behind him into the mirror. The grigori's gaze caught his eyes. In that instant, James realized he had made a very serious mistake.

4

CABAL

Azael clinched James in his arms, licentiously nudging his nose into the boy's ear. James cringed, trying to pull away, but the demonic Jinn was simply too strong. What James could not get out of his head was that while he was truly terrified, he was at the same time aroused – the monster's embrace excited him. Hot breath seemed to slither down his back, stoking his taught muscles.

"You know, boy, I can either hurt you very, very badly in this, or make you feel extraordinary…beyond anything you have ever known…don't resist me," the demon whispered into James' ear. His voice seemed soft and alluring.

James fought to resist the seductive spell he could sense the beast was weaving over him. "I'll do whatever you want," he replied, dread filling him. His own voice was horse from the strain of conflicted surrender. He remembered what Nick had told him. "Just don't hurt me….tell me what you want."

Azael slipped two fingers into the lip of his jeans and gently pulled the boy's hips toward him. James settled deeper into his clutches, feeling the bizarre, throbbing protrusion of Azael's s erection as it slid up and down against his backside. He could sense enormous power emanating from it, arousing some deep desire within. Suddenly James became erect himself. *This is what Nick meant about conjoining,* James thought, sensing how being bent over the sink would simply be an ephemeral formality for what the demon intended of this power.

"Ah, that's it, boy, now you realize...give it to me. Open your mind, and don't worry," he grunted as he pushed James forward, "I'll get to the part you will want too...in a minute."

James shivered, not sure if it was from dread or elation. He was losing the battle of wills with the demon. Desire consumed him. "Yes...take me," the boy replied with a shudder, astonished by the sound of his own voice.

"Trust me, I will do right by you this time...not like that impudent tool in the alley last night," rumbled the demon. "I should have just done it myself when I had the chance...and know that I would have been more than a match for Iblis."

James felt Azael's arms wrap even tighter around him, the embrace forcing air from his lungs. His mind began to rush with a flurry of images, moving so quickly that he could not make his own thoughts stand still in his head. It was like the pitched euphoria of ecstasy.

Azael growled in his ear and entered James' soul. The boy's head pounded. The turned angel was in so deeply that they were becoming a single psychic essence. James' jeans fell away and he was forcefully pitched forward onto the sink, face first. He looked up into the mirror, Azael's eyes meet his once more, and at that moment they boy realized that the grigori was in complete control of his every thought.

Azael smiled, gaining satisfaction from the boy's quick dread over what James was only beginning to understand of true darkness. After that came the first physical trust, James could feel the demon push inside of him viciously. The boy arched his back down and his hips up as the demon began to trust in and out. Without thinking or understanding, James reached back with one hand and grabbed the back of Azael's leg. He pulled the demon closer – drawing the driving dark enchantment into him even more. The instant he touched the beast, something thin between the two of them seemed to dissipate, and James suddenly no longer felt powerless.

Azael continued to surge into James' mind, clearly drawing pleasure from the assault as he prowled for something amid the boy's thoughts. James thrust backward, hard, to meet the penetration, causing the demon to quicken the rhythm of his attack again, driven by a need for more. As the grigori looked deeper and deeper into the boy's soul, James was astonished to find the mind of the turned Jinn equally open to his own curiosity. He need only push back into the darkness.

Perhaps the shock and dread of the first attack by Longinus had kept him from seeing this aspect of ethereal conjoining, or perhaps clarity was a function of Azael's greater power.

In either case, James became fascinated with the dark awareness he found there. Eagerly, he plunged further into the demon's knowledge and understanding. His head rushed with both conscious images as well as subconscious desire. A swift dismay fell over James, for he realized in that moment that Azael did indeed plan to kill him when they were done with this sinister, tawdry tryst. What they were sharing was simply too valuable to the dragons, just as Nick had warned.

Azael realized the boy was himself beginning to delight in the unseemly rendezvous. He too was being scrutinized profoundly. With that awareness, he lost himself in his own yearning, fed by James' unanticipated enthusiasm for this transgression. The boy enraptured him somehow; there was clearly more to this mortal than met the eye, yet he found nothing there of the prophecy they sought.

James was drawn into him and the demon into the seer. Fed by the heightened struggle between them, not just one of conquest, Azael and James climaxed together. As the grigori lurched forward in euphoria onto the boy's back, James regained his senses. In that moment, the young seer realized he must act quickly to save himself. He culled up the new power he found and was fearless.

⚓

The knot in Nick's stomach turned to a rage of ferocity as he raced downtown over the city. He could feel the beast's cruelty again and this time it had James. His attempt to find the boy by sensing his passage through the material plane was not working at all. He had to take another approach. The Accuser slipped fully into the ethereal plane and vanished. Once there, Nick found that James was emitting a powerful psychic signal; a very unusual thing for a mortal. He did not take the time to think-through what it might mean. The need to act was pressing. Whatever was happening, Nick sensed that James was seconds away from being extinguished in the corporal realm.

Since there was no time or space within the ethereal state, he used the powerful sense he had of James to bring his own essence near the boy's. He moved closer and closer to James, but was still frustrated. The demon was using some kind of dark ward. Nick realized there was only one way to get to James now. He would have to get inside of his essence, conjoin with his very source. It would be dangerous; he sensed the demon already had the boy in a coil.

The Accuser focused, probing toward the locus of the boy's distinct spiritual being, trying hard to ignore his own longing as he came closer to James' soul, which he could sense was already aroused by something else. Nick thought it strange he could not sense fear. *Am I too late?* he wondered as he slipped inside the boy.

Then and there, Nick came face to face with the dark spirit he had been pursuing, just as it pulled away from James. Azael, his brother, was truly Pythia now… lost to chaos. The Accuser reached, opened a portal to where the beguiling soul of the young seer stood within the mortal veil and pushed his form to it.

James flipped onto his back with such speed that he was free of Azael before the beast realized what was happening. Lying braced upon the counter, spurred on by a sudden adrenaline surge, he hefted his legs into Azael's chest. The grigori's bulky weight pitched backward, then crashed against the stall behind them, unhinging it as he fell through. Azael was stunned, but regained his faculties in seconds. He rose and looked down to find James scrambling for his jeans, clearly intending to make a dash. The demon reached out with his powerful coils, but found that he could no longer grasp the boy. He lumbered forward, drawing a menacing blade from its ethereal sheath. It seemed to materialize out of thin air. "If I can't choke the life from you, boy," he groaned, "I will cut your soul from your chest and consume it with my bare hands."

James rose, fixing the buttons that held the wrinkled denim snugly against his hips. When Azael reached out to taste the boy's dread, to savor the misery of his victim, he found none. It gave him pause for just an instant. He was uncertain, and in that hesitation Nick's full wraithlike form raged into a corporal state. The Accuser reached first inside of James to gain a footing there with the spell, then stepped out into the small room where they stood. He felt a strange rush of power as he withdrew from James, sensing something deeply ominous had transpired in those seconds.

The air exploded with raw energy as the Accuser forced his way through the ethereal portal, wings extended. Nick quickly turned to face his younger, twisted brother. The hilt of Haqiqah materialized. The blade flared with fury and flame. Azael stood eye to eye with Nick, tense fisted with surprise, wondering how the Accuser had found them so quickly.

Without hesitation, they both drew back to cleave at each other – now fully attuned to the other's power and presence. Just as they were about to strike blades, a voice wracked the room like thunder. The grigori and the Accuser recoiled painfully to the floor; it was like the voice of God himself.

"Get thee behind me, unclean spirit!" the voice roared.

Nick twisted to look up, wondering whether the voice had referred to him or to Azael. He'd been called by that name himself once or twice before. To his astonishment the powerful voice emanated from modest, little James, who was not looking quite so vulnerable at that very moment. A power raged from him.

As both Jinn watched in amazement, James abruptly turned to the sink. He waved a blessing over a pool there, dipping his palms to fling water at Azael. The turned angel writhed in agony, blinded as his face seared in his hands. The screech was horrific, echoing out into the streets and across time. James stared hard at Nick, fearless still. The Accuser could not as yet fully grasp the breadth of the supernatural change that had overtaken the boy. He stood completely paralyzed by surprise – *this* power was what Nick had sensed.

The young man twisted out his hand and pointed it at Azael, who was now poised to flee the scene of this apparent mishap, not understanding himself what had gone wrong.

"Sword of God," said the boy, "disobedient as you have been to Heaven...deliver the vengeance of your Lord!"

Bewildered, but realizing that the moment to strike was passing, Nick pushed forward and thrust his sword toward the demon's chest. Azael transformed into a great serpent as he was struck, the twisting body filled the broken bathroom stall to its brim. The Pythian quickly raised its head, like a cobra hovering to strike. Nick drew back his sword again, but not quite fast enough. The fangs of the monster extended as it lunged to strike, stopping only inches away from his exposed wing and shoulder. Nick stumbled backward a step to find James suddenly between him and the grigori; the boy's hands extended inches from Azael's venous mouth.

"Servant of the Abyss, I bind thee with the eternal, sacred name...*El-huit Zilo Pochtli*!" shouted James.

The demon's coiled body unraveled and spun, while the young man held its head firmly in place with a binding spell of unbelievable strength. Power suffused him.

"Now, Accuser! James bellowed. "Deliver the final blow of righteousness."

While the binding was strong, Nick could see the young man's power was beginning to fade as the demon pushed and wrenched desperately to break free. The Accuser reinforced his footing, cocking back the blade, and swung to sever the demons head with a powerful stroke. It sprayed the walls with poison and bounced onto the floor near the sink – the face twisted into fury.

Both the Accuser and the new seer were knocked off their feet by the powerful, writhing body of the great viper. Nick reached out as they spilled to the floor, taking James into his arms. He sensed the powerful essence that the boy possessed was now strangely fleeting away. James' eyes once again became colored with fear; they rolled clear of the beast together.

"Feed, feed now," James whimpered into Nick's chest. "Don't let his power pass back to the dragons."

Nick gently set the boy aside and scurried over to where the head quivered on the floor, its eyes rolling back in the sockets. He picked up the ghoulish scull and held it out in front of his face.

"Your own deeds have drawn a veil over your heart. Your name is marked upon the pages of Sijjin," shouted Nick.

The flesh of the head began to vaporize, even as the great-coiled body started to dissipate into a rank mist. Nick inhaled the dark vapor. The Accuser stood still for a moment. It had been thousands of years since he had consumed the hatred of such a powerful Pythian in that way, and never before a turned Jinn. Slowly, he twisted toward James, who was picking himself up off the floor finally, in a daze. Part of Nick was angry, part of him relieved.

The boy looked up at him as he tried to brush the grime from knees. "We have to get out of here, all the noise will attract attention," he said in an anxious voice.

"You think so?" Nick replied with derision.

The Accuser cloaked both their material forms as they left the bar, brushing past the police responding to the commotion. The bar patrons were mostly standing in the street at that point and never noticed as the dark exile and his young protégé made their way past. Nick reached out with his senses, trying to look into the boy again, but his probing power was instantly slapped away. James turned and glanced at him from the corner of his eyes, his gaze colored with fear and hurt. "Let's just get back to Nafees' apartment, I will explain when we get there," he groaned.

Nick did not try again, they simply walked west in silence, before hailing a cab on sixth avenue. "The Park at Columbus Circle," Nick growled as they climbed in.

Lurching forward, the cab made slow progress uptown. As they reached Radio City Music Hall, the ride ground to a complete stop and James took advantage of the stillness to nestle closer to Nick, resting safely in his warm arms. He laid his head against the Accuser's chest and caressed its strength with his hand. The dark exile did not feel the normal impulse to pull away. He simply wrapped James tighter into his grasp, heaving a sigh. *It feels so very good to hold this boy for some reason*, he thought to himself.

James inhaled the smell of Nick's body; it was musky-sweet and masculine. "Everything about you is perfect, Nick," he whispered, "the feel of you…your strength. You were crafted to that perfection, weren't you?"

Nick thought a moment, lowering his eyes toward the foot well of the cab. "I was made to serve my

Lord, and I have done that the best way I could. No, I am not a perfect creature. I am utterly fallible...as my exile demonstrates more than anything. I have failed both immortals and men over the years, but you already know that, don't you?"

James tilted his head in assent.

Nick grew still, thinking again about the boy's essence, before adding his own question. "So what are *you*, James?"

The young man sat up a little, nudged his nose at Nicks' chin affectionately, and smiled at the Accuser. They were so close at that moment their breath seemed to pass back and forth freely. "I guess I am what you would call an unwitting prophet...born from the power of the Jinn."

Nick appeared distressed, setting his sight straight-ahead. "We are all unwilling servants, every one of us," he grumbled. "So where does all this impulsive insight come from...Saint James?"

"I have consorted with the beasts of darkness in the act of conjoining. The Pythia mistook my meekness for weakness."

"A common mistake to make of your kind," replied Nick, "as I have learned the hard way." He looked at James again curiously – still wrapped in wonder about what he had seen. "But how did you escape Azael's coil? He had you, I felt it."

"Partly because he had grown smug in his satisfaction, and partly because his coil could not hold me as securely as he thought it might. Once he opened my eyes through our conjoining, I realized what he did not know, or at least did not take the time to see." He reached down to his pant leg and exposed the ankle bracelet of the goddess.

"Nafees?!" Nick blurted out in shock. "He made you Rafiq?" His brow furrowed as he spoke. "I was only gone a few hours."

"Yes. Nafees gave me the beads of Elat Astarte, the goddess, but did not explain to me what they could do. He simply said they were sacred and would keep me from harm. When Azael joined with my soul – unwilling as I thought I was – he was looking for something. But he didn't find it, Heaven has not anointed me. Since I myself did not understand what power the beads possessed, he was not able to see how they made me impervious to Pythian coils."

"Clever Nafees...so when he was spent from knowing you, you broke his grip." Nick stopped and looked at James. "You were letting him take you, weren't you? You indulged him." Nick felt a pang of jealousy. "Somehow you knew to use the demon's own Sijjin against him."

"At one level the beads compelled ziña...a desire in us for love too powerful to resist. I could not refuse him, but had Nafees showed me the purpose of the beads beforehand, the demon would have known the instant he took me. Coil or no coil, he would have killed me on the spot."

"But what good was breaking the coils? You could hardly bind him once you were able to wield that power...even with the sacred name you used."

"Just like you felt me in the Realm of Essences, I felt you coming like a storm on the horizon," replied James. "I only had to hold him off until you came through to me."

Nick sat stone faced a few seconds more, then looked down into James' tender eyes. He felt it there again, that sense of familiarity. It rattled him that he could not put his finger on its source. He thought of Joshu, but could not discern why. "So you are not the seer Gabriel said to watch for?" asked Nick. "This all seems a lot to be coincidence...too much in fact."

"No, I don't think so. There is another seer to be revealed."

"I don't get it."

"Their interest in me at first was purely to get at you...preying on me randomly near where they could draw you out. They fear you greatly, Nick. You're a wild card of fate, of which neither side knows what to expect. You will likely tilt the balance in the war to come...they all sense this...Heaven and Hell."

"None of this makes sense, James. Why so much effort to come at you a second time then...if you are not the prophet foretold of?"

"These are troubled days my, beautiful friend... only Allah knows for what reason men suffer," James said with a smile.

"Oh, damn it," snapped Nick with an agitated tone. "Stay away from that Sufi lunatic if you know what's good for you. I don't need the two of you mucking about my affairs...and by the way, mister my-eyes-are-open, you had better be very, very careful about ever evoking the name of God to bind another spirit like that. Did you learn that from Azael? I know you did not get that from Nafees. He would kill to wield the power of that name, and I *mean* really kill. Other than one or two other celestial beings, including myself, no one should know how to evoke the name of the nameless-god. If Azael knew that and you gleaned it from his mind, we are all in really big trouble."

"No, Nick, Azael did not know the name. Remember when you told me that I could never imagine what this was for?" James rubbed close to the inside of his groin.

Nick blushed.

"Well, Azael showed me what it is for an angel to 'know' a soul. No wonder it is forbidden to men! When *you* reached out from the Realm of Essences to me, after he withdrew, you showed me more than he ever could."

Nick turned white as the reality of what he had done set in. He was normally much more careful about sharing his essence and the use of conjoining.

"Don't be ashamed," said James. "You have given me a wonderful gift. I know now you are devoted to the nameless-one, and I know Him in a way that few ever could." James curled up even closer to Nick and buried his head into the Jinn's warmth.

"James, I am so sorry...I never do that. I did not even do that with...."

"Joshu? I know," replied the boy. "And I understand you could never love me the way you loved him. But Nick, you showed me more of the bounty of what is eternal in those few seconds than any human can ever hope to achieve in a lifetime."

"I don't know what to say," Nick replied, in disbelief.

"There is nothing to say, Accuser, but we have lots of work ahead of us. The time foretold is at hand, as you know well, and both sides are marshaling armies. This time you…I mean we…cannot let the Deliverer of Men fall into their hands."

"So if you have all this in your head now, why have I not come to know you from our joining?"

"You did not take the time to see, Nick. You were selflessly fixed on finding me and striking out at Azael, focused on that alone. If you look now, you will perceive me there inside of you."

Nick turned in, but was unable to distinguish this sense of James from his prior familiarity. It was baffling.

"When you came to me ethereally, right before you burst into the corporal field, I simply could not help myself. I should apologize to you, but when you touched me with that part of you that was meant for so much more…I simply could not set it aside. I looked into your essence…and took of it, fully."

The Devil just stared into his prophet's eyes.

James and Nick stood at a curb near the park for a moment. The cab pulled away from the brightly lit corner and the two dragged themselves toward the apartment building. Once inside, they shot directly up the elevator. Nafees sat waiting quietly in the apartment, looking out over the city as if commanding an army on the ground. The glow of the cityscape was the only thing that was lighting the room. He didn't flinch when they walked in together, as if expecting it.

James went right to Nafees and dropped to his knees, putting his head into the cleric's lap. "Thank you, Master Nafees. I would be dead now if you had not foresight."

Nafees stroked the back of James head slowly. Then he bent to kiss it.

Nick threw off his coat and fell exhausted upon a sofa. "So now is the time for us all to come clean, ah Sufi?" he grunted.

"Nick, I know you think mortals are beneath you," replied Nafees, "but I realized he was part of this plan in some way that none of us were yet privileged to see. I simply sensed it."

James raised his head, and looked at Nafees as he spoke. He smiled sadly at the immortal.

"We have never fully trusted one another, Accuser," said the cleric, "in spite what is between us. I suppose we may never, but we must work together now. You have your intention...I have mine."

"I suppose that is true enough. I have little choice it seems," conceded Nick, "so with that said...what does this all mean, Nafees? You are the diviner."

"Ask the seer...he has glimpsed into the mind of the serpents...into chaos itself." Nafees peered down at James; tears were streaking the boy's face.

"You should not have let him go," said Nick angrily. "I told him to stay here with you. You had no right to use him that way... to bait the Pythia with him. You knew they would strike."

Nafees just laughed, pushing a lock of stray hair out of James' eyes. He rose to his feet. "Nick, *you* are the last creature who should lecture me about using humans for sport. You have rarely thought more of them than animals...playthings to torment in your jealousy for their favored status. In that you have been no better than the Pythia. The time of being a rebel against Heaven is over, Jinn," Nafees said with disdain. "While there is advantage in the enemy thinking you are on your own side, I need to know if you are really on *our* side. I need to know that sooner rather than later!"

"And what exactly is your side?" Nick retorted bitterly. "I have never understood you, or what you were after. The priests of the old temple drove your kind into exile over three-thousand years ago, yet you turn up over and over again...like roaches. Why is that, cleric?"

"Because we are faithful to Allah and have charge of His will!"

"This Sufi bullshit is just a way for you to hide," Nick spat, rising to his feet as he spoke. "I want to know what the hell you want from me...and from him?" He pointed at James.

"You seem to forget that you have come to me, Nick. You brought this boy here, and left him in my care. I simply made sure he was prepared, even though I could not stand with him in his appointed trial. You cannot say the same!"

"ENOUGH!" shouted James. His voice parted the tension of the room with the same power he had used to bind Azael. "This gets us nowhere. You are right...I have seen into the mind of the serpents, but I've seen a lot more than just their plans."

Nick shot James a sharp, nervous look. The young seer returned it sternly.

"The Pythia have discovered a strange prophecy from the walls of some tomb," explained James "and have seen an omen of their own doom. The dragons fear the coming of a Deliverer who will topple the queen of chaos' power. They interpret from these prophecies that both the Rafiq and you, Nick, will be drawn to vie for him. So they have been watching you both, to see who found the prophet first. For some reason they think there is only one place where time and tradition will lead you to discover the truth. I am not sure why this is...but they think it has something to do with Twilo of all places."

The room grew very still. Both Nafees and Nick realized what this revelation meant.

"Of course," said Nick, "sema...the spell of corporeal ecstasis!" He grabbed at his own head and shook it, then looked up at James. "Mortals are more susceptible to the impression of ethereal communication under it," he explained as he turned. "It makes sense God would come to your men, Nafees...you have always been the best vessels of this kind of portent."

"And no one now weaves sema in pursuit of beatific-vision better than Jason Velenza," said Nafees of the club's popular DJ, himself a powerful Rafiq knight. As the immortal cleric spoke of Jason there was a hint of pride and affection in his eyes.

"What is ecstasis?" asked James, in a confused voice. He had seen much in the ethereal realm through Nick and Azael, but there were still enormous blind spots. The young seer fumbled with the power, trying to make sense of it all still.

"It's a meditative state," replied Nafees, "a form of ritual elation we reach as we touch Allah...a sacred practice that mortals have performed for thousands of years. The Rafiq call this use of sema, the rite of Zekhr...we've adapted it for the more modern trappings of Twilo. The mortal veil that normally keeps men from seeing into the ethereal realm is best penetrated with certain mind-altering substances. With them, as well as music and dance, mortals can work themselves into a state of ecstatic commune. In Arabic we call this state of bliss, wajd."

"They get fucked up and dance," Nick said snidely, to mock what he saw as the cleric's romanticizing of hedonism. "The intoxicants and drums appear to affect alpha waves in the brain, which somehow allows them sense beyond the boundaries of the mortal veil. Men literally feel God on that stuff or so they think... but it never does a thing for me."

"We both know why all rituals of rapture are empty for you, Nick," said Nafees.

The dark exile just answered with a sneer.

"Huh," replied James, with a chuckle. "I always did think there was more to that place on Sunday morning. Me and my friends have called it 'church' forever."

Nafees smiled at the young seer's attempt to break up the tension with some humor. Nick was unmoved; there was more at stake for him than anyone could imagine.

"I can't believe we didn't sense this sooner," said the Accuser. "It was right in front of us."

"Perhaps one of us did," replied Nafees.

Nick turned and made a face at the cleric. "What do you mean?"

"Gabriel has been making visitations there now for weeks. You've not been around, Nick...so you've missed them."

"And when were you going to tell me this?"

"When it seemed important," retorted the cleric. "Why would you think I owed you an explanation? You shun the rest of the Jinn."

Nafees did not understand how Gabriel was, and always would be different for Nick. The Accuser paced a moment – something still seemed out of place. "Why attack James, and then the boy in Hell's Kitchen? What were they after if this is not all connected in some way? They are being careless...too careless."

"I think at first to draw you away, just as you believe," surmised James as he delved into his visions. "If you were feeding, you would not be there to see Gabriel deliver the revelation. Longinus simply misjudged you, or perhaps was expendable to them...you have become predictable in so many ways, Nick. Your fascination with the men in this part of the city clearly heightened your lust to feed when we were threatened by darkness. The Pythians used that and your need of vengeance to divert your attention from the club."

"Your sympathies for *beautiful, beardless boys* betray you, Iblis," ribbed Nafees playfully, twisting the infamous quote from the Koran to tease the Devil.

"But they did not count on you bringing me here, Nick...to the Rafiq," continued James. "They didn't count on you and Nafees working together....that was not in their vision. Once you did, they surely assumed that there was something special about me...they needed to find out for sure."

"Nothing happens by chance," said Nafees. "Trust me...there must be more to this."

"Perhaps, but they attacked me that first time simply to lure Nick away from the club, of that I am certain. They knew you were close and it was a means to an end. Later, when they feared they had made a mistake by allowing me to escape, that perhaps I had been the anointed prophet after all, they tried again."

"I think we all know where this leaves us," said Nafees. "We must seek out Gabriel's prophet before the Pythia get to him...we must use sema to protect him."

Nick raised one hand. "Since were on the subject of revelations," he said. "I suppose I should point out Gabe recently came to me as well...minutes before the attack on James." He figured James would know anyway, he should bring it up lest he appear unhelpful.

"He told me the time was near, judgment is upon us. Yes, a new Deliverer *is* at hand…a prophet will be sent. The scrolls of God's plan are opened and read by the Jinn…that means the trumpets of judgment are not far off."

"He came to you?" replied Nafees in surprise. "Why would he come to you?"

"Yes, me," huffed Nick. "Contrary to what you think, I still have a friend or two in Heaven," he repeated of what Gabriel had said to him, then paused and thought before going on.

Both James and Nafees could see he was working something out.

"So tell me, have you seen who Gabe has been whispering sweet nothings to on the dance floor?" Nick asked finally.

Nafees' face fell. Nick had him with that. "Therein lies the problem," explained the immortal cleric somberly. "We don't quite see with whom the Jinn is conversing. It would appear that during the fog and daze of wajd, it could be anyone there on the floor. He is quite good at making sure none of us sees or hears anything of his visitations. In your own way, each of you Jinn seem to be quite astute at your given skills."

"Is that a compliment from an elohim to the Jinn?" asked Nick with a sinister grin.

"Merely an observation, Accuser," said Nafees.

"That is why they are trying to keep you away, Nick," added James. "If anyone will peg who Gabriel is honoring with revelation before they can, it will be you."

"Well that settles it," said Nafees. "I guess we all have a date Sunday morning."

"Sounds like a party!" replied Nick coyly, seeming to almost make fun of the cleric. He turned away and looked out at the city, suddenly feeling strange they could tell. Then Nick glanced back at them both sadly for a moment, before he spun and walked out of the room, leaving them alone.

James and Nafees watched him go; both accepting Nick was as much a self-imposed exile as he was truly banished.

⚘

The significance of what was unfolding needed to be communicated among the Rafiq ranks. Its senior members were all contacted and plans were made to meet in many places – some of the cabal in far off lands. Later that evening, while they waited for the knights in New York to assemble, Nick sat with James in the guest room that the young man would occupy for a few days. They wanted him close, while taking time to figure out what to do about Sunday morning.

"Are you sure you won't come to dinner, Nick?" asked James.

"Yes, I think I need some space. This team player thing is not my normal *modus operandi*. You are one of them now...best you cozy up to your responsibilities with your brothers. But remember, you made a deal with me. Nafees must never realize you know the name. He will use it for his own end...trust me."

"Scout's honor," replied James, as he smiled.

Nick rolled his eyes.

They both looked away. After a few awkward moments of saying nothing, James piped in and tried to break the discomfit that lingered between them. "You miss him, don't you? That's what this is all about for you...you want him back."

"Who are you talking about?" Nick raised his eyes, confused.

"Joshu," responded James, averting Nick's eyes, knowing he was touching a sore spot in the Accuser.

"Oh damn," grimaced Nick, "I am going to pay for those two seconds I slid inside you for the rest of creation, right?" Nick wounded James with the harshness in his voice. The Accuser was simply not used to being so upfront with a mortal.

James dropped his gaze and spoke without thinking. "I am sorry, Niko," he said. It just came out.

Nick was stunned to silence.

James' eye shot wide open. "Oh Nick, I am so sorry... I didn't not mean that either...I..."

"It's O.K...I know...let it go," he stopped the boy. "It's me, not you." Still, a hurt welled up inside Nick. *What is it about this kid that rings of Joshu?* he thought. Nick leaned forward and brushed James' golden hair from his eyes, smiling ruefully at the boy. He reached out with his senses and tried another spell of tranquility, to ease the boys mind. James pulled away. His face went pale.

"What?" asked Nick with a look of surprise.

"Don't do that, Nick. Don't just reach inside of me that way if you don't mean it."

"You felt that?"

"Yes I felt it...your ethereal touch is magic to me," James stopped and stuttered. "...I mean that metaphorically that is...I mean, yes, your touch is really magic...but what I mean is...it feels wonderful."

Nick raised one eyebrow at his awkward rambling.

James finally sighed and collected his thoughts. "I don't like it when you do it *that* way, like you are trying to calm a child."

"I suppose that's fair enough, I am sorry," said Nick. "What if I try it like this?" Nick leaned forward and laid his head against the boy's. They sat there for a few, quiet seconds. James went entirely limp as if he had fallen asleep. Nick turned his head ever so gently as he used his ethereal wings to embrace the young seer.

"My God," said James, as he began to rise up from the bed.

"Easy, easy...don't pull me," whispered Nick. "Let me control it. It's a spell...I learned it thousands of years ago, from Gabriel in fact." James' breath shuddered, as he looked up at Nick. The dark exile opened his eyes.

The boy could see a tear break at the edge of the angel's nose, trailing down, and dropping directly onto his own flush check. Nick drew in a shallow breath and withdrew himself from the ethereal plane where he held James' soul within his wings. James shivered.

"That was amazing, Nick," he said. "I'm sorry. I guess I made a mess of things."

"You made a mess?" growled Nick. "James, self-deprecation does not become you. You did not cause any of this disastrous affair...this is a battle much older in the making than even I am. We are all pawns."

"I guess I am only beginning to understand," replied the young man. "Actually it's fairer to say am only beginning to see. But if what we face is about the way I felt at the moment you reached out for me in the bar, then I am willing to fight for that."

"You sound so much like he did," said Nick. "Josh predicted the meek would inherit the world...I laughed at him."

"What was he like? I mean, I know you loved him, but I don't understand everything I saw inside you about him...it's confused and conflicted."

"I suppose none of us can fully understand, James. He was a man...but he was really more. The absolute impossibility of understanding how he existed both physically as a mortal and yet still occupied transcendence is beyond the knowledge of even the Court of the Heaven. There are so many things we cannot put into words, things that we feel and know intuitively. Most my understanding of God is that way. I feel it in my heart, even with my ability to see more. That, I suppose, is the hardest part of love, we all want so desperately to understand it and we simply don't. But Nafees said to me once, a long time ago, one of the only things that makes sense about all of this—*we can never understand Allah, who is so great he does not fit into all the universe, but yet he fits into a single man's heart.*"

James considered that for a moment, before looking up at Nick. "Does it bother you to be hated so by people who don't know you, who don't understand how much love is really in you?"

"It did once, but don't forget that hate is my sustenance...it is the role of the Accuser to receive man's hate. It is a harsh reality, one I face each time I have to consume a soul so twisted by abhorrence that it no longer resembles that spark of life God gave each spirit. Josh used to warn me of it. *If you live only by that sword, it's all there will ever be for you in the end,* he would say. But I've never felt I had a choice...God gave Haqiqah to me. I did not author evil, but it is the core of my purpose. It's hard to have something like that be at the center of your life and not be affected by it. Even my love for Josh can't change what I am...I have to face it. I am the Satan of *Diké*... the messenger of divine justice. That's all the word 'satan' really means James, all Jinn are simply envoys of destiny."

"You are nothing like what any of us are taught to imagine of the Devil," sighed the handsome young seer.

"Look, my beautiful friend," whispered Nick. "I am not making excuses. I have my flaws and I've been brutally selfish most of my existence. I freely admit it, but few creatures in the cosmos have endured more pain than I have...that is the honest truth and I accept it for what it is...His will."

"I can't say I understand...not just because I have in no way felt the pain you have, but mostly because

I don't understand how you endure it. All I can do is say, I'm sorry for it."

Nick made a strange face. James reached out with one hand and stroked the dark hair of his forehead. The boy extended his power and Nick wondered if he did it knowingly or if he was still learning how to control it.

"Believe it or not, that actually means a lot to me," said Nick with a grumble, not wanting to let on how good it felt. "But someday, James, you will behold the face of God himself. All that He made you for will be known then."

"I guess there is something to be said for what we're doing after all," James comforted Nick.

Nick rose from the bed and propped his weight up on one elbow. "I am going. I have something I want to do before Sunday. Stay close to Nafees. You are gaining strength, but there is safety in numbers."

He got up and walked toward the doorway. As if on cue, Nafees appeared at the entrance. They bowed to each other cordially before Nick slipped by and was gone.

"Are you alright?" asked the immortal cleric.

"Yes," answered James, "I'm fine, a little ragged around the edges, but I'll be alright."

"Good, the car will be around in a few minutes," said Nafees, turning to walk away. Then he stopped and gazed back at James as the boy got up to fuss with his shirt in the mirror. "You know," he said to the boy, "I've known Nick a very long time. I actually have always liked the wayward Jinn very much. To tell you the truth, I've always thought that he was by far the most attractive of all Allah's created creatures...I suppose that is simply a matter of taste. Anyway, he has always been very much...how do I say this?" He paused a moment. "He has always been quite a 'dick' as you say."

James bowed his head slightly in the mirror and heaved with a laugh. He found the always-formal Nafees to be most amusing when he was trying to be crass.

"Perhaps that is actually why I like him," Nafees went on. "It's the bad boys that always seem to entice us the most.... Am I right?"

James nodded and peered at him from the corner of his eye.

"Still, let me just tell you this about him, James. While he is not what myth and rumor have made him out to be, Iblis is most assuredly still *the* Devil. He will break your heart...trust me on that. Heartache is what he was made of, and for. Only Allah knows why."

Nafees stared at James with a very cold gaze and the boy instinctively knew not to return it. As alluring as Nick was to him, in his heart, James sensed the dark exile might well be his undoing.

"I think that is what he was just trying to tell me," said James softly.

"Good, that means he still has a conscience, despite the baleful leather-thing he has going on these days. He always struck me as too much of a pretty boy for that 'daddy' act."

They both laughed out loud together, then headed out the door to meet other the Rafiq. Fate called.

5

TWILO

A pulse from the strobe lights pierced Nick's eyes, as he shifted along the edge of Twilo's dance floor. He stepped away from the glare. The hypnotic rhythm in the music built from moment to moment, as Jason Velenza wove the sema of Zekhr, an enchantment filled the air and from it the club was steeped in its spectacle – a veritable circus of the senses. The ecstatic performance of each devotee's dance on the floor was as much about the pageantry of the ritual as was the thrill of the lights and music. The weekly revelry was further heightened by the intoxication of ecstasy, the smell of sweat, and the smearing of flesh on flesh.

Nick stood enticed with the scene, watching the enthusiasm of the men as they reached out. This was really an ancient custom; mortals had partaken in euphoric ritual for thousands of years, with dance and drum calling them into communion with something they understood was beyond their sensibility. In all of Nick's many years, it was *this* age of man that captivated him more than any other. For in it he felt most like them in their longings, as they were driven by the fevered sacrament. And yet in spite of its lure, all *he* could do was stand at the edge watching, for Nick was an exile from the very presence they sought. It was like a drug that would never hit him, no matter how many times he tried to indulge it.

On the surface, the practice of Zekr was pure self-indulgence: hedonism. Yet at the core of it was an age long mediation. Nick appreciated men for their ingenuity of the practice – how at times they transcended their own spiritual limitations and became connected to the nameless-god despite the mortal veil within which they were so haplessly trapped. He was also amused by the seemly reckless, unfathomable appetite some mortals displayed in performing the traditions, dancing along the thin line between Heaven, their own existence, and Hell's emptiness – all simply to catch a fleeting glimpse of the source from which they came. In Twilo, words meant nothing. Only the frantic pitch of emotions mattered as the rush that came with the drugs stripped away the prison of the mortal mind and allowed, just for an instant, communion within what for them was truly the holiest holies.

Yet in spite of how he could appreciate the ambition of Zekhr, Nick did find the practice crude at times. The intoxicants these men used often destroyed them. Their frenzied attempt to reach for meaning in this way was almost pitiable – but it was a desperation he understood all too well. As with the plight of his own existence, it seemed like watching some remorseful animal chase its own tail to no end. Nick sighed as he watched them. *Sometimes I don't know who got the worst end of God's love,* he thought of the drama, *them or me?*

The mob writhed as a single mass with the beat, pushing into him so tightly that Nick could do little more than sway from side to side in the gathering of bodies; never quite dancing as it were, just heaving within a wave of bare skin and muscle. The body heat seethed up over the floor, while arms and chests slid along one another like cobras trapped in a jar. There was so much sweat in the air that it condensed on the ceiling above them and fell like rain. In it, groups of delirious men hung together in clusters, huddled about the heaving throng of flesh in a state of elation. Nick stared with fascination, reminded of Dante's depiction of his second circle of Hell; the endless mass of body parts knotted into a storm of desperate desire. He was struck by irony that one man would imagine Perdition to be such a thing, while the souls in front of him sought it out so frantically. *They are such sad, extraordinary creatures,* he thought, watching the mass push back again in the opposing direction. *I will never fully understand them, I don't think.*

With poise, he slid his hand down into his pocket and retrieved a pack of cigarettes. Spinning the white box round in his fingers, he twisted to bang it against his wrist several times, tightly packing the tobacco inside. He raised the pack to his mouth and clinched one of the thin-skinned rolls in his teeth, pulling it free as the fury of the din climbed yet again toward climax. One of the mortal revelers caught a glimpse of the unlit cigarette resting along his lip. The man took it as an invitation. He had been eyeing Nick for some time. Pushing past two sweat covered bodies, he moved to break free from the constriction of the crowd. The light rained in on them as an array of crimsons, yellows, and blues: a storm of radiance.

Another strobe light cut quickly into Nick's eyes, blinding him a second time, while the man stole up from the mass of flesh and lifted himself up a single stair, so as to stand eye to eye with the infamous dark exile of Heaven. They swayed there, with the young stranger smiling glibly at Nick; his eyes falling over the Accuser in delight, taking in the Jinn's shirtless form – first the chest, then abdomen, and finally his legs. The broad, rounded bridge of Nick's shoulders supported a near perfect physique, crafted to please none other than God himself. Nick's own eyes never left the man's face – half indulgent, half disdainful – he smiled inwardly. *Run puppy... run, and run after what you cannot have,* he proudly thought to himself.

The young man raised his lit cigarette to mouth, pushing in just a little closer to Nick. He took a long drag, and tilted his head straight up into the air to exhale – a polite gesture in quarters so close. Then slowly he raised it to his mouth again, leaning in to touch the end of Nick's unlit cigarette. It was a proffer. Nick accepted it, drawing in upon the tiny flame bouncing at the end of his nose. He inhaled and repeated the same gesture of pushing the smoke up and away, then nodded to thank the man. The music reached for another ascending crescendo, and the crowd responded with frenzy, jumping in place and cheering for the skillful spell the DJ cast over them.

"Go, Jason! Go, Jason!" one group of young men shouted up at him.

The music roared with the crisp cadence of synthesized trumpets, sounding like they hailed some heroic knight at the door. Then a great hiss cut through the howl of horns; jets of dry-ice spewed cold vapor onto the floor. Revelers quickly rushed to the center of the platform to immerse themselves in the soothing spray. A mass of white fog spread out across the floor, its veil utterly unyielding. As it fell, the music slowly settled out again, low and trance-like, to begin the same cycle of ascension all over again.

The cloud of white cold parted gradually. Amid it the young stranger slipped away, smiling slyly and inviting Nick to follow, just as James had done with Azael earlier that week at the Round. The Jinn glanced away, disregarding the man's enticement. He moved into the crowd, turning his attention to the dance floor, casting his gaze out over the mass and seeking with his entire being for a sign…some hint of Heaven's satan.

Nick folded his lips around the cigarette, and began to inhale. The red ember at its end bounced to the music, glowing as he consumed it in one, single inhale: a trick he amused himself with, knowing none would notice in this state. He tiled his head up to release the column of smoke into the air. It mixed with the dying white of dry ice and became undistinguishable from the rest of the cooling cloud. Then the Accuser dropped the butt to the floor and crushed it with the weight of ages.

Nick turned slowly and moved around to where the DJ booth overhung the floor, looking up into its VIP lounge. There he saw Nafees and James surrounded by a ring of knights. These were Nafees' senior cohort, the most prominent members of the mysterious sect. Their ties as a community ran deep, both socially and politically. They were vain and seductive mortals, consumed with physical beauty as a reflection of spiritual potency. Most were indeed stunningly attractive; dark and foreboding characters, with sculpted bodies that were adorned with extravagant tattoos. Each man's markings were a sign of his rank. The more ornate designs denoted the most senior of the secretive cleric knights. Twilo was known for men such as the Rafiq; it was a veritable sea of the male form, and at the center were the two lithe but beautiful leaders of the cult: the ancient consort of the Queen of Heaven and the new dubious Seer of the Temple.

James nodded to Nick, signaling all was ready with the order, as they watched over the revelry of the floor like sentinels. Nick could also feel there were thralls in the crowd. He hoped the overwhelming presence of both the Accuser and the Rafiq would keep them from what they had planned– at least for the night.

As Nick looked up, he saw a large and imposing male figure step from behind James. The man wrapped his arms around the young seer. James laid his head back against the shelf of his chest and nestled it there affectionately. They moved together with the beat of the drums and the flare of lights. Nick felt an unexpected stab in the chest. He gave James a terse smile and quickly turned away to look back at the floor. For an instant he thought he might be jealous of James sharing his affection with this new companion, but then he brushed off the feeling as impractical. *Such sentiment for a mortal is beneath me*, he reassured himself.

Then something subtle, yet powerful altered out in their extended field of awareness – not so much in the corporal revelry, but in the Realm of Essences itself. An ominous shadow moved over the crowd. Nick reached out and took hold of James within his wings, stretching out through the dimness to insure his own wards strongest around the boy. James shuddered from the euphoria of ecstasy the instant Nick touched him. He shed the embrace of his companion and moved forward to the edge of the overhang. Nafees took notice, as he became aware of the presence as well, marshaling all his soldiers to the ready with a wave of his hand.

Nick turned his head slightly to glance up at James again. The boy leveraged his newfound power to bolster Nick's own. Together, using the spell of sema as a shroud, they all cloaked the floor from the coils of the Pythians.

A cold, cruel blast of enchantment seized Nick, as Shemhazai appeared in front of him out of thin air. The dark exile didn't even flinch, looking him straight in the eyes. He had been waiting for one of the demons to show themselves.

"Hello, Accuser," the grigori snipped snidely.

"Nick, if you please".

The demon smirked. "Your name is of such little consequence…don't you think?"

"Shem, Shem, Shem…well, it's been a long time," Nick hissed back. "I guess I shouldn't be surprised to find you behind all this...after consuming your pathetic twin."

"You won't waste your dwindling power on me here. I don't know what you and those Sufi fools think you can accomplish, but this war is only beginning, brother. I leaned in the last one how not to pick a fight with the likes of you without making sure you are alone...your time will come...but you know that."

"Like Azael thought to challenge me?" Nick replied with a deepening grin.

"He was useless...too consumed with his own lusts to be effective in this new struggle. You did us a favor by weeding him out of our ranks."

"He is not the only one among you who thinks merely with his dick...I'm not impressed with any of you new traitors, Shem...nor is Heaven."

"No, I suppose you're not, but overconfidence was always your weakness. Is that not why you are an exile?"

They stared into each other's eyes. The Accuser did not realize the grigori was stalling, hoping the thralls on the floor would find their quarry while Nick was distracted.

"Your little pet certainly seemed to like what he got," said Shemhazai, probing Nick's emotions for a weakness he could exploit. The grigori seemed to sense that if he could get the Accuser to lose his temper, he could force the spell they cast off balance.

The stab at James did work. Nick did become enraged. Shemhazai sniffed the air delightfully, reacquiring some of the power the Accuser had taken from Azael earlier that week. Dark energy flooded the floor.

Nafees surveyed the confrontation from above, feeling the surge of enchantment ebbing and flowing between the two potent Jinn. "This is not good," he said nervously to the James. "They will use Nick's rage to disrupt sema and take the prophet."

James could perceive Nick's potent wings enveloping him even more tightly, as if to shelter him, or perhaps even claim him. The boy was not sure which. It was at that moment James decided to do something he had only imagined he might. He probed at Nick with his novice power, enticing the dark exile to conjoin again; as farfetched as he knew the Accuser would find that impression.

Nick turned on the floor, wide-eyed, and spoke directly into James' mind. *What the hell are you doing?*

"You let me inside once, Nick. Do it again... just this one time ...trust me," the boy whispered simultaneously into the air and into Nick's mind.

Nick hesitated, and then without the slightest understanding of why, relaxed that part of him that held James' soul at bay – just enough to open himself. James entered; with him came a flood of light that fed along the ethereal path the grigori was using to siphon power. The instant James was inside Nick, Shemhazai's face turned grim and bitter. The seer's ripe power flowed into him; Nick had become a sudden conduit for it.

The grigori began to twist and choke as if he had swallowed something the wrong way. That source of true adoration was like poison to the beast.

"You and I will always have a special bond Nick...use that for what it is intended," James said into his mind.

For just that instant, the Accuser willingly and fully allowed himself to be filled by the spirit of a mortal, without a thought of consequence or pride. After centuries of defiance, he finally submitted, just as the nameless-god had wanted. Neither Nick, nor the world, would ever be the same.

"What was that?" Shemhazai barked as he spat out the taste of mortal affection that fed into Nick. The Accuser half smiled, not fully certain what had happened, but realizing it had helped give him a leg up over the demon.

"Well," said Shemhazai, "I can see these mongrels have taught you some new tricks, Accuser. You're not so obstinate after all. Too bad you didn't let Adam do that when you were told to...you might have saved yourself a few thousand years of misery."

Nick tensed with a quick fury and forced James out of his ethereal form, but the maneuver – if that is what it could be called – was enough to throw Shemhazai off balance and give Nick the upper hand. James backed away from Nick's harsh rebuke, feeling surprisingly sad and alone after being inside Nick again.

Nafees stared at James with a look of astonishment, sure in his head that indeed the end was at hand. He had lived to see the abduction of the Queen of Heaven and with it the decline of Eden. He'd seen the fall of the dark exile and how the earth shook in his wake. Now he had beheld that very Devil do the one thing Nick had been prepared to endure hell to keep from happening – he surrendered to a mortal's innocent love. Few but he understood the magnitude of that single act. Everything had suddenly changed; this was what he had really been waiting for all along. Nick *had* picked his side, and Nefees understood immediately what all this meant about James.

"By Allah," said the immortal cleric, "you have no idea what you have just done." He took the boy's head in hand, kissing him on the forehead. The others closed tightly around the young seer, the portent of Nafees' sentiment clear.

With Shemhazai off guard, Nick pressed his advantage. He reached into the Realm of Essence and took the form of a dark winged raptor, pinning the coils of the serpent in his talons. The two wrestled, causing a steeped measure of emotion to bristle on the floor. James felt Nick's struggle and tried to reach out to him again, but Nafees and the Rafiq held him back. They all understood the boy would only be in the way of what the Accuser must do.

Men had long assumed the eternal struggle to be one of black and white, good and evil, but the cosmos was not that simply composed. Every creature, including the Jinn and immortals, had a propensity toward anger, fear, and spite – the shadow of the great dragons in each living thing. It was choice that was sacred, to love and nurture rather than be consumed by rage. Nick and Shemhazai fell deeper and deeper into the ethereal void of timelessness, enveloped by that very struggle. It was then Nick realized he did have a choice, that while he had been made chiefly to serve the nameless-god, his heart could still decide its own fate. It was not a matter of submission, but of surrender...God wanted Nick to yield his heart, not out of obligation...but out of want.

Shemhazai plotted in his mind that if he could pull Nick into the void, the web of sema would collapse and dark power flood back through the strands the Rafiq wove over the floor. Nothing would stop who waited in the gloom from seizing the prophet if that happened. The Accuser and the demon spilled toward the frightful gap of the void, but using his last bit of power from James, Nick bit hard at the back of the viper's neck. The grigori screeched at him in wrath, as the Accuser used it to begin to devour the demon's essence on the spot. Shemhazai aptly broke Nick's grip with a surge of malice, blinking instantly away from the fight and fleeing into the refuge of the Abyss – where he knew Nick would not dare follow.

When the Devil reappeared on the dance floor again, trying to regain his senses, the music was climbing once more in its pitch. Two powerful Rafiq swiftly moved to his aide in order to insure the web of sema was maintained. Both stood supporting him with their shoulders, sensing Nick's legs were a little unsteady, as his power was unstable.

As Nick came around and his mind cleared, a bouncer walked up to them. "Is he falling out or something?" the imposing man barked. "Because if he is, he's gotta go!"

Nafees emerged behind the two men holding Nick, as if by magic. The bouncer immediately recognized the immortal cleric and backed away.

"He's fine," said Nafees. "He just needs some air."

Jon Godfrey rolled hard as the ecstasy pill hit him. His body pitched first left, then right with the crowd. He was not conscious of the human tide that carried him, lost in the heat and chemical euphoria. The restless young man came to Twilo every Sunday. He and his friends would sleep Saturday night until four or five in the morning, then gather at daybreak of Sabbath to make for the dim streets of the West Side. It was ritual for them.

Jon had taken the ecstasy about an hour before. He realized the pill was going to be a good trip, because it had just wrenched so intensely at his empty stomach – always a sign of quality stuff. The light began to fuse about him and he lost himself within the embrace of two tall men who did not seem to even notice him wedged between them. Their faces rubbed and nudged at each other as they kissed deeply, just above his head. Jon's bright red hair seemed like a flickering fire between them.

It happened so suddenly. His eyes rolled back into his head and he became lost to a place he could never identify – so deeply transfixed with its sense of elation that all he could do was release himself to it. He swayed to the music amid the euphoria of the high. The young man felt a rising sensation, as if he were being pulled away from his own body. The music infused him. He was no longer just listening to it – the beat became part of him, driving him. All he wanted to do was reach out and hold someone, anyone…in that moment it didn't matter who.

Once the Accuser gathered his senses, he moved away from Nafees and the knights, toward the huge columns set in the middle of the dance floor. He could feel the thralls as they lurked at the edge of the revelry, like wolves just beyond the outer rim of a wood. They were being very cautious now and yet a powerfully sinister presence lingered there. Its attendance infused them with malice, but would not show itself.

Radiance all around Nick altered into a new state, it was somewhere between light and sound. He felt the abrupt, unmistakable presence of an angel descend upon them, so he moved quickly in its direction. For the partygoers of Twilo, the manifestation of celestial power was indistinguishable from the strobe and glare of the club lights.

It was Gabriel. Nick pushed up next to where his manifestation fell upon the floor and saw a handsome redheaded boy wedged between two large muscled men. The Accuser was very relieved to see that they were not Rafiq. He didn't want to have to confront and wrestle God's anointed prophet away from them that night as well, but *he* needed this boy whatever the cost. Even the Sufi knights would not stand in his way.

Gabriel turned and noticed Nick as he approached. The Jinn smiled warmly from ear to ear, as he bent and began to whisper into Jon's ear. Nick stole up closer. A strange, unearthly voice issued from Jon's mouth, spilling out what to those around them was nothing more than unintelligible rambling. To Nick, it was a very clear presage from God.

"Can you hear the voice? It is like the sound of trumpets and rushing water…it speaks to me. The first and the last – who died and lives again – has this to say.

'I know you have suffered and that you have lived deprived of wealth in spirit, even though you are rich in power. Behold, I send to men word of His coming amid the clouds! Be wary of those who call themselves friend, you have but one true chosen in this world. Every eye shall bear witness to the sign, even those who deny Him now. All peoples of the earth shall mourn his coming bitterly!"

With those final words, Jon's legs gave out from under him. Nick reached to catch him, pulling him free from the clutches of the two kissing men. All the revelers were oblivious to what was going on around them.

Then Jon quickly stole from his vision; the bright angel hovering far above him now. Wavering in his step, the young prophet stared directly into Nick's eyes. The Accuser drove his gaze back, leaning forward to speak softly into his ear, trying to set him at ease with a spell of tranquility.

"Hello, beautiful," he said to the young prophet. "I've been looking for you."

Jon returned a smile from a foggy haze, lacing his fingers about the Accuser's shoulders and swaying with the rising music. Slowly, without a word, he lowered his head with its short bristly hair to Nick's chest, nuzzling it there tenderly.

At first, the Devil and the prophet were unnoticed by most amid the swells of flesh and sweat, but for two green glowing eyes that bore down on them from the far side of the floor, high from a shadowy perch. A voluptuous woman scaled down the bleachers and vanished into the crowd, never taking her eyes off Nick and Jon as they danced. When she slipped into the darkness, all the shadows of the floor left the room behind her.

Eventually Jon's ecstasy wore off; he began to respond to Nick's strong embrace. At first, he had hung loose on Nick's shoulders, but then he became more lucid and steady.

"My name is Jon," he said, trying to break-up the awkward silence between them.

Coming to your senses that way into a complete stranger's arms was unsettling. It happened a lot with ecstasy. "Thanks for lending a hand…I was a little out of it."

The Accuser tilted his head forward. "I'm Nick," he said.

"Pleased to meet you, Nick…you are hot," replied Jon, giggling like a child.

Nick grunted, amused at the sound; the drug ecstasy always brought out the bluntest speech imaginable from men, even as its intensity subsided. It was why men liked it – the sense of trust and ease if afforded them, to get over all kinds of inhibition. Sometimes it was just shyness, sometimes it was hurt, and sometimes it was more of a misguided self-loathing these men struggled to get past from the prejudices they endured. The pursuit of wajd was always about stepping outside oneself. It was a desperate ritual; wholly human Nick assumed.

The Accuser stared at the prophet for a time, relieved the drama was over for the moment. Jon was not really a boy in the physical sense, although he could not have been older than nineteen or twenty. His large arms and broad chest made him very popular in that crowd, even though he was not one to seek the trappings of what he considered 'cliques' – such as the Rafiq. He prided himself on being his own man.

"So, where are your friends? You can't be here alone." Nick finally asked.

"Ah, they are here someplace…two really tall guys."

"Oh yes them…they did not desert you. You were wedged between them when I found you. I guess I stole you away actually…I hope you don't mind."

"Knowing those two…they were probably so strung-out you could have been…like Lucifer himself…and they would not have stopped me from…running off with you." The boy's speech was broken from the drug's effect.

Nick's eyes became hooded. "Really," he replied caustically, "somehow I find that hard to believe."

Jon sensed he had upset Nick with what he had said. Assuming it was his usual bad manner, a talent for saying the wrong things at the wrong time, he tried quickly to find some way to retract the remark.

"I'm just kidding, dude," he said nervously. "They usually have my back. If you had really been bad news...they would have been right up in your shit."

"Well," said Nick, "I guess that means I must be an O.K. guy, right?" He maneuvered around so he could see up to where he knew Nafees and James would be watching. He didn't see them.

"You seem like a straight-up kind of guy," Jon finally said with a grin. "So was I babbling nonsense when you found me? I get so embarrassed sometimes when I get high. My friends all make fun of me for the crazy things that come out of my mouth."

"You were a little out of it, but you seemed just fine to me."

"That's a relief. I would hate for you to get the impression that I was a fool of some kind."

"I wouldn't worry about it," Nick said in a reassuring tone. "That's what we all come here for, isn't it...to lose ourselves?"

James turned from the floor, overwhelmed by everything that had transpired in that last week. The big man who had been holding him earlier plopped his weight down next to the boy. James took solace in his embrace; it was warm and comforting. Somehow he knew he belonged there, even though his mind drifted back to Nick now and then. The music had moved off the trance-like rise and fall, with Jason starting to play songs that had vocals laced through them. The words were sad, yet somehow the grief they bore was transformed in the pleasant cadence of the mix. It was the power of the spell.

The big man kissed James on the back of the neck. It was a genuine display of affection that caused James to melt there in the knight's strong arms, but the young seer nudged him away playfully with his elbows when the Rafiq knight rubbed his rough beard across the boy's back. James looked up at the man in the dim light with sad eyes. "Adriano," he said, "let's do another hit of e."

The man nodded and rolled over to one side, pulling a small plastic bag from his tight jeans. He fumbled for a time, producing two yellow pills, each bearing the stylized "S" of Superman. Ecstasy pills always had some strange sign or icon like that to identify what kind they were. James took one of the tablets from Adriano's hand and popped it in his mouth, then reached into his back pocket to remove a half full bottle of water wedged there. Each move was like a sacrament, practiced and ritualized. He unscrewed the cap and washed down the pill with a gulp, after that he handed the bottle to his new companion. Adriano repeated the steps of the custom, taking the other pill-like host and drinking. With a commanding strength, he reached over and took James by the face. "Body and blood," the man said irreverently, then kissed him deeply.

After a few impassioned seconds, the big man drew back and looked in to the eyes of the young seer. "I know this loss hurts," said Adriano. "We have all felt that pain, but you have to let the Accuser go...he is meant for something else."

James frowned at him, a little wounded by that reality. "I guess so," he replied, "but what makes all of this worse is I know that guy...I know the prophet. I've had a huge crush on him for months. I can't believe it's *him!*"

"You do?" asked Adriano. "Did you tell Master Nafees yet?"

"Not yet, I was too stunned when I realized who he was."

"Who is he? What do you know about him?"

"Not that much really. I met him a few times in a place where I hangout across town. He seems like an O.K. guy...he'll flip over Nick. I just know it."

"This will be important information," said Adriano calculating. "The Accuser will likely hurt the boy by using him for his own end. You will be able to approach the Anointed One later for us, if need be."

"Why do you think?" James started to say, but then stopped the question mid-sentence. "You are right," he finally sighed. "Nick doesn't care about that kid really. He is only after what he knows about the prophecy. When he is done with him, he will push him aside…just like he has me."

"Teach me how to reach inside your soul," begged the handsome knight. His arms clung fast to the young seer, adorned with its dark tattoos.

James blushed. "I will try in time…I'm still learning myself," he said, quickly losing himself in another kiss with the big man.

The young seer still didn't fully understand the significance of the role he played in the Rafiq, but he was overjoyed to be part of the order now. James had always felt like a lonely, awkward boy; he knew that had changed because of Nafees. The sting under his arm, where he had accepted in ritual the symbol of the Rafiq – a sacred bird called the homa – reminded him again of the pain he must endure for the order as well as for God's plan. It had hurt like hell he thought, but that was the point after all. Just as it would heal, his hurt in life over Nick would fade. That was the point.

"The pain of life in the mortal veil," Nafees told him, "scars men. Taking a tattoo under the arm in this way recalls to us that pain…so that we never forget what it has taken to become what we are. Only from the pain do we grow…do we gain wisdom about ourselves, and what Allah wants for us."

When James had asked what the bird signified, Nafees would only say it was an ancient totem. He promised the young seer there was much to learn, both about the order and about his newfound abilities.

It would all come in time, but for now there would be Adriano.

Not far from where James sat with the knight, Nafees stood in a lounge; he turned and stared at them as they indulged affection, enraptured by wajd. *This affair is indeed fortuitous*, the cleric thought. *The enchantment between them is strong...stronger than I thought possible.*

Nafees understood James would be instrumental to his purpose in the coming days. There was much that the immortal could not yet see, but he was convinced it was *this* prophet who could help him guide the order to unify God's people in the last days – as promised. Slowly, he turned and entered the back of the DJ booth that was suspended far above the dance floor. He gazed out over the crowd. It appeared like a writhing sea of flesh.

Jason Velenza was standing with his back to the cleric. The handsome knight wore a sleeveless t-shirt that exposed an elaborate, twisting pattern of tattoos. Nafees approached him.

"Did you see?" the cleric asked.

The man glanced over for a moment. His striking face adorned with a crown of distinguished silver hair. "Yes," he replied with a thick Italian accent. "It's just as you foresaw...there *are* two."

Jason abruptly turned his attention back to the equipment, listening for the transition of the music in the mix. Jason was weaving sema deeper over the crowd with it.

"What will you do?" he asked finally, eyes still fixed to mixing board.

Nafees thought a moment before again turning to search for James and Adriano. "James is Rafiq now... my instinct says *he* is the one we were told would come."

"Gabriel did not anoint James...the one on the floor with the Accuser seems favored by Heaven," answered Jason. "Doesn't that put a little wrinkle in your prophecy?"

"That all depends on your perspective. The omen given us from the knights guarding the Ark of the Covenant never said the anointing would be from an angel of Heaven, only that the prophet would come to us by way of the Jinn. Nick has been expelled, but is of the Jinn nonetheless...don't forget that."

"Intriguing logic," grumbled Jason. He turned and gazed over at the cleric. "I know you and you don't sound convinced about all this...what's wrong?"

Nafees held his breath; then released it after a few tense seconds. "I'm not fully sure...it's a leap of faith. I have to choose the right path now, there is no time left. We have to be careful...Nick cannot follow us once we leave here. The grigori are drawn to him, it will be too dangerous if they suspect where we're going."

"Well, if you try to take the one on the floor then, expect the Accuser will follow. Iblis clearly thinks that man in his arms will lead him back to the Court of Heaven."

"Yes, that makes James the obvious choice, given what we have seen."

"Perhaps too much so," said Jason. "Are you being a little reckless maybe, Nafees? You risk the frail destiny of the Rafiq on an intuition…on infatuation perhaps it seems to me."

Nafees looked at him with a brooding stare that told the man he knew what he was doing, not to question him.

"No, not just a hunch, beloved" he replied. "In over five thousand years, James is the only mortal I have ever known to peer into the heart of the Accuser. You saw it yourself… just as I did."

"The other half of the omen…you think James knows the true name of Allah already then?"

Nafees bowed his head. He spoke the prophecy aloud as if it were an incantation:

"Two seers will be led from the new wilderness by Jinn to serve God. The wiser one will bind the Devil. He will command the name of the Lord and the unruly Jinn will surrender his dark heart. The wiser one will lead the righteous, as a son of kings, and return the Tablets of Destiny to their rightful place.

The other will take the crown of serpents and crush the dragons under foot, taking his might too from the Devil's mark left on man. All is to God's end…He wills it."

"It will be useful for the Accuser to assume he is right about that boy," said the immortal. "They will lead the dragons away from us. I sense that boy's fate is uncertain…the dark rift rising in the sky, past which there is no sight, is where *his* destiny lies."

"That is assuming you are right about all of this, Nafees," Jason said, with a worried tone.

Nafees bristled.

Then both looked slowly out over the floor one more time. They were pleased with themselves for what they had done that night together, as the rhythmic trance of the sema drew the men on the floor deeper into wajd. The cosmic alignment of Heaven's fate and man's peril was eminent, and now finally they felt they were ready.

∘✵∘

Nick dared not take Jon back to Nafees' apartment, not just because he was reluctant to give any more away to the Rafiq than he already had, but also because he did not want to hurt James with this. James had helped him, just as Micah hinted the boy would. They did have a special bond. The dark exile had never let a mortal touch him the way James had – emotionally or ethereally. The improbable idea still burned within his mind. He tried desperately to ignore what it meant for him. Nick could no longer deny the truth – even the Pythia knew at this point that he had surrendered.

For thousands of years the Accuser resisted the idea that humans were more than ethereal mongrels, playthings created to amuse the nameless-god whom they serve. Now, he had come to see they were in fact much more. God had after all become one of them for a time, and was planning to do so again soon. Nick finally faced the fact that the nameless-god had a purpose in this – one which transcended his own needs, as well as that of mankind's. Whatever that fate was, it depended upon the precarious events as foretold. Still, he knew even prophecy needed a hand here and there. Somehow Nick was intended to lend aide – despite his disobedience.

At that point, the Jinn tried to push all his nagging thoughts about the fate of the cosmos out of mind and focus on Jon. He had what he had come for after all – the true prophet – ordained by none other than Gabriel himself. As long as Nick kept Jon away from the Pythia, the Accuser believed he had a second chance to make all things right – to find and protect the woman that would bring men a deliverer, and bring him redemption.

The crowd in the club was breaking up, men wandered around as if lost, still dazed by wajd. Nick followed Jon to the coat check; they took only minutes to retrieve their things from the now empty coatroom. The Accuser pulled the leather of his coat over his shoulders, then reached to help Jon with his light, sweatshirt – the young man's coordination still off from the intoxication of the drug. They both struggled a second with it.

"So, do you live close?" Nick asked Jon, as he tried to keep the young man's balance.

"I live in the West Village, but I don't think we should go home together tonight."

Nick's heart sunk. "What?" he snapped. The Accuser could scarcely believe his ears. After the entire perilous production and what waited for him out there, the damn fool wanted to go home alone. The surprise in Nick's voice was deeply apparent.

"Do you live with family or something?" Nick asked.

Jon laughed and stumbled a little again, still off his equilibrium.

"Seriously, it's not like I don't think you're totally hot," said the boy, "but I just don't go home with guys from the club like this. Look at me, I can barely put on my own coat…I don't trust myself in this condition."

Wonderful, Nick thought angrily, *with all of Hell bearing down on him…*this *prophet of God would have to be so fucking self-righteous that he won't go home with someone on the first date.*

Jon giggled naively a little upon seeing Nick's face – the noise sounded almost foolish coming from his rugged, masculine frame. Nick assumed the strange, juvenile gesture was because Jon was still high on the ecstasy. He ignored it.

The young prophet timidly leaned his head into Nick's chest, rubbing his face there again with affection. "You are not used to being told 'no' are you, stud?" he asked, sounding amused.

Nick watched him a moment, stunned and somewhat annoyed.

"As a matter of fact, Jon," he replied with an air of unease. "I am more accustomed to rejection than you could ever begin to imagine."

6

RAPTURE

A brittle energy flowed through Nick as he circled Jon's building. There the Accuser extended his potency into the material plane, like a marker. He wanted to be sure any supernatural force that dared venture too close would sense his presence immediately. Nick was also struck by how easily Nafees let him slip away with Jon. He remained vigilant that even the Rafiq be kept away for now. He did not like being so far from the prophet, but the Jinn figured that if he could not be next to Jon in his bed, he at the very least would envelope the young seer with a shield of ethereal protection.

The big question that burned in his mind was how could he now approach this anxious new prophet with the reality of what was unfolding? Jon was clearly not your run-of-the-mill mortal, besides being anointed by the Jinn. He seemed to have some innate ability to resist supernatural suggestion, as if his soul was somehow composed differently than other men's – Nick had tried to bend his will in the club and failed.

The Accuser was also aware the young prophet would come loaded with all kinds of superstations about him as the Devil. He had to tread carefully or risk turning the boy away into the arms of the Rafiq; or worse yet, into the grip of the dragons.

The young prophet's bedroom faced out on to a busy street, several floors up from its chaos. At least that made watching him a little easier. Nick thrust himself straight into the air, pushing his body aloft with his wings, moving toward the brick over-hang of the ledge on the other side of the street. His cloaking spell made him completely invisible to onlookers – even the pigeons that hobbled along the concrete outcrop passed him by without a second glance. There he perched himself like a great bird of prey, surveying the roof tops, scrutinizing the passing pedestrians in the street, and examining the shifting light as it broke through Jon's window where the young man lay fast asleep.

The wind picked up along the building and lashed at its crevices. The Accuser shivered a little, not from the cold, but from anticipation. Deep inside his being, he searched a heavy heart for what he should feel at that moment. He found a desire that was hopeful but foreboding. *Time alters all things*, he thought to himself, while the weight of loneliness pressed down on him.

For the first time in many centuries he began to really grapple with the unbearable pain – his bitter missing of God. It was a hurt that blotted out the light of all other feelings. The wayward Jinn began to slowly pull apart the emptiness of being alone in the cosmos from his other feelings of angst. For so long those feelings were all just bundled up into one rage. It had been over five thousand years now since his banishment; he realized it was time to let it all go and move forward. Still, Nick struggled in his own heart just how to do that. Joshu the Nazarene had been the only human – despite being demigod – whose presence had allowed Nick to push aside the loss of the nameless-god of old, for somehow that incarnation of the eternal spirit into the body of a man changed Nick's sense of the divine. In truth, the Jinn had never known the nameless-god to have that kind of compassion, that kind of.... *What is the word I want to use?* he thought to himself, struggling with his emotions. *Humanity... that's it... Josh lent to God a sense of humanity.*

When the thought finally formed in his head, he quivered at the significance of it. Now too even the missing of Josh, which at one time had been a second great wound in his soul, seemed to ease away. What remained was mostly a kind of purposelessness, an empty feeling distinguishable in many ways from grief by its hollowness. Strangely, he sensed it was as if he had gained something by losing Josh, in spite of the deep ache of helplessness it caused inside him. He could get past it. Nick realized anything was possible from the growth that provided him, even going home. That was worth the hurt to him at that point – if he could just find a way to redemption.

The Accuser glared across the street and watched the young prophet with an odd mix of pity and bewilderment. Something about the young man seemed out of place. The boy's refusal to leave the club with him set the Accuser's fears off. *How will this holier-than-thou mortal point the way to God's second incarnation?* he wondered. *His essence feels like a bull in a china shop…more likely to ruin than save things.*

A deep chill ran down Nick's spine as he sat there on the ledge. At first, he passed it off as the flurry of emotion surrounding his expectation, but then out of nowhere came a darting kiss. It was a simple disembodied peck.

Nick pitched to one side, away from the taunting tenderness – startled by it. He reached for his sword, only to freeze in disbelief at what his eyes beheld there; sitting next to him materialized his gentle brother, Gabriel.

The angel's cloak had been so powerful that Nick hadn't sensed him as he snuck up and stole that little bit of affection. There was a moment of unease over the fact that he could be approached so easily without warning, but then he remembered his curse. His eyes were blind to anything of God, unless of course God wanted it to be seen. Thralls and grigori would not be as adept as this agent of Heaven at hiding themselves, so he settled down a bit, realizing Jon had little to fear now the two angels sat outside his door.

"Hello, Nick," said the Jinn warmly.

"What are you doing here?" boomed Nick. His voice shook the building ominously, full and foreboding of his wrath. Gabriel simply laughed at him, seeing through his playful, menacing facade.

"First watch of the day belongs to me," he replied, "and the pigeons." He pitched his body from side-to-side imitating the ragged birds that dodged unaware between their feet. "But I am glad you finally made it up…it's been lonely sitting out here all by myself."

"How long have you been perched up here?" asked Nick, as he kissed the adoring angel back on his forehead.

Gabriel blushed and smiled at him, accepting the affection for its true warmth. The young Jinn seemed more at ease than he had been earlier that week; the somber business of heralding the Court of Heaven always took a toll on him. Guard duty was simpler.

"It seems I've been up here for months. You know me…time means so little, but to tell you the truth… that boy is a real bore to watch." Gabriel rolled his eyes in Jon's direction. "He simply sleeps…works… then broods around all the time. He is quite bitter for it…. he really needs to get a life."

Nick laughed at his tone. "It's common of God's prophets," he said sarcastically, the sting of Jon's rejection still fresh in the Accuser's own mind. "Suffering seems to be a prerequisite for the job…I can see this one is no different."

Sensing the true hurt behind Nick's words, the young Jinn pushed his folded feathers up next to him. Then in response, the Accuser instinctively extended his powerful wingspan out and around him. Gabriel laid his head upon Nick's shoulder. The dark exile opened his mouth to speak, but the Jinn just pressed one finger against his lips to silence him.

"Who is going to hear us up here?" Nick blurted out, dodging the touch.

"You've been out of it a long time, big brother. You forget you are banished from the eye of God. You don't see Him when He is near…as we do."

Nick tensed instantly. "He is close?"

"Don't work yourself up, you big coward…He is not that close," said Gabriel, "but you know…."

"I know what?"

"He hears all and sees all," Gabriel announced in an officious voice.

"Oh yeah, I forget that part sometimes," replied Nick with a half laugh. "I mistake His apathy for being short sighted."

"Be nice," replied the angel with frown. "He is still the Lord, Nick."

Nick rolled his eyes; then the two Jinn smiled at each other with affection, sharing in a single look all the things that did not need to be said out loud. They sat a long time on the ledge of the building, peering at the window where Jon lay, saying nothing more as the morning blossomed into day.

The roar of the traffic and high-pitched shrill of bus breaks slowly hedged out the eerie calm that rested over the city streets early that morning. The sky molted itself from grey to orange, then to a bright robin's egg blue as the sun rose high toward the tops of the buildings.

Gabriel pressed his lean form tighter into Nick's body, and the sleek turns of his muscles relaxed. He nudged the bridge of his nose along Nick's chest and took in a deep breath; he noticed the smell of God's euphoria still lingered upon the exiled Jinn after all that time. Gabriel relished it. Something inside his heart seemed to give way – a sense of defiance rose in the air about them.

"You know, Nick," Gabriel said without lifting his face, "it's been eons since we've been this close...and alone."

"Thousands of years," replied Nick tenderly, not afraid to let Gabriel know with his voice as well as his touch that he enjoyed that moment very much.

"I am feeling a little rebellious right now. Is that the influence you have on others that everyone fears so much?"

"So it is said," snorted Nick, making a sad face.

"Then let me suffer a little for the sake of remembrance," whispered the youthful angel, "after all...God is merciful."

"To you or to me?" replied Nick sardonically.

Gabriel did not respond in words, but instead lifted his face to look into Nick's dark gaze. He noted the loss and emptiness he found there, and grieved for it. The Jinn began to whisper into the Accuser's ear, very gently at first, so that no being further than a few feet away could possibly hear.

Nick smiled.

The soft almost erotic utterances teased at something deep inside the Accuser. They were the words of an ancient psalm. The deep-throated sounds of Aramaic speech turned from simple, coy phases into poetic verse. The meter and rhyme were perfect, rolling into stanza after stanza, spun together with such precision that after awhile it began to sound as if the angel was singing rather than reciting. Nick took a deep breath. The air seemed different – sweeter and fresher – as if the song was moving them very subtly through some sort of ethereal passage to another place. The canto turned to music, lush, like the roar and crash of a sea. The overture of Gabriel's voice rose in crescendo and as it reached its apex, the intonation transformed into a blossoming vision.

Nick's eyes widened. He could not believe what he saw. "Eden," he moaned with both agony and delight in a single word.

"Hush," whispered Gabriel, "say nothing…. let no one know we are here like this. You have been banished from the sight of God. He will be greatly displeased with me to know I've brought you back here, but I trust you will someday make my transgression worth the risk." His whisper was full of innuendo and desire.

Nick nodded, unable to take his eyes off the apparition.

They sat huddled upon a distant cliff, looking down into the valley as it spread away from them. Two great rivers rose and flowed away from its center, looking like serpents coiling across the landscape. The breeze was heavy with honeysuckle, as tiny wisps of dandelion shoots floated about the edges of the wooded paths, like sprites. Amid the placidity, Nick could see the fade and shift of images – the essences of all created life phasing from a fine ethereal hue to a semi-corporal state. The forms were cherubim that serve in the mind of man as legend and fable, but in reality were manifestations of Gods numinous dreams.

Eden was the divine plan unveiled, the very thought of God. Creation was an act of partition that began there, with God separating himself from one aspect of divinity to the next, each manifestation no less marvelous than the last. Thus it was all of creation possessed a deep sense of need for returning to that center – gravity pulling heavenly bodies down, chemistry bonding elements together, and life's yearning – this was all need of Him. This compunction that drove the forces of existence itself was in fact a subtle spiritual reflections of one principle: all things seek return to God, to conjoin.

Suddenly, Nick felt God's full presence and for a moment the guilt of banishment burned in his chest. A tear broke at his eye and it rolled down his nose. Gabriel reached up with his hand and caught the tiny droplet before it struck the ground, fearing even that simple gesture would be noticed. The Jinn held the tear firmly and consumed its grief. At that moment, he realized in his heart what Nick truly was. The power of that single tear filled Gabriel to his brim. There was more grief there than in all of man's despair combined. The sudden surge of that power passing between them almost caused Gabriel to burst at his brim. He fought desperately to contain both his ethereal form and his composure – Nick must not see this epiphany or all would be lost.

"We should go," said Gabriel sadly.

Nick hesitated a second, then tipped his head once to acknowledge that the young angel was right.

Gabriel waved his hand and Nick fell away from Heaven for a second time.

As they appeared again upon the ledge near Jon's building, Gabriel reluctantly pulled himself away from Nick, trying not to be conspicuous and convey to dark angel how much he truly wanted to stay in that embrace for all eternity.

"Thank you," said Nick, staring deeply into the youthful Jinn's eyes.

Gabriel made a comforting face, fighting back his own tears. "I have to go. Michael is near. He will see us and be displeased that I've consorted with you without his blessing."

"He always was a jealous little shit," replied Nick.

"Yes, he hates the thought of us together," said Gabriel in a tone that both agreed with and admonished Nick for his spite.

"He always wanted you for himself," Nick huffed.

Gabriel shook his head, wondering how such a powerful expression of God's love could be so lost, so misguided. "No Nick...of the two of us it's not me he really wants," he replied. Gabriel rose, hesitated a moment, and then vanished.

But before heading back to Heaven, Gabriel quickly slipped into Jon's room, cloaked again so Nick would not see him. The messenger of the nameless-god opened the sixth scroll, to finish reading the second half of the prophetic message from the night before. He read sadly, realizing this was a great leap of faith for him...the scroll contained a dreadful cautioning about Nick for the prophet. He bent and whispered dismay into the boy's ear, a warning of his doom, sad that he must do so.

Jon tossed in his sleep, lost to dreams as the Jinn spoke. He saw a dark presence holding a trumpet. The being – perhaps an angel, perhaps not – came close to him and spoke into his mind sedition. All of the images that Gabriel had visited upon him at Twilo filled his mind at once like a rushing river. Then the young prophet saw a wild beast that was part leopard, part lion, and part bear. He saw men worshiping the beast and saying that none could compare to its glory. Beyond the strange creature, he saw a woman appear in the sky, but he could not see her face. She escaped into a wild desert where an eagle fought with a serpent to protect her, the bird devoured the grigori.

The vision moved again swiftly; he saw her climb to the top of a mountain made of sculls. She was drenched in blood and raised her hands to the sky as if to plead for help. Tears ran down her face as both the sun and moon rose above her head in the sky at once. Yet another angel stood in the heavens between them, holding two lights. Every where he showed the lights men hid their eyes and screamed, "do not make us bare the sight of our own shame, Sons of Light."

Then Jon saw Nick, the man he met at the club that night. He held a sword and was standing with a stranger. Jon saw Nick was surrounded by anger and hate, like a flame. For some reason the prophet found he was jealous of the man, but he was not sure why. The man with Nick swiped with a rod at the strange beast Jon saw near Nick. He cut open its head. The beast flailed, but the man was merciless, raging with some deep and dark vengeance.

The righteous angel in the sky spoke to Jon saying, "all that you have been shown will come to pass with each trumpet. You will gain new wisdom, but you will have to choose the right path. Many will claim to be your friends, but judge them well...wickedness will lay closer to you than you sense. Your destiny is less than certain, for it leads to a dark rift beyond which there is yet no sight for man. You will wander there, as if it were a wasteland. There you will lead dark men to God's judgment, a doom you will share with the Devil."

Jon saw Nick's face again. He instantly recognized him for who he was…the exile of Heaven.

With that revelation, the prophet's ethereal vision stirred one last time. He watched Nick falling from Heaven like a comet, striking the earth and causing a great fire that spread over the land. He finally heard a voice inside his head, one which was not his own.

"The Accuser of God has come for you…all of fate fears God's wrath in him, loosed upon the world."

The young seer shook in his dream, filled with dread. Jon realized Nick would become his end, should he allow himself to be led astray.

When the prophet finally awoke, he leapt straight out of bed, realizing he was late for work. The disoriented boy began to scramble around his apartment. He pulled on a snug sweater that fit his body to show off his sculpted chest and shoulders, then fumbled for his shoes – not even bothering to change the sweat-pants he had slept in all night.

A thought struck him suddenly.

Jon pushed his hands into his pockets to look for something, becoming frantic as he realized he did not have his keys. The boy had a penchant for losing things, sometimes really important things. His problem was not really so much that he was absentminded – it was more that he could not stay focused on detail for very long. All the strange visions he kept having were driving him to the brink of insanity.

It was for this very reason he had started to do the drugs. Jon was constantly looking for some way to distract his wandering senses, and narcotics seemed an easy answer, despite how much he hated them. They alleviated his boredom, but not by making things more exciting – not at all. He simply cared less about all other matters when taking them – right then that suited him fine. Nothing made sense to him of late.

Shoving his hands into the sweat-pants again, reaching deeper into his pockets, he found the two tiny keys. He'd forgotten that he removed them from the chain the night before. They had been there all the time, even though he swore they were not just seconds before. Storming into the kitchen, he grabbed his coat and pulled himself together, filled with his temperamental wrath.

"Why are things always in the last place you look?" he blurted out loud resentfully. He quickly moved into the doorway, and headed out into stairwell.

At the far corner of the room, Nick drifted past the window still cloaked by his spell. *Because it is the place you find what you are looking for,* thought Nick in answer to the boy's strange plea. He was struck by the prophet's impatience.

Jon made an agitated sound, and bolted for the open corridor. The Accuser watched him go out like a hurricane. He suddenly realized this was a completely different boy than the night before. Nick wondered if he should not just turn around and leave this entire mess to Michael, whom he knew must have been lurking close by. Then he remembered what he wanted from this entire affair; he longed for the salvation this boy promised. Like it or not, Nick needed the boy now. It was too late to turn back. *I just have to learn to live with the frail faults of men,* Nick thought to pacify himself, *if I ever want to feel God's touch again.*

The Accuser pulled his material form out into the open air, just outside the apartment, and hurdled himself toward the ground; there he lit a few feet from the buildings' door. Jon tumbled out of the entrance, and down the stoop in front of him, awkwardly trying to button his coat as he stumbled along. Nick watched him turn and rush down the street, pulling and tucking at his own vanity.

Pitching his weight forward, the Accuser went aloft. He followed Jon, giving two enormous bursts with his wings for thrust, catching up just as the boy scurried down the subway steps. Then the dark exile descended into the tunnels, trailing the prophet into the bowels of the city.

There Jon swiped his metro-card at the turnstile and pushed through it, ramming into a woman he half overturned in his wake. He didn't even notice her. She glared at the back of his head as if to do him harm, but the prophet simply scuttled gracelessly down the raised platform, oblivious to anything but his own angst.

Nick crept after him in full cloak. The only hint of the dark exile's presence was the whirling of a candy wrapper that hung close to the yellow rim of the platform. It fell and spun away, drifting off the edge into oblivion.

A sudden wind filled the tunnel like an ominous omen, announcing the train that barreled in behind it. The subway came to a lumbering stop; the doors to a car where Jon stood hesitated for a few seconds before opening. He quickly darted through the gap when they did, expecting them to close behind him instantly. When they did not, he became even more impatient.

The boy nervously split his glare between the open doors and the sparse faces sitting about the train, shifting his weight from foot to foot. His irritation was palpable, looking like a child holding his urine. He raised his face into the air, twisting it into an angry mask.

"Ahhhhhhhhh," the prophet screamed out loud.

Jon's annoyance spread about the small enclosure like a wave of heat. The other passengers tired to ignore him, pretending they had heard nothing. The doors slowly closed, and then opened again. His look grew feral, like a trapped animal.

"Come on, let's go," he groaned through grit teeth.

"We have signals against us ahead," promptly came the voice of the automated conductor, "please be patient."

Jon threw his bulk into a seat, and glared into the air. His feet pawed against the floor like he had no control over them. Everything about the young man gave off an air of disquiet, but it was like the nervous rage of a little boy, not a grown man.

Nick floated into the car and thought to himself how ridiculous Jon appeared right then, tossing his temper about the train. Then he realized that the prophet *was* actually little more than a child, as young as he was. The life span of a mortal was so brief to Nick that he sometimes forgot how fragile human innocence really was – it came and went so fast. The door warning sounded again, followed by the same strange voice of the conductor.

"Please stand clear of the closing doors," it said.

The Accuser guessed that if he revealed himself to the boy at this stage, there would likely be trouble for it. Jon might think Nick was stalking him. The dark exile glared at the prophet, realizing he was in fact.

Without warning, the young prophet mysteriously settled down in his seat, calmed by something. Nick sighed; Jon's moods were exasperating. He watched the boy's eyes with curiosity, noticing how a man across from where he stood had seized the boy's attention. The prophet was taken with the handsome stranger, returning the man's bawdy, inviting stare with a coy looking grin of his own – and yet even that simple flirtation seemed awkward for Jon.

An idea came to the Accuser, a menacing one. It was the kind of notion for which Nick deserved his reputation as a sinister angel. He was known to men as the thief of wills for a reason: his ability to brutally imprison the mortal mind, to snare it for his own purpose. The spell was called *jinnd giritan* – ethereal possession – it could drive a mortal mind insane. Nick hadn't done it in centuries. *Desperate times call for desperate measures,* thought the Accuser, staring at the man on the train, pondering the devious idea carefully.

Nick reasoned that if the prophet would not willingly give him what he wanted, he might seduce it from the boy without his even knowing the truth. He could use this handsome stranger to that end.

Still, the spell of *jinnd giritan* was no easy feat. The push and pull of two wills within a single mind was maddening – it wasn't uncommon for the process to be fatal to a man. A mortal was most powerful in the seat of his own soul; ethereal creatures often found it too difficult to maintain the precision and focus needed to enter a man's mind, and at the same time maintain the hold. It was like trying to capture a butterfly with one hand; one false step could rip the soul in half, shattering the victim, and perhaps even leaving the invading spirit marred by the effort. It was one of the reasons the grigori tended to use forced conjoining to get what they wanted of men. Possession was simply too risky, and not worth the effort to most.

Nick's proficiency with the spell, on the other hand, was more brutal and exact than that of other Jinn. Heaven's exiled Accuser could grip the essence of a man like a lion holds an ill-fated gazelle. This ability had been intended by God as a tool of divine inquisition, when done in the name of the Court of Heaven. That is not what the spell had become in those later days; it was now just another means of violating a man's will. *But it's for the prophet's own good after all*, he thought. *The end will justify these means.*

Nick rose to his feet and reached deep into his core, where was stored the fundamental nature of his power. The stranger sat unaware of his fate, still luring Jon with a soft smile. The dark exile stopped for a moment to admire the man's extraordinary beauty. He noticed in that instant something odd, something otherworldly about him, but had no time to stop and try to figure out what the strange magnetism might indicate. The sooner this was over the better. Nick shrugged off the impression and hastily reached for the last thing he needed to weave the spell of possession: the hardening of his heart.

The Accuser needed to stop it from beating for just an instant, one cold and timeless second, to cloud out all compunction – for remorse would block the path of the spell. He focused on the pounding. It began to slow, and muffled. The sluggish rhythm drew cadence to a steady, low throb. Nick extended his ethereal talons as his beating heart came to a virtual stop.

One more beat, he thought, *and he is mine.*

But right then Nick's dying heart discovered at its center something he did not expect to find. At first he could not make out what the dim power was, hidden at the very edge of his existence and buried by fire, power, and rage. It curiously kept his heart from fully stopping the requisite seconds to finally close the circuit and lunge into the soul of the young man before him.

Nick forced harder, but it would not give way.

The power flickered and he realized something he could not explain, that made no sense to his being. This force was a spark of the divine he did not know was still inside of him, a tiny part of God somehow left from before he had been banished. It flashed. For an instant he thought he saw faces, the faces of men and angels…Gabriel, Josh, and even James. It broke his focus as something in it broke his heart; grief overtook him.

Nick quickly stopped what he was doing, the guilt throbbing in his chest as he did. He froze there in space and time, unable to complete the spell. The accumulation of ethereal power that he had been amassing receded, like the pulling away of a nighttime tide. The dark exile shuddered, suddenly mortified with himself for what desperation had made of him in those the last days of men. *I truly have earned my name, but I can't do this now*, he thought sadly. *It's wrong…it cannot be the right path back to Him.*

A crash suddenly tore into the Accuser from nowhere, as he was struck by a mind-numbing force. The next thing Nick realized, he was spinning out and away from the train, propelled by an object. Something had been driven into him about the midsection, and literally blasted him from the train doors like a canon.

The Accuser shook his senses, shifting his wings mid-air, using them to come to a stop. Nick's eyes quickly refocused, as his clearing head watched the last car of the train turn a downward curve away from him. It vanished with little sparks of light nipping at the wheels.

Something large was resting in his hands. Nick had gripped the projectile cast at him by instinct, and held to it fast as he had been thrown clear. He looked down and was astonished to find the near motionless body of his brother, Michael.

Nick landed on the subway track. The air rushing around him was like a storm.

Michael moaned.

"What the hell happened?" the Accuser hissed into the Jinn's ear.

Michael's eyes fluttered. The semiconscious angel looked up at him with confusion. Focus returned to his eyes slowly, then they opened wide. He tried desperately to speak, but nothing came out at first.

"What?" Nick shouted.

"The Pythia...are on that train," said Michael finally in an alarmed voice. "I was so amused with what I thought you were going to try on Shemhazai..."

"Shem?" Nick interrupted, instantly realizing what that strange glow about the man on the subway actually was. The grigori had been using a snakeskin enchantment.

"You could not see him under his glamour spell, not the way I could, and I wasn't paying attention to anything else but you two," choked the Jinn. "Shemhazai was not alone...there is a *serpent* on that train, Iblis. The dragons have descended upon the mortal realm."

"Shit!" snarled Nick. He looked after the train again.

Michael half laughed and half choked as Nick cursed. "It's a good thing you stayed that spell...no telling what Shemhazai would have done to you had you tired force your way inside his head. Strange he didn't seem to see you either...it's funny how the two of you think alike, both are so intent on stealing what that boy knows."

"What happen to you then?" snapped Nick.

"The dragon snuck up on me while I was watching you two fools." Michael coughed. "I think God's prophet is in need of a guardian angel right now. Oddly, you're the closest thing Heaven has to one."

Michael's voice had cleared. It rang with his righteous command. A sense of dread came over Nick all at once. He rolled Michael near to one side of the track.

"Go," said the wounded Jinn. "I am no longer important...stop that dragon any way you can. God cannot come to our aide now...trust me!"

Without a second thought, Nick bent one knee and threw back his powerful wings, thrusting himself aloft with such speed that he was gone in twinkling of an eye. The wind in the tunnel enshrouded him with meaning and purpose. The Accuser reached down into himself again for his essential power, but this time to draw his strength for the righteous cause of God. Whether by proxy of Michael or by fate itself, Nick found himself an agent of the Court of Heaven once more – if only for that moment. The dark angel felt renewed. His wingspan widened in the tunnels and he used the open space between beams to throttle up hard with more thrust, culling speed as he jetted though the dark entrails of Manhattan. His focus was mindlessly intent. When Nick finally acquired the train with his senses, he latched on to draw himself into it, ripping through the train with such force that the back wheels derailed. The car slid and slammed into the nearest joist.

The dragon was in mortal form and already had its coils around Jon, trying to push the young prophet onto his face and tear away at his clothing as the train shuddered. Shemhazai floated nearby with a look of triumph on his face. Nick's rage exploded, he dove at the grigori and swung the hilt of his sword, knocking the deomn so hard he crashed through the side of the train. Then the Accuser maneuvered the blade and reached to haul the monster free of Jon, but as he cocked and swung, the train pitched, smashing into another girder on the opposite side of the track. Jon's head slammed into one of the hard seats, his body tossed upward like a rag doll. The rear car uncoupled from the one in front of it and the screeching sound of breaks filled the air.

Nick wrestled with the serpent trapped in its mortal guise, as they heaved about the mass of metal, disoriented by its bounce and spin. Dread gripped him. Clutching the beast firmly, he dragged both it and himself forcefully into the Realm of Essences, away from Jon and the crashing subway car. *God alone is with you now, Jon,* he thought. *You at least have a better chance in this ruined tunnel than I will have with this monster.*

As he pulled the stunned, struggling serpent into the portal, the Accuser quickly realized just how over his head he was. The dragon assumed its true essence once they reached the other side, its scale in that place like a mountain of fire. What alarmed Nick the most was the fact that the beast was on mortal plane at all. In his time with the Court of Heaven, the presence of a dragon in the ephemeral world would normally draw the very presence of God himself, and yet He had not come. This was an act of war. The Accuser shivered for his plight. A dragon was the stuff of his very own genesis – a primordial power as mighty as the nameless-god himself in some respects. Nick doubted greatly he could do more than delay the hideous fiend without assistance – help that he knew would never come to him. As he maneuvered to strike at the beast with his blade, the question burned at his very center. *Where was God to allow this sacrilege of Tiamat?*

Nick had little time to mill over it before the monster batted at him with one of its massive wings, casting him back into the clouds of ethereal vapor – those primordial bits and pieces of matter that were left over after the creation of the cosmos. Then the dragon hissed as it drew in air, preparing to blast Nick when it exhaled the broil of Hell. The Accuser ground his teeth. *This is it,* he thought, *the very fire of Perdition will consume me, as foretold. God's curse is finally made full.*

No material or ethereal creature, other than God, could withstand the fire of a dragon. Nick expected to die right there and then, but oddly a part of him was pleased. Thousands of years of anguish could now come to an end for the Devil. He could not help but be both afraid as well as relieved. He closed his eyes and actually welcomed his end; he had served his Lord the best way he knew.

The monster pitched his head to one side and erupted like a massive volcano; the flame enveloped Nick. The sensation was horrific. His normal ethereal essence felt like it melted away instantly. Even the metal of the sword seemed to lose its substance, yet neither he nor it broke into fragments from the unbearable force. To his astonishment, something was holding his form intact, resisting it. It was as if some part of what was in his spirit defied the impulse to implode from the chaos issued around him. After several seconds, Nick was struck how the inferno was taking mercilessly forever to destroy him, and just when he did not expect that he could endure another second of the pain, it simply ceased.

Nick felt a sudden surge of energy that was so intense it actually replaced his faltering substantiality. The first thing the Accuser realized was that he was not actually burned at all, despite how painful the searing heat had been. His skin seemed to radiate with some strange new power that rippled off of him.

Then shockingly, he looked back at his own wings and they were consumed in flame, brightly alight. The feathers were completely gone; each one was replaced with a shaft of translucent fire – it actually felt glorious and empowering.

The Accuser drew his wings back and forth, then up and down. His form shifted with such force that a single beat of his wing carried him light years away from the monster. And yet he could still make it out, despite the distance he traveled, sitting there stunned by what it was seeing of the mysterious Jinn. Nick put the loose ends together; he had somehow absorbed all the intensity of the dragon fire. It made sense suddenly. God had fashioned him of dragon fire after all, following the first war in Heaven. The blast had simply reduced him to his utter essence. Even Haqiqah, the sword that God had gifted him, flared and sparked with flame as he wove it through the air in the monster's direction, challenging it.

Far off, he could see the beast was retreating, for some reason it either could not, or would not pursue Nick. The Accuser let it go, relieved as he was. He'd done more than enough by driving the beast off – he hastily used his enchantment to move out of the Realm of Essences. Nick needed to get back to Jon that instant, should Shemhazai not been as deterred by Haqiqah.

When he materialized a few feet away from the crushed subway car, he was comforted to see Gabriel and five other lesser Jinn had come after all. They were all huddled around the unconscious body of the prophet.

Nick approached, instinctively raising a cloaking and unwittingly using his newfound power to create a powerful ward. Then once he saw that things were clear, he shed it. Gabriel nearly fell over from fright. The other angels took up an immediate stance for battle.

"Nick? "asked Gabriel, with an uncertain tone.

The Accuser nodded to him, as he moved closer, paying little attention to the others. "How is the prophet?" he asked.

All the other Jinn looked to Gabriel for his response. They did not seem to recognize Nick.

"It's fine," said Gabriel to them. "The Accuser is one of us again."

They hesitated, but followed his command. They were made to follow.

"The prophet is well," said a younger Jinn kneeling beside Jon. "We've mended his injuries as best we could. He will be scarred by the quick restoration, but will live. I cannot say what it's done to his soul...his is like none I've ever felt."

Gabriel still could not believe his eyes for what he saw of Nick. "How did you see us, and how did we not see *you*?" he asked.

"What do you mean?"

"We were cloaked with the ethereal shroud of God. You are banished from its sight and there is no ward that we cannot ourselves see, except that of God and perhaps of a dragon. You came unseen to us now. What's happened to you?"

Nick paused, knowing that the truth would be met with skepticism, especially coming from him. "A dragon...I sustained its breath and somehow escaped harm," he replied. He looked down at his hands to notice something, a raw primordial power he had never felt before.

There was silence for a moment as the gravity of his remark settled over them. Something seemed to brew there among the Jinn. "Lord of Lies!" one of the young Jinn blurted out finally. "That is blasphemy in the eyes of God...no angel can withstand the force of a dragon."

Nick sneered back at the youth, ready to strike him for his insolence. The tension was thick, but then a familiar voice cut the air from behind them. It was their commander, Michael. "There is one among Jinn that could survive it," he said, strangely eyeing Nick.

The group parted. Michael limped among them, his wings battered and his brow broken. The tension seemed to rise even more, there was no love lost between the Accuser and Michael and all knew it.

"It would seem the Accuser was created all along to shield God from the fury of the dragons," he explained in a flip tone. "We see why and how that was intended now. Look at him! He is like a grigori, suffused with the might of Heaven and Hell."

"What do you know of this Michael?" asked Gabriel impatiently. "What is going on?"

Michael just smirked; it was his own smug expression. Nick had seen that face before and did not trust it. Then the commanding Jinn of Heaven's army drew a deep breath, as if what he would say caused him pain.

"Some time ago God issued a secret edict...it is called the Phoenix Decree," explained Michael. "It foretells of a divine homa-bird that would resist all power when the last war comes, even that of the dragons. I alone was entrusted with the revelation...to conceal its importance."

"What the hell are you talking about, Michael?" Nick snapped.

The other Jinn also seemed unconvinced.

Michael raised both his hands and waved at them. "Calm down, brothers...we're in too much trouble now to squabble with each other over our petty jealousies from the past." Michael stiffened and turned to Nick. "You will now have to forgive me for my lack of faith in you over the millennia, Accuser. But perhaps that is why I was ultimately the only Jinn God ever told. If I accept you as the fulfillment of His omen...then clearly all will follow the decree without question."

Both Nick and Gabriel were shocked. They knew their brother well and wondered suspiciously about his intentions right then, but something had clearly happened they did not understand. Gabriel walked over and took the wounded Jinn by the arm and helped to hold him upright a little better. It would seem the wounds of a dragon did not heal quickly for the Jinn, with their power alone.

"Tell us, brother, what do you know?" demanded Gabriel.

"The final battles draw near and we are left to our own devices to defend Heaven...until the return of the King of Gods," said Michael. "If he ever returns... there is a dark rift in all divination, past which even Lord Joshu cannot see now."

"Where has God gone?" asked Nick, alarmed by the portent in the voice of the Angel of Death. The other Jinn all looked at one another, then stared back at Nick as if astounded by what he did not seem to comprehend right then.

"It's begun, Nick," said Michael. "Can't you feel it?"

The others looked frightened. They huddled close to each other as the Jinn spoke.

"God has left Heaven once more," said Gabriel remorsefully. "The mountain at the edge of Eden has fallen silent. I was there. He called me to the throne. I thought to punish me.... you know...for what I did with you. Instead, He filled my heart with a great sense of hope and dismissed me. He told me to find *all* my faithful brothers. I was not sure what he meant...until right now. You have always harbored a different kind of fidelity...you will always love Him."

"Not good," replied Nick. "That's why this dragon descended in the mortal world. If God is no longer in the picture here, they have a free hand on the material plane – they will devastate it."

"Not completely free as your survival shows," replied Michael, "but we definitely have some trying days in front of us."

"I don't understand," said one of the younger angels. "The dragons did not descend the last time God incarnated into human form, why now?"

"They did not know last time what they know now," said Gabriel.

"Why does He do this shit?" snorted Nick all of a sudden. "Always with the enigma and games...I hate being played with like this!"

"We don't know the ultimate reasons," Gabriel scolded, "but we understand Tiamat fears this very much. You know as well as anyone the prophecies of old say that only the son of the nameless-god can subdue Her, and put down the Pythia. She has discerned that this move is all part of His plan to destroy Her somehow."

He then turned to Michael. "But what of this decree and what does it have to do with Nick?"

"As you all know, the homa-birds select righteous kings appointed the mandate of Heaven," explained Michael. "They validate a mortal's rule by lighting upon the shoulder of one anointed by God for kingship. In the same way, the phoenix is a *divine* homa. God foretold from the Tablets of Destiny that one of the Jinn would be chosen to face the fire of Hell. All blame would be burned away, leaving only the essence of that which he was made...his true heart. This very special homa-bird will wield power beyond reckoning...power the dragons will fear. Nothing is certain from what the tablets say on this matter beyond one other thing...that he must 'unravel' the knot of destiny within men to succeed."

"You think that's me?" huffed Nick.

Michael paused and looked penitently at Nick. "God decreed we follow the phoenix when he was revealed. It is His will for all the Jinn…like it or not."

"How can you suggest that *Iblis* is this chosen homa of God?" blurted the young angel that had challenged Nick earlier. His voice was full of indignation. "Are you all mad?"

Nick looked at the arrogant Jinn. "You want to you take a bath in dragon fire, you little brat?" he sneered. "To see if it's you?"

The young angel averted the Accuser's furious stare. In the distance, they could suddenly see flashes of light. The rescue crews were coming down the passage, combing the area for crash victims from the derailment. Michael bent down and stroked Jon's head, then he looked up at Nick and made a strange smile again. Nick continued to glare at him with an air of suspicion, as the archangel whispered into the young man's ears.

Jon stirred a little and made a warm, peaceful face. "Nick?" he whispered.

Gabriel tightened his eyes at Michael; then he stole a look at Nick. The Accuser was not at all pleased at what he saw, that was clear.

Michael rose to his feet and took Nick by the hand gingerly, kissing it with his mouth. All the Jinn stood astounded. "Like your censure is burned away," said Michael, "I've removed his dread of you…as only I have the power to do. Look Iblis, we distrust each other still, I admit that, but God's will is final to us…

we need to work together in these dark days. The prophet will receive no more visions...there is no God on-high to deliver them to any of us now. You must work with what he knows and has been shown thus far...soon Joshu will break the seventh seal and the Trumpets will sound in Heaven. The war will follow... there is no other way."

"Don't you Jinn understand what the seer knows as well?" Nick asked, suspicion still hanging about his voice.

"No," Gabriel interrupted, "apocalyptic divination is given in code. We articulate the cipher as given to us by God and the prophet's mind is a vessel for it. Only the seer knows what is revealed and how to give it meaning."

"You must earn his trust," said Michael, "and nurture from him what God intends for us all. That is what it means to be faithful for the Jinn...you must follow that path alone."

The Accuser kicked at the dirt beneath his feet. "I never really have had a choice in this," he grumbled, "have I?"

"On the contrary, brother," explained Michael. "You have one of two choices. That was your gift all along...you resist the will of God the same way you do dragon fire. I suspect there is a connection. You could never have defied Him unless He made you able to do so in the first place...you know that as well as anyone. That means you can choose not to help Him. Only the prophet knows now how to find the woman that will bear the holy child. You *must* protect him and lead us, or we are lost."

Nick grunted cynically. He was still not totally convinced of his brother's motive, or this strange decree.

"What of the grigori?" asked Nick. "How do they defy then?"

"They don't," said Gabriel. "They never have... God gave no command for you not to be followed out of Heaven, only that *you* were exiled. They are still technically under his command, despite their treason....only you have the power among the Jinn to defy him outright. Thus the dragons are wary of their loyalty in this war."

"But don't expect them to follow the decree," added Michael. "It was only issued for my ears...they will not believe it. There is some purpose in this deception that they must not see until the time is right."

"Nor can any of us believe it," grunted the unruly young Jinn again, but this time his impertinence was ignored.

"Now," added Michael, "we have to go. There is much to do to prepare Heaven for war." He looked at Nick and laughed, his expression painted with a humorous glow. "God has such a strange sense of irony," he said finally.

With that he grinned and slipped into the Realm of Essences. The other angels anxiously followed on his heels.

Gabriel turned and took Nick's hands. They gazed deeply into each other's eyes for a very long time, saying nothing at all. Finally Nick sighed, knowing what he must do.

"You trusted me enough to risk taking me into Eden... now trust me to do this," he said to the handsome young Jinn, just inches from his face. "As much as I hate to admit it, Michael is right...it's my time to right things."

"You will forgive me, Nick," Gabriel said with a laugh. "I just never thought I would hear those words come out of your mouth."

"Now *you* be nice," said Nick warmly.

Gabriel said nothing. He just leaned forward and kissed Nick, easily at first – then quite hard. Nick pressed back, filled with longing.

When Gabriel pulled away, he stared at Nick. "I love you, brother," he said.

Nick turned pale at the words, wondering what he could say back. He took the Jinn's arm. "You know more than you are saying, Gabe."

Gabriel simply raised one finger to quiet him. He took one last look the Devil; then vanished, following the angels back to Eden.

Jon moaned at Nick's feet, catching the Accuser's attention. He leaned down and stroked the boy's forehead with his fingers. The angel's touch seemed to rouse him. Jon opened his handsome green eyes and stared up at the dark Jinn. For an instant, Nick was not sure how the young prophet would react – so much hinged now on the Jinn being able to learn what this man had been shown by God.

The boy lent Nick a grateful expression, and the Accuser relaxed in its wake. It would appear Michael had indeed appeased the seer's fears of Heaven's exile.

"Hey, you down there," yelled a fireman from the far side of the car. "Are you guys O.K.?"

Nick raised his head and waved at the man, then returned his gaze to Jon's emerald eyes. "I think we're fine for now," he replied in a soft voice.

7

SEVEN SEALS

Washington DC – Early November 1999

The cell phone on Caleb Drake's nightstand sent a high-pitched screech into his darkened bedroom. He rolled toward the ring and fumbled on the stand. The phone fell on the floor with a crash. "Damn it," he stammered, still half asleep. Then groping around on the floor, he found the black device just under the lip of the bed, hitting the green answer button before it rang again.

"Yes?" he barked into it.

"Doctor Drake?"

"Yes, who is this?"

"You might be interested in the news, Doctor... CNN specifically." The phone abruptly went dead.

Caleb grumbled to himself and rubbed at his eyes. He stared at the ceiling for a few ill at ease seconds. Slowly, he turned his head in the direction of the other nightstand, looking for the remote. It lay there just out of reach. He inched over, before finally knocking it off the stand as well.

"DAMN! DAMN! DAMN!" he bellowed, hoisting his body over the opposite edge and feeling for the lost control, then raising it into the air defiantly to pitch the signal right at the set. The television blared on. Flipping quickly through the channels to find CNN, his impatient fingers were uncertain as they poked at the control.

"Reports are sketchy at this time," said a correspondent's voice abruptly, "with Pentagon authorities not saying how many servicemen were on board the C14 at the time it went down. The C14 Huron – a twin turboprop passenger and cargo plane – is the military version of Beachcraft's Super King...."

Caleb turned down the sound a little and bowed his head. His eyes seemed to flutter. The motion of his head appeared trance-like. "Father, please safeguard the soul of Admiral Eason, and his men," he said out loud, in a low somber voice. He seemed sincere. "They have given their lives in the name of Christ, so that his glorious second coming can be ushered to us."

Caleb raised his head and returned his attention to the television, increasing the volume with the remote as he did. The correspondent went on.

"Local officials and US Naval personnel are said to be in route to the location of the crash, giving the recovery and rescue the highest priority possible."

The video feed showed a mid-air view of the isolated crash site, high upon a mountainside. The faint glow of fire flickered as the camera zoomed in from high above.

"Confidential sources from inside the Kremlin are suggesting that the plane, on route from Moscow to an undisclosed Turkish base, was not only carrying several senior Naval officers but the components for two low-yield nuclear weapons recently procured as part of an effort by the US State Department to prevent these types of devices from falling into the hands of terrorists. So far, there has been no word from the White House or senior Pentagon officials to confirm or deny the Russian news leak...."

Caleb shut off the set and rolled out of bed, heading into a tiny bathroom attached to his suite. After showering, he dressed and went downstairs to his extravagantly adorned study – it looked rather like a French King's parlor. The office itself was situated in the center of what he and his follower called a campus – East Calvary Cross College – but it was really like a military compound.

There, in the dim lit office, he pulled out a ragged bible with scores of tiny yellow place holders leafed about its pages. Opening it to the *Book of Revelation*, he began to slowly read. The demure evangelist poured over the pages for hours and hours, completely immersed in the text; his soft, charismatic face transfixed by what he was taking in from the dark message concealed in its prophecy. There was a glow about his countenance; a kind of satisfaction over what he read in those pages all somehow finally justifying the things he had done at God's command.

After a long time alone, the door to his study slid open slowly and a thin young woman – plainly dressed – entered the room. Standing there in the faint light of the cubical, she appeared nervous and timid, but did her best not to show it. She cleared her throat and spoke. "Doctor Drake?"

He kept reading, making her wait before even acknowledging her presence. The silence was awkward, each breath an eternity. Gradually he looked up and smiled.

"Yes, Sandy?"

She cleared her throat again, this time from nerves. "The permits from the Iraqi government for the dig you wanted the College to sponsor were approved," she said. "The archeological team will be in place by the end of the month. It's quite remarkable."

"Excellent news!"

"We 'tipped' the local officials in Arbil with the customary donation...your contact there was useful to us...just as you said he would be." She was in awe of his power to move even nations.

"Good," he replied, "we will need to set up a base of operation there in the city. See to it the missionary team is assembled and a shipment of bibles prepared from the print office...the gospel must accompany us wherever we go, Sandy."

She nodded and began to turn away, glad to be dismissed so easily.

"Oh, and Sandy," he called after her.

She froze and tilted her head back, but did not look directly at him.

"Call upon that boy from the evangelical center we spoke to last week...the one who specializes in Old Testament finds. He should head this up...Luke Edwards, that's his name, right?"

"Yes, Doctor," she answered in a perplexed voice. She knew Luke was on academic probation for failing to live up to Drake's moral codes. The boy was a homosexual...it seemed strange to her Drake would call on him for anything. Perhaps it was to make an example of him, to show that his methods to turn men away from that sin we're in fact working. Many had criticized his brutal approach.

She waited, hoping that was all. Her stomach was turning with worry and grief.

"Now, is there any word from Brother Phillips about the plane?" His voice held a kind of raw anticipation.

"Yes," answered Sandy, with a hint of heartache that she seemed afraid to show. While the young woman had known the subject would clearly be central to his mind, she had avoided broaching it with him. Sandy was not sure she was ready to speak about her loss right then.

He knew it and pressed her anyway.

"They dropped the payload early," she said. "Our recovery team was in place and the package was secured in spite of the accident." She was still averting his gaze. Something about his eyes could paralyze a person. She always assumed it was the fear of God.

"Wonderful," he said, then stood, maneuvering out from behind the desk. "Your father died in the service of Christ, Sandy. Our boys need all the help they can get...your father had a master plan to crush God's enemies in the East. We should keep to it."

His voice was remorseless.

She looked up at him somehow unconvinced, falling to her knees. "Please, Doctor Drake," she begged, her voice finally breaking up. "Pray with me for my Father's soul."

He raised one eyebrow, looking slightly annoyed. "Of course," he said in a cold tone. "I would be happy to pray with you."

✴

James wrapped a blanket around his shoulders and walked down the long corridor of Nafees' apartment to the deck overlooking the city. The gray sky seemed to recline over the horizon, giving it a feel of heaviness... of sadness. The wind blew in fits of fury, first as if driven by some great gale, then it would suddenly stop to hardly be heard at all. He could not shake the chill. It grew and grew, seeming to penetrate into the deepest part of his being. James realized this was not a physical cold; it was something else, something inside of him. He closed his eyes and reached out to see if he could touch Nick's mind, but there was nothing. He began to cry, not sure if it was missing Nick that upset him or if it was the despair to which the coldness of the air seemed to cling.

Nafees appeared at the glass behind him, just inside the apartment. He stood motionless for a second, also feeling the strange chill. He slid past the door and tiptoed over to James.

"What is this thing in the air?" whispered the boy, without turning his head. "Such a horrible feeling extending out over everything I see."

"Death," answered Nafees, "the shadow of passing. A dreadful thing is going to happen soon, unless something is done about it, unless we move into the field of presence and act...tribulation is at hand and it must not be allowed to prevail."

"Why us...haven't we done enough?" begged the nervous boy.

Nafees shook his head and gazed out across the skyline. He saw more than just the gray cloud cover, he saw a hand reaching across and snatching at life – the paw of some great beast. The air was thick with a morbid hunger that had not been sated in eons, but for the trifling conflicts here and there at the edge of the mortal veil. "It is only starting, my young friend, only beginning," he said with air of sadness.

"Whose death? Why does it feel so immense?"

"It's hard to say precisely who. What you feel is a shadow of emptiness...a void created in the ethereal presence. I've suffered this before, but the air has not felt of such loss since the great wars of Heaven long ago."

"Is this death for sure?" asked James, turning slightly to Nafees as he spoke.

"It's never assured...there are always choices out there for men to avert the darkness, but we can only help those who must face this thing, by being guardians of the truth." Nafees wrapped his arms around the boy and pulled him closer. "Come inside, let's sit by the fire and chase away the shadows as best we can. Perhaps we will learn something of what is to be faced."

The two men turned and walked into the apartment. A rough gust of wind grabbed at the door and shook it furiously. They headed down the hall, away from it.

Adriano emerged from the room he and James were sharing as they passed, wiping the sleep from his eye. The knight shot Nafees a puzzled look, wondering if everything was all right. The immortal cleric waved him off and the large framed knight hastily ducked back into the room – he'd learned when to stand among the seers, and when to leave them alone to their consigned vocation.

James stopped where Adriano had been standing in the doorway and peered in at his new companion. The big man stood a few feet back, waiting for them to pass. He felt the young seer reach inside of him – it was an unsettling sensation to which he was still getting acclimated. James looked back toward Nafees and the cleric returned the look, understanding the implicit question.

None of us are truly safe, Nafees said into his mind, *but of this one I can say that I've seen what Allah has set in front of him…as long as you draw breath…this man will love you…even longer perhaps.*

The big man smiled, understanding suddenly what was happening. "My faith and my love are all yours, James," he said in a solemn voice.

James looked down, averting his penetrating brown eyes. He stepped to lean his head against the big man's chest, but Nafees pulled at him ever so slightly to come away. The boy hesitated, then followed after him.

They slipped out into the living room where the fire was already warming the air. As they huddled close to it, orange and yellow tongues licked the hearth. Nafees sat with his head bowed low, as if he were listening for something. The light danced on his face and his checks grew thick with shadow. Slowly, he opened his eyes and James could feel the cleric's attention wrap around him like an embrace.

"Come with me deep into the Realm of Essences, James. I need you to see something...I need your opinion," he said coolly.

"Is it O.K?" inquired James. A look of frailty came over him.

"No," said Nafees, "as I said, we no longer have the luxury of safety any place...come."

The cleric reached out and James took his hand. Both men closed their eyes. As they did, the veil of the material world fell away. James was always astonished by the way Nafees manipulated the Realm of Essences. Through the flames, he saw thousands upon thousands of people writhing in a blaze. It horrified him. Then the two seers stopped to notice that their vantage was from a ring of buildings on a height, looking down into an old city – one that James did not recognize. The fire ringed all sides of the community, flowing in and about its hills like a river of flame. In the distance, he saw angel-like creatures, but not with wings of white. They had emaciated flaps like sickly bats, with black skin stretched between bony fragments.

"Thralls," said Nafees, "passed to the other side and trapped in a state of perdition, neither able to fully enter the Realm of Essences or return to the material world."

"Is this happening now?" James asked nervously.

"No, not yet...this is a vision I am showing you. It has been at the corner of my ethereal eye for some time...only recently have I been able to bring it into focus and see it fully. I need your help to unravel it... so it can be altered."

"How?"

"Walk into the fire, use the Realm of Essences to shield yourself from the effects of dark carnage and go toward the source of the chaos. We have to know where and how this ruin might occur. Its cause slips from the center of my sight each time I try to hold it in my vision. So I will bind the divination here to anchor our sight. You must go in and find the source."

James turned to look down into the dark torrent. He took in one deep breath, as if he actually needed to breathe there, and began down the hill. He trusted Nafees beyond any doubt. As he walked toward the source of the inferno, he glanced back at the cleric. He saw that Nafees' eyes were closed and he was weaving something in his hands. James could not tell what it was, but as he walked away the fire seemed to recede in front of him. Bodies reconstituted from the ashes and buildings rose back into their foundations. The street opened up and the flame appeared to flee from James. It was like watching a film running backwards. In the distance, the fire seemed to sink further toward its source until it suddenly flashed bright as the sun and was gone.

"Now walk...follow the path of the flame to where you saw the flash...go to its source," James heard in his mind. It was Nafees, almost as if the cleric had become an extension of his consciousness.

James walked through the streets, turning instinctively toward the origin of the blast. He passed a schoolyard and stopped for a moment to watch a group of children playing some kind of game with a pole and ropes. They skipped and danced and wove the rope together, laughing with childish glee as they did. Then he saw a woman standing with a baby carriage, reaching for her child as it began to cry. She picked it up and cradled it gently, trying to quell its sobs.

He moved forward again. The young seer was deeply unsettled. He scurried down a street and rounded a corner, to see a long line of concrete barriers. At it there was a gate with a car stopped and soldiers all around it. Between where he stood and the gate James saw a man and women come into focus. They stepped toward each other, embraced, and began to kiss passionately – the affection distracting him as they did. He watched them with a feeling of warmth.

"The gate... the sign at the gate...what does it say?" The voice pulled him back to his body, refocusing his sight first close, then further past the kissing couple to the gate. He looked there for a sign. It was over the barricades, wrapped in wire. The bold text of the gate-marker was written in a wording he could not make out at first.

"Focus on the sign, what does it say?" came the power of Nafees' mind pressed against his own. His view of the sign turned blurry; the image of the words seemed to twist and contort against the white backdrop. Then as if by some enchantment, he inexplicably could read the words clearly.

NOW ENTERING JERUSALEM – SECURITY POINT
42

He was astounded with himself at the feat; then there was a swift commotion. The man and the woman stopped kissing and turned toward the gate. A shocking, quick burst of gunfire let loose. James suddenly saw the militiamen shooting into the car indiscriminately. Three figures seemed to fly away from the scene like ghosts. Without warning, came the same flash he had seen earlier, but erupting from the image just in front of him.

The radiance was so intense at first that James could see nothing but white light. It enveloped the car and the soldiers, then moving in slow motion, it swallowed the couple in front of him. James placed his hands in front of his face and was instantly pulled away from the epicenter of the blast, back to where he had been standing originally with Nafees. He looked down into the urban valley and saw the flare of light as it radiated out across the city streets. It rippled out like a wave. The red and yellow flame expanded outward with such force it toppled entire buildings, consuming everything as it went.

The wall of fire coming toward James was gaining speed. As it approached, he raised his hands again to cover his face, but this time he did not spirit away from the approaching explosion. It broke on him like a blast of hot wind and knocked him back a few feet with its force. He turned to watch the wave move away, swallowing cars, buildings, and schoolyard, leaving only melting metal in the swirling ash.

James saw in that instant the figure of a man standing about twenty yards away from him. He could not make out any features of the face other than eyes, which bore into him with a furious inquiry. The man began to walk toward the boy, his penetrating glare searching and probing. "Who are you?" the man suddenly screamed. "Who sent you?"

James shuddered for a second. He took a step back and closed his eyes. When he opened them again, he saw fire still, but this time it was the warm flames of the fireplace in the apartment. He turned back to look at Nafees, whose eyes were open and staring blankly past him into the hearth.

"Israel," the cleric said very quietly, "they will strike at the sacred heart of Allah's people...Hebrew, Christian, and Muslim alike."

James stood to face him, almost stumbling as he did. He looked down realizing his legs had fallen asleep from sitting in the odd position during the trance. "Now that we know where this death will visit itself...we have to stop it," said the excited young seer.

Nafees pulled his gaze away from the fire and looked up at the boy. His eyes narrowed and his posture seemed to tighten. "You saw something else...a man in the wake of the flame."

"Yes, he seemed surprised to see me," replied the seer, "like I didn't belong there. Who was he, Nafees? Will he do this?"

The immortal cleric shook his head. "I don't know, but we better find out who he is soon," he said grimly. His face was pale. For the first time, James saw the weight of age shown in Nafees' expression.

"It's as I feared," Nafees added. "We must go… destiny calls us home. I am sure of it now." He turned and looked up at James with a smile, "and of you."

The Rafiq left New York within the week. Never again did they take up a ritual presence within Twilo. The sacrament of dance that they called Zekhr fell into the hands of less apt devotees in the days that followed. The spell of sema was nothing but a memory there. The club was closed soon after a young man died carelessly chasing ecstasy. An era came to an end in New York City when Twilo was gone, but for the Rafiq…the kingdom was close at hand.

cXo

The doctor in the emergency room at the Westside Hospital took one last look at the CAT scan; then glanced back at Jon. The anointed prophet moved from a bed to the open window. His restlessness seemed to infect the room, exuding the feel of a captured lion pacing impatiently back and forth in a cage.

"Are you sure you've never had any kind of head injury before?" asked the doctor a second time.

Nick drilled his eyes into Jon. The boy simply froze in his tracks; his expression appeared pained. In time, the Accuser would come to know this expression well – a mix of anger and annoyance, accented by an odd, almost avian twitch to his head. Nick thought it appeared rather like the young man had suddenly smelled something putrid and was searching around the room for the source, but it was simply the way Jon wore his angst, an invasive state of anxiety he couldn't hide even if he tired.

"I am sure," replied Jon. "I think I would remember having my head cracked open."

He did not sound sincere, Nick sensed he was lying. The Accuser smiled to himself.

"Well, it's just peculiar," replied the doctor, pointing to the scan. "You clearly show the mended signs of trauma here, along the cranium, with scaring and adhesions on the frontal lobe….see along here." The man stared at the scan again nervously. "It's consistent with the kind of accident you have been in, and yet you say you have never so much as fallen off a bike?"

Nick realized this discussion was not a fruitful exercise. "The human body is truly a miraculous thing," he said with sarcasm. He rose and walked toward the out of sorts' physician. "We are both clearly fine…but I have to tell you that while the accident has left no physical marks…it has me a little un-nerved." Nick's tone sounded contrived. "If you don't mind, we'd both just like to go home now and try to forget about this entire ordeal."

The doctor looked at Nick for a moment – he was most concerned that *he* had refused care entirely. At last he glanced at Jon; the prophet's face was pleading in its agreement with the Jinn. He wanted to get out of there in the worst way, hating hospitals as he did. "Well, I see no reason to keep you," replied the doctor." I guess you can go...but if you begin to feel nauseous or become unusually sleepy...come back here right away. O.K? These kinds of injuries can be very serious if overlooked."

Both nodded to him.

Without another word Nick reached for his coat, slung it over one arm, and walked away into the hall. Like Jon, he was not found of such places. In seconds, he was out of earshot.

Jon moved to flee as well, but the doctor reached over and took the young prophet by the shoulder before he could walk away. "Listen, there is more," he said to the boy. "I just want to let you know that your scans present for something we call Frontal Lobe Epilepsy, it can happen with head trauma. It's a serious condition and causes a variety of seizures... some people even develop schizophrenia. You might need treatment for this at some point. If you begin to experience blackouts, or start to have strange delusions, you should seek help right away."

Jon's eyes seemed to glow. "What kind of delusions?" he asked.

The doctor made a face that was full of distress. "Delusions of grandeur perhaps...like voices calling your name...some people actually claim to hear God."

Jon twitched. He stared away for a second, thinking about what the doctor said. *No...it's real...He does talk to me,* the prophet reassured himself.

When Jon refocused his eyes, he laughed in the doctor's face. "It's a little late," the boy said with deranged amusement, quickly turning after Nick into the hall.

The Jinn and the prophet were halfway out the front door before the doctor had signed the release order. They left from the side exit of the hospital and darted a few steps over to Seventh Avenue. Jon's anxious pace seemed to lessen as they got further away from the emergency room entrance and the din of ambulances. There was an awkward silence between them as they walked, Nick noticed the bad-smell face again and wondered what could be worrying the boy.

"So, I was banged up pretty bad down there," said Jon suddenly.

Nick glanced at him and tried to feign ignorance by shrugging.

"My head," Jon added, "you fixed it down there...I remember hitting it pretty hard...like the doctor said."

This time Nick's eyes grew narrow. It was clear the boy knew things, but how much?

"I wouldn't say that I fixed it," the dark exile replied. "Let's just say you had one or two angels looking after you down there today."

Jon stopped on the sidewalk and folded he his arms defensively across his chest. "I suppose that is your way of being cute?"

Nick tuned to the boy, perplexed by his intension. "So what is it you think you actually know about what happened, Jon?"

"I know I'd be dead had you not been there with me," Jon growled. "I know *who* and *what* you are...and while every instinct in me says I should run from you this very instant, I find for some strange reason I can't. I'm still trying to figure out why."

Nick smiled and thought that Michael finally proved useful. He had consumed the boy's fear just as he said he would.

"I am not crazy...I don't think," Jon continued. "Although for many months I thought I was from all these insane visions. And lastly, I know I am in big, big trouble. All of this makes me very sad."

"You are a clever and perceptive boy," Nick replied coolly.

Jon glared at the Accuser. "Don't patronize me, Nick. I need to make it clear right now that I don't especially relish the fact that the only friend I have in all of God's creation is the fucking Devil."

"I would not say that is completely true," replied Nick, his own caustic reflexes beginning to rise in response to the boy's tone.

"Seriously...I suppose you are going to tell me you're not the Devil after all."

"No," sneered Nick, "I am the fucking Devil, but you do have one or two more friends than you think you have."

A great sense of consternation fell over Jon's face; Nick could not read him at all. One minute his aura was that of a little boy – fearful and timid – then the next his temperament filled with fury, as if he wanted to break out of his own skin like a wild animal. As his moods shifted there, the Accuser noticed something else strange. The color of his eyes appeared to molt from a soft aqua hue to a deep hazel-green, as if to announce he had become something else.

"So, what are *you* really after from *me*, Satan?" asked Jon in a haughty tone. "I am no one's fool!"

Nick lost his temper, and a little bit of his ancient animosity toward men seeped through the shell of his vanity – that calmly continence he normally wanted men to see of him. It fused with the new, dark power that enveloped him, he became truly terrifying to behold. This was the face of man's fear, the true devil he could be.

The young prophet's expression turned pale, his eyes horrified. Jon broke down and suddenly began to weep. The Accuser looked around anxiously – shocked and ashamed by Jon's reaction. He reached for the boy, but young prophet just pulled away.

"Don't touch me," Jon snapped.

A strange power suffused Nick as they touched briefly. A chill went down his spine.

"I'm sorry you had to see that," replied Nick. "Sometimes in my rage I become things I am not proud of...I can't help it."

Nick realized from that moment on, he would have to stem the dark tide that was inside of him, that part of his essence that could never relinquish its origins in the dragons. He knew Jon must never see that power rise in him again like that, or all would be lost.

"I know your kind, Nick," said Jon. "My father was like this...trust me it's not a good thing. He used to just snap when he was angry…horrible things came out of him then."

Nick dropped his gaze to the ground. He didn't know why, but guilt began to burn in his belly, filling him with remorse. The boy was right.

Jon stared at him a moment with soft eyes, his brow bent and his mouth down turned. "Let's go," he said sadly. "I just want to get home."

Then Jon turned and walked away.

Nick followed, like a punished hound – his tail between his legs – trotting after in the boy's steps. They walked in silence for a time, moving down the Avenue toward Christopher Street. Nick let the young man lead. After a time, the air seemed to calm between them; Jon spoke again.

"My father was a bad person. He did things. Things I will never forgive him for and always that kind of dark rage was part of it. I can't handle it."

Nick glanced over at him, nodding. Somehow Jon's every word gripped him now. "Anger is a two edged sword," the Accuser replied to the young man. "It cuts both you and the people you love."

Jon grunted.

"I wish sometimes that I could make it all go away," added Nick, "but it seems to drive my very breath. I'm sorry, again."

"Well, the truth is I know the pain it causes…I know it well." Jon extended his hands out in front of his body and began to play with them. Nick noticed how strange the strong grip looked, as he pulled at his fingers the way a nervous child might.

"My father had a demon in him…he terrorized my family."

"You specifically?" the Accuser asked.

"In a way," replied Jon, "but it was mostly emotional pain he inflicted on me. For some reason he found it impossible to touch me…but for once. Unfortunately, that was not the case for my mother…he beat her really bad sometimes."

"It is the sign of a coward to pick on the weak."

Jon turned and gazed at Nick, his eyes changed again – to a deepening green that glowed like a leopard's. It was frightful. "You would know," he said cruelly to the dark exile.

The remark sliced into to Nick, again regret filled him. The Accuser took a deep breath and tried to ignore the insult as best he could. He wondered if Jon was trying to provoke him, or if he simply did not understand his own boorish temperament at times. Nick reached and pulled Jon close to him. The boy did not resist this time, his warm, sweet aroma over took the Jinn. It was a clean and innocent essence, but Nick sensed this was a man who needed to believe *he* was in control at all times – to disrupt that belief would be disastrous.

"Please don't do that again," begged Jon. The firm resoluteness of the prophet's voice had returned. "I know what you are capable of…and while I honestly don't know if I can handle this, I want to trust you. You don't need to extend that dark power to make me understand anything about you or what is going on here. I've seen more then you realize."

"O.K." replied Nick softly in contrition, wondering if the boy really knew of what he spoke.

They turned up the street and headed toward Jon's apartment. The boy said little on the way. Finally they rounded an angled street and came to their destination. Heading inside, the outer door to Jon's building swung behind them and slammed hard. Nick looked back at it, startled. Jon was used to the sound. He paid its crashing noise no mind. They slowly walked up flight after flight of stairs, silence still hanging between them. When they reached the apartment door, Jon's face turned cold and expressionless.

"If I let you in, you have to promise me, for the love of God, you will not hurt me," he said.

"For the love of God?" asked Nick in shock. "Why for the love of *Him*?"

"I said don't patronize me. I know you think I'm beneath you, but I am not. God has prepared a way for me, whether you like it or not. I told you I know more than you realize...I understand that the only thing in this existence you care about more than your own hide...is the love of God."

"Vision or no vision...that is a novel assumption for a mortal," snapped Nick defensively.

"Really?

Nick just grunted now.

"Seriously," replied the prophet, "you of all creatures know the importance of an oath like this. You risk the loss of what you hold dearest over a sacred vow...PROMISE ME!"

"You certainly are an insightful one," replied Nick. "I have totally underestimated you, but it matters little to me. I've lost everything that was ever important to me, Jon." Nick raised one arm and extended it over his shoulder, pinning him to the door. "I will not hurt you and I promise *that* upon whatever love I have left for God. The truth is I think well enough of you right now to promise it without being bound to *Him*."

"I am a fool for this," said Jon as he opened the door, "a pact with Satan…what have I come to?"

Nick gave him a cruel look. He hated to be called that and Jon had done it twice now.

A clean, cool breeze drifted out from the small space as they entered. Jon threw his keys on the table. He kicked off his shoes and they tumbled dead center of the room. Then he tossed his jacket to the right of them – the boy was clearly not neat.

Sauntering to a small sofa near the window, he fell into it so hard Nick was certain the frame would give under the crashing weight. *Not long before he destroys that*, Nick thought to himself. In that same instant he was struck by how like men he was becoming, to worry about something as fleeting as a tattered old couch, while at the precipice of apocalypse.

Jon looked at him and smiled. It was an odd, artificial grin, but Nick sensed the boy didn't intend for it to look so foolish in its pretense. The prophet leaned back deep into the soft sofa, and then tapped the cushion next to him like he was calling a dog.

Nick fumed, but moved to sit next to the boy, just as he was beckoned to do.

"So what now?" Jon asked.

"What do you mean?" replied Nick, again taken aback by the brutal frankness with which this young man seemed to approach all things.

"What is the next step for us? We must find that woman before the dragons do. How do we do that?"

"Well, well," Nick huffed, "you do seem to know a lot more about this than I assumed. Perhaps you should tell me, prophet."

"Don't be an ass," Jon said, leaning close to Nick's face. If the boy pushed any closer, they would fall into a kiss – a thought that pleased Nick for some reason.

"Look," Nick said, "I appear to be the one behind the eight-ball here. I don't know what the next move should be. I was hoping what you knew might change our fortunes a little...you are the prophet after all. "

Jon smiled slyly. His eyes were saying to Nick that he should never forget that fact.

The Accuser knew the boy was twisting their interactions so that *he* would have the upper hand again, as if their affair was becoming a constant test of wills. Nick leaned back, ground his teeth, and groaned into the air. It was as if Jon's very nature had been crafted to unnerve his sensibility.

"I can see Michael has put more in your head than fearlessness," he said. "You remind me a little of his smugness."

Something about Nick's sorted agitation aroused Jon. The boy grabbed the Jinn by shirt and pulled him down. The Accuser was a large and muscled creature, but he fell easily to the prophet's embrace. Jon's own thick body pressed hard against his. Nick did not resist, there was something in the way the young prophet pushed and nudged at him that conveyed to Nick that the boy knew perfectly well the powerful Jinn was holding back. It was a hesitance, like testing ice, and behind it was a kind if reckless abandon. The boy needed his submission, and he knew Nick needed him. *God's fate is cruel,* thought Nick.

Suddenly, the Accuser felt the young man swell against him. Jon was stirred to desire.

Over all the centuries of human relations, Nick had always been the aggressor in these types of trysts, and never to conjoin with a mortal. He had always manipulated sexual expression with men, seducing them – usually to tease, or to appropriate something he desired. Jon was different. *This mortal will take what he covets,* Nick thought to himself, *or die trying. If I want what to know what is locked away in his mind...I clearly have to let him have what he wants first.*

The dark Jinn materialized his own erection, and as he did Jon made a gleeful face, realizing he had won... Nick would submit. The Jinn pushed back against Jon's body, signaling he would not go easily, but just as Nick's own weight was rising – slightly off center of balance – the prophet reached across his body and took hold of him by the shoulder. With force, he spun Nick down and away. The Accuser was flipped onto his stomach before he knew what had happened.

Then eagerly Jon pried his legs open.

Nick froze a second. He could not believe he was going to let this happen a second time so easily, but after a moment of consternation, all resistance faded in his heart. If God wanted this boy to see in the way James had, Nick would let him see it all. It was not quite trust, but it would do for now.

Still, Nick did have his pride.

"Don't push your luck," he grunted, putting up a front for the sake of saving face.

"Why not?" said Jon with a guttural rasp. "You like it...don't you? Beg for it."

Nick resisted; only enough to necessitate Jon using all his strength, so as to let him think he was powerful enough in will to wrestle an angel. The act was filled with hubris.

"BEG FOR IT," Jon barked into Nick's ear again. Then the boy reached up and grabbed the Accuser by the back of the hair, wrenching at it hard. At first, Nick had to fight all the dark impulses of Heaven and earth itself not to reach for the boy's spine and break him in half. He had a momentary image of the young man smashing into the dirt clogs from which God had made his pathetic fathers. It lasted only seconds, before need of want consumed the Jinn.

Nick found that he did like it.

"Fuck me," Nick groaned in a loud vulgar voice, as Jon tore away at his pants.

"Fuck me *please*," insisted the prophet. The boy seemed very amused.

The Devil hesitated. "Fuck me....*please!*" he finally repeated.

For a second, Nick felt humiliated...and he knew that is what Jon wanted. The Accuser had let James partake of him ethereally in the club for just an instant, out of the urgency of the moment as well as some kind of affection that he could not as yet name. But this was different. This was a twisted submission...what Nick had always feared of men. And yet he could not help but feel compelled to do so, both from obligation, as well – to his dismay – from a growing lust.

Jon positioned himself with his hand as Nick pressed back to meet the penetration. Then with a twist of both their hips, it was done just that quickly. Jon entered the soul of the dark exile of Heaven.

"No condom?" grunted Nick scornfully as Jon pushed.

The young prophet pulled his hair, even harder, and pushed his face forward into the pillow. "I am fucking the Devil...I believe we're past the point of worrying about what's sane, or safe...don't you think?"

Jon thrust aggressively, drunk with his own power and the implication of that act.

You are a fool, despite what you think, Nick thought as he felt Jon drive into him, *and so am I. You have no idea what you are about to find in here.*

Jon made no effort to be gentle, nor did Nick want him to be. The physical penetration was the easiest part of the humiliating process for Nick. The pain seemed to distract him from it. But in a matter of seconds it all changed as their souls conjoined.

The abrupt crash and flow of divine light overtook them both with such force that it seized their breath and took it away. An incomprehensible mass of energy filled Nick. In truth, neither was fully ready for what the exchange meant. As he felt God's mind enter him, Nick experienced only the raw want of more, not obligation or remorse, like he had seconds before. The Accuser moaned as desire took him, then sighed as he realized he had become enraptured with its pain.

All Nick remembered after that first furious surge was the instant realization that Jon would finally understand the power of conjoining at a deeply sacred level. The throbbing in Nick's head quickly shut out all other sensations as the power of his creator drove into him. Then the next sound that he seemed to make sense of was the noise Jon made reaching climax – it was loud and ecstatic. As quickly as it had begun, it was done.

Both of them froze a moment, heaving as they tried to fill their lungs with air; the rhythm of their hearts slowing together. Nick let Jon wrap his arms around him tightly as they fell and lay in the silence.

The Accuser suddenly remembered Heaven; the feel of the nameless-god near his soul in this very way. *My Ba'al...how is this possible?* he thought, calling to God in earnestness. *You are present here within this man in a way I have never known. I miss you so much...I am so lost without you.*

Out of grief and need of comfort, Nick had used an ancient name in his silent entreaty that meant "beloved Lord' in the old tongue – a name permitted only the Accuser long ago in their intimacy. The Jinn was astounded by what he found. He could feel God there in the man; Jon's mind was comprised of sacred eleventh light. It was the very source of prophetic enigma Gabriel had discribed – the code that bore vision. The sense and feeling of his God so close to him after thousands of years made the Accuser tremble. Nick whispered something in a low voice that Jon could mostly hear as inflection, sweet and gratified:

I am one remembered by Him... to who he said 'My curse be upon you!' For don't the 'you' and the 'I' coexist in that curse? I am pledged to loving and yearning... I am in Heaven and in Hell.

The young prophet stared at him a moment, surprised by the tenderness he sensed in Nick's tone. "What is that from? he asked.

Nick wiped his eyes dry and closed them as he replied. "Something written about me many years ago by a Sufi poet I knew."

"You liked that, didn't you?" asked Jon in a bawdy voice.

Nick's face was still twisted into the pillow, only half exposed. He opened the one eye facing up and looked hard into Jon's grin.

"Yes, I did, Jon," was all he would say.

As the day wore on, Nick and Jon lay in bed – the Accuser tenderly stroking the ridge of Jon's shoulders and the muscles tucked under them. It was quiet and peaceful, making the hours seem eternal. For so long Nick had held sacred the act of conjoining for God only, but now he had just done it with this haughty mortal as if his devotion did not matter. There – to his shock – found a part of the very presence of the divine he missed so much. The Accuser was trying to make sense of it.

"Arbil," Jon whispered finally.

"What did you say?" Nick asked.

"Arbil," repeated the young prophet. "We must go there...as soon as we can." He rolled over and faced Nick. His green eyes alight. "Do you know where Arbil is, Nick?" The young man looked more than a little afraid for the question. There was something disturbing and powerful under all those coded images in his head. Nick could sense it and was alarmed for him.

"Of all the places on this earth, where did you come up with that one?" asked the Jinn.

"We don't see into one another the way we're supposed to when we make love, do we, Nick? Something is not right...I know it."

"No, we don't.... you are very correct...something is wrong or at the very least peculiar."

"What?"

"This is a little hard to explain," replied Nick, "but I will try. Existence is composed of eleven concentric aspects. Think of them like fields of perception. Mortals exist almost exclusively in four...time and three space dimensions...the moral veil. Some creatures however sense others, like the ethereal realm or the chaos of the Abyss. The Jinn for example, we see in seven of the eleven lights. But it is God alone that sees in them all. I know this because I've had this power inside me before. It's as if all other meaning is blotted out by its intensity."

Nick hesitated a moment. Then let his face fall to Jon's back.

"Your soul is fully composed of it. That is why we can't become open to one another the way two sprits should...it's quite remarkable. In all honesty, it's the best thing I've felt in five thousand years."

"You mean that?"

"Yes."

"I think I understand what you mean," replied Jon. "Everything I see in you is confusing, as if both our minds are windows onto two different worlds."

Jon's expression changed, looking at Nick with deep wonder. He made another immodest face, as he rolled over and took a deep breath.

"Don't ever mistake me for an idiot, Nick. Trust me, I'm no fool."

Nick was confused for a moment by his tone. Jon was so hard to read with his sudden mood swings. The Accuser sensed he was now seeing a relationship though the eyes of a mortal, bound as they normally were to such narrow vision within the mortal veil. He and Jon would be denied the easy way to know one another and of discovering the truth.

"Oh, I trust you on that fact, prophet...I trust you on that completely," he answered. "But what of Arbil? Where did you get the name of that damned place from?"

"For just an instant when you totally opened yourself up to me, when I was inside you and realizing how connected we were emotionally...the idea simply came into my head. It was not a vision. It was like suddenly two small parts of our very different universes intersected in a meaningful way, just long enough to see it as the next step. We must go together to a place called Arbil."

"Damn," whispered Nick, "that raises more questions than it answers, Jon."

"So we go and we find out why God wants us there," replied the prophet in a matter of fact tone.

Nick laughed with a sense of uncertainty, but not out loud. The heaving of his inward chuckle registered in the bed as a vibration. Jon turned. "What's so funny about this, Nick?"

"Arbil is a very, very old city in northern Iraq...I know it well. It's a dangerous, war-torn region. Are you sure that is the right place we should go now?"

Jon shrugged his shoulders and look innocently into Nick's eyes. "No, but what choice do we have. Anyway, why would *you* be afraid of going there?"

Nick hesitated.

"Sins," he replied to the boy. "Old offenses I don't care to face, or relive." He quietly shuddered.

Jon sensed Nick's apprehension through their subtle bond. The boy got a sinking feeling in the pit of his stomach as he watched the Devil quiver.

8

QUICKENING OF DESIGN

Gloria Merodach turned in a restless sleep. Her pregnancy had been a difficult one so far. Thankfully there was her mother to help. She moved home after her husband, Rafael, had been killed in a tragic accident – nudged from the busy platform of a train station. Gloria had not known that she was pregnant until after his death.

Her anxieties were now growing.

Shifting in the heat of her room, trying to get comfortable, her dark dreams swallowed her again. The wind rattled at the window, as it blew sand against the glass. A nightmare had been haunting her for months, replaying over and over in her lonely nights.

She saw the train in the station where Rafael was killed, and heard a voice echo. "This is the train to Babylon," it would say. As the engine pulled away, she could see a faceless man pushing Rafael. In the dream, Gloria would reach for him as he fell in front of the train, but was never able to get to him in time. After that, she saw his disembodied head in a tree, as if it had been pitched there. Standing under it, she extended her arms, reaching for him – his face was twisting to speak. When she grew close, his frantic words would catch in his mouth, and all that would come was a spraying sputter of nonsense and saliva. Putting her hands up to block the spittle from falling on her, she caught it. With that she came awake, covered in sweat.

Gloria then rolled over and frantically reached for the ceramic water pitcher next to the bed. The glow of the moon fell over her from the warm autumn night, as the thin linen curtain seemed to dance in the beam.

As the light struck her, she felt her womb flutter, like the wings of a small bird were trapped inside. She felt a round of tight, coiling pain following it. Turning to the open door, she tried to call for her mother, but nothing came from her mouth. She was alone in the world that night, but for the powerful spirit that was filling the growing life inside of her body.

In pain, Gloria reached to her abdomen. *It is simply too soon*, she thought to herself in a panic. *I can't do this alone.*

⚘

A cold wind blew off the side of the mountain and into a decrepit shack only a few miles from the crash site of the American C-12. Two men dressed in military fatigues huddled near a fire. The door surprised them, as it swung open. They jumped to attention, raising their guns and clicking them from the safety. There was split second that cut time.

"Put those damn things away," an officer in doorway roared. The two men looked at each other and lowered their weapons. "Where is the package with the broken-arrows?" he growled at them.

The two soldiers crouched again by the fire, motioning with their heads to the cases in the corner. The gruff officer moved toward the containers, a second office – unseen at first by the other two – stole in behind him. The two dark figures scurried to close in around them.

The first officer picked one up and laid it upon the weathered table in the center of the room. There was a latch with a small shinny surface that glowed whenever it was touched. He rubbed it with his thumb and the sensor turned yellow in color. Then he nodded at the second man, who reached over, pressing his thumb to the same spot. This time the light turned green, and the case latch popped.

"Is it hot?" the officer asked the crouching men.

The soldiers both turned their heads to glanced at one another, but did not move their bodies. "Normal rads, Sir," one said. "They don't appear to have leaked during the airdrop."

The officers refocused their attention on the device inside, undoing the final safety cover and slowly opening it to the glow of the room. Then the two soldiers near the fire stood up, curiosity drawing them to see what lay under the previously sealed lid. All four men stood still a moment, looking into the black container. The shadows of the firelight hung about all their faces. Slowly, the soldiers glanced at each with suspicion, and after up at the senior men standing in front of them. Their expressions were painted with confusion.

"What are they, Sir?" One of the men finally asked. "They don't seem like the cores from any mobile-nuke we've ever seen."

"That's because the Russians don't use a lot of plutonium in these things to achieve critical mass...not the way we do with our portables," replied the officer. "These have simple tritium neutron-generators...just enough plutonium in here to get things going...most of the yield for the blast will come from these." He pointed to the cylinders. They seemed rather like harmless thermoses bottles. "They have been recently re-infused with tritium."

"Shit," said the soldier. "What the hell was all this for then? Those things are only good for six month...a year max...before that tritium degrades down and is worthless. " The two soldiers became anxious and began to pace. "Those guys back there on the plane... they were wasted for nothing."

The commander reached inside to deactivate the biometric security system, and slammed the case shut. He glared at the men, they were becoming a problem.

"Gentleman, what happened to the Admirals' plane was an unforeseen accident. This is a war...there are losses. Fortunately, Eason had the foresight to drop the package when he had a problem with the others. Now, let us worry about the timetable for the rest. We would never get permission from the Pentagon to use tactical nukes in those caves anyway. The Admiral gave us our best shot to clear-out those underground networks before they become a problem for us in the days ahead. We simply follow the orders from Black-ops Command now…got that?"

The two soldiers rolled their eyes, and then turned back to the fire. They sensed things were getting out of hand – there was a fine line between culpable deniability and treason. Neither of them wanted to spend the rest of their lives in a cell for a plan that made no sense.

The commander and his colleague walked toward the door. "You will be extracted in six hours…try to stay out of each other pants that long," he said turning out into the cold.

The soldiers flipped him their middle fingers, behind his back. They had had enough.

"This is bullshit," one said to the other. "Am I missing something here? Makes no fucking sense, I thought we were nabbing plutonium nukes to hit those cave networks in Afghanistan, so we can continue ops there. Those terrorist will scurry down them like rats the next time we go in, and we will be fucked."

"Shut up," the other replied, "you always ask too many damn questions."

The moment was tense between them; then he reached over and affectionately stroked the back of his partner's head, clearly loving the feel of the sort, bristled hair. The uneasy soldier leaned into the touch and smiled.

Outside the shack, the two officers approached an all-terrain vehicle. They pulled open the doors and climbed inside.

"Was it wise to clue them in on the tritium?" the second officer asked the first. "Drake won't be happy...this cover-story has too many loose ends. You know he has no intention of sending those things to Afghanistan...the way we have told half the men working for us, including the Russians."

"It's of no consequence," replied the commander, reaching into his pocket and pulling out a small remote device. He flipped the arming switch – a red light glowed. Without hesitation, he pressed the trigger.

One hundred yards down the road, the small shack exploded into a ball of fire. It rose up into the cruel stormy night like a sinister beast.

"Jesus Christ," said the second officer, jumping as he looked back into his rear view mirror. "Why the hell did you do that?"

"You are in Christ's Army now, Walker...trust in Him...and *only* Him," sneered the man behind the wheel, as he threw the detonator onto the dashboard. "Or you will end up in Hell with those two queer bastards. Why the hell do you think I picked them for this?"

Then the officer adorned a sickly smile.

❧

Caleb Drake sat back in his chair at the ministry office, waiting for news of the crash. Mike Eason, the US Admiral in the plane, had been a member of his congregation from when it was nothing more than a broken-down church in the middle of nowhere. Both men had become disillusioned with the government, and that is why they believed the angels had come to them. They had worked out a plan together to create an army loyal to their theology, seeing the political path of America as corrupt and weak. That plan was now in motion.

The Admiral's wife sat in a chair across from him, sobbing into her hands. He leaned forward at his desk, the air grew stifling.

"I am so sorry, Mary Alice," he said. "I know this is hard, but Mike is in the hands of our savior now. You and I both know he was steadfast in his faith...he was a hero."

"I know, Doctor Drake, I know...but I just can't believe he's gone," she replied.

"Mary Alice, God has a plan for the world and each of us has our part in it. Some of us take care of our families...some of us take care of our congregations. Mike was a man who took care of his country."

"You are so right, Doctor Drake," she sobbed on. "It was his life."

"Now why don't you head out with Judy....you should go on home to your fam..."

"What about Sandy?" she suddenly interrupted in a clear voice. "Can she come home from the retreat now, Doctor Drake? I know it's against the rules, but...."

"I spoke to Sandy just this morning, Mary Alice," he stopped her, "when I found out. She was devastated, but her place is with her sisters and brothers at the compound."

"I can't believe she wouldn't want to come home!"

"I will speak to her again, and see if she will reconsider," he said without a single strain of emotion in his voice. "Now go on out and have Judy call you a car home."

"You're a saint, Caleb, you know Mike loved you like a brother...he would have done anything for you." She trembled again.

"I know, Sister Eason...trust me I know."

Caleb slowly turned to ring a buzzer on his desk. When his secretary heard it, she burst in as if she had been waiting right at the door. She trotted over to Mary Alice and bent at the knees to draw the broken woman up from the chair, her dress straining from the bulk pressed into it as she did.

As Judy left the room with his mournful guest, Caleb turned toward the television behind his desk and flipped at the control. The box squawked on. "A broken arrow is the official term used by the US Military to describe when it loses a nuclear weapon... not something that has occurred often, but it has happened nonetheless. The Department of Defense lists its very first accident with a US nuclear weapon as being off the coast of British Columbia. The incident occurred on February 13, 1950."

Caleb switched the channel, as if bored with the discussion.

"White House officials are now saying that earlier reports about a broken arrow are completely unfounded. A spokesman for the President patently denies that the US government was negotiating with Russian officials to buy weapons of any kind."

Caleb flipped off the television and swung around in his chair.

He paused for a second, before picking up his phone for Judy. "Is Mary Alice on her way now?" he asked, then paused for her reply. "Good.... will you send Seth Slivers in now.... he is still waiting, isn't he?"

He smiled when he heard the man was, and set down the phone. Caleb composed himself a moment as he waited. He knew this was one of the most important things he had ever done, and the Israeli secret service's involvement validated that for him.

The door opened a few moments later and in walked a heavy-set man, with an emaciated face. His suit was a size too small; it pulled tightly at his chest.

Caleb motioned for him to sit. "What have you heard from the ground team in Turkey?" he asked the man, without even saying hello.

"Everything is going as expected," said Seth. "Walker and Pratt have the nukes. The recovery team has been," he paused, 'dismissed' as I understand it."

The two men looked at each other with distrusting eyes.

"I am told your people will have the weapons out of Turkey by morning...then you need to sit on them for a while before trying to move. I understand the Russians are upset. They are not going to like it when the weapons don't turn up in Afghanistan the way we both told them they would."

"Who cares what those old guard KGB thugs think...they are heathens," said Caleb. "They won't risk their own government finding out about what they have done."

"We went to a lot of trouble for you on this...our reputation will be damaged with them for a long time.

"We did this for *you!* You and your men will be heroes when this is over, and your government will get the support it finally needs from Washington to rid yourself of those godless Muslims."

"Just make sure to send me the manifest for whatever ship you plan to use once you have it chartered. I will intercept them at sea, as planned, and alert my government once I have the weapons... that should tie the State Department's hands and allow us to move forward with our plans to finally route the agitator leadership in Palestine."

"Praise Jesus!" crowed Caleb.

"You're playing a dangerous game, Drake. The Mossad does not want the CIA knowing we had a hand in this affair. Your connections in Syria better pan out or this will look like a set up from the start. You are sure they are Kurds?"

"I'm sure...and don't worry about US intelligence. They are useless."

"This whole thing is a house of cards," said Seth, "and I would never count out the CIA. Even a stopped clock is right twice a day. What of your men...how are they on all this?"

"Relax, my soldiers are loyal to God before they are to this morally corrupt country," replied Caleb. "We've been working for decades to get inside all the military academy's to recruit men to His cause. We've been vindicated of late anyway by this President and his plans to let deviants into the services...all the senior generals will be behind us when the time comes...I've been assured."

"If these weapons get into the wrong hands, this could go bad quickly."

"You worry too much, my friend. It's all in the hands of God."

"Really?" retorted Seth cynically.

Caleb grinned. His expression was contrived; it looked like he was holding something between his teeth amid the cheeky smile. Seth did believe in God, but the idea that the lunatic in front of him had a direct line to the almighty seemed far-fetched to him. He'd almost rather be dealing with the Devil sometimes.

"Somehow that does not make me feel a lot better," groaned the Mossad agent, moving toward the door. "I think it's about time I got back to the Embassy. It's best we have as little contact as possible now."

"Seth," said Caleb. "I think it's my duty and obligation to offer that we pray together...that you give your life to Jesus."

The remark sent a chill down the agent's spine, the very idea of giving himself over to whatever god Drake worshipped turned his stomach.

"Thanks, but I am at peace with my maker for now," he replied.

Caleb made a dreadful face as he left the room. *God has a rude awaking waiting for him,* he thought. *And for all the Jews that don't give themselves to Jesus.*

The evangelist sat back in the chair of his study. His face fell emotionless as he allowed his mind to drift into a trance. He spoke a meditative prayer – the low murmur of the mantra seemed to hang in the room like shadow. His head twisted as if channeling some power from beyond. The conspiring pastor prayed that way for hours, until every last soul was gone from the office…but for one.

At a certain point in his meditation, he felt a presence. He abruptly opened his eyes and stared into the cold gaze of Shemhazai, the Jinn appeared out of thin air. Caleb dropped his body, prostrating himself in front of the grigori. His chest was flat against the floor, as he squirmed there like worm. The grigori reached out with his powerful hands and took Caleb by the face – the eerie pose they struck was an ancient mark of supplication between mortal and Jinn.

"Great Gabriel, you honor me with your visitations," said Caleb as he slithered at the feet of the masquerading demon.

Shemhazai smiled at his keen deception, and the gullibility of Caleb's faith. "The Devil is moving." he said. "Iblis has captured the prophet of God and seduced him with flesh."

"You need only command me and I will do as God wishes. My followers are faithful…they have already acquired the weapons that you instructed us to prepare for use against the enemy. We will destroy that godless abomination on the Temple Mount!"

"Good," said the grigori, "I will insure the Lord's agents are ready to receive and use them at the appointed time. Do you trust your God, Caleb?"

"Yes," stammered Caleb, "of course...I put my full trust in you. I always have...my follows have proved it over the years in our efforts to send the godless to hell."

"You are not plotting to blow up abortion clinics anymore, Caleb. That was child's play compared to what your men must do now. The dark omens from the walls in the Tomb of Habil have been correct so far. Go to Arbil with your ministry, as we have been planning. We know the Devil will flee there with the prophet, looking for the woman clothed in the sun and moon."

"Yes, praise Christ...praise the Lord," Caleb intoned, with his disturbing grin.

"Now go. Send in that woman I asked for...so she may know the God you have delivered her to."

Caleb scrambled to his feet and made his way out of the dimly lit office. He found Sandy sleeping on a cot in a small room nearby where she had been cosigned like an animal, awaiting sacrifice.

His office was a bunker; no sound left that place. Cruelly, Caleb grabbed her by the arm. "Gabriel is here!" he hissed. "He has asked for you just I said he would. It is your time."

He hauled her from the room, kicking and screaming. She was all too aware now that he was a monster, but it was too late for her. As they approached the door, she managed to leverage herself against a desk. Caleb fought furiously to pull her free. Suddenly, Shemhazai was standing behind him.

"Hold her down," said the grigori.

"She is unwilling," replied Caleb.

"As she should be," said Shemhazai. "She is a sinner….is she not?"

The demon fell on her with brutality, while Caleb stood and stared in deranged awe. When the dark Jinn was done feeding, Caleb groveled there in front of him, filled with a blind reverence for the grigori's power.

"She is absolved," said the Pythian with a sinister tone. "I took the sin from her."

Caleb was pleased with himself, thinking that he had saved yet another soul. His great crusade had finally begun; she would not be the last.

☙

Far above the brim of Eden, upon the holy mountain, the angel Micah approached the throne. In his hand he held a gold censer that he swung back and forth, releasing an ethereal vapor. The delicate cloud drifted toward the throne, upon which sat Joshu, the living Lamb of sacrifice and steward of Heaven. An aura radiated out from Joshu with such brilliance that the air looked as if is it sparked like a precious stone.

A great host of Jinn, immortal elohim, and the souls of faithful saints fell down before Joshu and worshiped him, for he was the mortal embodiment of the nameless-god, who was vested with the power to rule over Eden in His stead. Having broken all seven seals upon the plans of the nameless-god for how to counter the rise of darkness, Joshu contemplated destiny for a short time. Then he summoned seven holy servants, with seven trumpets to stand before him.

Micah lifted the censer above the alter that stood before the throne, and spoke in a commanding voice to all assembled. "Here, Prince of Heaven, heavenly avatar of the one ruling God, are the prayers of your servants," he proclaimed.

As if by cue, Joshu stood and raised his hands. "Children of the nameless-one," he professed to them. "Hear my words so that you may understand. We are poised here at the very edge of being – the place that is *Sephirah of Yesod* – where the spirit of the nameless-god conjoins in the world, and from where all things draw substance. I stand before you to evoke the rite of my stewardship, in the absence of our Lord. I've seen his plan written here upon the seven scrolls. I alone see all that will come to pass before we descend into the time of darkness, beyond which no eye may pass. Let His will be done!"

With that Joshu motioned to Micah. The wise and powerful Jinn moved to invoke an ancient prayer before the altar. The smoke of the incense rose to Joshu and he heard the entreaties that were borne within it.

Upon the altar something seethed. It was a power that coalesced into radiant embers so intense that they burned white hot, like the sun. The Jinn reached out to the altar and took up the embers into his censer, causing the vessel to flare and resonate with power. Slowly, he turned and walked to the edge of the platform, raising the censer over his head, and then casting it down into Eden. The power of the one, true God quickened in the world – the time had come. Then the seven angels of prophecy took up their trumpets, and stepped to the edge of the throne.

There was silence in Heaven.

Joshu reached out and pointed to the first angel. The Jinn raised the long horn to his mouth and blew into it. It didn't make a sound to the ear, but instead reverberated ethereally throughout all being. The angel shed a tear, as he saw out over the plane of Eden hail began to fall, mixed with fire and blood.

Part Two: The Two Witnesses

Then the King commanded the high priest, Hilkiah, his vicar, and the warriors to remove from the temple of the Lord all those idols that had been made for Ba'al, His Goddess, and the whole court of Heaven… they tore down the dwellings of the (male) cult prostitutes which were in the Temple, and in which woman wove garments to adorn the sacred asherah rod.

2 Kings 23:4,7

9

THE ISLAND EXILE

London – Early December 1999

Jon sat across from Nick in the plush chair of the hotel lobby where they had been staying, his face bright red with irritation and impatience as he watched the Accuser reading the *London Times*. Sensing his angst, Nick finally lowered his newspaper.

"What's wrong?"

"What do you mean, what's wrong? We're sitting here doing nothing, that's what's wrong!" Jon's voice boomed in the crowded lobby. "I told you we needed to go to Arbil to find the woman...not sit around in some posh English hotel pretending to be aristocrats."

The Accuser rolled his eyes. Jon hated it when Nick made that face.

"Where the hell did you get the money for this place anyway, and for these pretentious cloths?"

"What's wrong with you, Jon?" snapped Nick. "That's a $3,000 suit. Can't you just appreciate something nice for once?"

"Ahhhh," growled the prophet, turning his head away. "I don't care how much it cost...I feel like a fool just sitting here!"

Nick heaved his chest in frustration. He laid the paper down next to his seat and leaned forward, taking Jon by the hand "First, don't worry about the money. I've had a long time to learn how one manipulates mortal finances. Second, I do realize you are bored and more than impatient to get this underway, trust me I want to get to Arbil faster than you realize."

Nick stopped and pulled at his sleeve to straighten it with his free hand, adjusting a gold cufflink as he did. He glanced up slowly into the prophet's eyes.

"But right now we have to be careful, governments are at war in that region and there is chaos all around it. It is a very complicated and dangerous affair... going there."

"What does any of the mess there have to do with us?"

Nick drew a deep breath, wondering if Jon could really be so naive. He painted a grin over his own impatience, and pushed on trying to make Jon understand.

"Believe it or not, there is a method to my madness... a sequence of events that we should follow if possible. You have to trust me on this part...we are going to Arbil like you wanted, the best way I know how."

"So why all this fuss then?" Jon replied, motioning at the clothing, then glancing around the hotel. "I feel like I'm trapped here on this Island...it is like a prison for me to not be doing something."

"If I must endure the painful trek back to face *my* past...something I can tell you that I am not looking forward to...I intend to do it in the lap of luxury for as long as I can manage. This is my favorite hotel in

Europe. Can't we do something for me just this once? There is some twisted purpose in us being drawn to Arbil...it's a place that harbors an ancient animosity toward me. It will not be 'fun' in the least."

Nick knew they were both being tested in their affair by calling them into that wasteland of human misery – a suffering to which Nick himself had contributed.

"Our 'confinement' here...as you see it," added Nick with sarcasm, "will be all short lived. When we leave this place, we will need to start blending into a world that looks nothing like what you are used to. If you think you're unhappy in that suit...just wait until we're slinking around the foothills of Northern Iraq, and you've been in the same clothing for a month without a shower."

Nick leaned back and crossed his arms. The dark exile was still trying to understand the hold this young man had over him, the attraction was unlike anything he had ever known for a mortal man.

"And one other thing you should know...."

"What?" the prophet sneered.

"...You are not going to like Arbil in the least once you get there, my friend. London is a carnival compared to where we're going. Don't be in such a rush to be bored senseless there as well. At least here we can entertain ourselves with some familiar trappings while we prepare ourselves for that hell."

Jon's face turned red again. "I know that. I told you not to patronize me," he said through tightly held lips. "I am not a child...don't treat me like one."

Nick chuckled and picked up the paper, ignoring his desire at that moment to run upstairs and rip the suit off the handsome man. For some ungodly reason, he found Jon irresistibly sexy when he was being difficult – rage was becoming like an aphrodisiac to them both. Sex was most intense when they were angry at each other – to say nothing of the vividness of vision.

"So why are we just sitting here in the lobby doing nothing?" Jon mumbled. "I'm hungry, let's go someplace and eat at least."

Nick stopped reading again and lowered the paper. "Jon, we just ate a few hours ago." The Accuser's tone deepened. "If you must know, we are waiting for a business contact, someone who is going to help us establish a cover for you being in Iraq…so we don't stick out there like sore thumbs."

The prophet's eyes narrowed, as his interest peaked. He grinned at Nick, his mood completely shifting. "Why didn't you say so in the first place?"

Nick shook his head and glared at the boy. Jon seemed so manic at times. The Accuser had never seen a mortal with such a perplexing essence, not a sane one anyway, but he had also never seen one composed so completely of eleventh light either. That captivated him beyond words.

Nick's look became very serious.

"So here is the plan if you must know," he began to explain. "We need a little cover, so we will head to Syria first by plane, assisting with the transfer of some rather sensitive cargo…cash. I've worked with this group before. They are not the most pious bunch of mortals, but they will get us into Iraq and help us keep a low profile as long as we need. We have to be very careful about attracting too much of the wrong kind of attention, at least until we figure out why we have to be there."

A concierge suddenly walked over and slipped Nick a note; Jon appeared annoyed with the interruption. The Accuser opened and read it slowly. "This would be our man," he said. "Let's go. You can get something to eat at the bar if you're still hungry."

They rose and made their way across the lobby to the bar. Jon's pace was quick and nervous. Seeing his contact, Nick moved toward the man. The gaunt faced stranger rose to his feet as Nick approached, reaching out and adorning what Jon thought was a very fake looking smile. The Accuser took his arms and embraced him. They said a greeting in a tongue Jon did not understand.

Jon wondered for a time if they would speak in the strange language to exclude him. The boy was pleased to find Nick was not so thoughtless.

"Nazim, this is my business associate, Jon York," said Nick, introducing the prophet with a fictitious last name.

The man reached over and took Jon by the hand as well. Jon grinned and eyed Nick. He felt a strange thrill for the deception, it was a rush.

"I'm pleased to meet you, Mr. York. We are most delighted to have you working with us."

"Thank you," replied Jon, trying not to show that he was more than a little lost.

"Please, sit...shall I order wine?" asked Nick.

The man bowed politely, to indicate that would be fine. Nick raised one hand and drew the bar tender's attention.

"So, how is the old man, Nazim? Is he well?" asked Nick, settling back and opening his jacket to relax.

Jon tried to settle back too, but the stiffness of his own jacket got in the way. Then taking the cue from Nick, he unfastened it and felt as if the weight of the world had come free. As he reclined, his stomach growled so loud Nick could hear it.

The bartender appeared. The Accuser leaned over, whispering in his direction not to appear as ostentatious in front of their business associate for his taste in wine. He also did not want anyone to overhear his rather boorish order, for the occasion, of chicken wings of all things – something he had to specifically instruct the kitchen to have on hand for Jon. Such fare was not normally on their menu, but it was the kind of place that was accustomed to catering to their clientele's less than seemly requests from time to time. The tawdry American cuisine was a small concession for this regular guest, who normally had more indiscrete requirements of his hosts. The prophet had pitched a fit more than once over the last few days about there being nothing to eat in London that he found palatable. Jon could be impossible at times about such things, as Nick was learning. So he tried his best to appease the boy with any gesture he could, it was simply not worth fighting with him about every little detail of the trip.

"My father is well," said Nazim as the bartender left, "but he spends little time with our business these days. Times are tough back at home."

"We've noticed that," replied Nick. "Perhaps we can help."

"Yes, you can imagine how pleased we were to hear you were interested in working with us again, on a limited basis that is."

The man's face turned grim Jon thought. "In the past, your price was steeper for such services," Nazim added. "We are happy to have such a reasonable offer this time as well, much more affordable than paying off every little bandit and public official between here and Bagdad."

"Look, I'll be honest with you," said Nick, glancing at Jon. "My friend here is the real reason we are doing this so cheaply...I am mostly helping him out." Jon turned white, wondering what Nick might say next. "I've retired from this kind of work mostly...I don't have the connections in the business all that much anymore."

"Really?" replied Nazim. "That surprises me, you were always the most reliable of suppliers. You never miss a delivery...a quality that is rare in our line of work."

"Well, I am still the best on the currying end of things," explained Nick. "I will be able to get your money into Arbil past the authorities and the local 'entrepreneurs' ...but this is the man that will get the guns and munitions you need. The first shipments should be ready soon...as agreed. They will arrive in Naples a few days after we leave...you can inspect them when they arrive in port. We will go ahead with the funds. That's a risky place to curry that kind of cash these days, so I need to be light on my feet over land...no flights this time."

Jon had been right about not liking the affair. He was in fact mortified.

The bar tender arrived with a tray of glasses and the fine vintage. There was an awkward silence as the man laid out the wine before them. Once done, he quickly vanished. Nick sniffed at his glass, then raised it. "To Kurdish freedom," the Devil toasted.

Nazim appeared very pleased with Nick's courtesy. He smiled and raised his own glass. Jon just sat quietly and drank, his eyes glowing with furry at Nick.

Looking back into the boy's gaze, a euphoric chill went down the Accuser's spine.

⚭

A short time after meeting Nazim, Nick and Jon sat sequestered in their room. Nick was lying down trying to ignore the boy; it was sometimes painful to be with him when he was upset. All Nick could do at times was pretend he did not notice the waves of aggravation pour off from the young mortal.

Jon was fuming. He paced back and forth at the foot of the bed as he began to rant. "What the hell are we doing, Nick? I can't believe this! We're actually smuggling guns into Iraq?"

"Not exactly," answered Nick. "We are simply supplying guns to rebels on the market. Not smuggling them ourselves…there is a subtle difference. *We* are running laundered drug money….that's all."

"Oh! I feel so much better about it when you put it that way."

"When mankind decides to raise his hand against his brother, does it really matter who puts the stone in his hand? Anyway, *you* said Arbil and I am getting us there. Fortunately, it's a place I've had a lot of dealings with over the years, even though I've not been their directly in eons. You must understand that I am not a popular guy with the locals, for reasons I don't think I need to go into now."

"Yes, I can tell," replied Jon sarcastically, "but can't we just take a plane like normal people?"

"No! We're not going sightseeing," said Nick sharply, sitting up and swing his legs off the bed. "I told you we were going to have to blend in there…that means we become part of their world and all of what I am sure you will find as its unseemly habits."

"So, the only people living there are smugglers and terrorists?"

"Of course not, there are people of all walks of life, just like in America, but not people like *you*. That is the problem. We're going to the Northern Iraq… how many times do I need to spell this out for you? Unless we come up with a really good reason why we're there… one that they will accept…you are going to be in trouble the first time I leave you alone. It will be really helpful if I don't have to worry every second of every hour whether someone is going to snag you on the street or put a bullet in your head. They need to be as afraid of you as they are of me…and trust me they *are* afraid of me."

Jon stopped in his tracks. "A bullet in my head?" he asked nervously.

"Kid, let's talk some sense here. I think the world of you, but this is a very dangerous place we are going. I don't know how long we may have to be there, so far neither us has come up with more than the name of this place to help us find what we're after, despite our repeated efforts to get into one another."

"You say that like what's between us doesn't mean more to you than just looking for that damn woman," replied Jon stiffly.

"What?" retorted the Accuser.

"What about me?" asked Jon. "Don't I matter enough to you without all this fucking intrigue? What about what we feel for each other?"

Jon shot a look that wounded Nick to the core. The Accuser got up and went to the window where the boy stood. He reached for Jon, but the prophet dodged him. He was hurt.

"You don't care about me…do you, Nick?"

The Jinn got a funny feeling in his chest. He had not realized until that very second–until Jon spoke those words aloud– how recent events had utterly changed him. For so long in his existence, everything was clear to Nick about men. Now the exile of Heaven was not so sure what he felt in his heart. He stood speechless.

"See," said Jon meekly.

"Jon," Nick replied, his heart seeming to break as he took the boy's hands. "I do think that I…"

BANG, BANG, BANG, a knock at the door interrupted him.

"Who is that?" asked Jon with a snort, pulling away from Nick again.

Nick took a deep breath. "Room service I think," he replied, almost with a note of relief. He turned for the door and opened it.

The waiter quickly pushed in a cart. As the man entered the room, he looked Jon up-and-down curiously, then gazed back to Nick with a suspicious frown.

"Who is the kid, Bliss?" he asked.

Nick's face grew stern. "I am not working alone this time," he replied. It sounded like he regretted it for a moment.

"Is he cleared?"

Jon stepped toward them both. This was no simple waiter he realized.

"You never cleared me, what the hell do you care?" snapped Nick.

"I don't know about this, you didn't say anything about working with someone who didn't have clearance from Langley."

Jon looked at Nick, as if to insist on an explanation. Nick ignored him.

"Look Mason," said the Accuser, approaching the man's face and stopping only a few inches away. "I am getting on a plane tomorrow heading to Syria and then Iraq, just like we worked out. Either you want my help this time or you don't. I doubt you are in a position to dictate terms these days...you boys have made a real mess for yourself over there."

"WHAT'S GOING ON!" barked Jon in a loud voice. "Don't talk about me as if I am not here."

"Christ, he's American! What the hell are you up to, Bliss?"

Jon walked toward the man aggressively.

Nick sensed that was a bad idea. "STOP!" he shouted as he used a spell of suggestion to try and bend both their minds. It was the first time he had tried that on Jon since Twilo.

The enigmatic waiter's head looked to swoon. The Devil pressed harder, twisting his will.

"Jon," grunted Nick in introduction. "This is Agent Anthony Mason...with the Central Intelligence Agency."

"Awe damn it Nick...tell the whole fucking world why don't you? You know we can't be a clandestine operation if you tell everyone who we are!"

"Shut up, Mason, you take this secret agent shit too seriously."

Mason looked around the room again as if stunned a little by something, appearing to relax slowly as Nick pushed at his mind with the spell. It was clearly working on the agent, if only distracting Jon.

The prophet paused a moment, putting the loose ends together. Nick was acting as some kind of agent against the forces he perceived as corrupt, not working for them. He had misjudged Nick again; the tension drained away.

"Agent Mason," answered Jon, extending his hand and pushing Nick out of his head. "It's nice to meet you."

Jon appeared to be relieved that this was someone he considered to be on the right side, despite having no idea what that actually meant. Nick did not have time to explain that there was no 'good side' when it came to mortal empires, whether governments or syndicates, but his seemingly favorable perception of Mason clearly would make this affair easier. So he left it alone.

The agent took Jon's hand. The spell had worked, at least in part.

The prophet studied Anthony for a time. He was a hefty guy, a little thick, muscle no doubt, but a plain looking fellow. Not at all someone you picture as an intelligence operative.

"Did you sweep the room?" asked Mason, turning to Nick.

"Yes," he replied, "nothing in here but your bug on the cart."

"How did you know that?"

"That's why you pay me the big-bucks. Now let's get on with this." Nick took a step back and looked at Jon as if to prod him to keep quiet. "I made contact with Nazim this evening. We're going first to Latakia in northern Syria, after that we are heading to Arbil... the matter of some cash that requires laundering from the heroin road. I need this to be a clean job, Mason, so stay off my back....like all the other times, you will get your cut."

"Fine," said the Agent.

"We are also arranging for a shipment of guns to the PKK at the port." He glanced toward Jon. "*Parti*

Karkerani Kurdistan" he said for the boy's edification, "Kurdish separatists."

Mason glanced at Jon. Even he could read the young prophet's surprise.

"This one's green, right?"

Nick turned to face Jon and after looked back at Mason. "You've been in this business long enough to never take anything on appearance," he answered. "Your future may well rest in this man's hands." The Accuser waited a moment, to let what he said sink in for both men before he went on. "We have business in Arbil, black-market stuff, none of your concern."

"Fine, whatever," grunted Mason again.

"Now, what can you boys tell *me* that I don't already know?" asked Nick.

Mason looked over at Jon, hesitated, then figured he might as well. Nick had never let down the agency in the past. It was a little late to be second guessing.

"We collared Abdullah Ocalan in Kenya, with the help of Turkish authorities."

"The PKK's syndicate boss?" asked Nick. "Has he said anything useful to you guys?"

"No, he's back peddling big time…they will hang him unless he offers something up soon."

"I would imagine," said Nick, "not a popular guy among Turks…they will likely string him up regardless of what he turns over I am guessing."

"True. The PKK are refusing to stand down and disband in Turkey even with him in custody," Mason added. "They plan to keep that heroin-road open any way they can. It's the only way to keep the cash coming in for the guns they need, as you apparently seem to know."

"That reminds me," said Nick. "I need you to supply me with the ordinance as well this time."

Mason shifted in his seat. The idea was not setting well. He laughed nervously as he answered. "Nick, it's not like the old day…that's not so easy anymore."

"Anthony, you go ahead and run it by your boys back there in the swamps of Virginia…but I'm no fool. I know what your pathetic hacks need…intell on Iraq. I will be as close to finding out the truth about what's going on there…short of invading Baghdad… and we both know no one in DC is that nuts."

"It comforts me, Nick," said Mason sarcastically, "to know you are such a patriot."

"Just tell me what I need to look out for," replied Nick in a low voice.

Mason drew a quick breath and settled down in a chair close to the door. "With Ocalan being held," he said, "the PKK leadership is effectively headless. They are still dangerous, but without him the Kurds are simply not going to put out the same level of effort against the Iraqis that they have in the past. They are especially not happy with us for turning him over to the Turks…but we had no choice."

"I can only imagine," replied the Accuser.

"You better watch yourself with whatever you are doing out there," Mason continued. "Ocalan did tell us there are splinter groups developing in the region within the PKK fold, with designs on taking over the heroin traffic…but the old-guard PKK makes hundreds of millions of dollars off those drugs…they won't let go of that business easy. It could get nasty if they set to fighting over it. Word is the Republican Guard is also trying to muscle in, along with some group of fundamentalists from Syria. I am warning you…watch your back with your Syrian contact there, Ibn al-Ghazali."

Mason's voice turned flip at the mention of the man's name. He did not approve of Nick's relationship with the operative; that was clear.

"Ibn is in Arbil?" Nick's face lit up. That was the best news he'd had so far about this trip. Mason handed Nick a file with a dossier.

"The Syrians are playing both sides…the Turks and the Kurds."

"Why does that sound familiar?" Nick said with a laugh. That was normally Mason's M.O.

The agent scowled.

"And what of the Republican Guard?" Nick inquired after looking at the file. "What are they up to these days that I should watch out for?"

"I got nothing. You're right about us having little on them. If there is a chance you can get intelligence on what they are doing, Langley will stick their ass in the air for you; I am sure. Something big is going down here, Nick…we even think the Mossad is up to something. Our intelligence suggests that the components for two low yield mobile-nukes, lost by the Russian's a few weeks ago, are in play. We strongly suspect PKK involvement in trying to traffic them to someone in the region. Washington is pissing itself right now."

"Those nukes were on a US military plane when they were lost," Jon spoke up, "not a Russian one. That is what the news said anyway." He had noticed a sudden change in Mason, one he sensed was dishonest. The prophet's power was growing; somehow Jon knew he was lying about US involvement in the affair. But Mason could not admit to them the CIA suspected Christian Zionists in the American military.

Both Nick and Anthony looked over at him, the agent seemed to squirm. The Accuser was strangely relieved when he heard the prophet speak. He realized Jon was paying closer attention than the boy let on to be, that was important to his survival.

"So then," Mason continued, "I am sure the brass will arrange what you need, if indeed you think you have a chance of getting us something on that mess. Truth be told, if truckloads of M16's end up in Saddam Hussein's backyard...causing him grief...we're not inclined to be too upset. But you can't let the Turks know we're supplying you."

"I realize that," said Nick to the agent.

Mason rose from his seat. He looked cagy, he could feel Jon's essence wrap around him somehow...but could not discern the source. His breath grew labored. Nick never noticed the boy extend that power; perhaps because he did not realize him capable of it. Jon found the man's reflections were transparent to him, as if he could reach into is mind without conjoining. The thoughts seemed to echo in his head, which at first unnerved Jon as he tried to sort out what Mason said from what he thought.

"I need this to go smoothly," said the Accuser finally. "Use the Libyan guns you seized three days ago, that should give you all the cover you need. Set up the connection in Naples, here is the contact that Nazim gave me." Nick slipped him a freight invoice. "The guns need to be out of port, and on the way to Syria in days…so move fast before they figure out you are the ones that took them. And if they smell you on this, it's over…no mole on the ship!"

Mason froze, staring down at the paper. Then shook his head and slowly turned for the door, wondering how Nick knew about the Libyan job in the first place. Passing the cart, he picked up a tin warmer and peered at the pile of chicken under it. He glanced back at Jon with a funny look about his face.

"Sorry kid, these wings are cold," he said.

Jon's expression became harsh, he distrusted Mason all of a sudden, but was not sure why. "I like them cold sometimes," he replied.

Mason made a smug face and glanced at Nick. "I can tell," he snorted with an unseemly laugh, as if to imply he knew something more of them. Without another word, he reached for the door and vanished like a ghost out into the hall.

There was a long span of silence in the room. Jon did not seem to know what to say for a time. He paced a little more, then twisted his mouth and finally spoke. His voice was low and full of contrition.

"I am sorry, Nick."

"For what?"

"Getting upset at you over running guns for terrorists...when it was all just a front for us to get here. I guess I should try to have more faith in you."

"Don't feel too good about it...this other arrangement with Mason is not much better. Trust me."

"I just can't believe you work for the CIA."

"*With* the CIA, not for them...there is a difference," retorted Nick. "It's a marriage of convenience more I would say."

"How long have you been doing it?"

Nick laughed at the question. Jon pulled him closer as if to beg of him what he found funny.

"Believe it or not, Jon," said the Accuser, "the US government and I have a long history of making dirty little deals." He waited for a response from Jon, none came. Then he walked over to the cart and reached under it to crush Mason's listening device between his fingers. "You should eat," he said finally.

The young prophet tilted his head and his eyes lit up. Nick then felt the boy grab him with a constricting power, and was shocked by the abrupt force of his ethereal embrace. It was abundantly clear from Jon's face something other than food entered his mind.

"Speaking of wings...that gives me an idea," the boy said in a menacing tone.

"What's that?" replied Nick, hesitantly.

"Next time we do it... I want to hold you down by your wings."

"You mean when we have sex?"

Jon grinned and nodded.

Nick turned and grabbed him about his square jaw. "And I am the one that gets a bad reputation for seducing men with my indecorous fetishes," the Accuser laughed.

Nick reveled in the prophet's mortal desire; he somehow enjoyed the surrender Jon required of their affair. The Jinn felt oddly validated by it, but was still not so sure it was such a good thing.

⚶

Nick and Jon spent one more restless night in London. They even tried to go out dancing at a hot spot in the city called Heaven. Jon wanted to tease Nick for the ostensible humor of it. *He better not get us kicked out of here too*, he mused to himself as they entered the club. Still, Jon thought better of actually ribbing Nick in that way, sensing the Devil would not find the joke as funny.

The entire scene at the club was a lot like that of New York, but no matter how hard they both tried to lose themselves in the music and lights, they simply could not relax. Nick seemed uncomfortable. There too a Rafiq knight supervened over the throng with his power, as the revelers searched for wajd in those most desperate of days. The handsome young man watched Nick from the DJ booth, with his crystal blue stare, wondering what the Accuser was doing there with the prophet. Nafees would surely want to know.

Nick finally thought it best to leave the club; they would find no peace there. The underlying tension over what was happening never left the pair, no matter what they tried. The only way that they were able to escape their anxiousness was through their intimacy. It gave them something that was theirs and theirs alone in a world of increasing discord. The presence of the dragons seemed to be growing all around them, even in the simplest of thing. As it did, Nick found his ethereal power waning more and more, and the impulses of the dark stronger. He fought to suppress its rising tide within his soul, uncertain of what it would do to him.

In a way, Jon distracted Nick from the reality of exile. It was a comforting form of denial, lending the wayward Jinn a sense of normalcy for once in his existence, even if he knew it was a facade. But despite the deepening passion between them, nothing new of the prophecy yielded itself in their impassioned conjoining. At times that frustrated Nick; he was intensely aware that something was simply not right. He did not know what to do.

Jon on the other hand appeared more focused on the simple carnal outcomes of their union, sated by Nick's submission, and the sense of power it afforded him. The Jinn could tell it made the prophet feel secure. Nick realized that no matter what, he must feed that allusion for the time being – there was purpose in it beyond his understanding.

They huddled in their hotel room alone, just feeling each other breathe in the dim twilight. Nick nodded off finally. He had been sleeping so much better than ever before within Jon's embrace.

Shortly after they had both fallen asleep, Nick was awakened suddenly by Jon as he violently convulsed in the bed. It was a seizure of some kind, a violent one that nearly tossed them both from the bed.

Nick tried to hold him down, but an unearthly strength consumed the young man's body. He uttered in an unrecognizable voice. The terrifying episode resembled a spell of possession to the Accuser, but he knew that to be impossible with how Jon's mind was composed – at least the way Nick understood the spell to work. Without warning, the prophet gripped at Nick so hard the Jinn swore it was coil that he extended for a moment; then the boy abruptly stopped moving, lapsing into a deep, coma-like sleep. Nick lay for a time watching him, distressed, realizing he had no way to control what was going on for Jon. Exhausted, he finally managed to settle down and fall asleep again himself. As he dozed there in the eclipse of despair, darkness deepened as light was emptied out of all being. It seemed to Nick in his dreams that he was trapped in the undertow of some dark ocean, the Abyss perhaps. He wanted to save Jon from it, but realized he could not. The boy must find his own salvation, and knew better than Nick where it was to be found.

For the moment, they slept peacefully. It was a deceptive calm.

When Nick brought up the issue of the attack with Jon the next day, the boy acted as if he was out of his mind. The Jinn felt even more helpless, fearing the power that was growing in the young prophet was somehow unraveling the very structure of his mind, something that happened to God's prophets frequently Nick knew. Most he had known over the years went completely insane from the touch of God's power – in some ways Nick felt he had himself.

The pair got up and left London that morning, both trying to focus on the task at hand. It was cold and raining – gloom seemed to follow them. They boarded a commercial flight at Heathrow Airport, traveling with Syrian passports, and flew to Switzerland. There they transferred to a private jet headed into Latakia, on the coast Syria. It was a quiet, quaint place to start their journey into travail.

Uneasy about their cover, Jon asked about the money they were supposed to be currying. He had been nervous about moving the cash from London to the Middle East. Nick assured him that his methods were foolproof.

They pretty much were. Nick never actually smuggled anything physically. After the money was passed to him by Nazim, he simply stowed it within a safety deposit box at the Bank of London. When it came time to hand it over to the contacts in Northern Iraq, he would move into the Realm of Essences and pass back to London, their retrieving it to hand off. No one would ever be the wiser, nor was there any risk of getting caught with the currency. Nick was not really afraid; he just would rather avoid the complication of having to deal with mortal authorities.

The flight to Syria was quiet and relaxing for Nick, but for Jon it was utter agony sitting still that long again. When they arrived in Latakia, they took a car from the airport to an area of town called Cote d'Azure – a popular tourist destination in that part of the world. There Nick had rented a small house overlooking the water, where they could try to lay low before making the trek inland. He did not want to fly into Arbil, that might alert local authorities to where they were heading, something he wanted to avoid if possible.

Nick was insecure about the entire trip. The very idea that the woman of prophecy would be there in Arbil made no sense to him. *Why would God take human from in that cursed place?* the Accuser wondered. *Even if she is there, it will be impossible to protect both her and Jon… it will likely crawl with serpents.*

10

BALAK

Calm lay over the sea, as if before a storm. Nick and Jon sat in their room overlooking the Mediterranean surf, watching the sun go down through a sliding-glass door just off their balcony. They were wrapped in an uncertain affection for each other, baffled by how their feelings for one another grew so quickly in ways that neither had expected.

The sky was colored with a bright red hue, as Nick nestled up to Jon in the bed – his head resting upon the young mortal's chest, listening to the boy's heart. He could not help feeling at peace in the prophet's embrace, but was wary to trust that emotion. It all seemed impossible, and yet there was the sentiment he had always feared of men. It was as if his curse had been turned on its head, and now always would be.

"This feels really nice," said the Accuser softly.

The young prophet squeezed Nick. The boy made an odd noise that sounded like assent to the Jinn. Nick felt as if he had conquered all of creation when he could calm Jon, for some reason all that mattered was making the boy happy. Nick had never wanted to please a man so much. "I could never imagine coming to feel so strongly about a mortal like this, Jon," he said. "I still don't know what to make of it."

"Why, am I not worthy of angelic attention?" replied the prophet.

Nick raised his head and looked at him. "You have such a chip on your shoulder sometimes. That's not what I meant."

"I know," said the boy. "I was ribbing you...lighten up. Seriously, just think how I feel about all of this. I am falling for the author of original sin."

"You're an ass," snapped Nick with a laugh. "You know that's not true."

Nick laid his head back on Jon's chest with a thud. *Not at least the original one,* the Accuser thought to himself.

"Perhaps, but you love me anyway...don't you?" said Jon in a sarcastic tone.

A spray of ocean brushed up past their window, distracting them a moment, and yet there it was...said out loud. True to form, Nick could not say it back. For him, it seemed to be admitting defeat in some way, despite knowing what he really felt inside.

Jon didn't seem to get upset when Nick said nothing. "I've never felt this way before either," the boy said finally, with a nervous quiver to his voice. "It frightens me."

This time Nick squeezed Jon to imply *he* agreed as well.

The Accuser rolled to one side, and Jon slid in behind him. The Jinn leaned his neck back. Then the young prophet began to nibble gently at the base of his hairline, until his tongue reached up for his ear. Nick's body loosened and welcomed Jon's strong hold. It aroused the prophet's mortal desire, gripping the Devil in that way. Nick's eyes opened suddenly as Jon pushed up against him with his hips. The boy wanted sex.

"Again?" grunted Nick.

Jon let out a guttural laugh and pushed at Nick's shoulder, trying to get him to lay flat on the bed. The Jinn obliged, and in seconds they were positioning to make love.

The Accuser continued to marvel at how much he had come to enjoy intimacy with Jon, even though they could not see into each other properly. The eleventh light inside the boy clouded their link, and yet at the same time enticed Nick. It afforded him such comfort, like recalling the familiar scent one associates with a lost love.

As the prophet entered the Accuser, their minds quickly fused. But there they only found a tumultuous sea of psychic energy. A bewildering fury fed their lust as they pushed deeper and deeper into each other's mind, trying to make sense of the visions that formed in Jon's head. Out of nowhere, they both suddenly saw a female face. It ripened out of the chaos. Her soft features seemed familiar to them both, but neither could sense why that was. Jon didn't break stride, pushing Nick's head forward and pulling at his hips. The prophet sensed that stopping would disrupt the apparition, bound as it was to their rapture. They both wanted more...of the vision, and of each other. Nick's mounting eagerness drove Jon into a passionate frenzy, as the Jinn arched his back down in submission.

The visions centered.

Next they saw her running, but from what they were not sure – neither of them could make out more than her fair face and a sense of her great distress amid their own yearning. With an immense gulp of air, Jon pitched his body forward, climaxing. He roared like a beast and fell atop Nick. They lay flat there on the sheets together, gasping – not only from the physical intensity, but from the ethereal strain as well. Both of their heads were pounding as they tried to make sense of the ecstatic portent, mingled with affect and desire.

"Did you see it?" huffed Jon, clutching at Nick's hair, his muscles still taught from the intensity. "It was the woman…clothed in the sun and moon."

"Yes," grunted Nick with exhausted exhilaration. "We seem to be making some progress at least."

He broke Jon's clutches and twisted around, grabbing the boy's erection so as to prolong the heighten sensation of the climax. Their bodies shuddered together.

"Maybe more detail will reveal itself as we approach Arbil?" Nick said with an evil grin.

Jon quaked. He took Nick by the shoulders, welcoming his grip as it did extend the rise of euphoria a few added seconds. He gave two quick breaths, and smiled back at the Jinn's flirtatious play before he spoke.

"Actually, I think the clarity of visions have to do with you and I," Jon said with a quivering voice and steeped breath.

Nick suddenly got a funny feeling in his chest, he released the boy. "What makes you think that?"

"I don't know," said Jon, "it's just a hunch...Arbil is about something else. I feel strange about that place all of a sudden."

Nick stopped. He thought his heart would fall into his stomach. Rolling away from Jon, he began to understand in his heart. The boy laid his head against the Jinn's back.

"You and I seem almost to be two distinct keys to some kind of code," the boy went on, "like we are unraveling something together...bound to a single purpose, but for a different purpose."

"Strange," snorted Nick, milling over Jon's words, as a deep sense of something being out of place rattled him. "Michael said something to that effect back in the subway wreck. He alluded to what he called the Phoenix Decree...an omen from God."

The prophet leaned onto his side and propped himself up on one elbow, trying to see around Nick's back. "What's it mean?" he asked, nudging Nick with his nose.

"I am not entirely certain, but after my encounter with the dragon that attacked you...my ethereal nature was altered. I've become infused with dragon fire. My wings flare and burn with it now. I am an entirely new being it would seem...like the myth says of the phoenix."

"Is that why you won't let me play with them when we do it?" Jon's voice was lewd and playful.

"Actually, now that you mention it," Nick replied with a crude laugh, "it is one more reason not to. The truth is I think it's disrespectful of divine essence in a way."

"Bullshit," snapped Jon. "You're so fucking full of yourself!"

Jon's tone struck the Accuser like a bullet. Nick's temper suddenly flared back. "I'm full of myself? You have some nerve asking in the first place...it's simply not proper of men and Jinn."

"You sure pick convenient times to worry about decency," Jon laughed to mock Nick. "What do you care? You break all the rules anyway. Come-on...it'll be hot. You'll love it, I know."

"Why do you have to be so vulgar about our involvement at times?"

"Oh no, Satan," cracked Jon. "Don't *you* start getting all self-righteous with *me.*"

"Satan is not my name!" snarled Nick. "It bothers me when you call me that...even as a joke."

"Don't change the subject," snapped Jon.

Nick was beginning to grow alarmed. He noticed the prophet's moods seemed to shift from agitation to amusement with more and more regularity, for no reason at all. The manic displays were inexplicable at times.

The prophet suddenly grabbed the Accuser, and started to reach around his back mischievously, as if to pull at the wings whether Nick liked it or not.

"STOP!" yelled Nick, pushing him away. "You are the one who changed the subject. We both saw the woman. She must be there after all...in Arbil."

"So what," sneered Jon. "I am getting tired of this fortuneteller crap...sometimes I just want to end this mess. It aggravates me. I like what's going on between us now. Why should we mess this up?"

Nick suddenly felt very sad. For once they agreed on something other than sex. Still, they had to stay focused; there was simply too much at stake. This was about more than them alone, but the Jinn could not seem to keep Jon focused. One minute he was obsessed with Arbil, the next he seemed to want to follow his own path.

Out of nowhere Jon reached over to kiss Nick very hard, and after looked into his eyes. There was a flash of deep sincerity there for an instant, before some feral expression overcame the boy's aura.

"I can't decide now if I want to do it again or eat," the young prophet growled into Nick's face.

"You're a machine," replied the Accuser, put off by the prophet's sudden warmth. "Do you ever stop?"

"No," Jon replied, grinning.

The Accuser pulled away. Jon made a face to resist, but they got up and dressed anyway; both went to the small kitchenette. The boy went right for the refrigerator. Nick watched with morbid fascination as the young man ate, and ate, and ate. *He is insatiable*, thought the Jinn. Nick just stared at him.

After a few minutes, the weight of their mission summoned Nick back to his concern; he turned away and walked out onto the deck that overhung the water. His mind was wandering, trying to make sense of the enigma that surrounded Jon's vision. The boy scurried after with a plateful of food, sensing something had distracted the Jinn's attention.

As they reached the deck, Jon stared off for into space for a time. The blue-green of his eyes seemed to color his entire face at that moment. His expression turned soft, Nick loved it when that look fell over him. And yet, the Jinn could tell something was suddenly bothering Jon, as his mind drifted away. Nick sensed sadness.

"What's wrong?" the Accuser asked.

"I was just thinking about my past is all...I am better than all of that now. This proves it."

"Bad memories?" asked Nick, sensing vulnerability rise in Jon. "Perhaps were not so different after all?"

"Yes, bad memories. The world is a wicked, evil place, Nick. Men will be punished for it...I see that now. I am being punished too, but I will never allow *myself* to be the things my father was. I am better than that...I'm God's prophet."

At times like this, Nick found he just wanted to hold the prophet in his arms and make that brutal truth that so distressed him go away. And yet the Accuser knew he could never do that. "I've learned we never truly understand what we can become until we face our own inner demons," said Nick. "Still, what did he do...that has you hate him so?"

Jon made his bad-smell face, then looked at Nick. "He was an alcoholic. All he ever could do was see his own pain. He drown it in that bottle...neglecting me and abusing my mother. It was pathetic."

Nick remembered that night at Twilo, and Jon being twisted out of his head on ecstasy, clearly trying to escape his own heartache at the time. The Jinn said nothing, again struck by what seemed to be such deep inconsistency in the way Jon viewed the world. Nick struggled to make sense of his logic, but accepted he perhaps might never. That was the purpose of eleventh light.

"He would come home, and beat my mother," said Jon. "When he got really angry, he would drag me into the room and sit me in a chair…then he would begin to hit, and hit, and hit her. He would say I needed to see how horrible she was…that she needed to be punished."

"Was she?" asked Nick. It came out without his even thinking.

"What kind of fucking question is that?" he roared, raising one hand as if to strike Nick.

Nick twisted his head and pulled away, more in surprise than fear. *He's not so foolish as to think he can do that to me?* thought Nick. *Is he?*

Jon noticed Nick's body language. His hand shook, as if restrained by some unseen power. Then he lowered it slowly.

"My mother was a saint," said the young prophet finally. "She would do anything to take away what hurt me, Nick…she is why God chose me to see the things I do now."

Nick looked at him with a strange face, sensing that discussing such a delusion should be avoided. It was a reality for Jon not to be challenged. The Jinn stumbled through his own thoughts for a less troubling topic. Nick thought of how comfortable Jon seemed to find their intimacy. *Perhaps that is a safer subject,* he worked out in his mind.

Jon turned to glare out at the water.

"How long have you been out of the closet, Jon?" Nick nervously asked.

Jon squirmed a little for the question, but did seem thankful for the conversation's turn nonetheless. He tipped his head and looked at Nick with questioning stare.

"What do you mean out? I have always been this way...what's to be out?"

"You don't at all seem ill-at-ease with your sexuality...like most mortals are."

"Yeah, well you got that wrong...I am," grunted Jon. "I hate being this way."

Nick quickly realized his ploy had not worked; there was just no winning sometimes. He noticed the strange shifting in the boy's aura, back and forth from warmth to ire.

"That really shocks me," he said to the young man, reaching out to take him by the arm. "It's the one thing I thought you would feel most secure about...given your sight and understanding. It's so simple really."

"Why, because I don't feel like marching in the street and telling the freaking world I'm queer? I hate this sometimes...the way people gawk at you, having to hide it all the time."

"One doesn't really need to hide it anymore, Jon... and trust me God himself is fine with sexuality...He made it for a reason. It's a powerful expression of what Heaven would have us be. It's mankind that twists it into something else…like all things it can be a source of joy, or a tool of malevolence."

"Whatever," retorted the young prophet.

Jon's tone grew colder, and more melancholy. Nick could sense shame unexpectedly.

"I'd give this all up in a second, if there was some way to make it go away," the boy added finally, "but I am stuck with it too. I will always be bitter for that. Let's drop this, can we?"

Nick recognized that tone, from how his own hurt caused him to rage. Jon was fused with a sense of helplessness; this mission somehow filled that void. His heart ached for the boy. They stood hushed awhile. The sea air smelled so fresh and invigorating, but there was a chill on the wind. To Nick's surprise, Jon drew closer and nestled up to him, feeling for the Jinn's heat.

The shame and anger had vanished as abruptly as it appeared. "So," said Jon, "what is this decree about the phoenix mean?"

"It has something to do with what is called a homa-bird," Nick explained softly. "They are a form of cherubim…a special kind of Jinn with very specific responsibilities. It is said that whenever the world is in need of a new king, a true leader, God sends a homa to anoint one. When the bird lights upon the shoulder of a mortal, the man is appointed a mandate of Heaven. Apparently, the phoenix is a divine homa. It anoints the king of immortals…at least from what Michael said to me."

Jon looked confused. "How can there be a god-king, when there is only one God?" he asked, clearly struggling with what he found a strange, new mysticism.

"*We* only have one God," replied Nick. "He is the immortal that made us, but there are still other divinities with great power that have existed side by side with our nameless-god for eons, much longer than even we Jinn have been around."

"So you are this god-king homa thing then?"

"I am not sure how I could be," replied the Accuser. "Why would God have done all that He has...rebuke and torture me...if I were in some way a spirit that could legitimatize His rule over the dragons? It makes no sense. But the rest of the Jinn believe it right now... that is fine by me...let them."

"Well," replied Jon, "we are looking for the mother of God in human form. Perhaps you figure more into this than you understand. Maybe I need you to 'unravel' the knot in me so to speak...so we can find her together."

The Accuser appeared wounded at that.

"What wrong?" asked Jon.

"How cruel He is then?" said Nick. "All I ever wanted was to love and be near Him...to serve Him, and be loved by Him in return. Now I learn that I have been cursed to never know true love, for what? Some pathetic prophecy?"

The young prophet shook his head and pulled away, suddenly insulted. "I get that I am not anything like God, Nick," he replied, his face pained. "But you and I have something together now, and there seems to be some purpose in that. I can feel it. Perhaps you need to learn to see love where it is and not where you want it to be."

Jon walked off the deck toward the bedroom. The Accuser followed. Just as the boy reached the door, he stopped and turned to face Nick.

"I need some time alone," said Jon, and he slowly closed the door.

Nick paced in the hallway, not sure what to do. He stewed a moment; then approached the door in anger.

"I don't get you sometimes," he said through the wood. "Take all the time you need. I'm going out anyway…I have something I need to see about. STAY HERE! I mean it."

He waited, but there was no sound from the room.

With his anxiety tailing behind him, Nick walked outside and ripped open the ethereal realm. He lingered there a moment in vast emptiness, then opened a portal and appeared high in the sky above the Syrian capital of Damascus, a short distance from where he and Jon were staying by the sea. He surveyed the skyline, looking for the hotel where Nazim had told him to send word about the arms shipment.

I need to know more about what Nazim is up to, thought Nick, *this Arbil thing is all to convenient for my tastes.*

As Nick soared in the sky above the hotel, he turned and dropped over the roof, cloaking himself. He passed down the halls looking for the suite. When he found it, the Jinn passed inside undetected. Nazim was there; he sat at a table with two other men.

"So do you trust Bliss?" one of the men said to Nazim in Arabic. "Is it wise to involve him? You know the CIA will be all over his every move."

"No," said Nazim, "but we can't afford to pass up this chance to distract him, even if it exposes us a little bit more. Our instructions are to keep a close eye on him and his companion....to keep them occupied." He glanced at his watch. "Keeping the CIA and the Syrians focused elsewhere is to our advantage for now anyway...they are all pawns to our end."

The other man noticed him check the time. A look of delight overcame his face.

"Is it time yet?" he asked.

"They will leave the harbor in Adan within the hour...those US ships will not yet be in position... timing is critical."

"We should turn on the news," replied the excited stranger. "I can't wait to see their faces."

"Go if you want, but it won't be on for hours," said Nazim. "You are too eager."

Nick realized something major was afoot. The only port of Adan he knew of was in southern Yemen, a long way from Syria and of little interest normally to the Kurds or PKK. *This must be big,* he thought, *hitting an oil tanker maybe? What is the connection to what's going on in Iraq?*

Nazim remained at the table with a second stranger lurking near-by, as the first one went into another room of the suite.

"Bliss is dangerous," said the man to him. "I don't care what you say."

"Yes, of course he is," said Nazim, drawing a deep drag on his Turkish cigarette. "But he has worked with us well over the years, and has no allegiances to anyone but himself – we see that now. *I* don't trust him, but no one does. Whatever he is up to can only help us; I doubt he will have allies elsewhere...he obviously tricked those Sufi knights by stealing the seer from right under their noses. We had worries they we're working together from what the master told us – thankfully he betrayed them. Bliss seems to have his own intention and we can use that to our end."

"Men can be bought," said the strange man.

"Not Bliss," replied Nazim with a gloomy look, "I know him...money means nothing to the bastard... he has a plan to extort one of the two sides somehow."

"How do you know that for sure?"

"He is not human really...he is a dark Jinn, a very powerful one," Nazim replied, exhaling a cloud of smoke, "not loyal to Heaven or Hell. The queen thinks he can be swayed it seems, but the grigori fear him and want him destroyed."

Nick froze.

"Really?" laughed the strange man nervously. "Are you suggesting Nick Bliss is the exile of Heaven himself?"

A dark smile slid over Nazism's face. "You ask too many questions. That's how slaves end up gutted like goats," he hissed.

As Nazim spoke, Nick felt the man extend a coil, hid behind a snakeskin spell – just like the one used by Longinus and the grigori. *Nazim is Pythia,* thought

Nick in shock, *clearly a great and powerful thrall…how did I miss that?!*

The man's eyes narrowed and he looked at Nazim as if he might jump across the table toward him at any moment. "Are you threatening me? *I'm* a thrall to the dragons, not just to a turned Jinn, like you."

"Only trying to be helpful for one of your kind," replied Nazim grimly. "There are bigger forces at play here than ever before…you will keep out of it if you know what's good for you."

Nick had heard enough. He hastily withdrew his presence from the room and stole into the evening sky. Thoughts were racing in his head – Nazim had pegged him for Jinn, and worse yet his old partner in crime was now a servant of the serpents.

What are the dragons up to in the gulf? he wondered. *And what trap is waiting for me in Arbil?*

He tried to push all the nagging thoughts out of his mind. Perhaps when he got back to Jon, he could call Mason and they could look into the threat. Then again, Nazim had said it would only be a matter of hours before whatever they were up to would be over and done. There was no way Mason could get word back to Langley in the States, then have that relayed to the US Fleet in the gulf. The only way to discover the connection to the Pythia was to go and see for himself, but leaving Jon alone too much longer was a gamble.

Nick exploded into the ethereal realm and made his decision on a dime. As risky as going to the gulf might be, something about his affinity for Jon was changing Nick. *I am the Accuser after all,* he reminded himself as his broke through the material plane amid the churning sea of the Gulf of Aden. *Is this not my purpose, despite what the serpents think?*

The four winds of the world were growing restless in God's absence, as if they sought to break loose of some binding. Nick tried to cast out his senses, but he detected nothing...not even a hint of ethereal discord. *Something is wrong*, he thought. *The world is never this calm...first my foresight fails and now my ability to even sense malevolence fades.*

Nick remembered what Michael had said about God not being on the throne, how it left them all alone and unable to effectively draw upon His eternal power. The idea made him feel uneasy, like all of creation was emptied out.

As the tempest tossed him, Nick set thoughts of God aside and focused on the issue at hand. He descended over the sea, trying to think of the best course of action. Suddenly it occurred to him. *If I cannot find these ship, perhaps they can find me*, he thought.

The Jinn came to a stop and altered his material form so as to sense the powerful radar signals put out by vessels navigating the waterways. When he did, he felt the electronic waves strike him from all directions, throbbing and searing into his body. He made for the intensity of the first signal, as if following an electronic trail of crumbs.

Coming up on the first vessel, right away he could see it was an Egyptian freighter, and not a US ship. He pulled high above it. Then without hesitation, he banked and soared for the second wave of signals – pounding like beacons. This time he found two Korean Oil tankers making their way north. The winds were rough, but the scale of the monsters kept them from hardly registering any motion at all in the angry seas. They just hulked along slow and steady.

Frustrated, Nick turned in the direction of the last three contacts that he could sense, hammering out with their radar. These last were very powerful signals, emitting an array of pulsing waves that tore into him with staggering ferocity. The Jinn ducked low to the waterline, out of the lobe of signal, and then bounced along the bottom of the energy field just enough to sense he was moving in the right direction, easing his way toward the ships. He could tell the signals were clustered together closely in a group.

Suddenly he saw a small craft bouncing in the waves below him; it looked suspicious out there alone in the storm. The boat was built for speed, but was lumbering along as if overburdened. It was then that Nick could see the small vessel maneuvering itself into the path of three ships appearing on the horizon. He was somewhat surprised to find they were US warships, and not tankers. *Damn, the bastards are becoming brave if that is their game,* he thought. *Clearly, they are no longer sated by feeding off the weak.*

Such a brazen move could only be intended to provoke more conflict there than usual, by drawing greater forces into the gulf. The Pythians were clearly trying to insight clashes in the region in order to feed off of the dark power it created for them, nesting in the chaos like vipers.

Nick glided down close to the hampered craft and extended himself into it. His guess had been correct; he examined the high-yield of explosives stowed in her hold for a moment. The tiny boat was loaded to the brim, so much so that it struggled to stay buoyant. *I must keep them from feeding in any way I can*, he thought, *until I know what's happening in Arbil.*

He moved out and circled a few times to survey the situation, looking for an opening. It was then he noticed the name – she was called the Parthian. A wave broke over her side. Nick saw two men in the back of the craft, frantically manning pumps. He seized the opportunity. Rolling his mighty wings along the edge of the stern, the Jinn dipped low to circle around to the front. Then he gripped the craft by its nose and used all his might to hoist the bow up and out of the turning sea. He could hear the engines roaring against the strain as he pulled the small vessel higher and higher off the waterline. A torrent of waves breached the aft where the men worked, and quickly burned out the pumps. The Accuser released the small craft and it faltered in the churning white-caps, with disastrous consequence for the crew.

The men on board scrambled to her deck. Nick dropped his cloak and revealed his true form to the frightened rabble. They fell to their knees in dread when they realized the Devil had come to claim them, wailing as the boat began to slip beneath the waves. Allah did not hear their prayers that day.

The craft vanished for a second, but then unexpectedly bobbed up from the gloom. An air bubble was caught in the hold, causing the small craft to linger a bit just below the crashing waves. One of the men managed to catch on to the hull, pulling himself up onto a portion of the rigging still exposed. The Accuser descended upon him as he clung there, thrashing in the water. The vengeful Jinn used his extended wings to nimbly balance along the keel of the capsizing craft, maneuvering his foot to force the man's head under the waves. Nick would not feed on this soul, he sensed the man had not taken on Sijjin willingly – he had been seduced by the Pythia with lies. *He is still entitled to grace…if not life*, thought the Accuser. *Whoever his god really is will decide his fate.*

The mortal reached up and pulled at his boot, trying to frantically break free, but Nick just pushed down on him even harder. They both shook from the struggle. After a few seconds, the man's efforts faltered and he slipped below the crashing surf.

Remorseless, Nick took to the air.

The Accuser hovered above the debris for a time, turning to watch the US warships slip past him in the night, still unaware they had been targeted. He glared at them, knowing no mortal nation would be blameless in the days ahead. The dark power of the dragons was settling over land and sea like an ominous fog, fed by man's own iniquity.

All Nick wanted right then was to get back to Latakia, to crawl into Jon's warm arms. *Even the second coming can wait for that*, he thought.

The avenging Jinn forced open the ethereal plane and vanished into it. Unseen by him, Shemhazai drifted about the wreckage of the small craft, his mind mulling over what he had just witnessed of Nick. *It would seem that the Accuser is going to be a bigger problem than we thought,* he said to himself. *Why won't the queen let us strike at him...what power does She fear?*

Jon had another seizure. This time he realized something was seriously wrong – the convulsions left him feeling disoriented and confused. Something was growing inside of him that he could sense – something frightful and wild. Against Nick's instruction, the prophet rushed from the house and stood in the street; his breath labored from the attack. Just wanting to escape all the frightful things he saw in his mind, he wandered away in a daze.

The streets narrowed and twisted as he walked. He became lost at first, but soon saw how the streets circled around in a way he mysteriously understood. Once he had his bearings again, he was pleased to find a place that seemed to serve some recognizable fare. He was hungry and wearied by the effects of his ebbing power. He sat at a café to ordered some flatbread and cheese...it resembled pizza in his mind.

When the waiter approached to take his order, he was nervous to utter a word...until the man spoke. Unbelievably, Jon's mind reached into his, and the prophet spoke in tongues. The man understood his every word. *I am God's chosen*, he said to himself in awe as the man returned with the plate.

The prophet watched the people all around him awhile; that area of Latakia was frequented by tourists of all kinds. Jon started to feel relatively safe as his faculties returned and he realized that he could make his way without Nick. The spirit of the Accuser haunted him. At first he thought the feeling was the ache of love, but now he was not so sure. What did he know of love anyway? It seemed to him more likely he was going insane. There was something within him that was at war with itself and he began to worry that perhaps *Nick* was at cause. When the dark Jinn had slipped away into the Realm of Essences a short time before, Jon noticed an uncomfortable flash of images in his mind, which appeared to set off the seizure. There was a room of men sitting around a table, then curiously out of nothing, a vast, churning sea. The visions didn't make sense to him, especially the disturbing impression of someone being drown underfoot, which kept replying in his mind over and over. He felt as if he himself was drowning. Suspicion grew at his core, fed by apprehension and paranoia about the Devil's motives. *Damn, I can't ever get him out of my fucking head,* Jon stewed. *Why is that?*

The young prophet pushed the half eaten flatbread and cheese out in front of him. He was suddenly not as hungry as he thought. As he did, a gentile wind blew though the narrow street and over his table. He glanced to follow it over the edge of the terrace toward a small cluster of houses, straining his eyes to see as far as he could. His sight became a mixed blur.

Reaching into his new and growing power, he focused harder and the structures all suddenly came into clear focus. He watched a boy playing with a puppy on a slab of stone, the dog flipped after a small ball. *At least there is some innocence left in this world,* he thought to himself.

"You came all the way to the Middle East to eat pizza?" enquired a strange voice in English.

Jon shot his gaze up to the man standing near him, instinctively reading his aura. It was pleasant and reassuring; Jon felt deceptively safe. "I know what I like," he warily replied, "no matter where I am."

"Typically American," the man said with a laugh, extending his hand to shake. "I am Caleb Drake."

Jon reached and shook his hand. "I am Jon Godfrey."

"May I," asked Caleb, motioning to the chair next to him.

Jon rolled his shoulders to indicate he guessed it was fine. The prophet hoped right then all those angels Nick was always talking about really were watching over him. He offered Caleb a slice of the pie. The man indulged out of politeness.

"So what brings you to this beautiful place," Jon smugly asked, studying the man.

There was a calm radiance about Caleb. He seemed so very self-assured to Jon.

"I am a missionary," replied Caleb. "I am heading to Northern Iraq, to help bring the good news of Christ's return to that sad, war-torn region."

Jon got a funny feeling. *This is too convenient,* he thought. Caleb just smiled at him, seeming to know what he was thinking.

"That's a rough place for an American missionary to be headed these days," replied the prophet, remembering all the things Nick had told him. "How do you intend to get in and stay out of trouble?"

"Oh, I have faith that the true angels of the Lord will watch over *me*," Caleb replied. He stopped and glanced around.

"Angels can't always be trusted," Jon replied, lifting a glass of wine and peering over its brim. "They are not all on the right side."

Caleb leaned in close to him. The man's aura changed just long enough for Jon to sense there was a lot more to this missionary – things he should perhaps fear.

"Some of us know that better than others," replied Caleb with his cheeky smile. His tone was flip, almost sarcastic, to imply some hypocrisy in Jon's remark.

A chill went down the young prophet's spine.

"So where is he?" asked Caleb coolly, looking into his lap and brushing away the crumbs of the brittle crust.

That chill now turned at the base of Jon's back and rose up, as his stomach knotted. "Who do you mean?" he replied, his own confidence fading.

Caleb's hooded eyes floated up to meet Jon's, the prophet could feel coldness settle over him. "There is no need for pretense between us, Jon," he said. "We both know why you are here...where you are going...

and who you are with. The question is…who do you really trust?"

Jon settled back into his seat, realizing he was totally on his own. "Fine," he huffed, "let's say we both do know all that stuff. That means the only other bit of information I need to understand right now is who the hell *you* are."

Jon quickly wondered what he would do if he had to run from Drake. *Can I go in to the Realm of Essences and find my way out again,* he thought, *the way I've seen Nick do in my mind?*

"I am a Christian soldier," replied Caleb, "plain and simple. The last crusade is upon us and the Holy Land must be saved for God's people. I intend to find the new Christ before your 'friend' does. Are you even thinking straight, Jon? Do you have any idea what you are doing with him?"

Jon began to squirm in his seat. Caleb was getting to him.

"You are leading the Devil himself to the New Christ!" Caleb added with alarm.

Jon tensed.

"Don't you see the lustful spell he's woven over you has seduced your senses?"

"I love him," said Jon defensively. "He loves me."

"Does he really?" replied Caleb, half laughing. "Does he love anything but himself? Does he serve anything but his own arrogance?"

The blood ran from the prophet's face. Caleb pressed the advantage he sensed in Jon's doubt.

"I *know* you have misgivings…and you should. This path you are on is not God's way…real love is between a man and woman only. What you have been indulging is a great sin…a horrible perversion. The Devil is using that weakness to manipulate you. That is his way…that is what he does."

Caleb rose from the table and glanced off as if to be looking for something. He was actually nervous; it showed for the first time. He realized Nick would not leave this prize for long. His face turned earnest and he smiled, sadly. "I am confident God will win this war, Jon, with or without you. But I am concerned for your soul…you are on the wrong path. What's more, you risk the world of righteous men by aiding our one true enemy…Satan."

"Why do you care?" snarled Jon.

"I am the good-shepherd," replied Caleb, "who cares for all his sheep. I have a group that can help you, Jon. It is specifically intended to assist men of your affliction. We are going to Arbil too, as part of our mission…all good men are being marshaled to the cause of Christ."

The prophet grew anxious and conflicted. Jon felt so alone in the world right then. This man suddenly offered him some hope that what he had suffered could somehow be fixed. *If I really could change,* he thought, *maybe things would be different for me.*

"I will see you in Arbil," said Caleb, "perhaps by then you will reconsider washing your life in the blood of Christ and breaking the Devil's hold over you."

Jon felt very confused at that moment; that made him dangerously angry.

"Goodbye, Jon," said Caleb. "Remember, you are *God's* anointed prophet...come to Christ."

With that he gave Jon one last pleading look and turned to walk away, down the narrowing stone road. He quickly vanished into the crowd of tourists that were wandering in the dimly lit streets. But a seed of doubt quickly was sowed into the heart of the prophet. It took strong root.

Jon grew quite agitated as he sat there all alone. He curled his lips and bit at them until they bled. His body shuddered with rage; it seemed any sense of peace or joy he held had faded. The young prophet began to blame Nick for the uncertainty. In frustration, he swiped at the air, catching a fly that taunted him – it had been staking out a spot of crumb on the table. Griping the little insect between his fingers with delicate precision, he slowly pulled its wings off one by one.

Jon's face took on a sadistic grin, he was suddenly not himself.

Gabriel stood in the distance and watched in grief. The prophet was in great peril. They could do nothing but watch the growing dark spirit empty his heart, praying he would not at lose faith, not lose his way.

11

LAYLAT UL-QDAR

Ethiopia – Late December 1999

James twisted unconsciously in his sleep, pulling free of Adriano's tight grip as he spun in the sheets. He woke himself finally, nearly falling off the bed. The young seer had been dreaming again, his nightmares were becoming intolerable. As he pivoted his feet off the bed, he sat up and stared into the gloom of the shabby hotel room he and Adriano shared. A dull ache filled him. *God, I'm home sick,* he thought.

The African swelter seemed to broil off the land even at night. The window on the far right of the room was open, only occasionally did a gust of wind drift in to intrude upon the heat's domain.

Half asleep yet, Adriano felt a lessening of the warmth as James pulled away. The knight stirred and opened his eyes. He was still jetlagged from the flight, his body screamed for him to sleep more. The big man grasped at his pillow and almost nodded off again before he noticed James sitting at the edge of the bed. "Is something wrong?" he asked, easing his frame closer to the young seer's body, his powerful shoulder coming to rest snuggly up against the young man's back.

James was filled with a renewed sense of promise the moment they touched.

The knight gently reached over and caressed his young partner in the darkness, encouraging him to open up. He ran his fingers along the lean ridge of James' shoulders, letting the tips linger there a moment, then dropped them until they touched the t-shaped dimples at the narrowing of the boy's waist. Adriano loved that spot, it rouse desire in him.

The wind burst into the room all of a sudden. It felt like a desert spirit slipping in through the window.

"Just bad dreams again," replied James finally. He leaned back and relished the feel of the calluses on the knight's hand. Still, the boy shook, he was uneasy. "Do you really love me, Adriano?"

"What kind of question is that?"

"I'm afraid," James answered. "I don't grasp so much of what is going on...I certainly don't know if I understand falling in love right now."

"I can understand that I guess," replied Adriano. "We're all afraid and a little lost. Really, James, I don't know if I understand love all that well either in the wake of this trial...but I will tell you what is in my heart."

James felt comforted by the genuineness in his companion's reply. "Fair enough," he whispered.

Adriano lowered his face to kiss the top of James' head. He let his nose linger there a moment, thinking how much he enjoyed the smell of the young man's hair.

"James, I wanted you from the moment I saw you. That night when we met for dinner to discuss confronting the Pythia at Twilo, I was instantly enamored with you. Then later, when you asked me up to the apartment...I thought my breath would stop."

James chuckled and seized Adriano tightly. "You big softy," he said, teasing the big man.

"When I learned about your relationship with Iblis and what he meant to you, my heart sunk. I knew from that first night that the two of you shared something special. I almost didn't pursue you, because I feared I could never compete with him, yet something inside me wouldn't allow me to walk away. I wanted you badly, despite my fear."

"That's the most amazing thing anyone has ever said to me," replied James. The young seer raised his mouth to meet the big man's and they kissed.

As Adriano rolled on top of James, the seer's tender frame seemed to give way under his weight. The boy pulled his legs free of the knight's mass, and wrapped them snuggly up around the back of his thighs. Then the big man shifted his center of gravity and pushed back one of James' legs, entering slowly. The boy gripped at his shoulders with a hand, and guided Adriano's lower back with the other.

"I love you too," said James, biting his lower lip to distract himself from the initial penetration, gripping at the bed suddenly as the big man struck rhythm.

In the passion that followed, the knight clung to James. Every time they made love that way, James' growing power seemed more and more exposed to him. The Rafiq soldier was uneasy at first with the deep intimacy it accorded him with spiritual forces beyond his understanding. Nafees had told Adriano that it was a rare gift, and that he should be honored for the chance to experience love in that way.

James had great ability, but he was not always in control of it the way he wanted to be. The boy was careful with what he let the big man see inside of him. Their sharing was at times awkward, like two teenage lovers clumsily fumbling with themselves trying to figure out what to do for the first time. But Adriano sometimes sensed the intensity of the young seer's visions anyway. He saw one right then that made him very uneasy about where they were heading, and about what they would have to endure together. At times he felt lost, clinging only to the connection he had with James, and his faith in the path God had placed them on.

In this new apparition, the Queen of Heaven called to the seer from the netherworld. The boy followed her voice down; Adriano's spirit did as well. It was only a reflection in the mind's eye the big man realized, but it seemed so vivid and real. James went to Astarte obediently and there in the darkness, she held him in her arms like a mother would a child. Adriano was in awe of her presence.

Then in the distance, there was a terrible roar. The malevolent Leviathan could be heard bellowing. She quickly hid him under the hem of her skirt as the monster came closer. The goddess comforted James, telling him not to fear it. So he stilled his soul, clinging to the legs of the queen as the great serpent came to torment her.

"Your king is about mischief from high upon his mountain," said the Leviathan to the queen.

"He is always about your end, Abaddon," she replied, "but sadly I have no knowing of Him in the world of the sun and moon, or of mortal men. So, I am indeed grateful for your kind news of Him."

"You lie, you contemptuous creature," hissed the beast.

She simply smiled back at him, taunting his rage.

Little by little, he brought his hideous form closer to her. James could smell his fetid stench, like the rotting odor of foul water. "Would it pain you to know, Queen of Heaven, that your king has left his throne?"

"*You* lie now, unclean spirit. The king of all gods only ever left the throne unattended once, and he vowed to all of creation never to leave it that way again!"

"Truer words could not be spoken," replied the Leviathan. "The throne itself is still attended by the Lamb as God, that whelp we should have consumed when we had the chance."

"Joshu the Son of God!" she replied. "So He is on the throne still!"

"Yes, but not as the nameless-one in fullness...His son alone has not the strength to bind back all the dragons. The full trinity of his power is required, the father, son, and spirit of logos."

"If that be true, then why are you still here plaguing me with your stench, and not assaulting the walls of Eden?"

The Leviathan was silent, she was clever. *Now what to say and not to say to her?* the dragon wondered.

James could feel the beast's breath. Something deep inside told him he must destroy this monster at any cost.

"Tiamat now gathers Her forces," replied the dragon, "but She is not yet ready to descend into the mortal realm in Her true, unbound form until She knows where the nameless-god will make Himself flesh again. She does however already move about men, concealed as we speak. Your king can no longer protect the mortal veil with what He stole from us. We will find the tablets soon."

"The great mother, Kishar, will not allow it!" said the Queen of Heaven. "Tiamat will never succeed as long as the spirit of the mother hides destiny for Him within her womb."

"The earth-mother will be the first thing Tiamat reclaims once He is gone…but first there will be war, brutal and cruel. The Jinn are already gathering in Heaven, and Joshu has broken the seals of His grand design to counter the ensuing darkness. Soon we will strike at Eden to prevent them from doing whatever He has planned."

The Queen of Heaven grinned at the dragon, playing with the hem of her dress, taunting him. She wanted James to hear what the monster was saying; he must know these things to lead the righteous Son's of Light in the world.

"It is a trap," she said finally. "The nameless-god makes safe for you the material plane – to draw you to

Him. Your arrogance will be your undoing, he will kill you like he did the others long ago."

"We know this much of Him, witch! That is why I am here bothering with you in any case. What is this trap He thinks to lay for Tiamat?"

"How would I know?" the queen snarled at the dragon.

Her smile deepened.

"You have eyes within the mortal realm," said the serpent. "We know your treachery. We will make your knights suffer if you do not tell us His intention."

She laughed.

"My soldiers are bound to the throne of the King of Heaven. They will not be turned or threatened... they will die to the last man for their faith. As for the trap, I am as bewildered as you truthfully, but I do love a mystery," she said to tease him. "It would be no fun if any knew the means of your end fully but Him."

The queen and the dragon stared a long time into the each other's eyes, there was little more either could do to rattle the other's sensibilities. Then the dragon turned to leave.

"It matters little," he growled. "We will devour the son of the nameless-god the instant the demigod arrives into the world, and then tumble the walls of Eden."

"Then what are you waiting for? You will find nothing here to help you!"

The Leviathan wailed in rage and crashed about the hall, toppling everything it saw as it stormed away. When it was gone, she reached for James.

He was trembling.

"Go now," she said to him. "If Joshu has broken the seals upon God's plans, you will be needed...but be wary for now. The angels will blow the trumpets soon, turning man's own sin upon him as the darkness of chaos is drawn over the eyes of God. Mortals have fed the beasts with iniquity and hubris –the coming darkness will be all the deeper for it. All those who have consorted with the dragons will be rebuked and burned before the light can ascend from the dark rift of Tiamat. You must protect the faithful as long as you can...those who honor God's true heart in desire. "

She kissed him. James was filled with the grace of courage.

"I will come to you as I can," she added, "in your dreams, and tell you what you should do as the Lamb commands the trumpets. You must then follow where I send you. I know not the plan of the nameless-god, his full designs are truly hidden from us all, but I trust in Him and in His will. You must trust in love as well, James...in your knight. He is sent to you with purpose. Take the warrior-priests that follow you and lead them to God's victory."

James was honored. He knelt before the queen to accept her command and commission.

"Good," she said to him. "Return to your companion and kiss him tonight for your queen... love is our only salvation, my princely priest. That is the nameless-one's ture purpose for us."

With those words the vision dissipated into the wajd made between the prophet and his sentinel as they made love. They kissed when finished, and James quickly fell into a deep slumber.

It was the knight's turn to watch his lover sleep in the dark, restless and unsettled.

∻

The next morning, James went to the lobby of the hotel. He watched the flurry of activity around the compound as the Rafiq gathered, making ready to disembark. A stretch of six black Hummers and four large cargo transports lined up at the gated entrance. James was still not sure why they were so far from Israel.

Nafees was very guarded about what he understood of their journey, but explained they would move north a day from there, to a monastery he knew. In its dark halls they would meet with more needed allies, rest, and gather spiritual strength for what lay ahead of them in the Holy Land.

The men climbed into the caravan's vehicles one by one – the departure was unceremonious. The first few miles of road were smooth and well kept, but shortly after they left the populated areas around the resort town, the path turned wild. James glanced at Nafees. He was seated next to him in some sort of trance, the boy marveled at his focus. Then he looked up at Adriano in the driver's seat, who was firmly gripping at the steering wheel of the ORV as he drove. He too looked intent in his concentration, even as his bulk was being pitched to and fro by the uneven grade of the roadway.

Seated next to his companion was the famous DJ, Jason Velenza – the powerful knight from Twilo, who James knew held the sect together as much as Nafees. He had come with a group of other Rafiq the night before, all said to be the most powerful cleric-warriors, weavers of sema. It was the first time James had ever spent any real time alone with him. He was a tall and handsome man, looking much younger than the seer knew him to be. The knight turned to Nafees now and then, speaking with a heavy Italian accent, frequently smiling at James as if he knew something the seer did not.

Jason seemed to have an unusually powerful bond with Nafees, so intense that James wondered from their feel if they were in fact companions. It was hard to tell much about the immortal cleric sometimes, but ever since the goddess had begun calling to the boy in dreams, James' sense of emotional states in others became heightened – especially that of affinity.

They traveled for hours, not saying anything as the ORVs crawled over the broken, arid landscape. James grew bored. His attention zeroed in on any inane detail around him to distract his wandering mind. He noticed the radio-piece dangling from Adriano's ear. The young seer thought it looked awkward hanging along with the large sterling-earring he wore. The vehicles in the caravan were all closely linked in the material plane through the shortwave devices, but somehow James sensed that Nafees was using more than radios to monitor things.

The big man glanced back and caught James starring at him. He smiled with guile. It made James shiver, goose bumps rose on the young seer's arms. *How could it be that I would fall for someone so hard, so fast?* he wondered. *It's almost corny... a knight sweeping me off my feet.*

Out of the corner of his eye, he glanced to Nafees. The cleric was no longer meditating; he was glaring right into James' enchanted grin, his look severe.

"Drama queen," said the cleric.

James narrowed his eyes for a questioning second, then became outwardly annoyed. "Stop reading my thoughts," he snapped. "It's impolite."

"You have to learn to hide them better than you do. When we reach the monastery, we will work on teaching you that skill."

"You're the drama queen," muttered the seer, "with this entire production." Then he cast he eyes out over the dry African backdrop with feigned indifference. They traveled on for hours without exchanging a single word after that.

As the day grew long, the ORV ahead of them suddenly lurched sideways. Dust and gravel rose around it, beating at the side of the truck. Adriano turned hard on the wheel and their Hummer came to an abrupt stop. The young seer felt relieved to not be moving.

"We need to stop," said Jason without turning back. "The bridge is out a mile ahead. They are scouting for a shallow crossing, but we're not far from the monastery at this point anyway. We might just as well follow the river."

Nafees nodded, tilting his head forward. His gaze took on a dark, menacing look for a moment. The cleric reached forward to Jason, touching his shoulder. The knight glanced back with affection. James sensed the feeling between them. *There is something there*, he thought, *distant, but now plain to see.*

Jason's eyes shifted to James, his look was calm and collected. There was great warmth to his face that told the seer he was right about their closeness.

"Come with me to the lead vehicle, Jason," said Nafees. "I want to speak with the other drivers. Let's leave the new prophet and his knight to themselves for a time."

Nafees swung open his door and pulled his taut frame from the truck. Jason did the same. Then they slowly sauntered forward. All the while James followed them with his eyes.

"You O.K?" asked the big man, shaking James' focus.

"Yeah," replied James with a frown. "Don't worry about me." His tone was aloof, but not from annoyance…his mind was simple someplace else.

Adriano looked at him angrily, misinterpreting his tone. "How long is it going to take you to stop treating me like a doorman?" asked the big man with a sense of exasperation.

James' face fell. He had not expected that kind of response. A swarm of butterflies rose in his stomach. James felt guilty, he stopped and focused on the big man's feelings, looking inside of him, following the agitation to its source. Then he froze in his seat as a realization overcame him from what he saw.

The boy suddenly detected something he had not noticed before, yet it had been there from the very beginning he knew. In all the time it had taken to come from New York, he had simply accepted what he sensed in Adriano, never questioning it. It was only in that moment – when Adriano questioned *his* intention – that his focus changed and became clearer. He was filled with a quick rage; not at Adriano, but at Nafees.

James reached up and touched the big man on the arm. His expression was severe. "Do you trust me, Adriano?"

Adriano was even more annoyed by that comment. "You know I do," said the knight with a huff.

"Then take my hand. I want to show you something.... something I honestly never saw until now."

Adriano looked around a moment, as if uneasy, then answered by doing as he was asked.

"Now close your eyes and just have faith in us... open your soul to me."

Adriano did so without thinking, nodding his head with a kind of euphoric expectation. It took only a second for the young seer to enter the big man. James had only ever intentionally attempted this sort of thing once before – with Nick – but that had been out of pure urgency.

Adriano surrendered to the boy as James nudged inside his essence, submitting his full heart. The knight's will was not nearly as potent as James had expected, after engaging Nick's strong essence.

The seer actually felt a little uncomfortable. James enjoyed the dynamic of their love as it was and did not want to upset it, but this was necessary. He needed Adriano to see.

The Rafiq knight sat in awe of his power. The big man nearly crawled over the seat as the sensation overtook him, but James held him back. *Wait,* the boy inserted into the knight's mind, *just feel me inside you.* Adriano relaxed and gave into the feeling. *There... right there... see that... it's us... you and me together as one.*

The knight's body seemed to loosen and relax even more. What James was showing him proved beyond a shadow of a doubt that there was more to their relationship than just his seeing Adriano as some sentry, or servant. James in turn saw in him the great torrent of affection that lay at the man's very center... it was real and true. For the rest of their lives, neither man would ever doubt the other's sincerity and that they were destine to love.

But then James gradually uncovered something there between them that neither had noticed before. Once exposed, the two instantly saw it for what it was... an obsession enchantment. Adriano's eyes flew open as they glared at each other. A tense sense of suspicion rose in them both as they sensed the love charm.

"Nafees did this?" asked Adriano in shock.

James narrowed his eyes a second. "Don't look so surprised. He has been doing this to us from the very beginning. We should have suspected." James' face grew stern. "Nafees knew I would be putty in *your* hands, but he did not anticipate our mutual love... so to be sure he put this enchantment to bind and control us both."

"Take it out!" Adriano demanded.

"Why should I?" replied James. "You knew what he was up to...I see that."

"Yes, I suspected he wants you to love me and to trust me. He wants us to be close and he wants to use that trust for the Rafiq. I did know that all along, but you see what is real...you see in my soul that truly I love you. As God is my witness, I did not know about this enchantment. I would have never consented to a spell like this, James...to fool you in any way."

James sat for a brief span of seconds, milling over this turn of events in his head. He could sense the raw emotions churned up in Adriano.

"I know...I believe you," the seer said finally.

"Then take it out!" said Adriano. "I don't want there to ever be doubt that I am yours until my last breath."

James hesitated. "We both know that now, Adriano," he said. "But Nafees clearly does not trust *us* fully. If I disturb his spell, he will know that we have discovered it and he may try some other way to insure that he gets what he wants. It's best to leave it for now, neither of us doubts the other's intention as of this moment and someday we might need to use it for our own purpose."

Adriano made an uncertain face.

"It's quite intricate," added James, stopping to admire the immortal cleric's handiwork.

The knight finally nodded in assent, amazed at how powerful James felt to him at that moment. "You are my prophet," he said proudly, asserting his fidelity to James.

"And you are my knight," answered the boy. "We will never be manipulated in this way again. I don't know what Nafees is after with this spell. It could simply be a kind of insurance policy for him, but I see that I can re-orient it to our end. You and I will not face one another with this thing between us, to be prodded like pets performing tricks. We must turn outward away from it…here in this way."

James maneuvered inside of the knight's mind, twisting his essence like clay. "We will face the world back-to-back, with this thing between, but at the same time behind us. We will love each other and we will know it for its reality…truest of trusts."

"Agreed," said Adriano, then he grabbed James with both his hands, kissing him with such force that James was quickly aroused. The big man climbed over the seat.

When Jason and Nafees came back to the Hummer, after their brief discussion with the other men driving the ORVs, the cleric opened the rear door to find the young prophet and his knight huddled together in the back seat. James was nestled close to Adriano, whispering into his ear. He studied them closely, all his wards were in place and so was his charm. Still, somehow the two men appeared different to him…

something had changed. It had nothing to do with his magic as far as he could tell, but oddly their orientation toward each other seemed suddenly realigned.

Nafees believed that if he could hold the mechanism of their intimacy in place with a charm, he could wield the prophet's power more fully. They were headed into uncertain territory, a place where other powerful agents of destiny held sway. He felt the need to be certain he was in control of the Rafiq, as well as their seer. As Jason had reminded him at Twilo, he was risking much.

The cleric then noted something else about James, a new and powerful enchantment that was not there before he left them alone. It was a ward around his mind, the very kind of mediation he had instructed the seer to work on earlier, to protect his thoughts.

"I see the two of you waste no time," he said. "But the truck does not smell of sex, so I assume you did not consummate your oaths yet again. I swear you are like rabbits rolling about Eden."

The two men glanced at each other and smiled. Their plan was working. He would not get to them. "Fear not Pir," said Adriano, using Nafees' formal title as Sufi master. "The prophet and his knight grow closer to one another without the need for ziña… alone."

"Not that we don't enjoy the fruits of the flesh as it were," James chimed in with a flip tone. He knew he had to feed Nafees' confidence in order to distract him, keep him focused on anything but his new ward. He was not yet sure of his power.

"Very well then, I can see we are all on our way to realizing the will of Allah," he said suspiciously.

One of the things that baffled Nafees most right then was their apparent resistance to strife. He had taken advantage of the charm placed between them weeks earlier to leave a small amount of enmity there with them. He was worried about what James could expose the knight to without his supervision. Now the seer's rather inopportune mastery of wards prevented Nafees from seeing into what *both* of them were up to. Not only was James casting a shield around his own mind, he encircled Adriano with one as well.

All of this made the cleric a little wary. He motioned for Adriano to move into the driver's seat. The big man gave James one more little nudge with his nose, to reassure the young seer, and then slid out of the back.

Nafees climbed in the Hummer.

"We are close to the monastery now anyway," he said. "Our mission to save the holy city begins there with the monks of Aksum."

James looked at Adriano in the rear-view mirror, their eyes locked. *I will be the judge of that,* he thought into the big man's mind with defiance.

Nafees never blinked.

One hour later, the caravan arrived at an ancient Aksumite monastery. It was late in the afternoon; the sun was high and still potent. James was not sure if he had ever felt heat so intense. They had clearly been expected by the monks, but there was little fanfare as the men unloaded the trucks.

James was in awe of the elaborate structure, carved out of volcanic rock, looking more like it was designed for a siege than for worship. Over hanging it were curved cliff walls, with cascading waterfalls and mats of green vine covering its crags. It all looked magical to him.

The knights made quick work of the luggage to escape the harshness of temperature, vanishing into the cool, dark halls of the fortress-like monastery. Introductions were unceremonious. Nafees presented James to the head of the monastery. "This is Father Aaron of Aksum," he said formally to the boy.

The Coptic monk grinned at James. The young seer sensed his raw strength, and shivered for some reason. The man looked to be in his mid-thirties, but the white hair of his short, stubbly beard made him look distinguished beyond that age. The monk studied James with inquisitive eyes, giving him a nod and a short grunt as greeting.

Keeping to tradition, the men all took off their shoes as they entered the monastery. Adriano carried the few bags they had with them down to the cell of a room they would be sharing, their eyes taking in the amazing frescos adorning the ceilings as they walked. When they arrived in their room, there were only two straw-cots. They pushed them together, then threw plush linen over them, and fell on top. The big man bounced to test the comfort as he embraced the prophet.

"Right now what I would do to have a shower with you, but I think we should do prayers," said Adriano, nudging his nose in close to the young prophet's ear.

James squeezed Adriano tightly, rubbing the high end of his check across the knight's rough beard. He loved the feel of the Adriano's whiskers against his own skin.

"I suppose you're right," James said. "It sure seems like a quiet enough place…out of the way."

"I'd not assume things will be dull…we're here for a reason," said the knight. Adriano's tone was dead serious.

"I realize that, but this doesn't look like a group of guys that plan to go clubbing in town tonight."

Adriano laughed nervously and rolled free of James, the cot groaning as he moved. The big man leaned over to his pack and pulled a small necklace from a side compartment. It had an ornate metal cross, fixed to a line of jade-colored beads.

"I've never seen those beads before, they are beautiful," said James.

The knight glanced down at them and seemed to sigh. Reaching, he held out the string for James to inspect. The young seer took them into his fingers with care, and admired the intricate crafting of stone – each fashioned in to a perfect oval droplet.

"They were a gift from the man who invited me to join the order…he was my first teacher and companion." Adriano watched for a reaction from James, but none registered. "They are tasbih prayer beads, but this one is made to work as a rosary as well as to perform meditations for glorifying Allah. It is a symbol meant to reflect the belief that you do not have to be Muslim to be Sufi...we are all people of the book."

The seer studied the fine carved beads. "How did he die?" James asked softly.

"What makes you think he died?"

James smiled sadly and reached over to take Adriano by the hand. "I felt it. I will show you how to sense things like this later. If you don't want to talk about him now...I will understand."

"It's not that, James. I am just surprised by the depth of your insights." He made a funny face. "There'll be no keeping secrets from you."

"I think that's the best way to love," replied James.

The big man's nimble fingers rolled the beads about his palm. They moved effortlessly there, as if he'd been praying with them a lifetime.

"We were careless," he said finally. "The compounds we ingest to reach wajd are crude and sometimes dangerous, but the mortal veil is just so difficult to transcend without their help." Adriano leaned back a little, to be closer to James. It was hard for him to talk about it. "The two of us had been at party on the beach back home...it was called Festival. For we Christian Rafiq, that time of year is to commemorate Serge and Bacchus...two Roman soldiers who were lovers and early disciples of the gospels of Joshu. For the others there that weekend, I suppose it was just another party."

James' face lit up, liking the idea of male-paired saints. It was a romantic notion. "You will have to tell me more about your saints sometime," said the young seer sweetly, "but first tell me about your former companion. What was his name?"

"Robert," replied Adriano. "I met him when I was in college at NYU. I was totally enamored with him from the first night we met, in the city at a club called Limelight."

"The one in the old church?" asked James.

"Yeah," replied Adriano with a sad face. "It was a space the Christian Rafiq could stand apart, away from Twilo. Robert loved the place. He was everything to me then."

"And how did he die?"

"We were on Fire Island with a group of other Rafiq; the order maintains a large house on the Grove side. We generally keep to ourselves during Festival... except for the one, big party on the beach every year. We prayed that evening, took private rites together, and then we went with the others to the party. Man, did we dance...until the sun rose!"

There was a touch of nostalgia in his voice. James smiled at him. The ritual of dance was central to their very being as Rafiq.

"Robert used something called GHB...gamma-hydoxy-butyric acid. It's a popular drug, even now, that heightens the effect of wajd. It was legal then, but was very intoxicating in its pure form, easy to misjudge the correct dose. It could be deadly if misused."

"I know," said James. "I've seen what it can do."

"Robert was fond of it...too fond of it I guess. Anyway, after we had come back from dancing, he took some more of it when I was not paying attention. I went to lie down and try to sleep. Robert went to the beach apparently...he enjoyed the feel of water on his skin in the wake of wajd."

Adriano paused a second, then looked off into another direction. His aura took on guilt. His expression broke James' heart.

"We found his shoes and shirt at the water's edge the next day," Adriano's voice cracked. "I was devastated...from that moment on the *order* was the only important thing in my life."

James could feel his companion's grief. "Come here, let me show you something." he said, grabbing a pillow and the linen cover.

Adriano pitched his weight from side to side on the cot; then gave himself to James. Up to that point the young seer had not allowed himself to conjoin fully with Adriano, even in the truck when they discovered the charm set by Nafees. But he sensed now was as good a time as any to try and show the knight its full power.

"Here," said James, "put your back against the pillow...so the corner of the wall is holding you up."

Adriano followed his instructions, at first a little confused by the change in conversation. James wedged his back against the big man's chest. They sat upright enfolding one another. The seer took the knight's hands in his own and spoke to him softly.

"Each time I take a breath, see if you can synchronize your breathing with mine."

They began together. It only took a few seconds to match each other's rhythm.

"Now close your eyes and relax, clear your mind. Don't let it rest on any one idea. Just breathe, and if a thought enters your head, simply sweep it out. Be present only to the rise and fall of our chests."

"Ah, like the breath prayer we do," said Adriano.

"Yes, we start that way. Just match my rhythm…I'll do the rest."

Adriano nodded and relaxed. James began to chant under his breath. The sound was like a very low chord, a frequency that was barely audible. An amazing feeling quickly overtook the knight. He began to feel sound. It seemed strange. The reverberations that James made were literally resonating into his physical form. Adriano could sense space and time alter around him, it felt astonishingly like he had begun to roll on ecstasy.

"Now hold on to me," said James. The seer gripped him and pulled both their essences into a state of total ethereal bliss.

The first thing that struck the knight was the vertigo. Time stopped, and space seemed to magnify. It was as if he could suddenly see aspects and details that had always been there, but he had never noticed before. The room was there, but it was not there. It became all the cosmos. He could clearly hear James now, chanting so fluidly his voice was like a symphony. Everything around them was answering his song.

Adriano gripped James even more tightly and the young prophet used that embrace to initiate full communion, conjoining with the knight. The seer spoke into his companion's mind. *"Babe, you need to come to me now...all you have to do is reach past yourself. It will seem awkward at first, but once you begin to move toward me, it will feel natural."*

James felt an eagerness rising in the knight, as he began to reach out for the prophet. Just as James had said, he moved through essence without effort. Adriano began to cry. He had crossed into pure wajd, unaided by any drug or dance. He even passed the normal point at which men were turned away from the eternal when using ritual drugs.

The next startling realization for him was that this was actually all inside of James somehow. It was all part of his companion's soul. Adriano followed the path of being away from his own contained identity and into James, then astonishingly to none other than the Accuser himself. He shuddered, startled to realize he was inside of Nick there as well.

Much of what the Accuser had known was accessible to James. Strangely, it did not make him feel jealousy or envy. There was something deeply comforting about the feel of the Jinn to Adriano. There too were the other spirits that had forced their way into James, hideous things that the seer had somehow acclimated into his spirit. Their dark power surged there like a raging sea, but James held it in check. In wonder, the knight felt another great presence that he knew must be Allah – infinite and awesome –knowing every man's heart and seeing beyond all the margins of being. They remained conjoined as long as James could maintain the meditation, but he grew uneasy suddenly. *"Enough,"* said the boy into the link. *"We must return to the moral veil."* He began to pull back the power. *"Someday we will be here together, for all time...I know it,"* James reassured Adriano.

"I love you, James," the knight returned, *"now and forever."*

"We must leave...this will seem harsh. Once you have basked in eternal light...your mortal shell will never again feel complete...but we cannot stay here like this."

With that, Adriano felt as if he had suddenly been pitched from a warm shower into a cooling bath. The knight's body convulsed. He held on to James tightly as his consciousness returned to mortal sensibility. Adriano's inhalation became quick and labored. His eyes were full of tears...tears of ripe joy.

"Just relax a bit...we will do it again, and again," said James, trying to calm his companion. The young seer knew that nothing he said would console Adriano. The soul painfully hungers for rapture in God; Adriano would always long for it now.

"Why, James, why do we bother with mortal life?" Adriano sobbed.

"That is the mystery...that is the plan we don't see and cannot understand. I don't know why, I'm still just learning to see. All I know is we have purpose here, each and every one of us. Don't be bitter or sorrowful, that will waste the gift we are given. You see now why Nick is what he is? Why he so desperately seeks relief from the pain of exile?"

"I have a new patron saint in *you*, James," said the knight lovingly.

The knights rested a few hours in the monastery's deep calm, then in the evening went to dinner in a dimly lit hall. Adriano and James sat down on either side of Nafees. The monks were gracious, yet humble hosts – there was little conversation.

Nafees carefully eyed first James, then Adriano – he appeared distressed about something suddenly. James paid him little mind, but it was harder for Adriano to avoid his scolding, sidelong glances. As Nafees finished his meal, he seemed anxious. The cleric leaned toward Adriano and looked into his eyes again, searching for something. The knight squirmed a little, unsure of the consideration. Then Nafees threw his cloth napkin onto his plate and turned toward James. His look was frightful.

"Will you walk with me in the garden, my prophet... by the light of the goddess-moon?" Nefees asked James.

"Of course, Pir," the boy replied with formality.

The cleric rose to his feet and leaned toward the knight again, near to his ear. "You are playing with fire...immortal fire," he said to the big man. "Be mindful of your vows to the order as well as to your companion. James has a sacred charge...*that* must be your first concern...not your own, selfish need for emotional escape."

Adriano's eyes grew large and nervous. He felt a little torn.

Sitting across from the big man, on the other side of the room, Aaron smiled to himself, appearing amused at them all. Nafees pulled his chair away and walked out into the garden. James turned to shoot Adriano a perplexed look. He rolled his eyes; then bounced on his heels to follow after the cleric.

The moon was high in the night sky. Nafees waited until they were a good way from the hall before turning to face the seer.

"Your untutored playing with ethereal power is becoming dangerous," he scolded James. "If mortals were meant to tamper with the ethereal realm that way...you would all be able to do it." His tone turned biting. "Believe it or not, I am actually fond of that knight...quite fond of him. I knew I was setting him in harm's way when I sanctioned his pursuit of you as companion, but I trusted in you when I did, James. Please don't make me regret that decision."

James studied Nafees for a second, unsure of him. He held back the urge to use his own power to probe at the cleric. His instincts told him the immortal was genuine, but there was something else there as well, buried in the gaze of the mysterious spirit.

The cleric just brooded. He was waiting for a reply.

James turned and looked him in the eyes. "Nafees, why are we here?"

"Don't change the subject!"

"I am not changing the subject, Pir," James said with a hint of sarcasm. "We're here precisely because of what you infer of as playing games. I realized some time ago there was a more direct route to the Holy Land."

James drilled his eyes into the cleric. Nefees felt a surge.

"I sense what we approach," said the young seer. "What is your *game* in bringing us to this place?"

"What might you think you know," the cleric replied, "that you see this as some reckless exploit of *mine?*"

"We are close to the Tablets of Destiny," said James. "I can feel them. They call to my essence....Why?"

Nefees' expression became a mixture of surprise and agitation. The prophet's senses were deep and precise indeed, for him to sense the source of fate that way. The cleric held his tongue a moment, moving to sit on the lip of the wall extending around the garden. He looked up at the moon and drew a deep breath; the light glistened about his lovely face.

"They are located a few miles downriver," he said finally, "in a vault that runs directly under a small Coptic church dedicated to a manifestation of the Queen of Heaven as Holy Mother. These monks here are related to the Rafiq. We share a common past. They have remained close to protect the Holiest of Holies – the Ark of the Covenant in which the tablets are housed."

"So why bring me here? I can't do anything with them. They are little more than a useless relic to me," replied James.

Nafees' face turned very grim. "We're taking them with us." The night became still as he spoke, all of creation had stopped to listen. Even the crickets seemed to fall silent.

"What?"

"We are taking them with us to Israel."

"Are you insane? We can't go near them," replied the seer. "If any one of us touches them, we're dead. I understand that much."

"Not you," said Nafees in a low tone. "You must do this."

James was stunned. "What are you talking about?" his breath seeming to fade.

"I don't believe that you will die if you touch them. In fact I think it is your purpose to do so…you are the prophet promised to reunite the Amo – God's people – not the seer with Nick."

James wanted to laugh out loud, but he dared not. There was a lot he didn't yet understand about the nature of the cosmos, and knew that Nafees was himself capable of sensing in ways that were not readily perceptible to him. The young's prophet's mind raced.

"You don't quite get it, do you?" asked Nafees.

James wondered if this was just another ploy for control, to get him to reveal more, or if the cleric did know something that was hidden from him. The boy shivered with self doubt.

"James, you're not the only one who lives with a veil, each and every one of us do," explained Nafees. "The nameless-god is more than merely another immortal. He is immortality itself. He is a great mystery to each of us precisely because none of us can see beyond the shroud of creation that emanates from Him. Not even the dragons possess the ability to look upon the full glory of Allah's eleven aspects, which is why they fear Him so. Man's view is the most limited…you must see the purpose in that now."

"What are you driving at, Nafees?" asked James. "And what does this have to do with those old hunks of fire and brimstone?"

"I don't truly know. That is the enigma…but in the same way you sense them, all of us who can sense the ethereal can feel them in varying degrees. That is why they appear to men as nothing more than stone, and yet each of us who has extended vision intuits that they are more."

James reflected a second. At some level he understood. In fact most of ethereal existence he could only as yet deduce. The young prophet was not completely sure how he understood – he just did. It was all simply there in his mind, as if poured and left to slosh around aimlessly. What he did know was that all of existence was controlled by a kind of resonance, a vibration that was not really noise, but more of an inner trembling that radiated out from the center of all things. The more you could feel of that resonance, the more things you could manipulate both in and across the frequencies of being. That was how James had learned to work the ethereal power. "The tablets tremble with unknown power within the source of God himself," replied James finally, thinking out loud. "They bind creation in some way."

"They bind fate actually, the one unknown dimension beyond all things but for Him…that is eleventh light," replied Nafees. "Allah alone has eleven eyes to see all things…the rest of us are simply stewards of His intention."

"So what makes you think I can touch them? And even if I can, that I should take them?" James asked.

"I told you once that long ago I served Astarte at the temple of the nameless-god in Jerusalem, before the power hungry king and warriors drove us into exile for our veneration of conjoining-rites. We were all one group then, called the Asirim, divided into two basic casts. The Rafiq, as the priestly order, were called the Rei'a, and the warrior cast called the Gadol. The high priest and head of the Gadol is still Hilkiah. Like both Aaron and I…he is elohim."

James sat enthralled, wondering what it had been like for Nafees to live all those years ago, changing theologically with time, but still staying committed to the core of his faith in the goddess. Now after all that time, it seemed the wheels of fate were in motion. James guessed that anticipation must be nearly boiling over within the cleric's ancient spirit. He reached across and touched Nafees on the shoulder, wanting him to know he was still committed to the queen as well.

"Right before our order went into exile within the Persian court of Babylon, the warrior cast themselves divided into two distinct factions over the legitimate possession of the tablets. The ark housing them was secretly taken away by a son of Solomon named

Menelik, and brought into Africa. Several Gadol split away from Hilkiah and accompanied the prince here, fully separating themselves from the traditional power structure of the old temple. They kept their secrets well…to this very day in fact.

"Aaron's men?" asked James.

"Yes," Nafees said solemnly. "Over time Aaron's warriors converted to Christianity…they saw the eleventh light in the first Deliverer, Joshu, long before anyone else. These humble men who now guard the ark go by the name of Tomar…Knights of Christ… actually a remnant order of monophysite monks that helped give rise to the notorious Knights Templar."

"Templar of the Crusades?" asked James with a look of surprise.

"The very same," replied Nafees. "It's actually a convoluted story…Aaron can fill you in on his sorted history later, if you like." He almost sounded annoyed, but continued. "The important thing for you to know now is that before the Asirim broke up, all the men in the order served the three of us as chief guardians to the tablets. It was our mission to protect them and the fate they wove…at all costs. As the priestly order, we Rafiq fashioned the ark's propitiatory cover and from that enchantment the ark takes the name 'Mercy Seat.' The lid was crafted according to the will of the nameless-god. Placed upon it were two cherubim that symbolize satans… messengers of His voice. Within them, I wove a strong conjoining spell…one that did not require ziña. From then on, mankind became able to converse with the nameless-god directly through them. In turn, the goddess' ritual conjoining fell from favor with Hilkiah; and he had the Hebrew King banish us."

"So the Rafiq were the first oracles of God?"

"The very first, but with both our order and then later the tablets themselves going into exile from the Holy Land...the Amo became lost once more, like before Moses. They suffered greatly for their arrogance, arguing among themselves about the nuances of contrived law and shunning the hallowed divination of seers. The Gadol sought only control, banning men from conjoining...only they could mediate with God...so they believed...in sacrifice."

"How did banning love between men afford them control?"

"In two ways," said Nafees. "First, many powerful spirits set themselves up as godlike kings among men at that time. They came looking for the Mercy Seat, and enslaved the Amo. You see James, empire building is simply another form of rape...it is the ravishing of entire nations of people. The Amo suffered that at the hands of many powers over the centuries. Every major kingdom of the time had to go over the Holy Land to get to each other. Using ziña to subjugate mortals was an evil, but effective practice for getting what they wanted. The Gadol – understandably I admit – became sensitive to the misuse of ethereal conjoining as a means of feeding power and greed. You saw yourself why with what Azael did to you."

James blushed.

"But then later Hilkiah went further," explained Nafees, "and banned it outright; he feared the Amo would return to ritual conjoining without the Mercy Sea. The warriors trusted no one, and feared the power of Allah was no longer theirs alone to dispense. Without the tablets, they were lost. As favor slipped away from them, they grew heartless...their ritual practices sterile of anything but religious legalism. They fabricated many holy writings to that end, which I today believe to be a form of idolatry...a greater insult to the truth than conjoining could ever be."

"I still don't understand what this has to do with me," said James, as the darkness took hold around them. "I have not received any vision about of this..."

"You will," interrupted a strange voice, "if you are the truly the emissary the Mercy Seat told us would come."

Nafees and James came to their feet quickly. They both turned. There behind them stood Father Aaron.

"Tonight all the knights will perform prayers to our Madonna, Queen of Heaven. Many of the Beja people who live near here have worshiped the goddesses-image quietly for untold generations... there is an ancient temple to her in Philae, not far from us now. We will gather with them in common rites at the full moon...petitioning the queen to name a new emissary among the Amo on earth...Hebrew, Christian, and Muslim alike. For the first time in eons, it looks like she may answer us our prayers. The signs in the sky are fertile for her portent."

James suddenly grew wary. He'd not told Nafees yet that she had come to him already. He was still trying to make sense of the visions, not sure at times if they were more than nightmares.

"Brother James," said Aaron, "do not let Nafees laden you too much with burdens from our past. We elohim have a memory that reaches back further than any should. We sometimes forget the frailty of the mortal veil...don't we, Nafees?"

"Yes, that is true, brother," replied the cleric humbly. "But we must help our young prophet understand the signs. Soon she will call him....I am certain in my heart."

James looked at his feet, wondering if he should speak-up now. He decided to wait.

"And only God knows why," said the Tomar. "The boy has had much put before him already. Try to relax Nafees. It is the eve of the Hadhar...our time-honored night of ritual and dance. If his destiny truly lies with the tablets – as it seems to you – then *she* will show us tonight as we reach together for wajd."

Nafees seemed to concede to some power in Aaron, as if to recognize his rank. "You are right, as always," he answered. "That is why Astarte chose you to stand as guardian over the Mercy Seat all these years...your pragmatism has always won out."

"Look up there," said Aaron, "lest we forget what we are up against."

He pointed up into the darkness and the lace-work of stars that ornamented the sky. Nafees and James looked up and followed his extended finger to the corner of night he had intended for them to notice.

"The stars are amazing here," said James, admiring the clarity.

"Use your ethereal sight and follow mine into the dome of the firmament... look to the constellation Cygnus, that faint star that quivers so...right there."

All three stared at the sky a time, as an uneasy mood settled among them. Aaron was casting a powerful spell about the breeze.

"We Tomar call that star Jonah," said Aaron, his voice weighted with grief.

"It is dying," whispered James, "that is why it trembles that way. I can feel it."

"Yes, can you see how it dies?" asked the Tomar.

James intensified his vision, focusing on the faint shimmer set against the darkness. "It's being swallowed," he answered, a sense of dread rising in his tone. "But there is nothing there. It's as if the fire of the star is being eaten by nothingness."

"A dragon," whispered Nafees, his expression wide-eyed and fearful.

Father Aaron turned and looked at them both. His eyes seemed to glow. For just an instant, the strong veneer of the monk-warrior vanished and James sensed something different about him, something almost maternal; that was the only word that came to mind as he looked at the man. It seemed a strange contradiction to sense something so warm and feminine from Aaron's outward appearance.

"It is the mouth of a great dragon," the Tomar said, "consuming everything that comes near it. This one we call Taninim, the Devourer, and that emptying of spirit is called Balak....it is what happens in the end when enough dragons are fully and finally loosed in their forbidden form. It's what *will* happen on a cosmic scale should the Queen of Chaos' power be unbound from the Abyss. Keep the Jonah star in mind, James – so that you understand the fate we will all share should Tiamat prevail in this war."

⚭

After dinner the knights all got ready for the rites. In his and James' cell, Adriano fumbled with his ceremonial souf. The traditional wool shroud was pulled uncomfortably tight across his shoulders, it fit too snuggly – to say nothing of the fact he hated the itchy feel of the skirted costume. His only solace was in the fact that it would keep him warm in the cool desert night as they partook of the ritual.

James stood behind the big man. He placed an elaborate headband over his forehead, then motioned for the knight to inspect it. Adriano laughed as he reached to turn it right-side up.

"The heads of the entwined serpents must face to Heaven," said Adriano sweetly. "They look to Allah in fear of his might."

James rolled his eyes. "I hope this doesn't take all night, I'm exhausted. I just want to curl up into bed."

"Try to relax, James...you love to dance."

"Jason cannot spin," the seer sighed, "it's the middle of the damn desert, and we're not dropping a pill. It's not going to be the same thing as dancing at Twilo…I really want to get this over with quickly."

"Just give the Hadhar a chance. I don't want to spoil the surprises, but you will enjoy it…I promise."

"Fine, let's just go," James replied, weary of resisting.

He handed the big man his ritual asherah rod. Each man of the order carried one of the sacred staffs to formal rites, such as Hadhar. It was a common practice left from when all three sects were still Asirim. Each initiate was given a staff when beginning his training as a knight. As they rose in rank amid the various orders, the rods were decorated, often like their bodies. Adriano's was covered with the image of a winged serpent.

The two men took one last look at each other, to make sure they were ready. "So explain this 'Hadhar' to me now?" asked James. They both pivoted and left their cell, heading up the stair toward the outer yard.

"The Hadhar is a large gathering of faithful men from different traditions," replied the knight. "The Beja rites are very illustrious. The people here are well known for their sacred festivals of dance and song. They weave powerful sema. Various sects of Sufi and Christian gather and reach for God, unified by homage to the Queen of Heaven as people of the book."

"Sounds intense," replied James. "Do me a favor? Please stay close to me tonight. I don't feel like being all that social. I could use you running some interference for me....this is all clearly more your thing anyway."

Adriano nodded and kissed him on the head.

"The Rafiq will perform our rite of Zekhr," explained the big man, "but we will observe more actual tradition tonight – these aspects of Rafiq ritual actually go back to the time when we were part of the Persian Court. They are related to an old sort of ritual game, called *alish-takis*...where young priests explore erotic play with each other as a symbolic expression of longing for the divine...true ziña between men was considered sacred in those days. It's also about the time our beliefs began to diverge from the early practice of conjoining in temple-prostitution rituals, and followed the idea of companionship as being sacred among warrior-priests. The court was influenced by the Greeks then – Alexander the Great had seized the empire. The epic examples from their traditions of Achilles and Patroclus, the sacred Band of Thebes, and Plato were all held up as the ideal. Like them, we became a warrior casts ourselves, for when two soldiers were lovers they were thought to be unstoppable. Sadly, most Islamic and Christian orthodoxy have come to see our time-honored traditions as aberrant and blasphemous...they consider ziña to be a kind of sinful love now."

"Yes, Nafees once told me this...it seems strange to me that love could be seen as sinful," replied James. "If it's pure and full of joy the way ours is, it must come from God."

"Yes!" said the big man emphatically. "The Rafiq believe that true devotion to Allah can be reached directly by loving Him *or* it can be reached indirectly by loving things Allah himself cherishes...like the beauty of the male form."

Adriano reached over and adjusted the seer's souf as he went over the nuances of the rite in more detail for James. He took deep pride in the Rafiq traditions.

"The Zekhr is rooted mystically in the idea that watching beautiful men leads to an apperception for the divine beatific-vision. In essence, the desirability of lovely young men, created in God's image, is akin and a part of Allah's' spiritual rapture...the ecstasy we all seek. In the Koran it says that in Heaven the faithful shall be attended by *beardless boys graced with eternal youth, who to the beholder's eye will seem like sprinkled pearls.*"

"You're kidding?" snickered James, with a look of surprise.

"No, there is a term for the ritual desire of men in Arabic. Let me see if I can remember...*al-nazar ia'l-amurd*...yeah that's it. It means 'contemplation of the beardless.' The Zekhr is for the Rafiq both an expression of dance and mediation on desire.

"Why do religions fear us so much?"

"Power I think," replied the big man. "Mortal men seek control over the sacred. They have always feared the influence of sema and wajd...as well as the strength it affords us."

James smiled at him. "How does this ritual work then?"

"It's very similar to what we did at home. We will gather close and touch each other, listening for the spirit of the music to fill us with rapture through the sema spell. We watch the beautiful men and boys dance, swirling into wajd, and sometimes we heighten the process with wine or other elixirs...to better part the mortal veil and experience the bliss of Heaven."

The big man grinned mischievously at the last remark. James shook his head, thinking Adriano was incorrigible when it came to mixing his potions and powders.

"What's so sinful about all of that?" asked James finally. "It sounds pretty normal to me."

"Sometimes watching and touching beautiful men leads to more...to ziña...just as they fear."

James thought a moment. "Does that mean then that some of us beardless boys get taken advantage of at some point in these rites?"

"Yes," said Adriano slyly. "It's precisely what that means."

They stood staring at each other for a moment with warm, longing faces. James furrowed his brow.

"Good," he replied abruptly. "The night won't be a total loss."

Adriano laughed at his companion's good humor. They embraced and kissed one last time before walking up hand in hand from the dark halls of the monastery to the courtyard where the other Rafiq knights waited.

Nafees looked annoyed as they emerged from the corridor. They were late.

Adriano motioned for James to climb into the ORV
that Jason was driving. They both scurried inside,
and then the caravan made its way into the night's
mysteries. James sat in a back seat, watching to see
if he could catch a glimpse of the landscape, but the
darkness outside was so deep that the earth appeared
to fade into nothingness. A chill went up the young
prophet's spine.

After a long bumpy ride, the caravan swung into
a shallow ravine, where the river bent. The light of
hundreds of bonfires came into view. Around each
fire was a circle of linen tents, which waved in the cool
wind of the wasteland.

The ORVs all rolled to a stop. Then Nafees turned
to them and spoke softly; his tone stern, with a hint of
worry. "There is something I must stress to you both
now...I have already spoken with the others. There is
a little matter of formality we must address here and
now. For most of the rest of our journey, we all need
to be careful about using the dignified, despite well-
deserved, distinction of 'prophet' to refer to you, James—
at least in front of others. It is a habit we have gotten
into from home, but could be met with some hostility
among other Sufis' who hail from more conservative
Islamic clans. For most Muslims, Muhammad was
the last prophet...to suggest otherwise will be highly
offensive to their faith. So, along the road to the
Holy Land, let us confer upon our messenger from
the goddess the title Walis when in the company of
others. It means 'friend of God' in Arabic, and is used

to describe the most revered of religious leaders in the Islamic world."

They all agreed, knowing it was what lay in the heart, not in a name, that really mattered. They climbed out of the vehicle one by one and headed down into the river basin. There were hundreds of men huddled amid the fires and about the tents. James was shocked. The affair was a much bigger deal than he had thought it would be.

They stepped in and around the fire circles. As they did, men turned and watched them, murmuring among themselves. James wanted to know what they were saying to each other, but did not use his ethereal senses to try and scry out what they whispered. When they approached a large outcrop of rocks at the far end of the throng, he noticed how the tents there did not form a full circle, like in the other areas. Instead, they arched like a crescent moon – the ends of each tent line stopping at the edge of the jagged precipice. The fire was bigger there, rising high into the desert night like a monstrous beast. Tiny bits of spark popped and flared toward the heavens as it danced in the cooling air.

They all followed Nafees to the edge of the blaze. There they found Father Aaron and many of the monks from the monastery. The immortal cleric greeted Aaron with a traditional kiss, then each man did the same was well. When Aaron came close to James, he grabbed the boy firmly by both arms, shook him a moment, and kissed him. The young prophet looked sidelong to see if Adriano would register any distress, but the knight didn't. The priest turned to

Adriano, they too repeated the greeting. Then as Aaron walked away to others, Adriano donned a joyful expression. His eyes seemed to gleam with devilish satisfaction.

Abruptly, the sound of drums and music rose up from all around them. James stared in awe – Adriano could see it in his face, so the big man stopped to take some time to explain the affair to the excited prophet. First he pointed out a man playing what resembled a flute; it was an instrument called a ney that was said to emulate the breath of Allah.

Others around the fire then picked up tambourine like devices. Someone standing close by handed one to James. The boy inspected it curiously.

"That's called daf," said Adriano, smiling.

James then shook it, and joined into the rising tribal rhythm. The sound touched some power deep in his being, as he was drawn into the ritual cadence. It was then a stranger on the far fireside began to pluck at something that resembled a lute. The sound was magical and lively; it seemed to cause the fire to whirl and glide.

"That is a tar" explained Adriano, "my favorite of all of them."

The music the instruments made did remind James of the sounds he had enjoyed so much back home in Twilo. He started to bounce a little with the beat. The affair did not seem so bad after all. He was suddenly glad that he had come.

Adriano took him by the hand and led him away. They dropped into an empty tent. The floor was covered in fine silk pads and pillows. It all seemed to gleam in the torchlight. The knight walked over to a stand in the corner; it held a small mixing bowl and several bottles of wine, with a shelf just under the canisters. He pulled a wooden box from the shelf and set it next to the mixing bowl, then poured several splashes of wine into the dish. He looked back at James, who was taking in all that he was seeing with studious fascination.

"Palm wine," said the big man. "It's tart, but is mainly for ceremonial purposes...not the sort of stuff you want to drink a lot of. It will make you puke."

"Nice,' replied James mordantly.

Adriano opened the tiny box and took out a brown-green wafer. He crumbled it into the wine.

"What's that?" asked James.

"Don't you know?" replied the knight. "You've seen into me...I've done the rite many times before."

"It doesn't work that way," explained James. "I prefer not to access the ethereal memories of others unless I need to...it feels rather like an intrusion. I would not have needed the history lesson earlier if I knew what this was all about, Adriano."

The big man scowled at him; worried his companion might stay in a bad mood the entire night. "It is from the Devil's Trumpet," he said, "a sacred plant. I think the actual name for it is datura. My mother used to grow the plant when I was a kid, but I'm sure unaware of its properties. I can remember the bright white flowers in the yard that looked like trumpets, and how at night the leaves mysteriously reached up to God.

The effect of its resin is similar to ecstasy...only more intense."

The knight seemed excited by the prospect of taking the strange preparation. "But it's temperamental," he added finally. "We have to use it very carefully."

"We should reach for wajd without a drug now...I told you that."

"It's part of the rite; it's tradition. Can we just go with it for tonight? You were complaining not more than half an hour ago we had no ecstasy."

James hesitated a second. He was intrigued by Adriano's child like enthusiasm, despite the growing unease he had about all this tampering with compounds they didn't fully understand. He was beginning to sense that they were a sword that could cut both ways – one truly never knew what was in them. The good such preparations did might in the end undo them before they reached their goal.

"It's the first time I've done the rite with a companion," the big man pled. "Please?"

"Really...you and Robert never did this Hadhar thing together?"

"I wanted to surprise you," said the knight, shaking his head vigorously to emphasize that they hadn't ever had the chance.

James did want so desperately to please the big man. "O.K, it can't hurt I guess," he sighed, setting aside his fatigue.

Adriano turned and let the leaves settled around the mixing bowl for a few minutes. The delight of his expectancy was palpable. He raised the porcelain bowl to his mouth and drank a little, then he reached out and handed James the wide brim dish.

"This ceremonial vessel is in an ancient style; it's called a kylix. It's cool, no? In the days of old the court it was tradition for men who shared affection to drink from a common vessel like this...it symbolizes the unity of brethren...our vows to each other to stand as one."

The big man watched James as he drank. The boy was lovely in the torchlight.

"Drink in small, shallow swallows." he said to the young prophet. "We will take turns...partaking from this one spirit."

When they had drunk the last of the Devils Trumpet elixir in the dish, Adriano led him from the tent. Once outside, the big man thrust his staff into the ground, and motioned for James to do the same with his. "This is our tent now...no one will disturb us here," he said, "unless invited."

James wondered what he meant by 'invited.'

They joined hands then, as Adriano took him to the fire. Men were already swaying and whirling to the rhythm of the drums. The revelers were clearly intoxicated; perhaps with the wine mixture, or maybe with other things James thought. Some men sat near the fire smoking a dragon's-tail – he figured that it was more than spice he smelled in the smoke.

The prophet and his knight began to dance the formal rite of Zekhr together, as it was truly intended. James had taken various drugs recreationally in the past, but nothing like the strange narcotic they indulged that evening. As it hit him he seemed to shift out of his body, the delirium was feverish. A drum cadence took him over; his dancing became wild, yet elegant. Adriano matched his vigorous, fluid motion. They seemed to flow into and around each other with grace. In his dizzy exhilaration, James lost control of his ethereal poise, the Realm of Essences opened around him and he drew first Adriano into the deepening euphoria, then one by one all the men around him. For a brief period of time, the devotees were caught up into a kind of ritual rapture most had never before experienced.

Aaron and Nafees stood on a rocky overhang, scrutinizing the festivities, transfixed by the power of the young seer. Aaron reclined near a large stone, which looked carved square by human hands. He stroked it affectionately; seeming to think it was alive in some way.

"How did he come by such immense enchantment?" asked Aaron. He was suspicious of something that he could not quite put his finger on. "This is not the prophet the omens from the Mercy Seat told us to expect...he is much more powerful than he should be, and he is touched by darkness."

"No, he is not the Anointed One," said Nafees, turning to the Tomar knight, "not at least as we understood it. The prophet revealed by Gabriel is still with Iblis."

"I don't understand," replied Aaron. "You know full well this cannot work unless the prophet has seen into the heart of the Accuser and can in turn speak the name of God. You we're to insure the Accuser showed him the way. Only Iblis is said to have that power now. The rite will kill the boy if he trics to touch the Mercy Seat without employing the sacred name."

"I know. He did conjoin with the Accuser. I saw it the night Gabriel revealed the other."

"But you aren't actually sure if he is capable of employing divine speech yet...are you?"

Aaron looked at Nafees with near shock. It was a little late for his brother to be admitting such uncertainty about the boy's true commission. The priest was disturbed.

"No, I am not completely sure," replied Nafees, "but I saw the other mortal that Gabriel touched... something was not right about him. There was a rage in his soul. I had to choose one from the two, from what I saw...I did what I thought right. The omen never specifically said Gabriel would anoint the true prophet...only that the Jinn would do so. We assumed that it had to be done the way it was every time before. But it was not this time; there is purpose of Allah in this deception."

"And what if you are wrong? Anger and wrath is often the way of our God...you may have misjudged."

"The river is crossed," retorted Nafees. "We cannot go back."

"You are not answering my question," replied the anxious monk. But Nafees was correct. They could not turn back – they must trust in faith now.

"There is a presence of dark power in him...why, Nafees?"

"The Accuser is not the only one with whom he has conjoined. Iblis brought him to me after he had survived a failed attempt by a Pythian thrall to feed upon him.

"That explains his feel. He is fused with darkness...I sense it. That is not comforting news, Nonah," said Aaron. The priest always called Nafees by his ancient, lost name whenever he wanted to stress something important to him.

"Yes, I realize that...but there is more. After that he was attacked a second time, forced to conjoin with the Jinn, Azael. The angel had turned and deserted Heaven...so Iblis says. That means two Jinn have anointed James – just not the faithful ones we assumed would."

"Busy boy," snorted Aaron.

Nafees glared. "James and Iblis killed the traitor together. I suspect they bound him first...it is the only way it could be done. Azael would have been too strong for the Accuser alone, bolstered with Pythian power. Iblis would need the help of Heaven, or an agent thereof."

"So you only *think* he used the name?"

"Yes," answered Nafees coolly. "This young friend of God is infused with both the power of the Queen of Chaos and the Queen of Heaven." He turned to the celebrants on the valley floor. "See now what he does to the Hadhar!"

"The question is...who will he follow now that he is touched by both chaos and light? You have risked much," Aaron sighed, "but the goddess will know the right path."

Both immortals looked down into the ravine, watching as the seer and his knight slipped away from the crowd to their private tent. The time had come.

James and Adriano stopped and hung their souf over their respective asherah as they entered the flap. The two were out of the rest of their clothing and on the silk pillows the instant they were alone. They rolled in each other's embrace, passion feeding their desire for one another as the potion stripped away the pretense of caution. The big man rolled over onto James and the seer took him into his spirit. Their lovemaking was pitched and furious. As they reached climax together, the entire Hadhar seemed to heave and moan with them; tied to a single conjoined state of wajd. From nowhere, amid the cries of elation, both James and Adriano heard a whisper – a woman's voice.

"Children," the soft enunciation called to them.

At first, they paid the voice no mind. The height of their rapture and the pounding of their hearts drown out all things around them, but then the voice became loud and emboldened. Every devotee heard it in his own head – the Queen calling for her chosen. James pulled his head up and looked at the flap of the tent blowing in the wind. There appeared a woman.

The goddess seemed different now, as loose linen swayed around her. Adriano rolled off of James and stared at her. He quickly fumbled to cover himself.

The goddess smiled for his misbegotten shame.

"Normally there aren't any women attending Hadhar," said the knight to James, a little confused and embarrassed.

"This is no mere woman," said the young seer. James scrambled and prostrated on the ground in front of her. "My queen...how is it possible you are here," he supplicated at her feet.

"I have not come to you, child. You have come to me. You have brought them all to me."

It was then James realized that he was holding open the ethereal realm with such potency that he had drawn the full rite to the very edge of the underworld itself – where the Queen of Heaven was waiting to hear their petitions. She met them at the entrance to the Abyss, pleased beyond all delights to see the men who still venerated her memory.

"It's time you came the rest of the way, James," said the goddess, "but this way is not safe." She opened her spirit and revealed to him the pathway; epiphany blossomed like a flower in gloom.

"Now close this portal," she sighed, "before you draw the wrong kind of attention here, my cherished child. The dragons will sense you, and all will be lost if they find you here."

James looked inward and saw the way in which he had unconsciously opened the gate. He abruptly closed it. As he did the sobriety of the mortal veil returned to the Hadhar. The entire camp grieved as the power of wajd faded and the presence of divinity slipped away.

"Get dressed," James said to Adriano. "We have to go."

The big man pulled his tight pants on over his legs, still in shock. He staggered out of the tent after James, who by then was rushing toward the cliff. The knight grabbed both their souf from the rods as they stole past, leaving them upright in the sand. Men emerged from the tents, most stumbled out of the darkness and fell to their knees. They bowed before the seer. James did not appear to notice, but Adriano was dumb stuck as they all emerged and prostrated themselves in the dry desert dust.

The two made their way up a path near where the tents met the crags. They climbed for a bit until they reached the ledge overlooking the large camp. At the top of the rocks, they found Aaron and Nafees waiting.

"Quite a spectacle," said Aaron to James. "I've not seen common rites such as that in many, many centuries."

"Not since the celebrations of Mount Sinai, I think," added Nafees.

James looked embarrassed. The big man just gaped down at the fires and the multitude of men. "Wow, that was intense," said the knight.

James shot him an irritable look.

"Then I was right," said Nafees. "It comes down to this moment after all, Walis."

"It's no time to be smug," retorted James. "You could have been more forthcoming before offering me up. Move out of the way... she is waiting."

The cleric and the monk stepped aside from the large square rock. James closed his eyes and reached into the ethereal plane. It was as if he had done all of this before. The rock resisted, but finally slid free, exposing a passage down into darkness. Nafees walked over to a fire near the rocks, glowing with white-hot embers. He reached for a torch shaft and stoked it into the coals. The bound end of the stick burst into flame. Proudly then he handed it to Adriano.

"You will need that," said the cleric. "No one has been down there for several generations."

They all looked at James solemnly.

"Go with God, prophet," Aaron said finally. Then turning back to Nafees, the Tomar saw the cleric's look of rebuke. "*Walis* that is," he quickly corrected himself, with a warm, apologetic smile.

The tunnel sloped down a long way before it flattened so that they could walk with fewer stumbling steps. There was a stale smell that had been trapped there for ages, but James paid little attention to anything other than the way in front of them.

"Where are we going?" the big man asked, "and what is this place?"

"We're in the Vault of Aksum. It's a tunnel that runs under the hills toward the city. It ends at the catacombs that lie directly below where the Ark of the Covenant is kept."

"Oh Lord," said Adriano. "I shouldn't have asked."

James put one hand on the big man's back and caressed him gingerly. "I need you here, Adriano."

The knight turned back and smiled. He would do anything for James.

After what seemed like an eternity of wandering in the dark, especially with both their heads still swimming from the datura elixir, the two Rafiq champions reached the end of the passage. The tunnel just stopped. James approached the wall, motioning for Adriano to bring the light of the torch near to it. Studying the surface, he located two vertical seams that partitioned the stone into slabs. The young seer focused a moment, concentrating on the center stone and reaching out to listen for its resonance. Then he pulled on it with his mind. It moaned in protest, but was gradually drawn back into passage anyway; enough room was left on either side for a man to squeeze through, and pass. James stopped moving the stone a moment.

"Hold your breath," the seer told his knight.

Adriano tipped his head.

With that James gave the slab one last straining tug. As the stone cleared the opening, there was a thundering crash. The tunnel filled with dust. Adriano gripped fast to James to shield him, but the seer was unwavering. They stood and waited amid the cloud of debris for some time, as it choked the torch. When the sand eventually settled from the air, they could see that a stone supported by the one James pulled free had fallen into a pit below. It was just slightly smaller, creating a bridge across the opening. Had they pushed the slab forward instead, the suspended stone would have crushed them in the shaft.

"You knew" said the big man.

James' face turned warm. He loved the look of wonder in Adriano's eyes. It was like the joy of young boy.

"There is more to see inside." James replied. The seer pushed along the stone to slip past. Adriano followed and his eyes opened wide as the light filled the tiny room. There they beheld a spectacle few men had ever lived to see – the Holiest of Holies.

The cubical itself was about fifteen feet square. It had a sealed iron door directly across from the secret entrance they had come through. Adorning the opposing walls were two intricate fabric tapestries, each with a strange design. On the one closest, Adriano could make out the image of a tree, but instead of leaves it sprouted flame. The representation seemed to quiver in the touch light. The second tapestry bore the image of an asherah rod, fixed into the ground like a pole. Two snakes were intertwined around it. But still more amazingly, laid out before him was the indisputable Ark of the Covenant, with its mysterious lid –the Mercy Seat. The gold radiated power. Adriano took a step toward the holy relic, as he did James grabbed at him frantically.

"Don't, Adriano," James said, "it will kill you if you so much as brush up against it."

"What are we doing here then?" asked Adriano nervously. His voice was soft, as if he were keeping it down so no one would hear them, even though no one could.

James looked into the big man's eyes. He wanted to tell Adriano he knew what he was doing, but in his heart he was suddenly not so sure. "It's a test," said the young seer.

"For whom?"

"Me," replied James sorrowfully. "Who else?"

"Oh no...if this thing is dangerous, let's just back out of here slowly."

"I can't do that," said James. "The goddess called me here. I promised to trust her...*you* must trust me." He reached up and kissed his strong, loving companion. "Listen to me. I am not completely certain I was meant for this task. In fact, I think everyone assumed this was a job for Jon Godfrey. Nafees believes however that Nick is wrong in his trust of Jon...that this is my path. I can't say I know either way, but the goddess called us here, Adriano. I have faith this is the right thing to do now."

Adriano looked afraid. He pulled James close to him. "I love you, James Kyle...I will always love you... no matter what."

The big man clung to him, but James managed to pull himself free finally and turned to loom over the Mercy Seat. The boy extended his hands, palms out, as if he expected the surface of the gold to be hot. Then he said the sacred name of the nameless-god, just under his breath. There was no fan fare this time, just the searing sound of God's power. Slowly, James pressed his hands against the Mercy Seat. He turned his head to one side and winced. The surface made an unexpected hissing sound, but nothing else happened. Both men breathed a sigh of relief.

Cautiously, James leaned forward and placed his face in between the two cherubim – the likenesses of the Jinn created for divination. He closed his eyes to listen.

"What is it?" asked Adriano, gripped in fascination.

"Nothing at all," replied the seer. "The nameless-god is not on his throne. He does not speak." James reached up and took hold of the two images. He braced both feet and pulled; the propitiatory lid came free. The boy slid it to one side and glanced inside – a mist of white light covered him.

"Do you know what you are doing *now?*" Adriano asked.

"Not really," was all that James would say to him. He slowly reached into the long compartment and pulled out a wooden shaft, a very old and apparently powerful asherah. He turned and faced Adriano, extending it out to him. The expression on the young seer's face was triumphant.

"But I do know *this* is for my knight," he said. "Take the staff. I need you to carry it for me...you are my Rafiq."

The knight reached for it. As he grabbed the ancient rod, its wood seemed to writhe in his hand like it was alive. "And you are my Rafiq also," replied Adriano endearingly.

James stopped for a moment and pulled the white souf over his head, he struggled gracelessly to free it from his shoulders in the tight space. Then he turned his back to the big man, and gently laid out the shirt in front of the Mercy Seat. Without looking over at his companion, James reached in and began to take out several stone slabs – the broken fragments of the Tablets of Destiny.

There were two carved stones, broken into six distinct chunks. They seemed to radiate the same strange aura that had originally surrounded the Mercy Seat. With the fragments outside the holy container now, it was clear that they had been the source of the glowing power all along. James bound the stones in the wool, and tied it off with his headband. He turned little by little to face Adriano.

"Now comes the real test," said James with a frown. "Take the staff and strike the tapestry of the asherah and serpents…hit it hard and slice it open."

Adriano looked at the staff, then up at the tapestry – he understood. With divine right in mind, he slashed at the image and the ancient textile was instantly wrenched in two. The halves flew open, as if he had ruptured the surface of a great balloon. Then they heaved inward. The air of the room was drawn into a mysterious portal to nowhere formed in the gap of the torn fabric. It hissed, and the torch flared copiously at their backs.

"Come to me, James," they heard the voice of the queen beckon.

The young seer faced his knight. "I have to go," he said.

"Reach inside your soul, James," the goddess whispered. "Find the fire of the Pythia. Wield to your purpose what they would use to destroy us."

James closed his eyes and reached into the Realm of Essences. There he gathered the dark heart of the thrall in Manhattan, along with the licentious power of Azael. Lastly, he looked to Nick's despairing heart – the exile of Heaven. Using the knowledge of all three, James enveloped himself in the Jinn's fiery essence, as his companion looked on in horror.

"If I never see you again," said James sadly. "Always remember I loved you best!"

With those words he leapt into the Abyss. The portal quickly seized and closed. Adriano watched, unable to believe is eyes. With the shadows of the torn tapestry dancing in the torchlight, his beloved companion was cast to oblivion.

12

PASSAGE TO ARBIL

Eden labored within the grip of cataclysm as darkness grew. Joshu looked out from the throne and down into His enigmatic realm. Its pain reverberated across space and time, rippling through the material dimensions like rain striking a standing pool. He raised a hand and commanded the next trumpet to sound. With its blast, asteroids shifted their orbits out amid the great belt of cold mountains circling the solar system. One broke free and fell into Heaven's ethereal gravity well. The Jinn opened the causeways to paradise and gave the falling stone passage. It dropped to the sea surround the garden's high walls, and shook all creation.

On the material plane the seas were filled with its wrath. Dragons descended in the form of hurricanes and cyclones, battering at the land to weaken it. The floor of the oceans convulsed and sent great waves to pound the coasts.

The Pythian Lord, Aboddon Naga, stretched out his massive form over the earthly seas, no longer afraid of Heaven. He became a great tempest, surging across the Indian Ocean and picking-up speed to delight in fury. Freely loosed upon the material plane in full potency, none of the serpents were bound any longer to their mortal shells, which had been God's law.

Aboddon's dark joy rose as he saw the distant African coast. He drove for land with crooked envy, feeding from the wake of his brutality all up the ravaged coastline. The great titan probed at the mortal world with his senses, drawing himself nearer and nearer to the pulse of power in the hidden Tablets of Destiny. *They are so close,* he thought to himself. *Soon I will have them, and the power they possess.*

Then impossibly, without warning, the ethereal signature of the tablets simply vanished without a trace. The beast was thrown into a rage. He mauled the land, and was merciless with his hunger for vengeance. After what seemed an endless fit of wrath, Aboddon gathered himself and ceased his vehemence, assuming the mortal guise in which both mankind and grigori would recognize him. The dragon set his feet upon the ruined land and took a moment to relish the feel of life snuffing out around him. He then tore open the Realm of Essences, and pushed inside it to find Shemhazai. The monster broke through to the material plane moments later, when he appeared there, several thralls stood gathered in the room. As they saw him, the faithless men fell to the ground and began to wail with fright and awe. Shemhazai was speaking with Nazim, his back to where the dragon emerged in humanoid form. When Nazim looked past him and fell to prostrate, the grigori turned and immediately extended his wings in supplication, bowing low for the serpent.

"Aboddon Naga," said the grigori, "we fall at your feet as tribute to your might, great Lord of the Pythia.

You honor us with your very presence." The term 'Naga' was a title all dragons bore. It was a distinction greater than even that of 'god' to those that followed them. By its use, the Pythia forced all that followed them to reject the rule of Heaven.

"Where is the Accuser?" the serpent grumbled.

"He is here...in Syria, Naga," answered Shemhazai. "All has gone as you commanded, but we must approach him very carefully now. There is a problem. He was fused with the breath of one of your footman serpents –Nadu, who you sent to us. Nadu mistook Iblis for one of the other Jinn when we tried to seize the prophet from them. It is as the queen's omen foretold...the sign She warned to beware. The Accuser is grigori now. Fortunately, he does not yet understand the power he possesses."

Abaddon smashed his fist through a wall. It crumbled. The men around him quaked in fear.

"Is something wrong, Lord Naga?" ask the demon. "Have you sensed something of him we have not?"

"Yes," bellowed the beast, "he has managed to conceal the tablets somehow. I no longer sense the pulse of their power. The Accuser has taken them for himself, as I feared he might."

"Ah, yes...that," replied Shemhazai. "I too felt their fading...but it should not concern us now. As dangerous as Iblis has become, I am certain what we sensed was not the Accuser, great Na...."

"You are as stupid as you are weak," the dragon interrupter him. "The Devil will seize the throne of Heaven for himself!"

The grigori thought on it a moment. The Accuser had always been rumored to covet the rule of Heaven, but something told him that was not what the dark exile was after now. "But Naga," he said, "neither the prophet nor the Accuser have gone near the temple. We are watching them every moment. He is on to us somehow about our intrigues for war...but I am quite sure the two of them are still moving toward Arbil, and not Jerusalem."

"How are you certain?"

"Perhaps we should not speak of such things in front of the thralls, great Naga," replied Shemhazai. "I would rather we dismissed them, but now that we are in your presence...only you may issue command."

Aboddon looked up at them. "Be gone," the dragon snapped. They scrambled away like roaches at the sound of his voice. When they had all left the room, the dragon spoke again to the grigori. "Now, what do you know?"

"I find it difficult to believe that they have managed to take and conceal the tablets outside of the Holy City," said Shemhazai. "The Mercy Seat holding the tablets must still be in Jerusalem, hidden under the Dome of the Rock. I myself helped to build the first temple and the catacombs under it – as a slave to the mortal king, Solomon. The passages there are protected by powerful eleventh light wards designed to confound intruders. I think it more likely the Gadol fear all our coming, and have hidden the tablets deeper in the vaults there...that is why we no longer sense them. There is no other way in all of creation for them to be concealed but in eleventh light wards."

"What if you are wrong? What if they are not there? What if the old rumor is true and the tablets *were* hidden elsewhere?"

"Wives tales, Naga," replied Shemhazai, "created by the Gadol warriors to distract their enemies. I counsel that we continue with the queen's plan to destroy the temple mount and any hope they have of ever using the tablets. We know God cannot make war on us without that power."

"What of the weapons we need then?"

"Drake has them...but does not yet know why we want them. He still believes we will use them to destroy the Dome of the Rock only."

"There may be another way than destroying the Temple Mount," said Abaddon, "in spite of the queen's wishes. I am more interested right now in the woman of the prophecy. The dark oracle of Kain has been right so far...if the woman is devoured before bringing His scion into the world, then destroying the tablets is unnecessary. I desire the might of the tablets to use for my own end...so I don't want them destroyed as yet."

"The queen believes otherwise..." Shemhazai began to say, but before the Jinn could finish his words the dragon flung out a massive burst of dark power that enveloped him. The energy disrupted Shemhazai's ethereal source. The turned Jinn screamed in agony, thinking he would die that very moment for his impertinence, but Aboddon loosed him before the grigori was completely obliterated. Shemhazai's wings seared and his skin boiled.

"Compose yourself you pathetic worm," said Aboddon. "Don't ever tell me what *my* queen thinks... you Jinn are not even worthy to speak Her name."

Shemhazai suffused himself with dark power to mend the damage done by the dragon, then prostrated himself in front of Aboddon's feet. "Forgive me Naga," he begged.

"I want the woman," snarled Aboddon.

"Yes, Naga," Shemhazai sniveled.

The dragon reached down and grabbed the grigori by the back of the hair and raised his head. "I mean it. You failed not once, but twice to bring me that miserable prophet. The queen was there in mortal form and saw your disgrace...She is most unforgiving. You had better get what we need from that prophet soon, before the Accuser does. If you fail again, I will pull your wings off myself and make you eat them raw. Do you understand me?"

"Yes, great Naga," said Shemhazai. "I will not fail your need again."

Aboddon released him; then slipped into the ethereal realm, vanishing with a wisp of foul vapor.

Jon went back to the house by the sea after his encounter with Caleb. When Nick returned from the gulf later, he found the boy even more upset than before. The Accuser assumed it was because he'd left him alone for so long. The prophet's face was grim. The minute Nick touched him; Jon's body was pitched into a fit of convulsions. The Accuser took him in his embrace, holding him tightly, but the young man's head just thrashed violently about, and his big hands tried to push Nick away. The convulsions caused his body to stiffen at first and then flail. This time when it was over, Jon was ready to admit something was wrong. Nick could sense a great storm of anger welling up inside the young prophet. It was directed at him, as if the Accuser himself were somehow the cause of these attacks. Jon stewed awhile, but eventually he calmed down enough that they could crawl into bed together.

Nick tried to calm him with his touch, holding the boy as they lay watching the sea from their room. But no matter what he attempted, Nick could sense something was not right with the young man. The Jinn wanted desperately to talk it out, to try and get past all that seemed to be ripping them apart. He tried to make pleasantries to break the tension.

"Do you know what your name means?" he asked.

Jon shifted, restless in the Accuser's arms. His eyes drifted up to Nick's face. "No," he said softly, "I can't say I do."

"It means gift-of-God," said Nick warmly. "It's true."

Jon gave him a cynical glare. "Who are you and what have you done with my devil?"

They both laughed. The tensions did ease a little then.

"Seriously, Nick," said Jon finally. "I am over this... let's use your power to go directly to Arbil."

Nick pushed the young prophet away. "I don't think that's such a good idea."

"Why?" groaned the prophet. "I am tired of all this running around. I just want to get there and find out what this is all about."

"But if we just show up like we came from out of nowhere," explained Nick," we will stand out. I don't know why He wants us in that cursed place, but it's clear the board is set for a confrontation. I know the Pythia are already waiting for us there." The Accuser's tone had turned to appeal.

"So," said Jon, his voice snide. "You're the Accuser of God...you'll take care of it."

"You make it sound so simple," sighed the Jinn, "like I can move Heaven and earth myself. My ethereal power is fading, Jon...I'm growing weaker by the day."

"If you can't, Nick...what good are you to me?"

The remark stabbed Nick in the chest. It was a cruel and thoughtless thing to say, but typical of the young prophet's frequent uncouth. He always seemed to speak without thinking, even when he was not angry.

"Fine!" Nick snapped. "I know someone in Arbil it would seem... remember Mason told us an old friend of mine was there. I can see if he might be able to help. I worked with him many years ago. Ibn owes me a favor. He's a good, God fearing man; he will find us a place to stay and help us keep a low profile."

Jon pulled free of Nick's arms and rolled over. "Then it won't be a problem for you after all....good night, Nick."

It felt to Nick as if all of the warmth between them drained out and was emptied, like bath water from a tub. He rolled over. They slept back to back.

❦

The next morning, Jon was up before Nick. The Accuser was becoming more restless at night. The closer they got Arbil, the more difficult it became for him – its mysterious iniquity ate away at his ethereal essence. He could hardly get out of bed, needing to reserve all his power. He simply lay there fading in and out of slumber. Nick knew that if he could just feed the dark fire growing inside his heart, he would feel better, but he continued to fear that if Jon sensed the serpent's spirit...it would alienate them further. So he endured the emptiness.

Jon left the house when Nick failed to awaken, deciding to look for Caleb again, hoping to discover more about the strange man's mission. He didn't want Nick to know what he was doing, so slipped out quietly. The young prophet wandered around for hours, asking questions and marveling at his new found ability to unravel human speech. What at one time would have seemed like inane babble, now made perfect sense to him. Still, even with being able to a pass as a native speaker and question others, he could find no sign of Drake.

When Jon returned to the rented house later, the Accuser heard the front door open and close. Nick's head was in a fog, but he instantly realized from it that Jon had been off on his own again. The Jinn was enraged as the boy entered the room. He rose to speak.

"Oh hey," said Jon to Nick causally, then swiftly turned into the tiny bathroom and shut the door. Nick heard the shower running. He spun anxiously in the bed, waiting for him to come out, grumbling to himself about his hurt. A short time later as Jon came back into the room, Nick launched right into interrogation. "Where the hell have you been?" he said in a raised voice.

Jon gave him a strange look. "Why?" he snapped defensively.

"Because half of the world would love to drown you in that sea out there right now," replied the Accuser. "That's why. What are you trying to prove?"

Jon's expression turned disaffected. He looked at Nick like he was being foolish. Then the Accuser noticed another one of his strange shifts in essence, the kind that often accompanied his rage and confusion. The young man's eyes glassed over and his aura darkened. Even his voice seemed to change. "I was just getting something to eat," he growled like a beast. "You are going crazy, Nick….you're losing it."

Nick instantly knew he was lying, but at some level feared Jon was right about something – he was losing his mind. The Jinn's anger turned to betrayal, but he held it inside.

"Who were you with?"

"No one," replied Jon, in anger. "What's it to you anyway?"

"What's it to me?" retorted Nick indignantly. "What do you mean what is it to me? I'm...."

Nick stopped.

"You're what?" replied Jon. "You're jealous maybe?" The words came out as if to mock Nick.

"No, I'm concerned for your safety," was all Nick could say about his feelings. "What's wrong with you all of a sudden?"

"Nothing is wrong with me," Jon snarled. "I am just sick and tired of this stupid game and frankly...I am tired of *you*."

"Tired of *me*?" screamed Nick. The Accuser lost his temper and dark power began to saturate his being, despite all his efforts to resist it. "You useless little pile of dirt. Who the hell do you think you are? You are not messing around with some trick you picked up off the fucking street!"

Defiance rose in prophet's hooded eyes. He was no longer intimidated by the dark, wayward Jinn. He'd been waiting for the Devil to show his true colors.

"Fuck you, Nick!" he slammed back. "You think I'm afraid of you? You sulk around and blame everyone else in the world for the misery you brought on yourself."

Nick rose off the bed. His wings began to swell under his skin. But out of nowhere, to Nick's surprise, Jon grabbed him and pushed him backward. The Jinn was caught completely off guard by Jon's brash surge of fury. They rolled about, with the Accuser somehow keeping his dark strength in check, doing everything he could to keep from ripping a whole in the wall with his pent up rage.

Jon sensed once more that Nick was not fighting back fully, like when they first met, bizarrely reveling in the control he held over the powerful Jinn. Staring down into the Accuser's gaze, his emerald eyes blackened to voids. "I love you, Nick," he said, but his voice was actually hurtful. It was a taunt, not a true confession.

This beast is not Jon, thought Nick. *What is happening to him?*

Both of them shook.

"What?" Nick then cried out, confused.

"I love you?" Jon repeated, but this time his voiced seemed to be imploring it of the Devil. He wanted Nick to say it back – he wanted Nick to fully surrender.

Nick couldn't, especially not right at that moment. The Accuser reached inside himself, looking for the words. He even opened his mouth, but nothing came out. He would not say it to a mortal – not one that acted like this anyway.

Jon's face twisted. *He* is *only using me,* the boy thought, *just like Drake said.* The prophet grabbed Nick and rolled him over. *I am God's chosen,* his mind seethed, *and I will not be a tool of the Devil.*

Then Jon pinned Nick down. The Accuser lay paralyzed by some feeling that was beyond his understanding right then, as the young prophet began to rip at his clothing. Nick just laid there on the bed, giving in to the irate whim that suddenly consumed Jon. He felt helpless, resigned to whatever would happen now.

With Nick's thin, cotton t-shirt and underwear ripped away, Jon mounted him. The boy seemed to take pleasure in being rougher than usual. Nick in turn felt strangely compelled to allow it, a kind of *mea culpa* for his inability to speak the words Jon wanted to hear. For the dark exile of Heaven, this was a different kind of submission – the kind he had always feared and resented.

After a short fit of exertion, Jon groaned and his body tensed. He'd not even made an effort to look inside Nick. The prophet made a deep, guttural sound – then thrust one last time as he climaxed.

Nick was numb with shock. He felt nothing. Just as abruptly as Jon had flipped him over, the prophet rolled off the Jinn. He made a silly noise at that point: part gulp for air, part nervous laugh. Nick turned and faced Jon, stunned by what had just happened. The prophet's black eyes showed green-blue again, he was cruelly pacified somehow by this. The gentile, innocent man was suddenly back, as if by magic, and he smiled at Nick naively, like it had all been a game.

"That was hot," he said, as he rolled out of bed, but the kindness in his eyes was short lived, lasting only seconds.

Nick wanted to curl into a ball. *He* was now the plaything of a man. The prophet's aura was steeped within a kind of unbridled dark ambition that Nick had never sensed in him before. It was a feral spirit, as if great beasts swiftly took shape in him, filling his being.

"I'm hungry," said the prophet, pulling on his shorts and a new t-shirt. "I'm going to grab a bite before we leave."

Nick took note of how he *had* lied about eating earlier – how easily the boy now set out to mislead him. Jon stopped and stared at Nick with contempt, remembering his conversation with Caleb.

The Accuser just glared back, too hurt for words.

"I want to know something, Nick," Jon said in a cruel tone.

"What?" snorted the Jinn.

"What do you plan to do when we find the woman?"

Nick froze. "Why do you ask that all of a sudden?" he replied nervously.

"I thought you would avoid the question," said Jon. "You are a bastard, Nick...this is not about us. It's about *you* and your pride. Men are just toys to you, but I've fixed that now...haven't I? "

"I...I...just want Him to love me is all," said Nick, his voice breaking up.

He is lying, thought the prophet as he turned and walked out of the room.

The Accuser lay lifeless and defeated. He noticed the shirt Jon had on when he first walked back into the house. He pulled his weight across the bed and reached for it. For some strange reason, all Nick wanted was to take in the comfort of the man's smell...to ease his hurt. As Nick did, dark power surged out of it into the Jinn – an image of Caleb Drake came clearly into his mind. Nick lay there stunned. Slowly, the Accuser shrank away from the shirt, more alone right at that moment than he had been in a very long time.

Only a few miles away, Caleb Drake stood next to a truck full of bibles. They were disguised in guns crates. One of his staff approached; Caleb looked over at him and smiled with his deceptively comforting grace.

"The Lord said beat your swords in to plow-shares, Luke. Is it not fitting?"

"Until someone starts shooting as us," said the skittish boy.

"Let me worry about that."

The young man appeared unconvinced.

"Now, Luke...when we get to Arbil, I have a special job of you. There will be another young man there who has been tempted by the Devil into the same sins that plagued you once."

Luke suddenly looked deeply unsettled. He avoided Caleb's gaze.

"This man is important to our mission," he added. "I need you to show him how you were able to change and turn away from that depraved life-style you were cursed with. Help him see God's plan for his life."

The boy nodded uncomfortably and quickly changed the subject. "A geologist from the UN Food for Oil program is here," he said. "He is waiting at your van."

"Thank you," Caleb answered. "They've been kind enough to help us survey the dig site." He gave the boy his customary smug grin, then turned and walked toward the van.

Luke watched him walk away. He was doing his best to accept that God had touched Drake, but the man just never seemed to feel right to him. His instincts told him the evangelist was up to something menacing. Luke could not help but worry that in his own pursuit of salvation, he overlooked too many things of Drake.

Caleb approached the van. His guest was dressed in a thin, cotton uniform. The evangelist reached up and set one hand his shoulder; the geologist looked at Caleb as if offended.

"Hello Drake," he said, with nostrils flaring.

"Alexander," Caleb returned, nodding to him. "Do you have the survey?"

"Yes, it's right here," replied Alexander. "Do you have the money?"

Drake gave him the same cold grin that he'd left Luke with moments before. The geologist shuddered.

"Show me," said Caleb. His voice had a sudden, brutal chill to it.

Alexander bent and pulled out several large sheets of paper from a cardboard tube and set them out against the hood of the van. The wind wanted to carry them away, but the man gripped at the edges to hold the paper in place. Caleb studied them a moment, recognizing the familiar topography of a valley north of Jerusalem. A red line forked in two places all along a ridgeline. There were little yellow marks, with numbers set along the bold red outline.

"These are the spots?" asked Caleb.

"Yes," replied Alexander.

"And these numbers?" Caleb's fingers ran over the line to the yellow slashes.

"Those are the critical fault points. I numbered them in order of what I think to be the most sensitive spots."

Caleb turned and gave the man a grateful look. "How helpful," he said. "Bless you."

"You would need to get the charges down deep into the rock," added Alexander. "I would say at least four or five hundred feet, but this is all conjecture. You would need an enormous explosion to set off that fault...I don't think it could be done without nukes."

"But it would work?" inquired Caleb coolly. "Theoretically...it's all conjecture of course."

Alexander shot Caleb a bothered stare. "Yes," he answered, "my guess is with enough yield in the blast... the plate would shift. It would send a shockwave all the way down the valley, amplified by the soil deposits and rock formations under the city."

"And the Temple Mount?"

"Depending on the magnitude, everything on it would likely crumble...the Mosque and the Church."

Caleb's eyes lit up.

Alexander felt sick when he saw the man's face. "You are off your head, Drake."

"Now, now...it's all simply conjecture...like we said. I'm only trying to make a point in my new book about Bible prophecy, and the end-days. You see, we evangelicals believe that the second coming of Christ cannot arrive until after the Jewish Temple is rebuilt. That gold dome of those heathen Muslims is an impediment to that end....so it has to come down sometime. I'm simply laying out one possible way it might happen....should terrorist get a hold of something like a nuclear weapon."

"What about your precious Church of the Seplica?"

"Oh, I am sure if something like this were to ever really happen...God's angles would protect *our* holy places."

Caleb turned and rolled up the maps, then carried them around to the passenger side of the van. He opened the door and reached for the glove compartment, taking out a white envelope. He handed it to Alexander across the open door.

"Please keep my name out of your book," said the nervous geologist as he took the money. "I find this crazy...if terrorists here ever got a hold of a nuclear weapon, only a fool would think they'd use it to set off an earthquake. They'd level a Jewish city instead."

"Don't worry...like I said, it's all just conjecture," Caleb replied with a chuckle, trying to pacify the man.

Alexander shoved the plans in his hand. A part of him ached to slap the self-righteous grin from Caleb's face.

Caleb walked to the back of a van. He looked out at the road; it invited him to his fate he thought. They would head north by night, and cross from Syrian into Iraq, convincing sympatric locals they were actually running guns for the PKK, paying them off with large sums of money. The bibles were actually harder to ship than munitions. The Muslim authorities frowned upon western influences, guns however were common currency.

He pulled the seat cover back and looked down at the two cases stowed there. Caleb smiled. *Thy will be done*, he thought to himself triumphantly, rubbing his hand across the brutal weapons.

❦

Jon returned from wandering the quiet streets after their fight and furious sex, still finding no sign of Drake. Both he and Nick sulked about the house, saying nothing to one another the rest of the day. The Accuser wondered if he could do anything right in the boy's eyes. It bothered him that he even cared what Jon thought, but for some strange reason he did.

They sat together looking out at the sea. It turned gloomy and rough.

"I'm not tracking across this god-awful country," said Jon finally. "I mean it. Are you taking me right to Arbil from here or not? I know that you can do it...I've seen it in my head."

Nick no longer had the energy to fight Jon. He dropped his head, glared, and nodded.

"Good," grunted the prophet.

Nick drew a heavy breath. "I should go ahead alone to meet Ibn first then," he said, "to make sure it's safe."

"I'm sure I can find something to keep myself occupied." said the boy.

Everything about Jon was different to Nick now. The Accuser had no explanation for it. He rose and walked to the bathroom without another word. After Nick showered, he put on some durable clothing. Standing in the mirror, he reached inside for the last of his ethereal power; he would need it. When the Accuser came out of the bath, Jon was laying on the bed flipping through some kind of guide he had picked up in one of the hotels nearby. Nick stepped close and pulled the cover back to examine what it was he had. It was a listing of baths and clubs catering to tourists. The Jinn gave Jon a wounded look.

"Watch yourself in the baths here, Jon," said Nick. "You are not in New York...things are very different here. You can get in some serious trouble."

They exchanged another cold, hurtful look; then Nick pivoted out the door. He cut into the ethereal realm, using it to bridge the distance to Arbil. It was quiet there, as if all of creation had become soulless. He soared high above the old city for a time, looking down at the massive urban sprawl that had taken over the land. *How different it seems,* Nick thought, *after so many years.*

At the center of the city was the tall, oval rise of the old citadel. It radiated dark power, resembling a festering sore upon the land – its walls held a sinister past. While it could not really be said the residents of Arbil were more errant than any other people, this sadly was the place that the mortal sons of Adam had first learned to subjugate and torment one another. Nick in turn had tortured them in horrible ways for their Sijjin...that much was true. While the fire of the dragons had burned away the blemishes of Nick's soul, it had not removed the stain of sin there where mankind first took refuge in selfishness. Arbil bore the iniquitous mark of Kain, and Nick was in part to blame for its horror.

The Accuser soared high over the city for awhile; then decided to try something he had been hesitant to do up to that point, because of Jon. The essence of the nameless-god was almost fully emptied, his power growing weaker and weaker. Even the simplest of things were difficult now for Nick. So reluctantly, he reached into the dark fire of the dragons and tried to use it consciously for the first time. He was not pleased with what he found as the power caused his senses to spring to life – the city was crawling with Pythia.

Trying not dwell on that disturbing fact, Nick quickly reasoned that he should be about his business. He moved north, toward the familiar Christian area he had known during the gloomy crusades, when he was last there in the city. The Jinn gradually spun down and cloaked his form, landing near an open market. He walked through the mass of teaming people and down a secluded street to a well kept hovel. Stopping, Nick paced outside it, not sure if he was in the right spot or not from the file Mason had left him. The Accuser finally looked in both directions and warily knocked on the door.

A few seconds passed; the latch rattled and the door slowly cracked open. There appeared a rather broad man, with a wholesome look. He struggled a moment with Nick's face, as if trying to recognize him.

"Nikolai?" he asked after a few seconds.

Nick smiled back at him. "Yes Ibn, may I speak with you? It's important."

The man stuck his head out of the door and quickly reached for Nick, pulling the Jinn inside. The room warmed Nick's senses. It always seemed to Nick that Ibn was surrounded by an air of peace and nobility. The continence of a truly faithful man could not be faked the Accuser knew. Just like iniquity bore its mark, so did righteousness. Ibn was descended from a long line of noble, Alawite warriors. He now served as an agent with the Syrian Military Defense Services. Nick met the man nearly three decades before, back in Syria during what was then called the October War. The Accuser was running guns to the Syrians at the time; they had become associates. Ibn's men had been pinned down in the fighting for a night, with no way to escape but through the advancing enemy line. He turned to the Jinn in desperation and the Accuser felt he could not refuse the mortal a pact in order to allow them an escape – now Nick understood why he had felt so compelled to help the man. War often can make for the most unlikely companions, but there was something else to this Ibn – their fates were somehow tied then to this day.

"What are you doing here?" said Ibn nervously. "Have you any idea what's going on?"

Nick tried to look surprised, shaking his head to indicate that he did not. He was not sure what Ibn understood of what was unfolding, but the man was no fool. He knew Nick well enough to realize this was no social call.

"By Allah, Nikolai," Ibn responded, "things are spiraling out of control, but I am glad you are here. I spoke to my superiors in Damascus just last night. They have been monitoring radio-chatter from the Mossad and the CIA. Something dreadful is on its way here. It feels of the vipers again…like all those years ago. Damascus believes the Kurds have gotten a hold of at least one or possibly two portable nuclear weapons from the west!"

Nick made a funny face. "The trumpets have begun to sound," he said. "Something dreadful *is* on its way…judgment draws near and the Pythia are nesting chaos in the world, preparing it for war."

Ibn collapsed to a nearby chair, his face looked lost. "Allah save us," he whimpered. "The day has finally come."

"Believe it or not, I'm working on something. I am bringing a powerful seer here who may be able to help us. I heard you were here from our friends at the CIA. I need a place to stay. Can you help, Ibn?"

"For you anything," replied the Alawite. "I owe you my life. Whatever is between you and Allah…you proved to me long ago the true essence of your soul, there in the Golan Heights." He turned to a pad of paper next to him and scribbled something on it.

"I'm not so sure I agree with your assessment of character," replied Nick, "but you have saved *me* now."

Ibn nodded and grinned back, handing him the paper. "My son, Mohammad, has an empty apartment that he uses for his business dealings…black-market I admit, but he is getting essentials to people here that the government withholds. Here is his address. He will know how you can keep a low profile in the city, but Nikolai, he is a devout young man and won't understand our relationship. I will tell him you are spies for Damascus, that is all he can know…he will not trust you otherwise."

"Better that than telling him you are repaying a war-debt to the Devil, I suppose. Thank you, old friend."

"Who would have thought me minion of the seducer of men all these years?" Ibn laughed.

"Not funny, you old fool…you are a minion of Allah alone and you know it."

"Nikolai, I have to find these ungodly weapons they say are on the way here. If the Republican Guard gets a hold of them, or worse yet they are set off anywhere in Iraq…it will destabilize the entire Middle East. Damascus says it will be Armageddon. The Arab world will blame the United States and Israel. Already they are saying a new crusade is afoot…that men of faith should prepare for jihad."

"Nothing will galvanize the Muslim world like the memory of those brutal years," replied Nick. "I will see if I can discover if the Kurds actually have these weapons and if so, where. I've a need to meet with them soon to pass off funds for a transaction. Even though I know they are in league with the Pythians now, I don't want them discovering I am on to them, just yet. I will go through with it to keep them off guard as long as I can. So I will see then if I can determine more about what they are planning. Anything I hear I will pass back to you by way of your son, agreed? That will add to our cover for him."

The man frowned and nodded to Nick sadly, holding to that smallest of hope at least, which God's Accuser gave him, that the dragons would fail. Then the Devil slipped out of the door and was gone. He split open the ethereal realm and headed straight for Jon. The prophet sat in their room waiting. He saw flashes again in his mind. A strange city from a high vantage; another man he did not recognize; then Nick fleeing the scene back. As the Accuser broke into the room, Jon was ready for him.

"It's bad," said the prophet to the Accuser. "Time grows short."

"Yes," answered Nick.

"Let's not waste anymore time. This has been driving me nuts...I need to know why God wants me there."

Nick walked over to him and took him in his arms. They held each other tightly, despite all the recent tension between them. Then the Accuser opened a portal and stepped inside; Jon followed on his heels. When they emerged on the other side, they fell into the last thing they imagined to find. Nick had materialized in a square not far from where Ibn said Mohammad would be. There was a successive series of pops as they stepped from the portal; the entire area was riddled with gunfire. It was mayhem.

Iraqi military-police were opening up on a group of rebels. Bystanders scurried in all directions away from the hail of bullets and the rain of blood. The

Accuser fell on top of Jon and warded them both with his wings as best he could. As he did, three small boys ran from across the street toward where they both lay near a low wall, looking for cover as well. When they were about ten feet away, a spray of gunfire let loose. They were caught by its crossfire, mercilessly cut to ribbons in seconds. Blood seemed to cover every inch around the spot where they lay.

"Welcome to Hell, Jon," said the Accuser. "I told you this was no Sunday picnic…it was a bad idea to come this way."

❧

Mohammad was right where Ibn said he would be. Just as promised, the young Alawite hid them in a tiny flat. A few days after the commotion caused by the fire-fight, Nick felt safe to move around the neighborhood with Jon. That particular area of Arbil was called Ankawa; home to a small community of Assyrian Christians – a place the authorities would mostly avoid unless there was trouble. The prophet became despondent. Each time Nick went near him, the boy shrugged him off. The attack and subsequent death of the young boys seemed to rattle Jon; his aura was dark and impenetrable. At times Nick could feel such rage seething from it that it frightened him.

Jon and Mohammad became fast friends. They were an unlikely pair, but it reminded Nick of how he and Ibn had found camaraderie once. The young Alawite was Jon's guide and to some extent babysitter

– the young prophet clearly needed one there in Nick's mind. He was not yet aware of Jon's immense power, how the boy was grasping much more of what was happening around them than even Nick was.

Jon affectionately called his new friend 'Moe' for short, as they wandered the streets selling contraband together like a couple of mischievous school boys. The effort preoccupied Jon and clearly seemed to break up the anxious rage he held. He needed constant distraction.

It was then the Accuser decided to retrieve the funds from London, and deliver them to the PKK contact in Arbil that Nazim had given him. He wanted to get the affair over with, to put some distance between him and the Kurdish rebels now that he suspected their leadership was bound up with the Pythians. Nick also realized that the last of his ethereal power was emptying out – he had been barely able to pull Jon away to safety when they arrived. The time to act was on him, before all ethereal ability completely subsided in the wake of the dark-matter enshrouding the material plane. He still feared what Jon would do when the young prophet saw how much Pythian fire was beginning to build inside his essence, and he realized more and more he would be forced to use it.

When Jon seemed most distracted, Nick left him with Mohammed. The Jinn quickly made his way to London. He returned with the money and passed it off, then lurked about as best he could, using the smallest portion of dark power to cloak his form. But he was still unable to discover more than the fact that the Kurds were amassing weapons – nothing about any nuclear devices. He hoped Ibn's information was merely rumor, but after seeing what the serpents had attempted in the gulf...anything was possible now he feared.

Jon acclimated himself to Arbil under the watchful eye of his new friend. Once Jon and Mohammad were on their own, with the afternoon sun rising high, they drifted around the square where the young Syrian dealt his array of goods. Jon grew bored quickly, even with learning how to barter in the street. He'd made Mohammad promise not to tell Nick that he could speak Arabic fluently. The young Alawite simply thought it was all part of their intrigue. Jon wandered off a bit, and sat scanning the crowd. It was then that he happened to catch the eye of a strikingly handsome young man, lingering near an open air café. Something about the stranger struck Jon as deeply alluring. They kept exchanging glances and grins, the young man's interest emboldening the prophet.

After a time, Jon got up and walked toward him, fearless. Mohammed jumped to stop him, but the impatient prophet waived him off. Jon was smitten, as if drawn by some spell. He sauntered up to the table, then stopped and smiled down into the man's dark eyes.

"Greetings," the young man said to him in very poor Kurdi.

Jon instantly knew he was not a local. The prophet twisted his head to indicate he didn't understand – but he did. "Sorry?" he said out loud in English.

"Are you an American?"

"Does it show?"

The young man grinned again and nodded at Jon, not wanting to tell him it was more his mane of bright red hair that made him standout.

"I am Luke," the handsome stranger said. He stood and extended his hand. As they touched, a surge went through Jon. Luke stared into the prophet's eyes; he too seemed to be enchanted by something.

"You're from England?" asked Jon, recognizing the accent.

"Yes," replied Luke, "South London originally, but I study in the US."

"Seriously? I was just there. Interesting place, London…it reminded me a lot of home."

"And where in the US would that be?" asked Luke, as he motioned for Jon to sit.

In the distance, Mohammed became very anxious and paced with this pack. It was precisely the sort of thing Nick had said to avoid. They did not need any attention from outsiders.

"New York," answered Jon.

"Wow," said the handsome Englishman. "I love New York."

Jon just smirked at the coy euphuism, which he knew was meant to be clever. Then the prophet looked at the young man's exotic features intently. "What's your ethnicity?" he asked, "if you don't mind my asking."

Luke laughed nervously. "My mother's family was from Pakistan," he said, "and my father is originally from as small town near Manchester in England, called Holmes Chapel…I am half-and-half actually."

Jon leaned forward and drove his own eyes deep into Luke's. "You are very hot," he said bravely. "I'm into guys with dark looks."

Silence followed.

Jon wondered how the man would take the frankness of his advance. In the end, the prophet didn't really care if he was offended or not. Luke leaned back in his seat, never taking his eyes off of Jon. "I was hoping you might," he said. "You want to get out of here?"

Jon glanced at Mohammed with his characteristic nervous twitch, but the young Alawite's attention was usefully elsewhere that very second. Luke stood and they both wandered away together, quietly. A mass of people swirled around them as they walked down a hard packed side street toward a hill that sloped up in the direction of the old citadel. Both were taking a chance by wandering away from the market. Luke glanced back over his shoulder, sure that he had seen someone following them.

They came abruptly to an area where the path crested and curved – a good portion of the city could be seen far off in the distance. There a small stair zigzagged below them into a kind of vaulted space. Without even realizing it, Jon cast a cloak and they moved out of view from the street.

Luke sat upon the top step. He seemed to relax, as if to senses the prophet's power. The young American made him feel safe somehow; safer oddly than he had in years.

With a warm expression, Luke looked out at the span of urban sprawl around the old part of the city. There in the distance, the center of the old citadel rose like a mountain above the rest of the newer urban cityscape. Jon could sense that he was in awe of the city.

"This is said to be one of the oldest continuously inhabited communities in the world," said Luke. "It's rich with spiritual history."

Jon smiled, watching his delicate lips move, basically unaware of what he was really saying. "Oh Yeah?" he said with almost no emotion, pretending to care.

"Local legend says the city was founded by Kain. North of us, in the foot hills, is the tomb of his brother, Abel. The locals here call him by the name Habil."

"Really?" said Jon, still disaffected.

"Yeah, they say the city was here long before either the Sumerians or the Akkadians ever began to build their empires." The boy smiled at Jon. "I study biblical archeology, I'm here with missionaries."

All of a sudden Jon's attention turned, he narrowed his eyes. "Tell me more," he said, realizing the boy could help him.

Luke then went on explaining what he understood of Arbil and its dark past. Jon was fascinated. After about an hour of intense conversation, Luke reached over and touched Jon on the leg. "Can I show you something?" asked the dark eyed boy.

Jon nodded. A chill fell over him and goose bumps rose along his arm. Jon wanted the boy suddenly, like he had never wanted anyone before.

Luke took the prophet by the hand and led him down the stairs a few feet. As they twisted past the vault opening, the boy pushed Jon gently against the wall, out of sight of the street and stair. He went down slowly on his knees in front of the prophet and starred longingly up into his eyes. Jon shifted his weight back against the hard, cold surface of the stone, then reached over and placed his hand softly along the side of the young man's head. Unconsciously, he deepened the cloak and they *both* marveled in how safe they felt together.

Luke leaned into the caress as he reached up for Jon's belt, never taking his eyes away from the prophet's. Jon harshly grabbed a handful of the boys black hair and encouraged him. Luke stopped a minute, a little surprised by the forcefulness; but his expression quickly turned to abandon. Jon took that as a sign of submission, and after that was anything but gentile with the boy. Luke was more than accommodating. The prophet's ward seemed to suddenly envelope all the light around them. They slipped off to some other realm for awhile, dark and to themselves, neither realizing they had left that place with their indiscretion.

Twenty minutes later, sated of yearning, they both walked back down the path toward the market. The young missionary anxiously looked over at the prophet, who seemed to exude such strength – a magnetism the young man was trying hard to ignore. He wanted Jon desperately, but knew in his heart it was a bad idea to pursue this affair.

"I like you," said Luke, "but we can't do that again. I am here with a special missionary group...one in which I am working to free myself of...well...of these desires."

"Oh yeah?" asked Jon, trying not to laugh.

"Please, be discrete. You know our Pastor... Doctor Drake."

The prophet stopped in the path. "Caleb Drake?" he asked.

"Yes," answered the boy.

A range of emotions came on Jon so fast that he could not make them out: fear, anger, curiosity, even twisted glee. Luke shot Jon a guilty look as he leaned close to him, seeing the prophet was less than pleased.

"Then you know why he is here?" barked Jon, ignoring the fact that at some level he felt like he had just been played for a fool.

"Sure, we're surveying the tomb I told you about, as well doing the normal missionary work we always do when traveling aboard: bibles for the locals, saving souls...that sort of thing. The bibles were a lot of trouble smuggling in...the Muslim authorities frown on western Christians meddling here."

"Right, the tomb you say...what's so big about that?" asked Jon, his curiosity about Drake peaked.

"Well," said the boy, "Arabic legend holds that when Kain wanted to kill his brother, he actually didn't know how. So, he prayed to the Devil, who they call Iblis here."

Jon suddenly felt sick to his stomach at the mention of Nick. "I see," he said in a shallow voice.

"Iblis gave him two stones and told him that the way to kill his brother was to crush his head with them."

"How gracious of him," said Jon sarcastically, remembering what Nick had said in London about putting stones in some ones hands. Luke laughed out loud – unaware of Jon's intent.

"The mark of Kain," Luke went on to explain, "is his despair for the sin of killing his brother…the word Iblis actually means 'to despair' in Arabic. Legend says the stones were burred with Abel's body. Kain was blinded and sealed in the tomb as well, for all time. He received dark omens while trapped there…cursed with a kind of immortality to prolong his suffering. He wrote all over the inside of the tomb with his own blood. It's a frightful place. The scratching on the walls say the stones are the only thing that can send the Devil to hell forever. Drake believes the second coming of the Lord is close at hand – the relics will be pivotal weapons in the war against the Devil, and those that follow him."

Jon was not sure if he felt afraid or relieved to learn Nick had a weakness. "Does Caleb know you were spying on me, Luke?"

"He actually told me to watch for you and to help you," answered the young man. He looked ashamed. "But that's not why I did what I did…I like you, really I do."

Jon twisted his head, looking at Luke with his deep green stare. *He will be useful,* thought the prophet to himself. "I like you too," replied Jon back, in a half-hearted tone.

Luke didn't notice the bad-smell face, or understand what it meant.

"How can I find Drake," asked the prophet, "should I need to?"

"The compound is on the east side of the market," replied Luke, with a warm smile, "near the Assyrian Church...you can't miss the high walls."

13

SHEOL

When James opened his eyes, Astarte was holding him firmly in her arms; his head nestled upon the fullness of her breast. He could feel the cold darkness all around him. Her embrace was comforting.

"Hush now," the goddess said to him, stroking his head softly. "It's over for now...you have done well, my child."

He dared to look up into her face. Her radiant smile was pure console. She was the spirit of Heaven itself, lost to the darkness. James began to sob.

"I can't do this anymore," he said through his tears. "It's killing me!"

"Yes, James," she said, "it is...it's called the mortal veil. You all must face death, but there is more for you to do before that. Be still."

She was trying to comfort him with her tone, but James didn't find her words reassuring. "Thanks... just what I wanted to hear," he replied with a gasp of grief and laughter all together.

"I promise you that before this is over, you will be with me and that in time all the people you love will join us. But for now, we must struggle against the dark heart of the dragons alone. You hold destiny's hope in your hands."

"I can go back to him, can't I...to Adriano?"

"I think so, I am not sure of that yet. We have to find a way first...but you are not yet bound here. You cannot be until you partake of this place. Did you bring the manna from the ark of the Mercy Seat...as I instructed?"

"Yes," said James. He produced a handful of seeds that he had surreptitiously taken from inside the ark when Adriano wasn't looking.

"Eat one seed...it will sustain your hunger for the length of a day. Each time you find that your stomach rumbles, eat one. Count them so you will know the passing of days here amid the nothingness of Sheol.

"Where is that?" asked James.

"We are in the deepest part of the Abyss," she replied, "adrift in the void of the dragons...swallowed into the very bowl of chaos. But here you are sheltered by my embrace. Rest for now."

With that she waved her hands and around them appeared a magnificent hall, with a burning fire and lush beds at the center. She pulled him close and set him next to her on a soft pillow, one like he remembered in Nafees' apartment. Then she brushed his face gently with her hands.

"You are so brave and lovely," she said, "the first of my children that I have been able to touch in many, many years. Were you not one of my own priests, I would lay with you now."

James looked at her sidewise. She was truly lovely, but not enough for that. He suddenly wanted Adriano's hand in his own at that moment, very badly.

"I want to dance," the Queen of Heaven announced with a grin.

The hall unexpectedly filled with lively song, the thunder of drums, and the hallowed breath of a ney. She roared up from the soft seating and began to twist and spin, her motion was so graceful that James found himself wanting to cry for it. He sat transfixed, reminded of the consecrated dance he had shared with Adriano, both at Twilo and also that night at the Hadhar.

James was blessed to bask in the source of wajd. It was as if he had entered some strange trance, never sensing the passing of time. He knew only by the number of manna seeds he had eaten that many timeless days went by. The queen danced joyfully all that time, her grace and finery endlessly captivating him.

When she stopped, it was as if a spell had been lifted. He was drained, but sustained in his soul. Astarte slipped up next to him on the bedding. Worry was suddenly painted all over her face.

"Aboddon draws near again," she said. "You remember the dragon? You must go now, but I have one last task for you...here in Sheol...to please your queen. After that you must find a way to return to the mortal veil, and defend it as best you can from the dragons."

"How do I escape this place?" replied James with excitement.

"I am not certain," she said. "*You* must find the way...it is your fate. I don't know the path out...only in. If I did I would tell you. It is said however that the Jinn, Iblis, will understand and can find a way out...

look into his true heart. I know you have that power, you alone now know what the Devil truly desires."

"What must I do for you, my queen?" asked James.

"Take the fragments of the tablets and go into the vast void. Carry them as far away from me as you can, until there is no more manna. Then leave them there alone. The chaos of the Abyss will enshroud them... even the dragons will not be able to find them in the nothingness. When the time is right, the nameless-god will come for them. He will know how to pierce the depth of this dark place."

"I don't understand...you had me bring them here to hide them?" asked James.

"Yes, once the dragons are fully loosed, the tablets will be vulnerable in the mortal veil...they must be hidden here until God is made whole again and can use them."

James looked down at the tablets, wrapped in his souf, wondering what he would do. The queen kissed him on the forehead, and motioned for him to go. He picked up the tablets; they seemed weightless. The enchanted antechamber dissipated quickly like a mist, and she drifted way. Her face was contorted by her grief. James could smell rotting wood and swamp gases for a brief moment, like in his dream. Then there was nothingness all around him. He drifted endlessly.

In that great darkness, the deprivation of sense caused James to slip into another trance-like state. Images came to him and then spilled away. Feelings clung to him, then were forgotten. He would become hungry now and again. That single urge would rattle him back to a lucid state long enough to reach for another one of the seeds. Once he had eaten of the manna, his soul would float off again into the delirium.

Finally, the time came when he had eaten the last hallowed seed. He let go of the souf and its contents, wondering how in Heaven the nameless-god would find them there. As he did, a chilling realization came over him. He was suddenly alone in the void, just as the queen had been. He had not eaten of that place, but now the miraculous food was gone. *What will happen to me?* he thought to himself.

James turned in, drawing on his ethereal power. He searched the collective memories of every creature that had ever been touched by Nick or the two servants of the Pythia. Nothing came to him. He was confused, because the queen had said that Nick might have had some knowledge of that place. As he realized there was nothing in his soul that could help, he became angry. His rage built as he thought of Nick. Suddenly it hit him that anger was in fact the key...like Nick's fury. It could be used.

The bitter feelings of the Accuser commingled with his own and swiftly led him back to one soul: Adriano – the man he missed more than anything else in the world. James found this rage was not, at first, directed toward the knight he loved. It was more about being kept apart from him, as Nick had been kept from God. As his ire simmered however, the young seer found that he was becoming angrier and angrier at the knight for some reason. *Where is he?*

thought James. *Why has he left me here like this? He– of all people– should be able to find me.*

His mind raced in a panic.

James understood suddenly what was happening inside his soul. The spell put there by Nafees was causing a kind of angst toward the big man now; he concentrated on the enchantment, remembering that he told Adriano they would put it too their backs, facing out into the world so that it would never come between them again. James instinctively re-oriented the spell to face toward him. Again, he touched it and with all of his ethereal focus, spoke into the immortal magic woven between him and his Rafiq.

"Adriano?" he said. "Are you there?" His voiced echoed across the endless void.

Dimensions away, in the small Aksum vault, Adriano sat weeping. It had only been a few hours since James leapt into the mysterious portal, not days the way it had seemed for the lost seer. His grief was turning to irritation all of a sudden, for how James had left him there with nothing.

Neither man fully realized it was the spell drawing them together.

The torchlight had gone out, but the strange flaming tree seemed to still cast light into the room. As he raised his head to look at it, it appeared to flutter, almost as if in a breeze. He heard a voice. It was James. Adriano jumped to his feet and whipped the tears from his eyes. The knight reached for the asherah that he had used to split open the first portal. An idea came to him. He turned, and with a frantic stroke tore at the flaming-tree tapestry, splitting it open. The fabric ripped, exploding outward with unimaginable strength.

The knight was blasted back from the force that erupted out of it, as if something had been pitched from the open gash with great velocity. It swept him off his feet. Gripping to it, he carried the object backwards to a standstill, his body landing in the corner. The powerful blow knocked the wind out of him; he gasped for air amid the murk and dust. The light gradually dissipated as the tapestry fell into tatters, and the room sank into darkness. The knight was totally lost in nothingness, alone and frightened – his hope emptied out. The object in his hands trembled; then the smell of something familiar and comforting caught his attention. It was the scent of James' hair.

"Adriano," said the seer, shivering in his arms. "Is that you?"

James had passed the test, but not with the outcome the immortals had expected. Nafees and Aaron decided it was best if they go ahead of the others with the young seer, leading only a small group into the Holy Land. The boy had proved their faith correct, but both understood it would be difficult now – there was a catch...no tablets.

Since they had seen the goddess themselves, they trusted James. But this would all be a hard sell to the immortal lord of the warriors in Jerusalem – the Gadol – who they now needed to rally around them for what they knew of God's plan to work.

The group traveled north by small plane to the port of Bar Sudan, and there picked up a cargo ship bound for Israel. Things seemed to be moving, they were finally underway for the land of Amo, God's people.

Adriano stood at the aft of the French freighter, watching the great surge of water that was thrown up by its propellers as it lurched out of the harbor. He was reminded for a moment of the aircraft carrier he had been stationed on only a few years before. The smell of the sea air comforted him, but his mind was rolling like the churning sea beneath the screws of the ship. He was griped with increasing trepidation as he began to sense that James was somehow slipping away from him.

At the corner of his eye, he caught motion. He watched Father Aaron approach.

"How is he?" asked the Tomar Knight, as he settled along the rail.

"Shaken," replied Adriano, "but coming around. He still won't see anyone but me."

"He is a brave soul," said the mysterious Tomar knight. "None have been to the underworld and returned to speak of it…but for Joshu himself."

Adriano glanced over in Aaron's direction. He was not sure how to respond. He drew a deep breath; none of what had happened seemed fair. The knight found himself beginning to resent what their quest was doing to the young man he loved so much. Turning away again, without saying a word, he grunted his agreement into the brisk sea air.

"So, how are *you* doing?" Aaron asked. His voice was heavy with concern.

Adriano dropped his chin to the rail. It was apparent the responsibility placed upon him was also taking its toll.

"I feel worthless," said the big man sadly. "All I want is to take the pain away from him…to dispel that shadow that lingers within his spirit. But I can't."

"Sometimes the wounds of our companions burden us more than our own," said the Tomar. "War is an ugly thing."

A shiver ran down Adriano's spine as he realized that his affection for James had caused him to forget the true pith of war – its brutal, senseless chaos as it weighs hard against a man's spirit. Adriano was no stranger to it. He was a veteran of Desert Storm, a more conventional mortal war, but still very dreadful in its own way.

"It all feels worse than what I remember," said the big man. "I've seen battle…this is something else… something even more unspeakable."

"You are right," said Aaron. "It is something else. It is beyond anything we as souls understand of war. The stakes are not fully knowable to us…thus we must act from our faith."

"Must we really?" asked Adriano. "I am not sure that is true for me. I am beyond faith." He stiffened and spread his weight across his legs. "To act on faith," he explained to Aaron, "suggests we are compelled to something we cannot see, or sense, moving toward an end we *believe* righteous, no?"

Adriano tipped his head toward Aaron to see his response.

"True enough," replied the Tomar.

Adriano sighed and continued. "It may be true we don't understand the full end to which we work for God, but this is no longer a matter of faith for me, Aaron. I am fighting for something much more tangible right now. It's not about what I believe any more. I am fighting for the man I love more than life itself...that I know!"

Aaron smiled and reached over to place his hand upon the Rafiq soldier's back. He spoke in a reassuring tone. "You have clinched it, my friend. You have touched upon the one thing that separates the Tomar from the rest of the Asirim Brotherhood... what separates you from the rest of the Rafiq I suspect."

"I am not sure I follow," said Adriano.

"Come on Brother," replied Aaron, "you see perfectly...you just aren't letting your mind follow your heart. That is why *we* are different from other sects, divided by a subtle but central principal that drives us."

"For the old Hebrew order, the Gadol, salvation has always been a matter of legal obedience. They follow only legalism, as they understand it anyway, and that alone compels them to this day. They see the destruction and exiles that we have endured as the price paid for disobedience – penance for breaking that law. So to them reconciling with God's commandments is the only thing that matters now, before the end...but their legalism is a form of denial. It blinds them to the truth."

"For the Rafiq, on the other hand, devotion has become about submission to the will of God... as supposedly espoused by their great prophet Muhammad. Again, as it is interpreted by men.... you understand that he never actually wrote anything down himself. Muslims trust the word of others for truth, passed down to them in the Koran. To Muslims, it is about submission to the will of *those* words alone... but like always they are tinged with the ambitions of men, the pursuit of empire. Hence the Rafiq's misunderstood alliance with the Accuser, you see... Iblis represents to Nafees and his men the last stand of unwillingness to surrender to God's will. It is the Devil's redemption that signifies the plight of all men. If *he* submits, the kingdom of God is truly at hand in their eyes...ironically they may not be wrong about that."

"But we Christians of the lost Asirim, even you as a rare representative of our faith within the ranks of the Sufi knights, believe we have a slightly different charge to follow...made exemplary by our Lord, Joshu. While we too have had our share of men who have distorted the truth...bishops, popes, and emperors...it is in the end love alone that brings us to God, Adriano...pure adoration in all its forms. The others all seem to have forgotten the gifts of the Queen of Heaven, and the grace of God's love in her."

Adriano looked at him pensively. Aaron's words did seem to strike some resonant chord for the knight. He needed to look past his hurt and fear of loss to love, now more than ever.

"Don't get me wrong," Aaron went on. "I am not saying that the path either of my companion orders has chosen is totally errant – as they might contend of us. Only that we have all come to understand ourselves and our purpose here on earth differently. Nafees would even argue with me about the Sufis, and their devotion to love and the goddess. It's all a matter of perspective in the end, and faith. Don't you see, my brother, you have not lost your faith... you have justified it."

"Then why does this all seem so senseless?" said Adriano, looking up at the handsome Tomar Knight with sad eyes.

"Because love is irrational and often senseless," he replied, "purely and gloriously, absurd. Acting out love and compassion is the greatest leap of faith you will ever perform...the most supreme of acts to which God would have us commit ourselves." Aaron reached over and hugged Adriano with one powerful arm. "Shalom my brother," he said to the big man sweetly. "Peace be with you in this terrible time of chaos."

Adriano did suddenly feel a little better with the gesture, not completely sure why. He liked Aaron a lot, for he was truly a righteous spirit.

"So in the end what is this all for?" the big man asked.

"See here, there is one underpinning truth we all face...whether you come at it by way of love or law. God's will is actually very simple. The essence of what should be is freedom...we must resist that compulsion to subjugate and harm our brothers. War and empire are evil things...there can be no holy wars, no holy empires. The original Torah, the New Testament, even the Koran really have a simple message...love thy brother, love thy God...and all else will be well. Men have twisted God's simple intention to mean otherwise. In that, they have turned on each other for the sake of power and avarice."

"It's even hard to blame the serpents at times, for while they tempt and seduce, it is man himself who reaches for those forbidden fruits...power and ambition are the true root of evil. Moses led us out of captivity in Egypt, Joshu lead us away from the tyranny of religions hypocrisy, and Muhammad the cruelty of greedy pagan fiefs. These holy men were all actually after the same things. Yet each of their ways eventually fell into man's trap...the need for power."

"*Man* draw the dragon's here...they would have no sway if not fed by mortal ambition and what mankind so often is willing to do for it. Now the battle is taken up to Heaven at last...each soul must decide for itself, and face the consequences for ill or naught. This judgment is not brought down by God, it's a consequence of natural law...every action has an equal and opposite reaction. I see justice as a pendulum, swinging back on man for is selfishness."

The Rafiq knight drew in another heavy breath, relishing the sea air as Aaron tried to comfort and counsel him. He embraced the solace offered. There was a long pause as if both men let their minds drift off to some other place and the tasks that lay ahead of them.

"I am glad we decided to fly to Bar Sudan," said Adriano after a moment, "and to take a fast ship north."

"I agree. James needs rest now, and he needs you close, without the rest of us making a fuss over him. It's better the orders enter the Holy Land in small groups anyway, not like a crusading army."

"Isn't that what we are?" asked Adriano.

Aaron smiled at him, and half laughed. "Of course it is," he said, "but we don't have to tell the entire world that...do we?"

"No, it won't go over well here at all. Trust me... I've seen how much they resent the interference of any outsiders."

"As they should...but we are not here with our sign to divide and conquer. We come to unite the captives of the serpents this time."

That seemed to impress a thought in the big man's mind. "Speaking of outsiders in this land...how is it the Tomar are actually related to the Knights Templar?" he asked. "I thought they were all gone."

Aaron paused to reflect on the change of subject, then was happy to tell his story.

"After the Templar were accused of heresy in 1307 by the Pope and King of France, for our conjoining rites and for monophysitism - the belief in the total divinity of Joshu – it became even more important that we remained hidden. The relics we protected, and still do, must never fall in the hands of the dragons, or of power hungry men. I will share with you later why that is true."

"So, we changed our name to conceal our past... became the Order of Christ. Our Templar headquarters in Tomar, on the Iberian Peninsula, was rededicated to our new cause...we took the name Tomar Knights."

"How did it all start? How did you become Templar in the first place?"

"During the Crusades, a group of nine Frankish knights discovered the location of the Mercy Seat from a buried scroll in the Temple of Jerusalem. They came looking for it and when they found us guarding it, my order was pleased to merge with them to form the Christian Knights of the Temple of Solomon. It seemed quite the natural thing at the time. My monks here had converted to Christianity long before the Franks arrived. I myself saw Joshu, in Egypt. The satans on the ark told me to look for him there. He was a boy at the time, fleeing the serpent, Harrod. The Deliverer laid his hands on me...knowing me for what I was: a guardian of the Mercy Seat. I never doubted Him after that day. We became his servants for all time, so we in turn trusted the Franks to help us, and they did. It did not however turn out well for the rest of the region, I am afraid – the wars were senseless."

Adriano's eyes lit up. Of all the amazing things he'd heard on this mission, the idea of Aaron being touched by Christ enthralled him the most. The Tomar Knight sensed it and reached over to let a little of that spirit pass into the big man.

"So it seemed an easy paring between the old order of Solomon and the new nine from Europe," he went on to say. "We Christians of the east were persecuted by the orthodoxy in Rome and Constantinople for years…we were glad to have the nine see the truth of Christ. There is only one god as God, not begotten, or begetting…his human nature is absorbed by his deity, like a drop of honey in the sea."

"Somewhat like what the Rafiq believe," replied Adriano happily. "There is no God, but God."

"Yes, this is also why after the rise of Islam, it was the Muslims that sheltered us as a people of the book – while the Christians of the west tried to kill us. When the nine arrived, neither they nor we could afford to let the secret of the Mercy Seat get back to the corrupted powers of the Church in the west. We alone had access to the satans upon it, and the knowledge it afforded the Templar made us strong in ways the church feared."

"It still all seems so unbelievable to me."

"Well, there is in fact more to the story. I also became rather taken at the time with one of the young Templar: Hugues de Payens. The first Grandmaster of the order was also my first companion…I had never taken one until I met him."

"Ah, the real truth comes out," Adriano replied with a playful grin. "It's funny; as I recall the symbol of the Templar order was two soldiers of Christ on a single horse...I never did buy the poverty explanation for that."

Both men laughed.

"Especially when we were the wealthiest order of the time," said Aaron. "People see what they want to see. When the Christians took Jerusalem during the Crusades, it was a bloody ordeal. Many evil men found pleasure in the killing, on both sides. Sadly, the Christians bear a great deal of the culpability for what transpired then...there was nothing about it that was even remotely Christian. Nafees and I tried to broker a peace between Muslim and Templar, but the wicked wounds of the conflict ran too deep...they still do."

"We Rafiq were never told any of this, but it is all behind us. James will unite the Asirim now."

"There is one more obstacle to that...the Gadol will not be convinced easily. They have borne more suffering than all of us...for God's name and their wayward hearts. But yes, it would seem the time is at hand and I agree James is the one to do it."

Adriano paused a moment as a brisk breeze off the sea enveloped them. "What happened to your companion, if you don't mind my asking?"

"He died, Adriano. All mortal men die. I loved him dearly, but he returned to our source in the nameless-god. I did not take another companion until right before that brutal black Friday, when the King of France seized all our leaders in 1307...nearly two hundred years later. And I've not taken another since...it is hard, I admit that."

"And who was your second companion?"

Aaron's eyes looked sad. "Jean Walid...he went to his grave defending the honor of the Templar. He was burned at the stake." Aaron's voice broke up, after all this time it still brought him pain.

The big man squirmed. Then they both sat quietly looking at the waves. He understood the implication.

"Now see here, brother," finally added the Tomar knight-commander, "there is something else I need to speak with you about. Each of our orders has secrets, as you can tell, circumstances that have made us what we are. But the time has come for us to aside our philosophical differences and do what we know is before us."

"And what is that?" asked Adriano.

"Let me just say this," replied Aaron. "We trust *you*, Adriano. The poor-fellow soldiers of Christ and Tomar will follow you when the time comes. So to you we will entrust what we know of the battle ahead...the final test men, Jinn, and elohim will face together."

"You know more about what's to be faced when we get to Israel?" begged Adriano curiously.

"Here," he said, handing the knight an object wrapped in fine cloth. "I brought you something."

"What is this?"

"It's a gift...of sorts."

Adriano unbound the cloth. It was a small curved blade, well worked and engraved with elegant symbols.

"It's lovely...and remarkably balanced," he said, as he pivoted the blade in his hands. "I don't understand...why me?"

"You will someday. It's the blade of Joshu the Nazarene...one of the relics we have protected over the years."

"What?" asked the big man, in sudden awe of the weapon. "Christ had a blade?"

Aaron gave him a scolding look. "He was the messiah, not a fool. Sometimes men of faith must defend themselves...especially in the Judea of that day."

"I guess I am just surprised....it runs contrary to everything we believe about him." His hands shook as he ran his fingers over the handle, where Christ himself had gripped it.

"Really?" replied the Tomar Knight. He reached over and put one hand on Adriano's shoulder; then he recited scripture to the big man.

"Do you think I come to bring peace on the earth...I come not to bring peace, but to bring a sword, said Joshu unto the apostles."

"The Gospel of Mathew," answered Adriano in a low voice. "My God...chapter ten, verse thirty-four...I never really read that passage literally."

"Good boy! Nafees was right...you are more than a pretty face. "

They laughed together again.

"How did you come by the sword and why are you giving it to me?" asked the big man.

"That I can explain, but not here...come with me," said Aaron, as he pulled the Rafiq Knight away from the rail.

They wandered from the aft of the ship foreword, to the small cabin where the priest was staying. There both talked for hours about how the Tomar Knights had protected more than just the Ark of the Covenant for thousands of years. Adriano listened in wonder. It was during that discussion that Aaron reached for the rod, the sacred staff that Adriano wielded on behalf of the prophet. His touch seemed to pull back a veil, as if he had opened the lid of the Mercy Seat itself. There the Rafiq soldier found hope, where everyone else found despair.

The knight was filled with new resolve.

❧

Forces from INS *Hezt*, an Israeli missile cruiser, scurried over the deck of the Italian freighter, *Artemisia*. The ship had been bound for Syrian waters. The Israel defense forces combed through the hold for hours, while Seth Slivers sat on the upper deck of the cruiser, watching the eleven mariners from the freighter all standing in row at the stern. He pulled his coat closed in the brisk wind, then motioned for a sailor near him to bring a radio. The agent checked in with his men below, flicking his half-smoked cigarette out into the sea.

After no news of use, he turned inside the pilothouse and made his way to the cruiser's radio room. There he pitched is bulk into a swivel chair that was bolted to the floor and picked up a headset.

"Command, this is *Sa'ar*," he spoke into a microphone, "respond...."

"Go ahead *Sa'ar*, this is Command," answered a voice.

"We've swept the target...she is a clean, no radioactive signature. We've turned her upside down...there is nothing here."

"Repeat last update, *Sa'ar* ...what is the status of the broken arrows, confirm..."

"They are not here, Command...we recommend Jericho go to high alert. The broken arrows are in play, repeat the broken arrows are in play."

"Affirmative, *Sa'ar*. We will notify Jericho to go to high alert...confidence is high...out...."

Seth placed his head down on the table and rubbed the back of his neck again. *I will put a bullet in Drake myself*, he seethed in his mind.

Just then an intelligence officer walked in to the radio room. He stood in the doorway with a troubled face.

"What now?" asked Seth.

"These men are defiantly PKK, but no nukes on board. We've swept through three times and found no radiation signatures. We did however hit a mother-load of munitions...Libyan marked gun and gas canisters it would appear."

Seth looked up and made a cruel smile. "Better safe than sorry...take them below to the engine room. Shoot them and scuttle the ship with charges. Plant them in the boiler room."

"Any S.O.S?"

"No...lost souls, one and all. Get it done fast, I need to get back to Tel Aviv soon. Jericho is going to high alert...we've been setup."

"Yes sir," barked the officer.

The Israeli agents went about the grim business of executing the men and setting charges. Then the *Hezt* made a quick escape from the blast.

As the *Artemisia* sank, the gas canisters were ripped open by the explosion. They leaked a cloud of degrading arsenic compounds into the water. The plume floated south into the warmer fishing channels, poisoning the sea up the coast.

⚭

As senior knight of the joint campaign, Aaron led the Tomar and Rafiq from the ship, where it was moored in Eilat, Israel. As the handful of men reached the end of the gangway, there stood Hilkiah, Warlord of the Gadol. Security forces swarmed behind him; the Mossad had met the ship long before it entered the port and searched it top to bottom under the pretense of looking for weapons.

Hilkiah was a tall, dark featured man. He and Aaron bore a striking resemblance – both were dark browed, with chiseled cheeks that made them handsome beyond words. Hilkiah stared past Aaron right at James; his eyes penetrated the young seer.

"Hello, Brother," said Aaron cordially.

"Where is it?" replied Hilkiah, spinning to face the Tomar knight. His tone was hostile. "I don't sense it."

Just then Adriano step around Aaron and Hilkiah's glare fell upon him. His eyes surveyed the man's body; stopped for a moment as if to admire something; then glanced out along his arm to where the knight held the asherah staff.

"Plainly the mortal has been into the Holiest of Holies," he said finally. "But somehow you have managed to conceal the tablets from us. How is that possible?"

"God moves the hand of the prophet," said the Tomar.

"Oh yes?" the warlord laughed smugly. "Then show me the proof...take me to the Mercy Seat."

"Right to it then," moaned Nafees, "always the faithless voice." With that said, their eyes finally met.

"I've taken them to the goddess," James spoke up boldly, before any more could be said. His voice boomed amid the roar of sea spray and wind.

The Gadol warlord split his gaze between Nafees and Aaron. Then he laughed again, sounding grim. "You are joking," said the confounded immortal. "What are you talking about?"

"You cannot sense them," replied Aaron, "because they have gone out of this world, into the darkness of Sheol. The goddess came to the seer and showed him a way into the underworld. There they were left... hidden from the Pythia until God's time is nigh."

Hilkiah's face turned white. However mortifying and improbable, it *was* the only thing that could explain what he had felt. As bad as it sounded to him, he had little choice but to accept it. A long silence followed. Hilkiah studied James. *How meek he seems,* thought the imposing elohim, *just like Moses appeared... and how wrong was I about him.*

"Let me make something plain," said James finally. "I do not take my authority from the Asirim, or any part of it. It is not I who needs you...you need me."

With that he reached out and touched Hilkiah on the hand. He opened up his spirit and poured out the shadow of the Abyss upon the immortal. It caused Hilkiah to shrink in stature for just a moment. The seer then pushed past the warlord, heading to the waiting cars without another word. Adriano followed quickly on his heels.

The three brothers stood alone on the gangway, as it swayed in the wind. The pith of the reunion somehow brushed aside by the magnitude of the prophet's portent and his ominous touch.

"That's the goddess in him," said Nafees, smiling toward his two older brothers.

"All the mortal prophets spoke like that," said Hilkiah, shaking off the cold. "They never truly understand of what they speak."

Still, the intent was clear – James wanted Hilkiah to know the depth of loss with which they were all threatened at that moment. He also wanted the warlord to feel the hopelessness of the Abyss, which those who loved God endured. Most of all, he wanted Hilkiah to know *he* was there for the people of that holy land, nothing else.

The Gadol warrior abruptly turned his back on Aaron and Nafees, sauntering down the ramp behind James and Adriano. They could sense he was shaken, but still uncompromising.

Nafees took a deep breath and grinned. "It's good to be home," he said.

"Don't taunt him, Nonah," said Aaron, using the cleric's ancient again. "None of this is about us now."

Nafees nodded, as if he recognized authority in Aaron. They were now in the land of Yhw...the ancient home of the elohim, named for the one true God.

It took under a week for all the Tomar and Rafiq knights to file into Jerusalem from abroad, rejoining the older order of Gadol warriors. It was the first time all three branches of the Asirim had been assembled since Aaron fled Israel with Menelik into the Aksumite kingdom thousands of years before. All the knights seemed to understand the enormous consequence of the homecoming. They feasted, drank, and danced with unimagined joy, as if the world would never end. The gladness it seemed to cause in the men lightened even James' mood. He and Adriano sat watching the Asirim as they mixed and laughed, wondering what would come next.

Hilkiah sat alone in his apartment overlooking the city and the Temple Mount, as the men celebrated. The warlord could not allow himself to share in that joy as yet – despite its true portent. He glared out into the cityscape. The gold from the Dome of the Rock seemed to gleam all the more that night, taunting him with what was buried beneath it.

He nestled into a large wingback chair, his mind drifting off to the past...to Sinai and his mistake then. The elohim was not yet convinced James was the true prophet. The Gadol had their own sources; they knew about Jon and the Accuser. Hilkiah understood the prophecy as well as anyone – one of them was a great danger to the Asirim.

I must be sure, he thought. *I've been wrong before and cannot afford to be so now.*

14

THE PARCAE

Jerusalem – January 2000

Aaron, Nafees, and Hilkiah walked along the Wailing Wall a day after they arrived in the Holy Land, watching people praying and pushing tiny portions of parchment into crevasses along its face. Aaron reached out and brushed the wall with one hand.

"It's hard to believe this is all that is left of the second temple," he said somberly.

"It was horrific to watch," replied Hilkiah, glaring at Nafees, "both times they destroyed it."

"*You* brought it on the Amo," said the cleric, "with your own arrogance....don't look at me. That was always your way...from the very beginning. You simply brought them all down with your insolence."

"What hand did you have in those downfalls, brother?" replied the Warlord. "Did you whisper rumors of wealth and power into the ears of the gentile nobles, as you eagerly presented them your ass?"

"You flatter yourself, Hilkiah," said Nafees. "Were it I'd that kind of power over the kings of men in those days. We were slaves in exile because of you! You know as well as anyone the Babylonian kings, the Pharaohs, even some of the Romans drew upon great power of their own. They were elohim, children Kishar, just as we were, and didn't need my help...nor did I offer it.

423

This was all *your* doing! You had to raise great temples and make a spectacle of things. Allah told you the price to be paid for that when you pulled your stunt at Sinai. Your zealots tempted the powers of the world well enough with rumors of Solomon's wealth and the extravagance of these temples without the seductive powers of my ass....that is for certain."

"Silence!" shouted Aaron.

Nafees and Hilkiah grit their teeth and glared at each other.

"The two of you are impossible," said the Tomar knight. "You talk as if the years have meant nothing, as if there was something left of that kingdom here worth fighting over. You are both pathetic. It's gone... all gone...and lays crushed under this rubble because the Amo do what we're doing now. We taught them well to squabble, did we not?"

"It's time you both faced the truth. The nameless-god sent us here to help these people, to protect them alone. Now you both bicker only over the lost stones of empires. None of us have cause to take the high ground after all that has happened...things have gotten away from each of us. Even if it was true that the Nafees enticed the Babylonians and Greeks here, Hilkiah, you clearly curled up close to Harrod and the Romans all those years later...when Ba'al returned in mortal flesh to reclaim the people. All three of us have failed in seeing the plan and fulfilling His command."

Nafees and Hilkiah were suddenly mortified. The name Aaron used for God right then had not been spoken aloud by any of the elohim for over twenty five thousand years. It was forbidden to call Him thus, but for those who God held closest to him. It was His most intimate name, holding a generative power many misunderstood – one they had learned from their sister long ago. God had punished many races of men as well as elohim for the hubris of evoking that name...Aaron had simply lost himself in anger. He too missed God.

"None of us," snapped Hilkiah defensively, "had any way of knowing that the nameless-god would take a mortal form that way," responding to Aaron's half accusation about Joshu. "Even to this day His intensions are unclear to us. We had no choice but to do as the Roman's said then. Besides, the Gadol were well in hiding amid caves by the time Joshu came into the temple with his message to chastise all. You know we had nothing to do with His death...whatever he was in the end. I resent that implication, and always have. Your Templar certainly left their mark here, Aaron...they were among the worst."

"I know," replied the Tomar. "My point is simply what's done is done. We're together once more just as the Mercy Seat divined that we would be. James is the leader we were told to wait for. Our great and loving sister blesses him...I've seen the proof with my own eyes. He touched the tablets. What more do you need, Hilkiah? This strife between us must end!"

"It's not that simple," replied the warlord, "and you know it."

"I told you, Aaron," Nafees hissed indignantly. "He will never listen. Nothing changes."

"What's not that simple?" asked Aaron calmly. "Pray tell me, brother."

"There is a reason we three were given this charge," said Hilkiah. "You know full well why I stayed true to His command...despite both you and your mortal fads. I and I alone bare responsibility to install the rightful king, the true messiah. The power only passes in birth rank to either of you...and I need to be sure first."

"What's he mean by mortal fads?" asked Nafees.

Aaron turned and gave the cleric a harsh look, as if to say he was being coy. He knew the Sufi was taunting the Gadol warrior. "Our choices in honoring a different faith to Him...Christianity and Islam," he answered in a low tone.

Nafees laughed out loud and raised his hands to Heaven. "We followed prophets...you made up your own rules!" he said.

"You are hypocrites...both your traditions made up their own rules. Whatever our past mistakes, His edict to us each is clear," Hilkiah said. "The Asirim will only be led by a son of David. Either James restores the Tablets of Destiny to the temple, or he proves his linage and leads our men to war with the voice of Heaven...the War Psalm of David's House. Those are His conditions."

"He had the tablets and he hid them," said Nafees, "where they will be safe. That should be proof enough for you."

"So you say," replied Hilkiah as he turned his face away, "but I am not convinced by what could be mere parlor tricks. We've seen impostors turn their rods to serpents in the past. I don't have your luxuries to follow the whims of folktale gospels and desert legends. I must be certain…and frankly, the two of you are of questionable faith in my eyes!"

Aaron just shrugged and walked off, away from the ruins of the past. There was no point in fighting with Hilkiah – God would find a way he knew.

❧

James tossed in his sleep, so Adriano pulled him close. The big man knew where his prophet was going – to their queen. At least it was only in spirit this time; Adriano would never willingly release him to that place again in body. A peaceful breeze drifted in and brought with it the familiar smell of honeysuckle.

James opened his eyes in his dream. He was there again, in the underworld. The seer could feel an immutable chill.

"Hello, James," came the soft voice of the goddess.

He sat up and glanced in her direction. She was sitting upon her dark throne. He smiled at her, albeit not from delight, simply in veneration.

"You found a way out…I am so glad," she said.

"Love found a way for me…through unlikely means."

"It always does, James," she said. "Faith in those we love always will."

He smiled again. This was an awkward conversation. The pain was still fresh.

"You are in the Holy City," she said warmly. "Is it not wonderful even now?"

"Yes, more beautiful than I ever imagined."

"And you have at last brought the unruly Fates home to Yhw," she said.

He looked at her, a little confused. "Fates?" he asked.

"You've not figure it out yet?" She seemed to relish the idea he was still blind to things. It added to his sense of innocence, which she found endearing. "The three stewards of time – future, past, and present – are together again at His *omphalous*...the center and source of God's power on earth."

The realization fell over James. "Damn!" he said out loud. "That's what's going on with them and that is how Nafees sees what he sees." The prophet milled over the idea a few seconds. "Hilkiah is so stubborn," he surmised. "He must be the guardian that resists change...the Lord over the past."

"Yes...he is the winged-bull who honors His traditions," she said, "the keeper of Kings and law. He is the true high-priest of the House of David... headstrong as he is."

"And Aaron keeps the present full of hope," he said in answer to that, "always the nurturing optimist...but grounded in his sensibilities"

She grinned. "The nameless-god selected them from His court to lead the Amo from bondage long ago, and to protect them. They are petulant, quarrelsome siblings...sometimes more like a trio of fighting hens."

"I had assumed the visions about the Holy City came from you," replied James

"I did help Nafees some," she said, "but he is a powerful seer in his own right. My oracle is limited in this place...I rely mostly on what my heart tells me of Him. Nafees is the weaver of fates...but alas even his power fades."

"The Holy City," he said anxiously as he thought of Nafees' power, "the dragons will destroy it."

"They will try," she replied. "You must stop them anyway you can."

"How?"

James could tell from her face she was not sure. "Go to the site of my old temple at Megiddo," she said finally, "and place the great asherah rod in the soil... cull together the power of all my former alters. The dragons know this must be done to unite the power of the sacred places, so the prophet may fulfill his propose, but they will not know it's you...they expect another that is clear. Then and there the nameless-god will make all things clear to you I think...what you must face."

She began to sing a soft tune under her voice with that, ever so gently, a lovely and enticing song. James sat and stared at her exquisite form, enchanted by the sound of her voice as if it reached inside of him. He was filled with familiar warmth, feeling the words take shape in his head.

"It's beautiful," he said to her. "I've heard the notes before...but I can't place the words. It's like something my mother used to sing to me as a child."

The goddess crooned more boldly, and the sound began to fill the room. "It's actually a powerful sema spell, James," she said, stopping for a moment, "an enchantment that you will find useful when you get to Megiddo. Not just anyone may use this mystical psalm, but you can...by right...something you don't know of yourself as yet fully."

"How do you know then?" he asked.

"I just do," was all she would say.

A chill fell over him and he felt the goddess become restless. He watched her spirit swirl amid the hall with the sound of the psalm.

"I can't stay," James said finally. "Darkness is growing in the world...the dragons will strike soon."

"I know," she replied.

He bowed his head in his dream and stirred in Adriano's arms, then awoke abruptly. Vision was still ringing about his head. Adriano noticed his eyes where weighted heavy with worry.

What now? the big man questioned into his mind.

"Megiddo," James whispered to his companion out loud.

"What?"

"Find Nafees, we're going to Megiddo...they are coming for us!"

cৠৎ

Aboddon stood in the dark catacombs that stretched under the Christian compound of Arbil. His thralls had been secretly tilling and toiling all over the area for years, waiting for the tide of darkness to rise. He'd unearthed the labyrinth remains of the old temple structure to the storm-god king and his goddess long ago, where devotes once ceremonially traced her passage into the underworld to commemorate mortal loss. The serpent chose that place to desecrate and insult her. He had discovered from the twisted oracle Kain that it was one of the last places ethereal light could be bound once the king was dethroned. God's prophet would seek refuge in its emanations.

Like in Jerusalem, strange wards culled together eleventh light in that place, for some unknown purpose. The years of human habitation and spiritual power had made it into a kind of ethereal thin-space, a world between worlds. Aboddon opened a portal into the ethereal realm, then used festering dark-matter to prop open a gateway out onto the plane near the walls of Eden itself.

The dragon stepped out from it, and drilled his gaze balefully at the high smoldering mountain where Joshu, the Lamb of God, would make his stand. He knew that if he could topple Eden and the elohim, little would stand in his way of destroying the incarnate nameless-god, and then overthrowing even the Queen of Chaos.

Aboddon drew to him intense energies he could now harness from the sinister weapons they had stolen; its power feeding into the net-like mesh of ethereal wards in the temple precincts. Few realized their true purpose and power but he. The serpent began to weave a powerful disruption in space-time, lacing though eras of mortal existence and drawing time taught into a web. He bound all ages with that spiteful spell, pulling together battlefields where war lingered as an undying phantom, rich with chaos.

Still, the time was not yet ripe. He did not possess the full means to call up his timeless army of the dead, with which he would assault Heaven and launch his insurrection. Aboddon knew he must wait for the way to be opened – as was promised to him by Kain. Only then could the serpent complete the spell and take the powerful, mortal weapons to beat down the walls raised by God, protecting the heart and source of creation: the two trees.

If need be, Aboddon could also send from there one of the weapons into Jerusalem, obliterating the tablets he thought were hidden there – the way the queen insisted. But that was of course if he could not find them first, to render what use they were to his own end: rebellion.

In the distance, waste was laid behind those walls from the great woes that befell Eden; the darkness weakened Heaven already. Joshu knew it was time; he raised his hand a fourth time and commanded the next trumpet to sound. The angel holding the great horn walked to the edge of the platform. He set it to his mouth and blew. Hopelessness followed the vibration down into the world of men – it was the last of immortal mercy. Heaven could do no more for mortals.

The earth's atmosphere became gorged with pollutions in every corner, as iniquitous poisons rose from man's callus industry. Humanity grew sick, and the land festered with plague. Droughts and famines spread over the nations, until every place was touched by death. Mortal pride was yet unmoved as their great cities stewed in hazy broths of soot and vapor, chocking their own children, and their children's children. The seething air churned the sky into raging tempests, which then hammered the shores with remunerated fate and drowning the land in suffering.

The dragons were finally and fully loosed, delighting in unhindered wrath, drawn down by mortal failing. Eleventh light faded but for only in the most righteous sources, as the Pythian shadows grew long on the land.

Nick found Arbil daunting; the growing darkness was beginning to choke him with guilt. He was burdened beyond measure with what had happened in that place – the blood of his own sins stained the land. As soon as they arrived, Nick noticed Jon begin to change before his very eyes. They stopped trying to conjoin ethereally. The dark exile grew more and more anxious about the prophet's erratic personality. One minute the Jon's aura seemed warm and peaceful, then the next he was unrecognizable. The frequency of the strange seizures was also increasing; occurring almost each time Nick tried to touch him. Worse yet, blackouts plagued the boy, where he could not remember where he had been or what he had been doing for long stretches of time. Jon snuck away from Nick whenever he could now, trying to hide the instability of his sanity. Paranoia wracked both their spirits like venom in the blood.

Late one morning, the prophet wandered away while Nick slept, down a hard pounded road, to the collection of buildings where he knew Drake's mission was working in secret. As he rounded the corner and stood in front of the cement-brick building, he saw Caleb standing in the doorway, waiting it seemed.

Jon approached him, his eyes unable to meet Caleb's dark gaze.

"Good morning, Jon," said the evangelist. "I am glad to see you."

"Good morning, Caleb," said Jon meekly. He brushed at the ground with his feet like a nervous child.

"What brings you by today?" asked Caleb, his voice calm with assurance.

"I wanted to talk...I need to ask you some things."

"Of course," said Caleb. "Come in, it's cooler."

They walked into a small, plain room just off the street. Caleb motioned for Jon to sit. "What is it you would like to know?" he finally asked, settling into his chair. "Can I get you something?"

Luke appeared at the entrance of the kitchen and smiled at Jon. Caleb noticed the way they looked at each other; he was uneasy about their attractions but pleased that his baiting of Jon with Luke had worked so well.

"No," said Jon, "I'm fine, thank you."

Caleb then motioned for Luke to leave them alone. The boy vanished.

Jon knew Nick would be furious about this, but he had to find out for himself what was going on. None of this was turning out as he had planned. His mind was being wrenched in to pieces. He sensed things were getting away from him.

"It's O.K, Jon," Caleb said in a soft tone. "Relax... God brought us here together for a reason. We both know these are dreadful times, but the faithful will be rewarded."

The young prophet's head twisted nervously before he spoke. "What exactly does it mean to be one of the faithful?"

Caleb's face turned sad. "It means to wash your life in the blood of Christ," he explained. "It means to follow God's commandments, and it means to follow the will of his appointed servants."

"How do you know what God's will is?" asked Jon, "if everything in your head from Him is messed up."

"We both know why things are confusing for you," replied Caleb. "It's because of *him!*"

"Who?" rasped Jon, "Nick? That's not true, he..." Jon stopped.

Caleb raised his eyebrows and stared at the boy. "What would you say if I told you that I was in touch with another angel, Jon," Caleb said with an air of superiority. "One that I know is true and loyal to God."

At first Jon looked unconvinced – then slowly his expression turned wanting. He was not sure what to think.

"Gabriel led me here," added Caleb, "to help draw *you* away from the power of the Devil....to save you."

"So what...Nick says there have been angels all around us ever since we left New York...Nick says..." Jon stopped again.

"The Devil says what, Jon?"

Jon's face turned red. He realized then he was being manipulated. What aggravated him most was that he was not sure all of a sudden who to trust. Was Caleb messing with his head, or *had* he been simply seduced by Nick all along?"

"Talk to me," Caleb said warmly. "Why did he bring you here? What have you told him?"

"He didn't bring me here," said Jon. "I wanted to be here...I heard the name of this place in a vision and told him to come." Now Jon really was becoming uncomfortable. He began to get a sinking feeling all of a sudden.

"He wants to find the woman, doesn't he?" Caleb was tightening his grip.

"Yes," said Jon. The boy could not look Caleb in the eyes again.

"She's not here," said Caleb. He smiled victoriously. Jon's eyes lit up.

"But you already know where she is.... don't you, Jon?"

"I swear, I don't," the boy said nervously. "The vision said to come here, for me to come and...to choose...it never said she would be here."

He had answered Caleb's sly question about the woman. Jon did not know where she was yet, but Caleb still suspected that there was a purpose in bringing Satan there: to trap him.

"And the Devil does not know *that* part of your mission," asked Caleb, "does he?"

"No," replied Jon sullenly. "I was not sure I could really trust him in the beginning."

"There is nothing wrong with not trust'en the Devil," said Caleb, his southern accent finally breaking through his manicured speech. "Son, I don't believe we're looking for a real live, woman anyway. I think the prophecies are all misunderstood...and the Devil does not want us to know the truth. He is a deceiver. I have explained all this to Gabriel in his visitations, but he too is unconvinced by my inspired studies of the word of God. It seems not even the angels know for certain what God's will is...not the way I do. The Lord protects secrets closely...but I know He's revealed the truth to you too...in His way."

"That is what everyone seems to think," replied the young prophet," but I'm not so sure."

"The *Book of Revelation* says the woman is clothed in the sun and moon and on her head a crown of twelve stars. I think, and have always thought, that the woman is simply a symbol...a metaphor for a place, not a physical person."

"A place? But we've seen her face...Nick and I together."

"Perhaps that was just a trick of his, Jon," replied Caleb. "Gabriel is here...let him try and help us. Let him see the vision of the woman to be sure."

Jon stood to his feet, almost as if to flee. "Where?" he said nervously.

"Calm down, son," replied Caleb. "He is watching over us…but I can call to him anytime."

Jon looked again at Caleb's aura; he did not sense the Pythia. This man truly believed his path was righteous. He finally nodded assent, choosing, and the instant he did Shemhazai materialized behind Caleb. The angel used a powerful snakeskin to make himself appear glorious and wonderful. Jon was in awe. *Nick never appeared like this… so lovely,* he thought.

"Glorious Jinn of Heaven," said Caleb, kneeling before the Jinn. "It is as you foretold…the prophet has come to us." The evangelist turned to the prophet. "Jon, may I present Lord Gabriel, messenger from our Lord in Heaven."

Shemhazai smiled with a deep, calm grin, pleased with how such hapless mortals were so easily fooled by outward appearances…they were usefully gullible in that way.

"Is what Caleb said true, Anointed One?" asked Shemhazai through his disguise. "Are you ready to choose the correct path to God?"

Jon froze. Nick had never called him 'the Anointed One.' Suddenly his head began to throb; something was ripping at his mind again, tearing it into fragments. His body shook. Shemhazai noticed the curious shift of his aura, as Jon's face turned cruel. He waved his hand quickly at Caleb.

"Leave us," said the grigori so harshly that it almost broke the spell he wove over the room.

Caleb disappeared just as he was instructed, darting into an adjoining area to wait. Shemhazai walked to Jon, and took him into his arms. The angel did not even wait to put Jon on his knees in supplication, as was his custom. He pushed inside the prophet, using all his ethereal power right where they stood – victory was finally his.

As the grigori entered Jon, he ran straight into the wall of the celestial ciphers that plagued the boy's mind, that storm of light and images. The demon was instantly taken aback. Nothing was clear there the way it should be; there was no portent that he could discern at all.

What he sensed shocked him. Shemhazai had seen that type of ethereal maze in the past, but never in a breathing creature. It was as if Jon was a living labyrinth, crafted of the very wards that protected the temple itself.

Shemhazai became enraged; the grigori grit his teeth, ready to rip Jon's head from his neck. He'd been tricked again.

Then just for a second, there was a glimpse of something lucid amid the thunder and lightning of Jon's mind. *The woman*, the prophet thought into the grigori's head as he too saw the aberration.

Something strange occurred to the vision the instant they saw it together – the soft turns of her face changed suddenly. It was as if this vision had been hidden away, waiting for that very moment. Jon's past glimpses were so quick and always wrapped in Nick's rapture that he thought perhaps he had misunderstood them all along. *No, not a woman at all"* he thought. *"We were mistaken… a beautiful young man… that's James Kyle.*

"How did I not see this before?" Jon asked the Jinn. As soon as he spoke the question aloud, all his thoughts and impressions started to suddenly become clearer. The lines of his prophecy seemed to unravel for the demon. Shemhazai waited, as Jon fumbled with the lines of sight laid bare. The new vision came into its clearest focus ever. The image of the woman's face had been so like this young man's. The only answer could be that Caleb was right about Nick; the Devil had been keeping the truth from Jon all along.

As the likeness of James became clearer, Shemhazai was also shaken to his core. He too knew this young man. It was the very boy from New York that Azael had first suspected of being fused with prophetic power. Jon and Shemhazai sat in bewildered silence a moment, as they saw James standing at the gate of Jerusalem, holding the Tablets of Destiny in his hands...the tablets they now knew *he* had. *Caleb was right all along...there is no woman. That boy is the Deliverer,* thought Shemhazai, *and the Rafiq took him while the Accuser distracted us.*

The woman was Jerusalem after all, and so the *city* must be devoured to prevent James from becoming what they feared. The queen had been correct all along. Shemhazai withdrew harshly from Jon, but not before leaving a part of himself there to claim the prophet as his own – the darkness filled his soul and exploited the growing infirmity of his mind.

"What does it all mean, Lord Gabriel?" asked Jon, in awe.

"It means God will return to Jerusalem," he replied. "It is a plan so brilliant in its simplicity that we should have guessed it. The best way to hide something is to put it in the most obvious of places."

Jon felt he had finally done what he was intended to do. He was relieved. Nick had caused so much discord in his life he surmised; Jon would rid himself of the Accuser now – that was for certain.

No wonder Tiamat simply wanted the city destroyed, the grigori thought to himself. *Aboddon is wrong about all of this, and will pay for his treachery if he fails to do as She commands.*

"What do we do now?" Jon begged. He was excited to be finally on the side of what he thought righteousness, not realizing his mistaken trust.

"We go to our Deliver…to this James you know, who is now in the Holy City. We protect him," Shemhazai lied, to deceive Jon, "but first God has something else for you to do, Anointed One."

The grigori turned for the door and called through it. "Get the Stones of Kabil, Drake" he said in a sinister tone, "and give them to *our* prophet."

15

THE MORNING STAR

Walking back to the hovel near the square, Jon was filled with new conviction, believing that he deserved better than Nick. He was God's anointed, and would not be seduced any longer by the exile of Heaven. As he burst into the bedroom, the prophet was determined to exorcise the Devil. But when he entered it, he sensed something was dreadfully wrong. He could tell Nick was very weak, as if he were ill.

Suddenly a vibration in space-time caused the earth to shudder around them. Nick came awake with a start. The fifth trumpet had been blown and it seemed to nearly shake the life out of him. The Jinn rolled over and reached for Jon, but the bed was empty. He raised his head and looked for the prophet in the early morning gloom, his eyes unfocused as he searched.

Jon had turned away and was sitting at the window, gazing up at the dim sky. His face was pensive, as if he were counting the stars. A faint light fell over him and Nick could read sadness all about his aura, something was eating away at Jon, something horrible.

"What's wrong?" the Accuser asked in a weak voice.

Stillness held Jon, but he shook himself. "I have not been able to sleep at all, something is really messed up between us Nick," replied the prophet.

"You've simply been troubled by the death of those boys, I think," explained Nick. "Come and lay here with me. I will hold you."

Jon did not move. He just sat there shivering. "No, something else is wrong...I can tell. Will you look inside me?" Jon turned his head slightly and glanced sideways at the Accuser. He was so unsure what to do right then, doubt wracked him.

Jon's sad expression made Nick's heart ache. The Accuser sat up in bed and swung his legs over the side. The Jinn's body pained him so much. As he stood, he felt weak and weathered. The last of ethereal power was fading fast...blotted out by the strange iniquity of Arbil...but he still refused to draw from the spirit of the dragons that burned inside of him.

"Come here," he said finally to the boy. "Sit on the edge of the bed."

"I don't understand. I can feel something different suddenly inside me...it is like a thorn in my mind." Jon got up and stumbled the few feet to Nick. "It is annoying me, I try to pick at the apparition with my power...but it eludes me."

"What could it be?" Nick asked. Frankly, the Jinn was exasperated with the prophet – it always seemed to be something. Jon had become the essence of malcontent since they had arrived. "You just need to stop pushing yourself to gaze into the Ethereal Realm so much," Nick said to him in a scolding tone. "That's all...the visions will clear in time as they are intended. Look, I know this is an ordeal, but you seem to want to blame me for all of this at times. I am as lost as you are, Jon."

"Yes, I know," said the young prophet.

He sounded guilty for some reason, but Nick didn't give it a second thought. The Accuser took the young man's head in his hands and pulled him close. The prophet opened himself to Nick in a way made possible only by the depth of their intimacy, fading as it was. Nick conjoined with him and probed for a bit, prying at the strangely structured logic of his mind... or illogic depending on how he looked at it. The eleventh light flowed out of him, in looping waves of magnetic energy.

He is a living code, thought Nick, watching the strange field that enveloped the boy's mind.

"I don't see anything," said Nick.

"Look deeper."

Impatience was making Nick even more uneasy. "Wait ...there...that...open it to me," he said. "There *is* something lodged within your essence, but it's closed off...hidden from me...on purpose. It's a ward, how did you get that in there?"

Jon squirmed in his hands. "It hurts...be careful," he whined. "I know it's there, but I can't open it myself. Force it open."

"What? Are you sure?"

Something about the strange ethereal node was familiar. It was a kind of dark scar that had formed within the eleventh light. The Accuser nudged at it, but it resisted. So he pushed harder. "Hold still, let me try to..."

Nick stopped short suddenly. His heart sunk into his stomach as he pried the eerie protuberance loose from Jon's thoughts. In a state of shock, he pushed Jon away with cruelty.

The prophet spun and rolled off the bed, irritated with Nick for the harsh handling. "Shit, that hurt! What are you doing?"

Jon's voice seemed distorted as he spoke. He just stared at Nick with a kind madness the Accuser had never seen before in him, for all his strange mood swings.

Nick's fast fury was unbridled. "You stupid son-of-bitch," he snarled at the boy. "What have you done to yourself?!" Raw emotion twisted there in Nick's gut, between rage and heartbreak. The truth was settling in on him. Everything he'd set out to accomplish with Jon now fell into ruin…it was over.

"What are you talking about?" Jon yelled back, confused.

"The mark of Sijjin," cried Nick.

"What the hell is that, Nick?" Jon growled. "You're not making any fucking sense to me."

Nick could stand no more of the hurt; the floodgate of emotions broke and spilled out of his being. It had all came down to betrayal again. To Jon's surprise, Nick broke down and began to sob uncontrollably in front of him.

"You've consorted with the Pythians" the Jinn said through tears. "You've become a thrall!"

The words sounded absolutely unbelievable to both of them when they spilled out of Nick's mouth. The prophet stared at him defiantly.

"You have entered into an pact with a grigori, Jon" explained Nick. "You took his mark in your soul. Why?"

"You are crazy, Nick...I've done no such thing."

"You are condemned in the sight of God... you stupid, stupid boy. I SHOULD KNOW WHAT DAMNATION LOOKS LIKE...I am the Devil!"

Jon got a pained expression on his face. He couldn't at the moment fully grasp what Nick was saying, or perhaps would not allow himself to anyway. Then slowly, very slowly, it came to him. It had been Caleb Drake and the angel that did this to him, but Nick was the one he mistrusted. It couldn't be a mark of sin...Nick was lying; he *was* the Devil.

"I am born again," said Jon indignantly.

"Born again to what?"

"Seriously, it's not my fault. When this started, I was too naive in spirit to understand what it all meant... what I really wanted. You never wanted me to actually know the truth anyway...did you?"

"What truth?" asked Nick through grit teeth. "I thought we were looking for the same things."

Jon began to pace nervously. "That I did not have to live this way...that I could have more of life...that I could be normal."

"Live what way, Jon? I'm completely lost here."

"Like this...you seduced me away from what I really should be doing. You should have known better, Nick!"

Nick's ill feeling grew. Maybe Jon was right. Perhaps he did know better and had ignored his own judgment. He knew he loved Jon, but had he pursued this all out of self need alone? Was Jon right?

"I met the Christians soldiers in the square," snapped Jon. "The true angels are with *them...* Satan!" Now Jon's aura was ablaze with Pythian power. "I finally feel like I can be what I was meant to be, and you won't stop me. *They* are the beautiful, good angles of God. You don't know what it's like to be part of that...do you? I was meant for more than this!"

Jon walked over to his pack. He began stuffing it with articles of clothing. When it was full, he nervously fumbled within it for the stones that Drake had given him.

Nick was filled with such heartache. He walked to Jon, just wanting to stop him from leaving. He was desperate to try and make it all right somehow... perhaps Jon had not taken the mark willingly. He could still fight their power.

Jon raised both hands high as Nick approached, and without warning struck him wildly about the head. Nick never saw it coming. The force of the blow reverberated down through the Jinn's body. The Accuser had little inclination the prophet could access such power, and had even less that it would be used against him.

Jon looked down at Nick, with cold disdain in his eyes. He opened his hands and they were covered in blood...human blood.

"Do you recognize these, Nick?" the prophet said in a voice full of icy ire.

Nicks eyes blurred as he tried to focus. He shook his head, attempting fruitlessly to bring the two wavering images of Jon together before his eyes.

"They told me you would try to stop me. They gave me these...the Stones of Kabil. Yes, Nick...the very stones *you* gave Kain to kill his brother."

Nick gave-up trying to right the blurry images of the mortal he loved and was now losing. They were utterly uncontrollable, swerving and swaying around his woeful senses. Unsure if it was his broken head or his broken heart, he finally succumbed to the shadows that were pulling him down. Nick fell to his face and everything around him turned to darkness.

Three hundred combined Tomar and Rafiq knights assembled at the base of Mount Megiddo. Every man was anxious. The earth seemed to sigh below their feet.

"Now what?" groaned Aaron, looking out across the vast plane.

Both Adriano and Nafees turned to face James. The moment had come. The young seer walked over to the ridge where his companion stood; he reached over tenderly and took hold of the Adriano's sacred asherah. "Do you still trust me?" he asked.

"To the last trumpet," replied the knight with a warm smile.

"Something is in the air," Aaron interrupted them, "a growing darkness that is moving toward us."

"It is the timeless ghost of war," explained James as he took the rod with confidence and drove it into the earth. Then he began to sing soft notes under his breath, the sound resembled the mantra of the breath-prayer meditation. James opened the ancient channels of power to all the goddess' former temples in the region, the way she said he should. The staff was suffused with ethereal light; it would become a source of power to those that followed them – when the light of the nameless-god faded.

The dragon was waiting in Arbil for the prophet to reach for that power. He too had foreseen that moment, the parting of space-time with the joining of sacred thin-spaces to amass the last of ethereal enchantment. He understood now that James was moving the hand of fate, but he didn't know from where, or fully how. Abaddon realized he must act quickly – topple Heaven, and then use the paths to travel to the Holy City and destroy them all.

Being shifted as the plane before the knights was transformed, and filled with Pythian enchantment. Their field of vision wavered in front of them. Then suddenly laid out over the valley floor was a vast spectral army that seemed to appear from thin air. The bait was taken. In the distance, Nafees and Aaron recognized the high walls of Eden as they came into view; the gates closed and the fiery mountain silent. A sense of solemn purpose inundated time.

"Somehow," said Aaron as he walked to the edge of the overhang, "I always pictured this moment differently." The Tomar smiled as he turned; his ethereal sword and armor materialized. The bright, red cross upon his robe seemed to light their way.

Adriano and James came up on him, looking out at the embattled rift between them with its distant towering cliffs. Their eyes were filled with wonder.

"Where the hell did that mountain come from?" asked Adriano.

"The real promised land," said Aaron. "That is Eden and those are the gates of Heaven."

"Is this the last battle then...Armageddon?" asked the big man, suddenly afraid.

"No," replied the Tomar, "this is but the first of many tests for the Sons of Light, before Heaven's gates. Armageddon is not the last battle, it is the soul of all war itself...and much suffering yet lays ahead us before the conflict will be done."

With that he started down the hill to stand with his men like he had so many times before in that very place. "The Bible calls *this* the Battle of the Locusts," Aaron said with resignation as he walked. "It is the beginning of the end...and you my friend know what that means, Adriano."

When Nick came to his senses again, Jon was gone; and yet something about the prophet still lingered there like a phantom. The Jinn's head throbbed as he looked up. The dawn was starting to glow in the east, and the first ripe rays of sunlight began to warm the day. The sounds of people in the street rattled his sanity.

Nick looked around nervously. Jon had taken all his belongings. The Accuser's spirit sank. Somehow all the heartache he had come to know over his lifetime culled into that one great wound. He reached out with is senses for Jon, but something was shielding the prophet by deflecting Nick's thoughts away from the young man...the dark ward of a dragon no less.

The Accuser grabbed for his clothing, which was strewn around on the floor. He dressed in a hurry. Then bursting from the tiny hovel, Nick emerged on to the busy street. The local people were beginning to go about their day, oblivious to the exiled angel in their midst. Sand whirled into the air as Nick took flight, leaving only a cloud of dust floating where he had been standing.

The Accuser made his way north, toward the missionary compound Jon had once mentioned – it was the only place Nick could think of going. When he reached the square fortification of buildings, he immediately noticed something was wrong. From above, the site looked deserted. Nick spiraled down to the center of the compound, where a single well dropped into darkness. At its edge stood a boy, staring transfixed with its dim depths.

The Jinn lit next the boy and materialized. The youth turned white with dread and fled. The Accuser reached to grab him, but the boy pulled away and darted off into the crags of the building. Then Nick turned and looked for what the child had been fascinated with – a fuming broil of Pythian enchantment deep in the well's recesses.

Nick thrust himself over the edge.

The ground at the bottom of the well was hard and stable. The passage radiated so profusely with the power of the Pythia that the very substance of the material world seemed to bend around it. He turned curiously in the shaft toward a distant light source and the sweltering surge of power coming from it.

The light was an ethereal opening out onto some brightly lit landscape – a gate to an extended thin-space he guessed. Nick braced himself and moved into the brilliance. As he poked his head up and out of the opening, he saw a long, flat stretch of land extending for miles. To the north was a high rim of mountains, over which the he could see the crest of a smoldering peak – he recognized the palisades of Eden immediately.

To the south, he could scarcely believe his eyes – it was Mount Megiddo standing still and at the ready. This was no ordinary landscape; it was a mystic battleground – a nether-field. He understood such a spell was possible, but he had never imagined a power on earth strong enough to weave it. Eden was bound to the earth once more.

The Accuser extended his sight to survey what he knew could only be intended as a theater of war and realized he was standing in what was planned as an escape route for the Pythians, should things go badly. They were cowards, never picking a fight from which they could not flee, but he would fix that. Nick took two steps away, drew on a little dark power, and turned it inside out like a shirt. The gate imploded in front of him. *Those bastards aren't getting out this way*, the Accuser seethed in his mind.

He spun around. Not far, he could see the last ranks of a horde moving into position. The forces were an odd array of battle groups – an army of all ages it appeared – souls called up from the underworld for some dark end it was clear. Nick saw tanks from all the great twentieth century wars rolling along like scorpions; behind them marched infantry in uniforms that spanned thousands of years. He saw Assyrian footman walking in lock step with German storm troopers; Roman centurions defending ranks of Napoleonic artillery lines; and Macedonian cavalry escorting Russian surface-to-air batteries…all with the roar of apache helicopters overhead that made the sound of thundering warhorses.

At the head of the great twisted line was a man seated upon a black war steed. Nick focused his attention on the figure. He recognized the dragon straight away. It was Aboddon Naga, the Leviathan of the Underworld. *He* was behind all this carnage.

Nick was not surprised.

In front of the dragon walked a massive Carthaginian elephant, with a grand platform on its back. It emitted a strange, dark pulse – raw Pythian power that was somehow being focused through the device. The power was generating the enormous static sphere of energy needed to maintain the nether-field's hold. The beast abruptly stopped, falling into position as the dragon began to bark orders at the scores of footman around him. Then the columns of troops began to take up positions around the pounding heart of dark power, gathering strength for the attack.

Nick cloaked himself as best he could and took flight. He made his way north, toward the great gates that closed off Eden from the siege. As he came up upon the base of the cliffs that walled off the sacred lands, two flashing strobes caught his attention at the gate. He focused on the light. There he saw Michael and Rafael, the two most powerful warriors of God's guard, standing point before Heaven. They each clasped a burning sword that showed brightly; behind them stood one hundred and forty-four thousand warriors.

Nick made his way toward the line, staying close to the ridge to keep from being spotted by any but the two Jinn. He lit about one hundred meters from where they stood. The Accuser saw someone step around Michael – it was Gabriel. The two archangels looked at each other briefly; then Gabriel turned and walked alone toward Nick. The lithe Jinn took a few steps and pushed off with his wings. He stumbled a little from the forward inertia as he lit near the dark exile.

"We were wondering if you were going to come," said Gabriel.

"No one invited me," replied Nick, "I just stumbled on your little party by chance. Mind if I crash it?"

"Somehow I find that hard to believe, Nick. You heard the fifth trumpet. It was the heralding of man's infidelity...mortals reach to toss down even Heaven. Did you not hear it?" Gabriel's look was scolding. "You knew what it meant...that is all the invitation any Jinn would ever need to return home."

"I was pre-occupied," replied Nick. "The anointed seer has gone over to the Pythia, Gabe. He is fallen and with him goes all hope...he will lead them to the woman."

"We know," replied the handsome angel. "Don't take it personally, Nick...you of all creatures should understand his fate. None of us knows God's full plan in this, but whatever else Jon Godfrey will be about before this is over, he provided a diversion that was necessary, for something none of us saw until now. While we were all trained on him and you, the Tablets of Destiny were secreted away by another...the dragons are denied their prize."

The Accuser felt something twist in his chest. Jon too was a pawn, just as he had been. *Perhaps it was me who let him down?* thought the Accuser sullenly to himself. *I led him to this. Would it have made a difference if I told him I did love him?*

The Tomar Knights took up fortification lines along the Carmel Ridge, which overlooked the great valley and plane before Megiddo. Dark power surged up from the mass of red-bannered forces that were coiling along the valley floor. James thought it rather looked like a river of blood, horses swimming in it up to the bridle. In the distance, a haze gathered and in it he saw the mysterious mountain line.

Adriano extended himself higher on the balls of his feet and hooded his eyes with his hand. "Where did that army come from now?" he asked nervously, as he eyed the peaks of Heaven beyond it.

James shot him an uneasy look, unsure himself.

"They are drawing together a nether-field," said Nefees, "an ethereal sphere where time and space are warped by wounds of death in war. These are not real weapons, but shadows of them from the past. Make no mistake my friends, they are far more deadly. It takes tremendous celestial energy to hold a nether-field in place. I'm not quite sure yet how they are doing it yet, it would take a thousand dragons to do this."

"Why here?" asked James. "How could they have known we were here?"

Nafees rolled his shoulders to indicate he did not know and stepped between them. "Perhaps for fear factor," he replied. "I doubt they do know we are here. You opened some sort of cause way just now, James. They seemed to be expecting that somehow. Who knows for sure what the dragons plan with this, but for destruction and death?"

He jumped down into the hole near where Adriano stood and cast his gaze up at the sun, then motioned for James to step down behind him. As he did, the cleric turned to face the vast plane before the sacred mountain.

"Look with me, Walis," said Nafees, "at that power which radiates from ahead of the force. Let's see together what its source lies in...of what this spell is woven?"

James narrowed his eyes and extended his sight. "It's coming from that war elephant," he said.

"Not precisely," replied Nafees, "from what it has on its back I think. There is something in the plated ark on the platform...they mock Allah with it."

"I can't make it out," grunted James. "I can't see past its strange radiance." Then there was a quick flash in his mind. He saw the man from his vision, back in New York, the omen of the Holy City burning that brought them all there. "It's the weapon they will use," he said anxiously, "the weapon of the vision."

They both released their hold on the ethereal power they were using to spy out the object and stared fretfully into each other's face. Nafees sat slowly, rubbing at his eyes as if they pained him. He was trying to work through something. It was there at the tip of his thoughts, but it was James in his simple innocence that blurted it out.

"How could any mortal device, even a nuclear one like this one, focus dark power so intensely into being?"

"By Allah," said Nafees, "of course...it makes sense. I've never been this close to one before to sense it."

"What?" Both James and Adriano said at once.

"The dragons can focus the power of chaos through the weapon because the device is dragon essence itself...in material form. It's like a lens for sunlight."

"I don't understand," replied James.

Nafees turned and looked over the plane toward the line of mountains. "The effort to harness the atom as a weapon has a dark history," he explained sadly, "even its creators understood they were unleashing a monster. When the mortal developer of the atomic-bomb saw the first test of his weapon, it is said that he wept. He later wrote of the moment that he had done so because he was fearfully struck in his soul... reminded of the *Bhagavad-Gita*...and a passage in it where God assumes the form of *Shiva*, the multi-armed goddess of chaos, and says '*now I am become Death, the destroyer of worlds.*'"

"So man actually harnessed the might of Tiamat that day, to our eventual doom?" asked Adriano.

"Yes, it would seem so," replied Nafees, "a trick of the serpents no doubt. Man has always sought a more gruesome way to strike his brother, since Kain struck Habil...by taking the gift of this fire mankind has seeded this world with weapons that are now *Dracocardia*...the very heart of chaos."

"You see...man's intentions make both evil and good strong by the paths they choose. God is ethereal reason, trying to save you from yourselves. Made both of mortal and dragon essence, these weapons will disrupt the mortal veil, and break its very foundation if unleashed. Eden will fall if they get it inside the walls without God in his full potency on three thrones of Heaven to protect it. With Eden subsumed, all of creation will crumble at its source."

"War breeds desperation in men. The dragons used fear to deceive us, and they are using it now," said Adriano. His voice rang with a confidence that heartened all around him. "But all it takes is one righteous soul to turn the tide…we have to have faith in ourselves now, as God has had to bring us here."

Just then Aaron ran across the fortified line where the two re-united clans of the Asirim were dug in. He looked worried. "Nafees," the Tomar knight grunted, half out of breath, "they are fanning out and moving into position. They will strike at Heaven soon…we need a plan."

James stood and raised his staff, nobility glowing in his face. All eyes seemed to turn to him as a presence filled the prophet. "God has a plan," he said boldly, his gaze cast across the plane. "We simply have to keep buying time…whatever it costs of us."

At that same moment, the full multitude of bizarre forces encircled the dragon-heart and began feeding off of its sinister energy. Aboddon rose in his seat and pulled out a long trumpet. His every gesture seemed to goad at the Jinn warriors in front of him…the defense of the gate was the key. He raised it to his lips and blew. With the sound it made, a line of cobra helicopters thundered past him. All hell broke loose and was emptied onto the plane.

Nick drew Haqiqah; the blade sliced the material plane as it scorched the air. He extended his wings and let out a menacing war cry. The Devil then entered the fray. If Nick must use his dark power, he would do so to the Pythian's end. He hurtled himself at the approaching cobra air machines, touching the spirit of the dragon at his core and filling his senses with it.

Behind the Accuser, a mass of angels took flight to follow, advancing on the helicopters at full speed. The flying machines released a hail of automatic gunfire as they drew close, but the warriors of light extended wards and repelled the heated shots. Simultaneously from below, batteries of surface-to-air weapons released a volley, like a line of archers. They fixed upon the Jinn and slammed into their shielded wards, but the ethereal barricades managed to hold. Nick knew each extension of their power would weaken the Jinn, the dragon was deliberately forcing them to expend their waning ethereal power.

Nick advanced undeterred, only able to visualize Jon in his mind right at that moment. He was filled with rage and guilt for what had happened to the proud, well intended mortal he had loved...now consumed within the dragons' power.

As the lead cobra maneuvered to slam headfirst into Nick, he let his weight fall suddenly and rolled over onto his back in midair. He thrust his sword upward into the belly of the craft, halving it with the sheer force of inertia. The wreck exploded over the battlefield.

Along the ground, the various battalions of the ages lurched forward, making for the gate. They fed off both the power of the dragon-heart and off the death that was now splaying across the sky. The dark heart drew up and channeled all the chaos into the force, and unwittingly into Nick. His strength burgeoned at the limits of his physical form. He turned his attention down toward Aboddon, who sat taking delight in the carnage. The avenging angel raised his weapon and bore straight at his hideous mortal guise. The wind surged over his wings as he descended from his embattled perch to strike like a meteor.

Seeing Nick, Aboddon thrust his arm forward and a large war-hammer extended from it – the gesture gathered strength and slammed full force into the Accuser, but Nick continued to drive down at the dragon's position. Aboddon then began to pummel at him again and again with all his might; each time the Accuser's hurt over Jon swallowed the blows – dark power countered with dark power. Nick drove even harder at the beast, intent on both their destruction, if that is what it took.

The dragon knew if the Jinn reached him with God's sword, he would be vulnerable to an enchantment even the queen feared. He turned and calculatingly pulled Jon up from below his feet, where Nick had not seen him hidden. Aboddon displayed the prophet like trophy kill. The boy squirmed as if he were a small animal in his coils.

Nick's focus was quickly broken as he saw Jon struggle that way, and the dragon used that opportunity to hammer at the avenging Jinn with unbridled potency – fed more and more by the destruction around him. The force knocked Nick mercilessly backward; he spiraled up and away from the ground. The Accuser reflexively strengthened his ward just as he was sent crashing through the wing of a Mig fighter. The plane's ordnance ripped open and caused a massive fireball all around him. His flaming wings simply soaked in the inferno as it too scattered over the battlefield.

Nick struggled and quickly righted himself. As he did, he sensed something new with the infusion of power from the flame – a recognizable presence, warm and comforting. He extended his sight toward it, down along the undefended flank of the dark army. There Nick could see another group of ethereally armed warriors entering the battle. They crashed into the exposed rear guard of Pythians, surprising them. Then gradually the band began to cut a swath toward the central source of the dark army's power.

"James?" asked Nick aloud to himself. "How is this possible?"

Below, a line of shellfire rapidly drew his attention, as a battalion of Panzer tanks finally ripped open a hole in the Jinn lines at the gate to Eden. Simultaneously, Nick felt time and space waiver. The nether-field had suddenly and inexplicably weakened for a moment – Nick realized the dark-matter Aboddon wielded was growing unstable. He drove downward again, toward the gap in the line of defenders at the gate, hoping to repel the progress of the enemy. If they could stem the assault a little longer, the dark-matter may imploded and dissipate on its own.

On the far ridge, the Rafiq had left a handful of Tomar Knights to defend the crags, so the group themselves would not be outflanked. The advancing knights cut first into a disorganized, yet ferocious cluster of Celtic footman at the rear of the battle array. They surprised the barbarians. No one had expected a military force – as small as this – to be so effectively embedded within the foothills. James led his tightly knit force into the very bowel of the enemy force. As he did, the fabric of the nether-field seemed to shift, its energy somehow tethered to the army's cohesion and effectiveness. Even pulling slightly on a fraying string of dark power seemed to destabilize it.

Aboddon *had* over extended its enchantment – the spell was powerful, but utterly unsound. Nafees was reassured by that fact, as they moved along various scattered units of time strewn marauders, cutting them down and moving closer the dragon-heart.

At that very moment, James raised his voice and began to weave sema with it. A strong ethereal resonance spun out of him; and its pulse seemed to echo in the head of every soldier on the field, creating a deep tactical focus within their charge. Aaron was not surprised by what he heard, but thought it certainly would have made things a little easier had the boy done so sooner. Nafees acted like he had known James capable all along, plowing forward into the lines infused with light.

"By Allah, boy," shrieked Nafees, "you are the voice of David himself!"

It's the goddess, Nafees, he replied into the cleric's mind. *She is my strength in our moment of need.*

James then extended the trancelike psalm out even further into the field of conflict. The Rafiq used his hypotonic power to harmonize their driving assault. They synchronized to the sema, just as they did in all their ecstatic rituals of dance. Each warrior reached a choreographed stride, cutting into the enemy line with brutal precision. The spell was altering time and space, slowing its flow, re-casting the tempo of motion to the knight's favor and powerfully warding their form. The dark army unraveled as the Rafiq and Tomar reached wajd.

Adriano was most in tune with the potent cadence; his asherah in one hand and the short, curved blade of Joshu in the other. No one knew its secret but for his companion and the Tomar knight who had given it to him. His weapon strokes were led by an unseen-hand, disrupting the dark-matter around them.

James suddenly felt Nafees slip off of the nether-field into the ethereal realm. He wondered nervously what the immortal cleric was up to, but kept his voice high and clear. In the distance, they could all see the raised platform set upon the war elephant swiftly rearing up above the swarm of soldiers. The beast was panicked, men scattered around it.

Just as quickly has he had vanished, James felt Nafees slip back again. He had used the Realm Essences to cloak himself and strike unseen at the war elephant. When the cleric re-materialized a few feet away from James, the young prophet saw the far-off platform falter, and then slip. The beast had toppled forward. Nafees grinned, a delightful smile that was reminiscent of a mischievous child.

"Well at least that is not going anywhere now," he said, as he waded back into the assault.

It took the Rafiq a fair amount of time to push up past the different forces to where the strange ark lay. Each of the first newly encountered troops would throw the knights off their stride, but once they had a few healthy cleaves into the fresh line, the way seemed to clear for them. It was only taking James a few measures to keep them in step, as he orchestrated the Pythian ruin with the spell.

The dead elephant was now within a stone-throw of them. It was only then that Aboddon realized he had been outmaneuvered, his army's might becoming more and more defuse. The dragon quickly moved to counter. Troops were called back from their frontal assault on Eden – more effective squads, with devastating weaponry and skill. They moved toward the Sons of Light with all deliberate speed. But because of the Rafiq and Tomar proximity to the dragon-heart itself, Aboddon dared not use enchantment more potent than dark infantry to stem this surprise assault.

As the crowd of scattering ghosts split near the counterfeit ark, James stopped and stood in disbelief. His focus faltered. Standing about ten feet away was a familiar face. The man looked back, with even more astonished eyes.

"Jon?" shouted James.

Adriano froze in step. He could sense the confusion rise within his companion.

"James?" replied Jon back to him, even more surprised.

"Where is Nick?" asked James quickly, his voiced pitched with excitement.

Jon's face turned red. Shemhazai appeared, cloaked in his snakeskin glamour still, and stepped in front of their new prophet. The grigori's hands were holding fast to the second case that housed the other dragon-heart; its power somehow concealed from James until that very moment.

Dread fell over the seer. "You!" he said to the grigori. "You are the one I saw in the vision of the burning Holy City."

Shemhazai glared, looking nervously between James and Jon. Sensing this was not a confrontation he wanted to allow. He reached into the Realm of Essences, fixing on a point well past the ridge defended by the Tomar Knights, and pulled Jon in to it. They stole away into thin air as their master's plans unraveled.

James gathered himself from the shock and returned to his battle psalm. As he did, he noticed a stranger scurrying after Jon and the mysterious Jinn as they vanished. The man appeared stunned that he had been somehow abandoned there on the battlefield – it was Caleb Drake.

At that very second, Gabriel descended over the man and looked upon him sadly. "You were a fool," said the angel, "but alas there is no grace this day." His sword fell and gruesomely cleaved the man in half. "God will sort you out on the other side…of that you can be sure!"

The shift in the tide of battle was palpable, but Nick feared it a hollow victory, he sensed the power of the heart. He used his wings to pull himself up a few feet into the air, looking for the dragon again. That loftiness gave him the advantage of higher ground. After a few frantic strokes of his sword to ward off a volley of attackers, he could see that there was a gathering force around the fallen elephant. Knowing he had to move quickly, Nick motioned to Michael and Rafael to follow.

Then, out of the corner of his eye, the Accuser saw Aboddon suddenly crashing forward on his horse. Like the elephant had done moments before, it too fell and he vanished into the grinding mob of soldiers fighting their way back toward the source of Pythian enchantment. It was as if someone had cut the legs out from under the beast. Nick could not have known it was Nafees yet again.

As the three angels reached the dead hulk of the war elephant, Nafees materialized there. Without missing a beat, he began wrenching at the compartment on the platform, trying to pry the lid free.

The Jinn lit next to him.

The cleric glanced over after a moment, but did not stop wrestling with the compartment. "A little help if you please," Nafees said sarcastically.

The angels looked at each other. Then the three of them took hold with Nafees, and together pried at the lid until it broke into fragments. The whole dome that made up the nether-field seemed to tremble and groan as it fell away. The spell was coming apart.

"Nick!" James stammered when he saw the Jinn, breaking focus a second time. The Rafiq line paused as he did.

Adriano turned and faced the Accuser. The Devil looked back at the knight. There was a moment of strange jealousy that raged between the dark exile and the mortal before the urgency of the moment took hold of both. Adriano drew a deep calming breath, for he realized fate now was upon them.

Nick slowly turned away and stared down at the throbbing mass of circuits and working wires. For a moment, it looked to be alive, as it pulsed out wave after wave of dark power. Drawn to it, the Accuser reached to touch the device. As he did, the dragon-heart let loose a single pulsing quiver, it convulsed under his fingers, going into what looked like mechanized spasms.

Everyone around realized there was a problem the instant he raised his eyes from the bomb. The forces of the Pythia on the field felt the surge instantly, and with it their power faltering. Nick was consuming its essence without even knowing it. The army began to withdraw – to the escape pass – the spell was giving way and would trap them there if they could not get off the neither-field. With the rush of troops away in retreat, the three angels and the line of knights quickly found themselves there alone.

"That can't be good," said Michael looking at the weapon as is seized. "What the hell did you do now, Iblis?"

"I didn't do anything," replied Nick angrily to his brother. "I just touched it and it took something from me."

"It's going critical!" Nafees shouted. The cleric began to motion frantically for everyone to fall back. "Your touch has somehow destabilized its dark essence, Accuser. Flee! Everyone Flee!"

They all began to run – but for Nick, Adriano, and James. Even the angels pushed off and made their way back to the gates of Eden, driving their troops away from the fearful epicenter. God's high walls would protect them, they knew.

Without another thought, recognizing that the moment Aaron had foretold on the ship was at hand, Adriano reached over and took Nick's head in his hands. There was no time to even speak. The big man pushed his mind toward Nick's in the fashion James had taught him for conjoining.

Nick's first instinct was to knock the mortal senseless, but when he felt the curious thrust – Adriano's feeble attempt to penetrate his mind – he took pause. He wanted to laugh out loud, and he would have had he not suddenly seen what the knight was holding. He instantly recognized Joshu's blade. Nick was no fool. There had to be something behind the knight's intent, for him to be trying this now. He looked into the dark, handsome eyes of the impetuous mortal. Then something inside the Accuser's soul seemed to give way. *Oh, what the hell,* he thought, *once you let one inside you... what difference does another one make?*

Nick anxiously relaxed his wards.

The conjoining thrust was fast and furious. The climax of information was instantaneous. Neither of them had time to feel more of each other's desire.

The Devil and the knight recoiled away, repelling with such force they appeared to revile what they had both just done. Then they stood for two breaths, looking into each other's eyes sadly, understanding what they both must do next.

Adriano turned and pushed James away. The seer was still trying to piece together what he thought he had just seen.

"Run!" screamed the big man.

James resisted only for a few paces, encouraged along by Adriano's firm hand, before he began to finally run.

Nick turned and took hold of the dragon-heart. It flared violently. Fire erupted all around him – again he soaked it up as if it were made for him, or he for it. He planted his feet firmly, threw his wings back, and went airborne with the powerful, dark heart in hand. As he rose, the sinister matter within it built to both a material as well as an ethereal chain reaction. He soared high into the sky, trying to get it up and away from the land, waiting for the knight.

On the ground, the scattered Rafiq and Tomar climbed back into the crags of the Carmel Ridge. Only James and Adriano remained running at the edge of the broken nether-field, which was beginning to dissipate. Adriano stopped short. James bolted on unaware that the big man was no longer following him.

The Rafiq knight then did something that absolutely astonished them all, but for Aaron. The companion of the prophet opened the Realm of Essences, by himself, and slipped inside. As James ran squarely into Nafees, still unaware, the cleric grabbed him and pointed him back to where Adriano had vanished.

"When did you teach him to do *that*!?" he barked.

James just stared out at the scattered battleground in confusion, watching the nether-field begin to collapse. Adriano was gone.

"I didn't," was all he could muster to say, "as God is my witness."

Adriano re-emerged on the far side of the battlefield, where Nick would not miss what he was about to do. Above him, the dragon-heart began to glow. It looked rather like a star rising in the morning sky. Adriano turned and ran toward the vanishing edifice of mountains that surrounded Eden. He drew the asherah, and used it to trace along the ground. It sliced open a rift into the Abyss. The wound in the earth looked like a crescent moon from a thousand feet in the air. As he reached the end of its path, the knight slipped back into the Realm of Essences, leaving the open fissure for Nick to spot from above.

Nick bowed his wings and drove for the gates of the Abyss just as Adriano had shown him in their conjoining; never question this sacrifice for men... his final submission. It was the only way to save the others.

As the bomb flared, Nick noticed something odd – the device was actually composed of dragon fire.

He began to consume it from the weapon almost as quickly as it erupted out, feeding from its pulse at an unprecedented scale, as if it were Sijjin. It made him stronger and stronger, beyond anything he had ever known.

As he drew close to the opening in the earth, he cast himself down inside the fissure. The bomb went fully critical and a blast-column rose up out of the hole enveloping Nick as he fell. While most of the force of the bomb had been subsumed into the nothingness of the Abyss, a fair amount of energy scorched up and across the shallow plane of the dissipating nether-field. It created a pooling effect along the land. Smoke poured up out of the shaft like a bellowing furnace, consuming the dark army as they desperately looked for the escape route Nick had calculatingly destroyed.

The last remnant of power in the field winked out, just as Adriano reappeared amid the ranks of the Rafiq. He saw all were pale as ghosts as they stared back toward the battle. Every soul watched the ethereal spell shutter from existence and Nick descending into the void amid the flaming turmoil.

Nafees began to cry. *"And behold,"* he said quoting sacred verse, *"I saw the Devil was cast to the lake of fire."*

From atop the holy mountain, Joshu looked down upon the flame. He saw Nick wreathed in it. The nether-field had faded and the material plane was immediately restored to its rightful alignment. Megiddo was gone from the horizon, but a great sea of flame broiled at the rim of the high Heavenly walls.

He raised his hands and pointed to the sixth angel. "Release the four foul winds that are tied at the great river," he said with a booming voice. "Man's judgment is at hand."

With that the angel blew his trumpet. The four horsemen of apocalypse were fully released upon the world.

cNo

Adriano sat upon the ridgeline, his mind racing. Aaron appeared from behind him. The Tomar lowered his weight close to the big man, and set a hand upon his shoulder.

"Why do I feel so full of sadness all of a sudden?" asked Adriano.

"You looked into the heart of desolation...the Accuser," said the Tomar. "Now you know the grief of eternal loss...a hell without end."

Nafees and James rushed to the knight's side. "How did you know to do that?" asked Nafees.

Aaron looked up at him with a calm stare. "I told him," said the Tomar knight. "The dragon-heart had to be cast into the Abyss and Iblis was the only one who could do it. He was crafted of dragon fire...made for this purpose and this purpose alone. The Devil is all that stands between us and the dragons now – along with the tablets. That is the truth we Tomar protected, and handed down from the secrets in the hidden *Book of Revelation*, the version we alone have. Adriano is Rafiq, but he is also a Knight of Christ...I gave him the power to conceal that knowledge and to use it when the time was right."

"We trusted you," said Nafees, as if betrayed by this in some way.

Adriano looked up at James, still trying to read the lines of his companion's face. His eyes seemed to implore pity and understanding of the prophet. The young seer walked between Aaron and Nafees to him, shaking his head as he did.

"None of us fully know what lies in our deepest soul," he said, "put there by God. We all conceal truths we don't understand ourselves. Don't you see? That is what this is all about. We are edging toward something none of us can see in whole by ourselves. That is God's plan, for us to come together, each with our part. No one of us can discern the full scope of His designs, because the dragons must never find out what He is about."

The young prophet walked over to his companion. He wrapped his arms around the big man. Adriano began to cry.

"We need to have faith," added James, with a comforting voice.

"What now?" asked the big man, shuddering as he spoke. "I don't think I can stand to lose you, James."

"I know," said the young seer. "The fear of loss you feel comes from what you saw in Nick...the unimaginable grief he shoulders. It will pass and I will comfort you. Just as important, I know now how to give Hilkiah what he wants."

"You do?" Adriano begged.

James just stared back at him a moment.

"Of course he does," said Aaron. "The song... that battle cry was the War Psalm of David. Only a descendent of his house can employ the powerful sema of that psalm. Hilkiah can no longer deny James...the unity of the Asirim is finally at hand.

"You will just have to trust me now, Nafees," said James calmly, "to lead the Sons of Light."

Nafees smiled warmly at him, and nodded.

☙

Jon sat on a high rock over Megiddo, hidden by the power of Aboddon. The knights of the Asirim fled in the distance. Drake was dead. Nick was gone.

"I am not the prophet of light," said Jon, shaking all over. "Nick was right about the mark of the dragon."

Anger burned inside of him. His head ached inconsolably. He'd been lied to, but was now trapped by his carelessness – he could not go back.

Shemhazai reached over and touched him on the shoulder. There was almost affection in the gesture. "No," said the grigori, "you are not the prophet you thought you were, but you were anointed by the nameless-god nonetheless. Now like I am fallen, you are fallen. But you were meant to come to us, Jon. We saw it in our divination. You are the dark prophet who will lead the world to us. You are not on the wrong side seer...trust me...you will see that in time."

"I don't understand," said Jon to the grigori.

"When Iblis left Heaven," replied Shemhazai, "a third of all Jinn eventually fled as well...seeing that we did not have to serve men, or serve Him. We were sickened by the self-righteous piety of the other Jinn, and realized we had a choice. The nameless-god thinks He is above the dragons, but He is not. They are the primordial powers that control all things. They alone are truth and eternal power. Without the Tablets of Destiny, God is nothing...soon we will take them, or destroy them...and then toss Eden down."

Jon sat and stewed. It now occurred to him that he had been played all along – by God and by the dragons. *I will no longer be a tool,* he thought in his mind, *of any of them...not even these foul creatures.*

"I am *not* a prophet," said Jon aloud in a disheartened tone, "nothing makes sense to me....I feel like I am coming apart."

"Oh, you *are* the anointed seer we were told to wait for," said the Aboddon as he scaled down the hill behind them, "who will usher in the rule of Pythia."

They jumped at his voice. Shemhazai grabbed Jon and drug him to the ground before the dragon. The prophet resented it, bowing grudgingly, but knowing he had little choice right then.

"You've revealed much to us," said the dragon, "and thankfully before you were able to give Iblis anymore information than you did. He is more dangerous than you can ever imagine."

Jon looked even more perplexed.

"You saw the face of the woman that signifies the Holy City, and you saw it change into the face of the scion of David. We have deciphered from this that God is in Jerusalem already...this James you know protects Him somehow. *That* seer's death is the key you will deliver us. The nameless-god needs two things to defeat us. He needs to be mortal and he needs the Tablets of Destiny. It appears both will be accomplished unless we act soon to destroy James and the Holy City. We will look for the tablets first, but if I can't have them, no one will...especially the nameless-god.

"What good are they to you," asked Jon, gritting his teeth.

"Witless mortal," replied the dragon. "Whoever controls destiny controls the cosmos...immortal, dragon, or even mortal. Now that we suspect they are hidden in Jerusalem after all, the easiest way to end all of this is to simply wipe the city from the face of the earth...that is if we cannot manage to find them there first."

"That should be no problem for you then," said Jon, his heart filling with bitterness.

"Believe it or not, it is a problem," said the dragon. "The Holy City is a thin space ...the dragons cannot simply destroy it by normal means. It would take the breath of a thousand dragons to do so."

"So I take it there are not a thousand dragons handy for that," said Jon sarcastically.

"Oh yes," said Shemhazai, "there are." Then he handed the weapon in its case to Aboddon.

16

THE LAMP STANDS

Nick wandered in the chill of the Abyss alone. The Jinn had expected to feel more rage – but did not. He was at one level resentful for Jon's betrayal and yet in spite of it, Nick could not hate the young man. Something inside the Accuser simply would not allow that to happen; something he had not felt in eons.

His senses adjusted as a man's sight does in the dark. The underworld was not quite as empty as he had assumed it to be. Slowly, the gloom rendered a sense of primordial form. He steadied his footing and surveyed the eerie, unending world that took shape in front of him, walking down a roughly cut road. Every time he approached a turn or a fork, he seemed to know in his heart exactly what to do next. The sensation was deeply unsettling for him. After what seemed endless hours, perhaps even days, he turned a corner and ran right into the back of man standing still in the path. It happened so abruptly that it startled Nick. He dodged a little to the side so as to see if the man sensed him, but the stranger did not appear to notice a thing.

Nick stepped cautiously around him. His expression fell as they stared into each other's eyes.

"Hello, Iblis," the man said.

Nick's mouth dropped. "Habil?" he answered. "What the hell are you doing here?"

"I am right where both you and Kain left me, satan," replied the phantom.

"I had no idea," said Nick, "that you had come here."

"You are such a fool, Iblis," replied Habil. "The stones bring us all here...to this place of desolation. Don't you recognize it?"

Nick looked around. "I don't get it," he asked nervously. "What does this all mean?"

"Hell is not really a place outside us," said the ghost. "It's a world within... a place crafted from our own grief and rage."

Nick hefted his weight upon a large stone near the man. "I'm fucked," he grumbled.

Habil laughed.

"Yes, you most certainly are," relied the ghost, "but fortunately I can help you."

"You can?" Nick looked surprised. "Why would you, after what I did?"

"Oh, not because I am some kind of saint...there is something in it for me. You owe me. I want out of here and you hold the key."

Nick looked at the ground and felt a twinge of raw guilt, something a mortal could never do to him until now. *What's happened to me?* he thought.

"It takes two strikes of the stones to bind you here, Iblis. You need to leave this place."

Nick jumped to his feet. "I can get out?"

"Certainly, anytime you want."

"How?"

"Look around," answered Habil, "all of this is familiar because it's simply a reflection of your own hurt. Hell adapts itself to our pain. Just walk Iblis...the roadways will seem like ones you've traveled before... because you have. It may take time, but just follow the path of your own heartache and it will lead you to a way...eventually. You have all the time you need."

Nick looked around. Habil was right. He glared at the road as it twisted away over a distant hill. He'd seen it all before. The Jinn stepped close to wrecked mortal, whose expression seemed almost gleeful.

"I should be the last guy in hell you'd want to help," he said.

"Fulfill God's promise," said the phantom, "and this ends for us all."

"What promise?"

"Find the woman, protect the child, and help Him re-bind the Pythia. Then and only then will those of us trapped here be free."

❦

In Jerusalem, Hilkiah paced back and forth in a vault that was hid amid the dark catacombs of the old city, not far from the Temple Mount. The immortal high priest was surrounded by twenty of his best Gadol warriors. A man suddenly burst into the room and strode right to him.

"The Tomar and Rafiq have arrived," the man announced. "The assembled knights are waiting in the upper compound, but the cleric and the priest are on their way down now."

It was finally time to face the truth. Hilkiah stiffened and faced the door. Moments later, his brothers came through it – behind them followed James and Adriano.

"We came as soon as we got your word," said Aaron.

"We were a little busy," added Nafees, with an air of sarcasm.

Aaron gave his younger brother an angry, sidelong glance.

James leaned close to Adriano. "Ever notice how Hilkiah brings out the small boy in Nafees?" he whispered.

"Older brothers have a way of doing that," he replied into James' ear.

"We have a problem," said Hilkiah. "An hour ago, a car rammed a check point outside of the city. There was an exchange of gunfire, but three fugitives managed to escape into the city with what I suspect is a bomb of unimagined yield."

James looked at Adriano nervously. His vision was unfolding.

What Hilkiah did not tell them was how he was aware of the bomb in the first place. His own men – agents of the Mossad – had a hand in acquiring the weapons. Hilkiah had wanted the portable nuclear devices for himself; to use as political capital in strengthening support for the Gadol and their hardliner beliefs within the Israeli government. His intrigues had gone all wrong. The dragons were too powerful now, and without Nafees, he could not see the Day of Judgment closing in on them to know he was playing into the hands of the Pythia.

"Then why are we huddled down here," growled Aaron, "and not out there after them?"

James and Adriano stepped into the room a little more. There was a deep tension. The prophet sensed this did not all add up, there was more to it.

"The Seal of Solomon was broken a short time ago," said Hilkiah. "Someone is in tabernacle maze under the Temple Mount."

"How can that be?" asked Aaron. "Only a prophet anointed by an angel of God can break that ward."

There was a brief span of quiet. Then Adriano cleared his throat.

"Jon...the Anointed One," he said. All eyes turned to him. "He's obviously here with them. I saw his betrayal of the Jinn....he has deserted the way of light."

James' expression turned red. *We will have to talk later about what else you saw there,* he said directly into Adriano's mind.

The knight looked uncomfortable, but he went on. "Jon attacked Nick...with the Stones of Kabil... the dragons found them in Arbil. The prophet's mind is wracked with some dark madness the Accuser would not allow himself to see. Jon took the mark of the Pythia in his bewildered despair."

"Not good," gowned Aaron.

"At least he does not know how to use the stones properly as yet," said Hilkiah, "or you would have never been able to conjoin with Iblis the way you did out there...he'd be trapped forever in Sheol."

"He is now anyway," replied Adriano, for the first time feeling sadness about Nick.

All of the men in the room grew silent – there was a flood of emotions. Some of them clearly thought the world would be a better place without the dark Accuser. Others realized he was the key to salvation.

"The blast will not have killed him," said Aaron. "The question is will he find his way out of the underworld in time to do what he must...we know it's possible." He glanced at James.

"He will," the young seer said, looking inward with his own power. "I've seen it, but we need to worry about Jon and the dragons right now."

"Agreed," said Hilkiah.

"What difference does it make that they have gotten in?" said Nafees. "The maze is only a ruse. The sealed passages were only intended to keep people sensitive to that power thinking that the Mercy Seat might still be down here. The tablets are safe....we know that."

"I came for the Amo, Nafees," replied James. "We need to stop them from using that weapon against God's people...all three faiths."

Without warning, a wave of chaotic energy suddenly surged up and out from the maze tunnels. Shemhazai had just armed the detonator.

James' body stiffened as he felt it. "They are not bothering to find the tablets now," he said. "They will simply blow the entire Temple Mount, and most of the city with it to try and stop us. Your deception has worked too well, brothers. They think the tablets lie here still and will stop at nothing to destroy them...if they can."

"As we saw in the vision," said Nafees, dread coloring his eyes. He realized James had finally and fully come into his power.

"James," snapped Adriano. "We can use the Realm of Essences to go down to the weapon and stop them."

"No, you can't," said Hilkiah. "The maze is warded against ethereal intrusion. If it were that easy, the Pythia would have been down here long ago. That false prophet has opened the front door for them. There is only one way down or out now." The warlord of the Gadol turned and slid open a secret entrance, sealed with his own powerful spell. He motioned for the others to follow.

"If we block them in," he said, "they may not unbridle the force of the weapon, fearing they have no other way to escape."

"Or," said Aaron, "they may just blow it up and sacrifice themselves. We might be walking into a trap if we face them down there now."

"If they do the deck will be evenly stacked in risk for both sides again," said James, stepping toward the entrance of the catacomb.

"How do you figure that?" grunted Hilkiah.

"Because Jon is too important for them to lose.... now that he is turned, the prophet is a great danger to us. The tablets are safe, but the dragons obviously don't realize that yet. Nick will find his way out of the Abyss...he is fated to eventually lead one of the two of us to the woman. So we have to try to stop the dragons here. Jon is their only chance to get at the woman before we can...they won't risk him."

"I don't share all this new found faith in the Accuser," said Hilkiah, unconvinced that such a mission could ever be trusted to the Devil by God, "but you are correct about the plan of the dragons... we cannot allow them to destroy the Temple Mount. It would seem we have come to the same truth by different paths, prophet."

The Gadol warrior suddenly turned and rushed down into the shaft, followed by his guard. The others were quick to do the same.

"We have a problem, Hilkiah," said Aaron as he followed close on his older bothers' heels. "We are at least twenty minutes from the seal stone from here, and as I recall there are two other entrances before that shaft. They might get out one of them before we arrive to trap them in."

"I know," Hilkiah said in a low tone. "I thought you were usually the voice of hope, Aaron."

Aaron pushed playfully at his brother, as they all moved down the stone-carved tunnel. Something about that place seemed to slowly wash away all vehemence between them.

"James," the Gadol warlord finally grumbled, "now would be a good time to show me you can unite us after all...the way you intend. Both the Tomar and Rafiq above are less than a few minutes from the entrance to the other tunnels. If you are who they say you are, use the sema of the psalm to send the men into the shafts and cut the Pythia off."

James hesitated, trying to focus on the sacred cords. Hilkiah glanced back with a discerning eye.

"Sing, boy," called Nafees, "with all your zealous pride."

❦

Darkness filed the shafts of the old maze. Shemhazai rose from bending over the weapon. They had searched the maze and found nothing, the wards were too strong, and time was running out. Aboddon was deeply frustrated; he lost patience with them all.

"I thought you knew this place," he grumbled to the grigori, then turned from the Jinn. "Never mind... the weapon is armed, let's get out of this hole."

As he spoke, a group of thrall burst in on them. They were out of breath.

"What is it?" growled Shemhazai. "Why did you leave your posts at the seal, you worms?"

"Knights, my Lord...the Sons of Light are advancing down all three shafts. We are trapped."

"What?" snarled Aboddon. He paced anxiously. All became tense watching him. "Leave the device," he said abruptly. "I will deal with them myself, we can detonate the bomb remotely."

The band of Pythian sentinel and their dark captains made it around two twists of the maze before the combined force of the Asirim fell on them in the narrow tunnel. The Christians and Muslims mowed into the first line of thralls together, fighting side by side. But just as quickly as the warriors of light cut into them, Shemhazai and Aboddon crashed back against the knights like a storm.

The Asirim knights fell back.

Aaron, Hilkiah, and Nafees quickly took up the front line, trying to repel the Pythian Lords with a powerful discharge of enchantment – the three together were potent beyond measure. James thought about binding the serpents in that darkness, but worried that might cause the Pythians to panic and detonate the weapon in desperation.

Hilkiah looked at Aaron, quickly working out a plan as the dragon and grigori were taken off guard. "Can you hold them here for a while, brother?" shouted Hilkiah.

Aaron nodded.

Within seconds Hilkiah fell back behind yet another line of knights waiting in the tunnel. He scuffled though the mass of men and found James, still muttering the cadence of the psalms' mantra.

"James," said Hilkiah, "you stay here...you must maintain the meditation. It's the only thing that will keep the dragon and his minions at bay…. Adriano, you come with me." With that, he grabbed the big man and hauled him back up the shaft. James tried to stay focused. His voice rose, and the knights surged against the Pythians.

Once around a corner and out of view of the others, Hilkiah stopped suddenly. Adriano looked confused. The immortal pushed at another stone on the wall, a second hidden passage gave way. He pulled at the big man and ducked inside it.

"Do you mind telling me what we're doing?" asked Adriano.

"This passage circles around to where the Pythians are pinned down," answered Hilkiah. "Our little standoff cannot last...that serpent has the ultimate advantage of time. We will grow weary...it will not. They will eventually overwhelm us."

"So you want to hit him from behind?" questioned Adriano, "just you and me?!"

"Not quite," said the warlord. "We need to out maneuver them, not simply out flank them."

Just then they surged into the main passage, on the other side of the Pythian line. As they stepped into the tunnel, Hilkiah motioned for Adriano to follow again. They made one quick turn, and there sat the weapon, pulsing with an eerie glow. It was completely unattended.

Hilkiah reached for it and slammed the case shut, then made back in the direction they came. When he reached the secret passage, he stopped and handed the case to Adriano. "Now listen to me," he said to the knight. "I realize you know how to use the asherah... the key to the Abyss. I was there, unseen, and saw what you did. Take this back around to James. Once there, get rid of it like you did the other one. When it's gone, let Aaron fall back and these beasts will follow as you retreat."

"Of course," said Adriano. "They won't even realize it's gone until it's too late." Then the big man paused and stared at Hilkiah. "Tell me one thing before I go."

"You are kidding, what do I look like?"

"Will you stand with us and unite the Asirim behind James now?"

"You are not as bright as everyone says, Rafiq," Hilkiah snapped. "You already have Adriano...now get the hell out of here...even fate has its limitations."

With that he pushed the knight into the passage and moved back to the main shaft, intending to out flank the Pythians once Adriano had the weapon out. He would push them out of God's city for this offense.

As Adriano reached James, he showed him the case. The young seer's eyes lit up. The big man handed it over. He then pushed past the boy a few feet to where Aaron sliced and hacked at Aboddon, driving the dragon back. *Give us ten minutes,* he said into the Tomar knight's mind, *and then retreat slowly up the shaft...that's all we will need.*

Aaron nodded. He trusted the knight without question.

Then Adriano made his way back to James. Together they headed up and out of the maze.

∘⋇∘

Nick had been walking for what seemed lifetimes. The endless and empty road appeared to go on forever. It weighed heavily on his heart. *It's like being trapped in a dark dream,* he thought to himself.

Sheol was a place where the gravity of nothingness was greater than any other force – such that not even ethereal light could escape unaided. Then it occurred to Nick, he did know a force strong enough to come and go from the Abyss at will. Joshu had come long ago to free souls from this place. The dark exile fell to his knees, and closed his eyes. He took a deep breath, calming his head, looking for a quiet place inside his heart.

"Lord, hear my entreaty...forgive me," Nick prayed. "I beg of you...reprieve me. I have paid for my foolishness...my hubris. Please Josh, give me another chance. I was wrong not to trust your word then. I was wrong to think I knew better than you."

Tears filled his eyes. After a few seconds, he felt something take hold of him. It was a powerful feeling – two arms in a disembodied embrace.

Soft words filled his head.

"Niko, all you ever had to do was ask, but you were always so proud...so defiant."

Nick opened his eyes and looked around, but there was nothing there – just the soft sound in his mind. And yet Joshu's words filled the darkness. "Where are you?" asked the Accuser.

"I am in all places where you are, Niko...even in Sheol."

In the distance, Nick saw a light suddenly take shape. At first it was only an orange speck, he thought it was Joshu at first. Gradually it became larger and larger, growing into glowing ball. Nick finally realized he'd seen this sort of thing not so long ago. It was a massive spray of dragon breath, directed right at him. The fire enveloped him and his form burst into a raging conflagration.

Nick then saw the great beast approaching, haplessly drawn to the presence of Joshu's voice in the Abyss. The dragon's scales bristled, as it turned its head to strike. Nick drew Haqiqah, the sword flared.

Twisting on itself, the serpent arched its head away, wary of the blade it seemed. The dragon's two front feet planted firmly on the ground as its head swayed around, scrutinizing Nick, looking for an opening to strike.

"No, not the sword...not yet," said Joshu into his mind.

With those words a force bound the great dragon's head. Its tail lashed forward, but Nick dodged the swipe. The beast began to flail as the unseen force seized it and drew its head to the ground, binding it as if under God's foot. The jaws of the beast were pried, while its entire body heaved trying to break free from the binding.

"Inside, Niko, you must...it is the only way for you now."

The Accuser hesitated, then realized what his beloved Lord was showing him – a way out.

"Thank you, Josh," he said warmly.

Nick reached inside for his power and caused the dark fire to rise around him. He turned and shot directly into the gullet of the monster like a dart.

Joshu released it.

Once the hold was broken, the dragon charged into a blind fury. Everything around Nick became merciless flame, an inferno that seemed to roar beyond all reckoning. He sensed nothing but the burst of atoms colliding – then ripping apart. Even with his resistance to dragon fire, being at the center of a great serpent in that way threatened to tear his soul apart. His torment seemed to go on forever and ever, but somehow he held his composure deep in the serpent's fiery bowel.

Since he had no sense of time in the Abyss, Nick was not sure how long he had been swallowed by the beast. Yet at the appropriate time, he did seem to acquire a sense that the monster was rising out of the sea of nothingness. Joshu's voice reminded him of that place deep inside, where he had found the light of affinity. Then Nick also remembered how Shemhazai had reacted when James entered his essence in the nightclub. Mustering some deep and vast need within his soul, Nick touched that spirit at his very center – affect for James. He released it into the dragon.

That tiny spec of light that he managed to gather from within his soul lodged into the endless nothingness of the serpent. It became an instant irritant to the creature. The dragon twisted and pushed its head up and out of a thin-space fissure on the material plane. There it belched Nick from its mouth into the fury of a volcanic fire. Nick pitched and rolled with molten rock as it cascaded onto a sloping landmass and pooled like a lake of boiling sulfur. Gradually, he stepped up out of the flame to shake himself. Then he stopped and tried to draw a breath, but there was nothing in the air there except for ash and toxic vapor. The land was dark around him but for the pale light of the eruption behind him and the strange yellow glow of the soil.

Nick looked up and through a brief parting of the intense fume he saw a startling sight. A massive orange ball filled the sky. He paused, disoriented for a time, as the distinct spot of Jupiter's eye came rotating into view. The Jinn watched the massive storm on the gas-giant rage and saw it too was a dragon laying in wait, all the way out there. He shuddered and kicked at the soil of Jovian moon beneath his feat, testing the firm ground.

Close enough to home, he thought, as he split open the ethereal plane and stole away from the yellow dust of Io. *I can make it the rest of the way on my own, Josh.*

Adriano and James rushed past the open seal of Solomon. They must hurry. If the dragon realized that the weapon was gone, he might try to use it then and there. As the two men reached the outside, they looked at each other. Adriano moved to use the asherah, but James stopped him. "It's time we rid ourselves of Nafees' silly spell," he said.

They looked into each other's eyes, took hands, and kissed. The young seer slowly reached inside of his companion and took hold of the barbed charm. He wrenched at it, but it did not come free. Then his eyes seemed to sadden. "Babe," he said, "I cannot take it without some part of you coming with it."

Adriano just pulled James closer. "Take what you must," said the big man, "I don't want this between us any longer."

James focused, then pulled quickly – as if to rip off a bandage. The big man's expression turned white. He gasped for air.

"I'm sorry," said James, kissing the knight again.

"That hurt like hell," said Adriano, trying to laugh at the pain.

"My turn," replied James. "You do it for me."

"Are you sure?"

James nodded. He led Adriano's ethereal hand to the spot. Adriano hesitated, not wanting to hurt his companion. The sound of battle abruptly rang from behind them. The knights were retreating, giving ground to allow the Pythian retreat from the magically sealed labyrinth.

"Now," squawked James.

Adriano pulled, but the spell would not come free. He tried and tried. It was no use.

James looked at him sorrowfully. There was not time to keep trying. So he linked Adriano's part of the spell to the device, and pointed to the wall. "Now," said the seer, "open the way."

Adriano struck the stone with the rod and tore a hole into the surface. The dark portal yawned horribly, and James pitched the weapon in it. The portal slammed shut just as the knights poured out of the shaft of the maze. On their heels raged Aboddon and Shemhazai, with the near lifeless body of Jon being drug behind. The two sides faced off. The dragon smiled and held the detonator out in one hand. Then the beast ripped open the ethereal plane. Shemhazai threw first Jon and then himself through. The thralls scurried after like insects.

The serpent held the tiny control and pointed it at James. He gleefully reckoned this was his moment of victory over the nameless-one, killing James this way. He flipped the switch with his long fingers and stepped into the Realm Essences.

The portal slammed shut.

As it did came the embrace of silence, but for the labored breath of the knights scattered around the prophet. In that settling calm, the Asirim stood united.

⟳

Nick hovered in the Realm of Essences for a moment, reconstituting himself. Now that it was over, the haunting image of Jon rising to strike him kept replying over and over again in his mind. He began to argue with the man's ghost in his own head, as if the prophet were there to hear the plea. *Why Jon? Why?*

After the intensity of dragon fire faded, Nick forced open the passage home. He thought for a moment about going to Israel, but then shuddered at the thought. The Accuser had seen into the knight guarding James, and knew he would be of little use to them in the Holy City now.

Stepping through the portal, he stumbled out onto the rainy corner at 46th Street and Broadway. It felt strange after being away.

The surge of people about the avenue was so thick, no one noticed the Jinn appear out of thin air. He shook his coat and looked west toward the Hudson River. *No place better than this to leave the past behind,* he thought to himself, *the woman is still out there....I feel it.* No longer afraid of the dark power he now knew could be controlled within in him, the Accuser reached out, feeling James and Adriano. They were safe –both somehow part of him now.

Nick dodged a cab and vanished into the teaming human horde – just another face on the street. He lost himself quickly in the glare and din.

On the other side of the world, a familiar feeling settled over James and Adriano as well. They felt Nick re-enter the material plane. The young seer and knight were profoundly relieved. For better or worse, they had both seen into Nick's soul and there found something endearing, something that God had loved...and still did.

Will he come to us? the big man found himself saying into his companions mind.

James just stared back at him with an uncertain look, then glanced around for Nafees among the injured, stumbling knights.

A strange wave of ethereal power washed over the seer – it was dread. He turned back to the big man, his expression pale. "My God, Adriano," he said.

At that very moment Adriano sensed it too. They bolted back into the temple passage as if with one thought, making their way down the clammy passage. It seemed to take longer than before. The open shaft to the seal was just ahead of them. Bodies were gathered in several places.

Then they saw Jason trying to pull Nafees away from that place. He was caught up with grief. The cleric sat slumped over Aaron's crushed corpse. Hilkiah was lying nearby, still and lifeless. The Tomar had fallen defending his Gadol brother. They wilted together – back to back – like fallen companions. The immortal siblings of fate, after centuries of separation, died within inches of one another.

When James reached Nafees in the tunnel, voiceless tears streamed down the cleric's face.

"Are you O.K?" the young seer asked, trying to draw Nafees toward him at Jason's urging.

The cleric did not budge.

"They are gone," he cried. "They are guardians of mortal fate no more."

"How?" asked Adriano, grasping at Aaron. "They cannot die….they are elohim!"

"No," said Jason somberly, "they cannot. Death is a human thing… immortals do not die. They simply cease being…extinguished in this existence. Aaron knew their time was close…he had warned us. The dragons are swallowing the world…one soul at a time. If they find our nameless-god in mortal form…we are all doomed to this end."

"They are gone," wailed Nafees again, pulling at his hair. "My immortal kin are gone forever. We are lost!"

Little by little, the Asirim gathered around. They took up the bodies of all the fallen and carried them to a great hall under the holy site. The knights washed the bodies and clothed them in their traditional garb –

the armor of the great Sons of Light. Then Nafees led them deep into the catacombs. There he laid his brother to a true eternal rest, in a tomb prepared for them long ago under the temple they had all served together.

James, Nafees, and Adriano stood alone at the sealed crypt doors after the ceremony of goodbyes ended, comforting each other. Nafees placed his hand upon the seal. Both James and Adriano watched him with sorrowful eyes.

"Are you O.K.?" asked the big man.

Nafees lowered his head. "Yes," he said, "it is the way of things...someone is always left behind."

"Where do we go from here?" asked Adriano, reaching to steady Nafees as he spoke.

"We go home," answered James abruptly. "We take all the knights to New York and we wait for the next revelation."

"Nick is there...in New York," said Adriano to Nafees in a comforting tone, trying to reassure him. "James and I both felt him return from the underworld...he got out."

The immoral cleric smiled, finding comfort in that knowledge somehow.

17

TEMPEST

New York City – September 2000

Months had passed since the great battle, but for the first time in centuries the Asirim were united together in one city. The Devil was there too, still lurking alone in the streets. He was waiting for a sign.

Fall was in the air, a cool wind blew up Twenty-Third Street where Nick stood remembering the night the thrall had pounced on James from that very spot. A part of him wondered if he had missed some opportunity for love in the boy, had he made a different choice. Nick no longer clung so tightly to the idea that he could only share his affections with the divine. In the end, he submitted fully to a mortal, just as the nameless-god had intended.

I miss you so much, Jon, thought the Accuser, speaking to the prophet like a ghost again. *What will you become now?* He could not help worrying about the young man.

A long black car rolled to the curb, and the rear window came down. Nafees stared up at Nick, his smile warm and comforting. The lights on the avenue flashed green and a line of yellow cabs shot past them.

"I am glad you decided to come," said Nafees to Nick. "We need to talk....a sense of something powerful grows nearer to us...a portent of Him."

The door popped open and Nafees slid to one side, letting Nick drop his weight into the car. Adriano and James sat curled in a corner at the far end of the limousine. They smiled. Nick returned the grin. *They deserved to be happy,* he thought. *They are mortal after all. Who knows how much time any of us really have.*

He took pride in his newfound emotional strength. The dark exile really felt that they all could be friends now, and work together for the good of things. Of course, pride was something for which Nick was never in short supply.

The car rounded on to the street, heading east for the mid-town tunnel and the Long Island expressway. They were headed to finally meet James' family, to celebrate the prophet's birthday.

"So, what's new gang?" asked Nick in a playful voice. Then he threw his arm around Nafees and pulled him close, imitating the way Adriano and James sat in their embrace.

The cleric looked startled for a moment. The prophet and his companion laughed at the sight of the two, staring at each other with wild eyes. Nick turned and smiled back at them again.

After a moment, Nafees realized the affectionate gesture was sincere and lighthearted. The two of them then shared a little innocent warmth, remembering better days together.

"Will Jon really lead the Pythia to the woman, Nick?" asked James nervously. "Is he capable of betraying everything?"

"I am not sure," replied Nick. "The truth is I can't say I ever knew him at all. His heart and soul were filled with torment, and his mind seemed to be torn. He was being driven mad by something – at times I thought it was me. He pretended to be one thing, but in the end was not who he said he was."

"It's been said of mortals like that," Nafees huffed, "such hypocrisy is the homage their vice pays to virtue."

"If all this is true," said Adriano, "then we are all on even ground still. They have no better chance than we do at finding the woman, even with the anointed prophet. They need you Nick as much as they need him to discover the truth...*you* must lead the prophet to her."

There was at least some comfort in what the big man said.

"How are you, Nick?" asked Nafees finally. "I have to tell you. You seem changed."

Nick laughed and blushed a little. "That would be an understatement, old friend," he replied. "It is as if I have become change itself. I really loved that boy, Nafees, genuinely. Nothing will ever fill the gap of losing God or Josh, I realize that, but it's as if Jon forged out a separate heart in me...a place that is all his, no matter what he does now."

"That is the most humane thing I have ever heard you say," replied Nafees.

Nick turned from flush to bright red, then got a funny look about him. It almost appeared as if he had eaten something that didn't agree with him.

"Awe, look what you've done, Pir," said Adriano, "gone and insulted the Accuser."

The four laughed together.

After a few hours on the road, the black car wound its way through the serene streets of Sayville, James' hometown. Something about the place seemed to lift their spirits. It was untouched as yet by the great tribulation unfolding in the world. Even Nick could not help but feel at ease there, as if some burden was lifted from him.

The sound of gravel popping announced the car as it came to a stop in front of the small, well-landscaped house. The four agents of the nameless-god trickled out from the car and walked toward the steps. As they did, the front door opened and a frail, lovely women of about sixty bolted from it. She shrieked with joy and took James into her arms. A mysterious strength seemed to overtake her; she nearly lifted the young prophet off the ground.

"Honey, it's so good to have you home. We have been so worried!" she scolded.

James' three companions seemed to stiffen, unsure of what to do next.

"Mom," James said, motioning toward his knight, "this is Adriano, my boyfriend." The term seemed so inadequate, but how else was he to explain it to her?

She reached over and smiled warmly, taking the big man by the hands. "It's so nice to meet you, call me Lilly," she said warmly. "I have to admit, I am at a loss...James hasn't really brought us up to speed on what's been going on with him over the last year."

Adriano smiled politely.

Then James turned to Nick and Nafees. He was not quite sure what to say about these two creatures – at least anything she would understand. *How does one introduce your mother to the Devil?* he thought.

"These are two very good friends of mine, Mom," said the young prophet finally. "This is Nick and Nafees…they have been like family to me this past year."

Both men looked honored by the sentiment.

"Well," she replied, "let's all go in and get acquainted. Are you boys hungry by chance?"

"I could eat something," answered Adriano eagerly.

Nick looked over at the big man, something about the way he had spoken up reminded him of Jon – the dark exile's heart sank for a moment.

The five of them tuned toward the door and went inside. They made their way through the house and its collection of reminiscences. The family had clearly lived there a long time. The home had a nurturing feel, safe and fruitful.

On the back patio there were an array of metal chairs and a table. The smell of food filled the back yard. In the corner, a tall column of smoke rose off the grill like a sacrificial pyre. The aroma was heavenly. Lilly motioned for the men to sit. They did so graciously – all but Nick.

The Accuser stepped to the edge of the patio, following the interlaid brick as if it reminded him of something he could not completely recall.

A splay of discrete motion flashed at the corner of his eye and he turned to focus on it. There stood two small boys, each about one year old. The taller of the two stared intently at Nick, with unwavering nerve. The other pivoted back and forth nervously on his feet, a few feet behind his brother. The boys inched forward toward Nick. The bolder of the two reached up and took him by the pant leg, while the smaller, anxious boy continued to just smile at him.

The dark exile stooped low, so that he was near face to face with the boys. He smiled tenderly at them. The others noticed the twins approach Nick, and the unexpected warmth with which the Accuser received them. There was something striking about the image. Nafees let out a sigh.

"The lion shall lie down with lambs," he said, with a voice full of mirth.

Before James could get to his feet to run and meet his nephews, a voice trumpeted from behind them. "My God!" it sang out crystal clear. "My little brother is home."

James was instantly on his feet, he ran toward the young women. The moment came so quickly – so effortlessly – that no one was ready for it. Nick knew profound events frequently had such a feel, as if time were stopped.

"Gloria!" James cheered. He reached her and they embraced with deep affection.

Nick's bowel tuned in on itself at what he saw, as if he'd been hit in the stomach. He looked down at the boys in astonishment, disbelieving that after all they had been through, it all came down to *this* simple gathering near the sea.

The boys both smiled up at him again, as if they knew what he realized.

At the throne of God, Gabriel walked forward to the edge, tears streaming down his face. He raised the last trumpet and blew.

"The hope of the world now belongs to our Lord," proclaimed Joshu on the throne, "and the ones he favors."

The moment Jon sensed in his soul that Nick was standing in the presence of the woman, he drew upon the powers given him by the Pythia. Drake had been wrong; there was a real woman after all. Aboddon would reward him well. He ripped open the Realm of Essences, like a wild animal disemboweling its prey, and issued fourth an ethereal summons to both Shemhazai and Aboddon. *Nick has found the woman!*

The Accuser felt Jon coming like a storm. He extended his wings, as the sky above the small house turned blood red. The two small boys reached out and clung to him, knowing safety would be found there.

God kept his secret well, thought Nafees, as he raised his eyes to the darkening sky.

The clouds suddenly opened and the air above them was filled with terror. The dragon fell upon them with all his rage, like a great cyclone ripping at the roof and shutters of the tiny Long Island house. He became a fast tempest delivered up from the sea, unforgiving and murderous. At his feet hovered Shemhazai, with his host of traitorous grigori. Standing in the doorway, beyond where James clung to his sister, was Jon – the Stones of Kabil hanging from his neck, affixed by a chain.

Nick was filled with a fierce fury.

Nafees rose and laughed out loud, understanding reached him. His wild eyes bore into Adriano. The events clearly had taken even this fate by surprise. "For eons I trained scores knights to stand with me in this moment," the cleric said to the big man, "and yet as the faithful hour arrives…you and I stand alone before Him."

Nafees then drew his curved sword form the Realm of Essences and pointed it in the direction of Nick and the boys. "To Allah!" he wailed.

Adriano faltered for a second. His instinct was to go to James, but his hesitance drew a quick rebuke from Nafees in the form of a slap with flat edge of his blade.

The knight turned and leapt toward Nick just as Shemhazai was about to crash into him. The Rafiq warrior met the blow, fully expecting the might of the grigori to crush him. His block somehow held. He was fused with Nick's power, surging into their bond.

Shemhazai looked down into the knight's eyes and saw his resolve. The big man would die there if he must. Then he looked to Nick and the twins, all three glared at him with defiance. Adriano retaliated methodically with his blade, driving the turned angels back, away from the Accuser and the incarnation of the returned nameless-god.

Nick was unsure of what to do; he just stared at the mobbing traitors, working it out. Should he stay and defend his friends, or should he flee and carry the boys away from the storm? At that very moment, he sensed two hands on his shoulders and a second set of wings envelope him from behind. Two of the assaulting grigori pushed past Adriano and hammered into Nick. The blows crashed against the outer set of feathers shielding him like an artillery round, but the ward upon of those very special wings didn't falter.

"Keep faith, Accuser," someone whispered in his ear.

Nick looked back. It was Javi, the Guardian of the Innocents. The Accuser was relieved beyond words.

"When did you get here?"

"I've been here all along," replied Javi.

"You knew then?"

"No, not until just now...the nameless-one crafted his trap well, as was promised us all. I will take Him where He will be safe, away from the Leviathan's dark rage. My power endures...because of them...a purpose remains for both you and I from among the Jinn."

Nick went to pull the two boys close to him, as if to deny Javi his charge, but they were in the angel's arms before Nick could stop them. They smiled at him and reached out with their tiny fingers together, touching his lips to silence him. With that, Javi folded the Ethereal Realm around him like a cloak, and was gone. His stewardship was beyond the reach of inequity – that was what *he* had been crafted for.

The Devil rose in wraith, and drew Haqiqah. Urgency filled the air like the torrents of air from the dragon's vehemence.

Nafees quickly realized that all would be lost if the dragon released his breath upon them, so he flung himself at the beast's great maw. Aboddon parried away from the immortal's slashing blade, and Nafees used that moment to summersault upon the crown of his head. The cleric's moves were artful like a whirling dervish. The monster made two twisting convulsions with its neck in an effort to shake the immortal, but failed.

Then Nafees hastily thrust the long blade through the monsters nostrils, pinning his massive mouth shut with a binding-spell before the beast tossed him free. Twisting to land upright, like a bird on a branch, the immortal lit right at the feet of James and his sister.

James' face was painted with horror and disbelief; he was extending a powerful ward, as if by instinct. The cleric reached for James and took his hand. He smiled mournfully at the prophet; while all around them chaos mauled the earth.

"I always envied Adriano," he said sadly. It was as if he had somehow slowed time around them.

"What?" replied James in surprise.

"Of all the mortals I've met…you are the most fair. You never saw it in yourself. Your vanity never consumed you, perhaps because your inner elegance exceeds your outer self. In any case, you have enchanted us all friend of God."

James shook his head, trying to collect his thoughts. "This is one hell of a time to make a pass at me, Nafees!"

The immortal clerical snickered, then reached across and kissed James on the forehead. "Give her to me, James, I will make her safe... there is more for her to do."

At that very moment, something passed between them...an omen of sad portent from the last surviving Fate. James looked back at his sister. She clung to him, clearly in shock from the unbelievable carnage about them. He knew in his heart it was the right thing to do. With trepidation, he handed her over to Nafees. She snatched at the cleric, as a child clings in a fall.

"Go to your knight, and go to Allah...you are his champions," said Nafees, and with that he assumed his true material form.

James stood in awe of the great winged eagle that stood before him – Nafees was a true homa. His heavy eyes were bearing down on the seer through a feathered brow. Then with two great strokes, Nafees and his sister were aloft. The prophet watched them rise into the turbulent sky, and then vanish behind a thundercloud. Somberly, he turned his attention to Nick and his companion, who alone fended off the relentless attacks of the assembled turned Jinn.

It was at the moment the dragon managed to break the ethereal blade that clamped his great jaws shut. Aboddon's fury was unbridled. The woman and the reviled fruit of her womb had escaped again. He would make these miserable creatures that stood in his way pay for his failure – the Queen of the Pythia would be unforgiving. His frenzy made him blind to the danger he faced from both Nick and James. For unknown to each, their full power remained untested. The dragon ignored the peril Tiamat warned him to avoid – the union of the Devil and his true prophet.

James stole up on Jon. The two men stared at each other a moment, then Jon turned and looked for Nick, trying to understand what was happening. The Accuser and the Anointed One met eyes. *I love you,* thought Nick into the boy's head. *There I said it... please don't do this, Jon.*

The young man seemed to shrug off the gesture, as if to say "it's too late, Nick." He had become something new and frightful from the trivial they had faced. His own hurt was too entwined now with his rage to feel anything but hurtfulness and bitterness. Before Jon could raise a hand, James delivered a decisive blow right to his nose with his own righteous staff. Caught off guard, never expecting it from James, the green-eyed prophet fell to the ground instantly, the stones of Kabil scattering at his feet.

The dragon took noticed of Nick and Adriano, fighting back to back as the grigori assailed them with repeated blows. There was something there between them. They fought as if conjoined, but Aboddon thought that impossible. The Devil was not so weak to fall for another mortal so easily. Whatever power it was they wielded, he would use his own might to crush it once and for all. Aboddon knew dragon fire alone would only consume the mortal, and not the Accuser. He needed to do more. The serpent reached back with his tail and swung. It appeared to sweep away the stars.

Then from nowhere came a powerful voice. It boomed like thunder amid the clouds. "Unclean spirits of the Abyss," James roared into the squall, "I bind thee with the power of God's eternal name. *El-huit Zilo Pochtli!*"

The Dragon was swiftly pulled from the sky, his great mass heaving about the ground wildly. It crushed the surrounding houses with its weight, including James' family home. The fallen angels too were bound with the dragon, their outer forms now taking on the appearance of great snakes, thrashing and flailing like worms on hot pavement.

Nick and Adriano jumped back, out of the way of the monsters as they tore and ripped at the earth.

James *was* truly the prophet of God. Still, his hold was not without limit. They could sense the ethereal shackles would not last long on the might of a dragon. Adriano ran to James, seeing his enchantment wavering. He motioned to Nick for help, but the Accusers could do nothing but swing his blade to strike at the heads of the various grigori he could reach closest to him.

"This will never work," screamed Nick. "There are too many and I am not even sure how you kill a fucking dragon!"

"They must be subsumed into their own chaos," said James in a stern, somber voice.

"How then?" Adriano begged.

James reached out and took his companion by the face and held it in his hands. The knight's heart filled with a grief beyond any he could ever have imagined. Gently, James kissed him. Their heads fell together as Adriano began to sob, imploring James not to do the thing he now saw in his own mind.

Nick himself had still not worked it out.

James turned slowly to the Accuser, with Adriano pulling at the sleeve of his shirt. The look on the boy's face was grim. "Satan," he shouted, with tears in his eyes, "rebel against Heaven… I bind thee in the name of *El-huit Zilo Pochtli.*"

Nick's face fell into shock, as his material form was reduced to its essence – a great flaming bird. The phoenix rolled on the earth next to the serpents as James thrust Adriano aside, his face filling with determination.

"Now, my eternal Rafiq!" screamed James.

"Please no, James!" Adriano replied with dread in his voice.

"NOW!" James' voice roared back like thunder.

The earth shook.

Adriano drew out his staff. He looked down and stared at it few seconds, then reluctantly turned and tore at the earth with it. The Abyss opened at his feet.

With one final glance into the big man's eyes, James cast himself into the void. The twisting mass of the mighty serpent and its minions followed him in as if all were linked by a chain – so too did Nick. Just as

ill consume you" the dragon f

hing you have ever loved, whelp o

quickly

No, you won't," said James, with a re

n his eyes.

e young seer's strength was almost g

eemed the beast would finally break

on of primordial spirits crashed into the

fathom of the Abyss—the dreaded seas of

It was the place where James had cast the

deadly Heart of Dragons. He had followed

e remnant of the barb-spell with its tiny part

l Adriano's comingled essence still attached,

way he had followed it out of the Abyss all

nths before. The young prophet could

st of his strength leaving him, as the great

ings broke the ethereal binding and began

im with fury.

ody would not last long under the frenzy

n. He used his last bit of power to thrust

the heart, deep in the bowels of gloom.

ldo, Nick's proximity to the heart caused

tonators to erupt. It sent the plutonium

ical mass; dragon fire erupted instantly.

ness with one enormous flash. The

e serpents disintegrated into a fuming,

– consumed by the chaos from which

r.

een's own prophecy was fulfilled.

l conflagration simply passed into

him with raw energy. He felt for

s it had been wrenched open.
rworld slammed shut.

Adriano sat amid the wreckage of
the storm faded away. The big man
at his hair. His sorrow was incalcu
to the end of his days. Through
saw a rush of motion in his periph
turned to see Jon rising to his
opened upon the false prophet
a few feet and noticed the knig
deadly flail lying before him
surged with all the fury of He

Smiling with a sinister
knight's head as if the lir
something. *Thank James fo*
for him to finish this and get
vanished into the Realm
man could deliver a sing

The churning air c
world. Adriano dropp
prophet had escaped
rage. The wrath of
scratched at the br
bled.

"I will kill him
my entire life."

In the void of
power as they fell
into its cold gri
close to James.

ev
god
"
tears i
Th
as it se
collecti
deepest
Sheol.
second,
down th
of his an
the same
those mo
feel the la
dragon's w
to beat at h
James' b
of the drago
Nick toward
Like at Megi
the tritium d
cores into cri
It lit the dar
dragon and th
sulfurous boil
they drew powe
The dark qu
The primev
Nick, engorging

James, but to his horror there was no substance left of the boy, only essence – true essence. The young man's soul lingered there in its pureness, close to the Accuser. They conjoined for just an instant, Nick's wings around him in the same embrace they had once shared. The Jinn struggled, trying to save some part of the seer that he might then restore.

Niko, he heard James' soft voice say into his mind, then fade away.

The brilliance of the blast sighed with one last gasp of bedlam. Nick drew a stilted breath and then was alone in the Abyss – for a second time. The cold of nothingness enveloped his soul.

EPILOGUE

New York City – One Month Later.

Nafees sat quietly reading a newspaper as the train pulled out of Pennsylvania Station. His lithe body swayed, as the car was pitched from side to side.

Adriano was perched across from him, stone faced, looking out at the open track as they passed toward the tunnel under the Hudson River. The train was momentarily immersed in darkness as the halogen bulbs above their heads flickered off, then on again.

The immortal cleric lowered the paper and peered over it at Gloria, who was nervously pacing up and down the aisle of the near empty car. It had been over a month since the freak-storm destroyed her home on Long Island. None of it would have made sense had she not seen the dragon with her own eyes, along with the angels that fought amid the wreckage of their lives to save her. Gloria's mother had been killed in the storm. James had vanished and was presumed dead as well. Worst of all, the boys were missing. But Nafees had assured her they were well. The immortal gave her his solemn word that she would see them again soon. What could she do but trust him now?

"Gloria," said Nafees in comforting voice, "come and sit, dearest. It does no good to work yourself up into such worry. He will come…that I can assure you."

Her face turned pale, the wait was killing her. She moved back to them and sat in the seat next to Adriano, something about the big man always calmed her. She edged closer and laid her head on his shoulder. Adriano closed his eyes. He was always struck by how, like James, the bouquet of her hair hung pleasantly near his face. The big man hurt so much from missing James that sometimes he was not sure he wanted to live himself.

A man entered the car from behind them. Gloria jumped to her feet. She turned anxiously, and then sighed when she saw him. It was simply another of the Rafiq knights. He approached the group of them and leaned over Nafees' shoulder to whisper something. The cleric appeared relieved as the man spoke.

"The car is sealed and guarded at both ends," said the cleric. "We are alone and will be alone for the duration of the trip."

Gloria settled down, nudging even closer to Adriano. When she did, Nefees laid the paper in the knight's lap and motioned for him to look. Adriano glanced down. The headline read: *USS Cole Attacked in Persian Gulf.*

"This is a bad sign," said Nafees, "the dragons are loosed upon the world. Even the mighty American Navy is not safe from their audacity. War will breed war and the dragons will feed from it."

"Who of us is safe anymore?" was all the big man could say. "Who of us really ever was?"

Out of nowhere, a dark form materialized in the rear of the car. Nafees noticed Nick first, but studied him before saying a word. The Accuser looked battle-worn and exhausted. He hunched forward and appeared a bit older than usual. A line of grey hair streaked up the center of his dark black locks.

What had happened to him in the bowels of the Sheol? the cleric wondered as he looked up into the sad, drawn face of the Devil.

Nick held both boys in his arms. They seemed at easy with him. David, the older of the two boys fidgeted with the Accuser's beard, fascinated by its course texture, while the other, Jeremy, lay next to him fast asleep. The younger boy's head nestled close to his guardian's heart. Abruptly, the rambunctious David let out a gurgling squeal, and all eyes turned toward them.

Nafees smiled at the tenderness he saw there in Nick. *No creature is beyond Allah's grace*, he thought.

Gloria was up out of her seat in an instant. She rushed and pulled first David, then Jeremy away from Nick. The angel's instinct was to cling to them, but he knew deep in his being there was no place safer for them than within her embrace.

As the heavy eyed Jeremy came free of Nick, he began to cry at first. Ecstatic, Gloria could care less. All she wanted was both of them in her arms. After a moment of shifting agitation, the boys quickly recognized her and climbed gleefully about her shoulders.

Adriano came to his feet and walked straight to Nick, grabbing him by the face. The Accuser suddenly felt a determined probing of his wards – just as the knight had done before on the battlefield. This time it did not strike Nick as funny at all. It touched and saddened him. Adriano strained with his unripe power, but Nick could sense there was nothing hostile in the man's advance. He was simply looking for James, hoping beyond hope that somehow the prophet had survived.

Nick lowered his wards and let the big man enter. Adriano pushed inside of Nick, as if he were breaking down a door – rough and hungry. The Accuser reached up with both hands and grabbed the big man by the shoulders to brace himself from the forceful penetration. It took only seconds for Adriano to see that James was nowhere to be found. The seer had passed beyond to some unseen place none of them could now reach.

The knight's eyes turned red, as he labored at his breath. A tear escaped one eye and trailed to the end of his nose, where it broke free and fell. Nick dropped one hand and caught it before it plunged to the ground. He held it there in his powerful grip a second, then reached up gingerly and cupped the nap of the big man's neck, drawing their heads together to comfort one another. They stood that way for a while, conjoined and sharing in the grief, as well as the beginning of something new – a thing they sensed James would approve of somehow.

As if by unheard summons, they all looked at the two boys, bouncing happily in their mother's lap. Those hallowed champions drew a tight circle about them.

"Have you sensed which it is yet?" askcd Nafees, his voice barely audible in its reverence for the twins.

Nick reached over with his hand and the boys both grabbed nimbly at his fingers. He shook his head and grinned down at the playful, loving pair.

"God only knows," the Devil answered.

9737512R0

Made in the USA
Lexington, KY
23 May 2011